THE BEFALLEN

CAMBRIA WILLIAMS

IMMORTAL WORKS
SALT LAKE CITY

To Hannah,
Anyone can be a hero!

Immortal Works LLC
1505 Glenrose Drive
Salt Lake City, Utah 84104
Tel: (385) 202-0116

© 2023 Cambria Williams
www.cambriawilliams.com

Cover Art by Ashley Literski
http://strangedevotion.wixsite.com/strangedesigns

Map by Mayank Sharma
https://dzign.in

This book is a work of fiction. Names, characters, businesses, organizations, places, events and incidents either are the product of the author's imagination or are used fictitiously. Any resemblance to actual persons, living or dead, events, or locales is entirely coincidental.

ISBN 978-1-953491-59-6 (Paperback)
ASIN B0CBKYR69K (Kindle)

For all the Unsungs who dare to dream.

CHAPTER
1

In Mohn, Village of Deogol: Sloane

S loane squinted against the first traces of dawn's light, scarcely able to believe today had finally come.

She and her father stood outside the family's small hovel in the tiny village of Mohn, a place that—according to what Father said—wasn't even on some maps of Deogol. Sloane had never seen a map of their island country but had heard many tales of its scattered diverse landscapes. The only place Sloane had been besides Mohn—whose only fortification from the outside world was that of makeshift, yet permanent, wooden poles—was Asana, a village that could *almost* be called a town, at least to Sloane's imagination. Its outer wall was constructed from rock. Not that defensive walls were much use nowadays in Deogol. They couldn't stop the Befallen; it did not work like that.

"I'm still not certain this is a good idea," Father said as he put the last two items in the satchel, leather belts commissioned by the elder of the village of Asana for their night watch. There was still *plenty* of room in the satchel in which more items could be packed, but Sloane said nothing to Father. He thought he was helping her by not filling it.

"You speak like I've never walked to Asana before. It's not *that* far."

"I know." Father tugged at his left ear as he tended to do when making decisions. "But I've always been with you, and you didn't have to carry so much."

"I'll be fine. And you're needed here to help prepare the village for tomorrow." Sloane gave an exaggerated smile.

He scratched his chin, but Sloane knew the decision was made. Hence, the half-full satchel. So, she waited, allowing him to believe she didn't already know she would go to Asana's Market Day alone to sell their leatherwork.

"Besides," Sloane dared, "I'm a much better barterer than you."

"You cheeky girl." Father laughed. "You most certainly are not."

"Aye, I am. And to prove it, I'll come back with a surprise—"

"Now, Sloane."

"—*and* coin leftover." She crossed her arms in front of her nearly flat chest for good measure.

"'Tis a bit late in the summer to spend coin we should save. What kind of surprise?"

"Something for Sherik?" Sloane said. Father would have more difficulty saying nay to that idea. She'd been wanting to surprise her little brother for moons.

As if sensing he were being spoken of, Sherik came out of the family's hovel, rubbing his sleepy eyes.

"Can I come with you, Sloane?" The little boy yawned as he scratched his mess of curly hair.

"Nay, little brother. But if you're very good and help Father get ready for the Prodigal Moon Celebration—"

"Celebration?" Sherik made a sour face. "How is starvin' for a whole day a celebration?"

"Sherik." Father knelt so he was eye-level with the child. "Fasting is only *part* of tomorrow's celebration. We have much to be grateful for..."

Even if we are half-starved most of the time, thought the part of Sloane who was looking forward to her complimentary meal from Nagel, Asana's pub owner.

And don't forget about the Befallen, added the other part of Sloane who was anxious to be back in Mohn before nightfall. *That terror is nothing to be grateful for.*

Don't even think about the Befallen. She couldn't let fear overcome her. She was going to Asana *alone*. Finally. Trusted to go alone. It'd only taken her almost eighteen years to do what Joah had done at age twelve.

Joah. Best not to think of her older brother, either.

"...besides, next moon at the Harvest Moon Festival, we shall feast and dance and sing to our hearts' content." Father finished his speech.

"You can't sing." Sherik laughed.

"Stars help me, two cheeky children," Father exclaimed as Ma came out of the hovel, carrying a small potato muffin on a kerchief. The warm scent, which had awakened Sloane before dawn, made her salivate.

"This will have to last you," Ma said, wrapping the small muffin and handing it to Sloane.

"Don't worry, Ma," she said, enjoying the warmth in her palm against the crispness of the early morning air. How would she make it to midmorning without eating it?

Her parents shared a glance that Sloane knew all too well. She better start off before they changed their minds. Besides, she'd have to rest at least twice before completing the half-day's walk. And she needed to be in Asana's square by midday.

"I need to go, Father," Sloane said, rebalancing herself onto her good leg.

"Remember to get the boar. And be aware of your surroundings," Ma said, tucking a loose strand of Sloane's brown hair behind her ear.

"I will."

A second silent exchange was shared between her parents as Sloane lifted the satchel. It was heavy enough, she hated to admit.

"Oh, I almost forgot." Father snapped his fingers. "I told Lewis— you know Lewis, his cottage is the fourth one from the baker in Asana —that he could borrow my large stitching needle. Will you stop by the stables on your way out to take it with you? Tell him I'll collect it after the Nay Moon."

"Won't you need it?" Ma's brow furrowed. It being late in the season, commissions from the few neighboring villages for Father's work were trickling into Mohn less and less, but there was still a chance to make more coin before the weather turned.

"'Tis fine. I have the other two, and that's enough for me." Father winked at Ma.

Sloane's chest warmed. Father was a master leatherworker; why, he'd even been commissioned once to make a saddle for a baron. For leagues surrounding Mohn, it was said no one was better. As Father's new apprentice these past two years, Sloane hoped that someday her work might be as well sought-after.

"You know the needle I speak of and where to find it in the workshop?" Father asked.

Sloane nodded.

Is Lonn in the stables right now? She wondered.

That was unlikely. It was so early no one had come out of their hovels yet, but Sloane ran a hand along her plait, ensuring her dark hair was still in its tight braid down her back. There was a chance.

Ma took Sloane in an embrace. "Ma, I'll be back tonight."

"I know, but..." Ma's eyes darted around as if expecting danger to appear. "Be careful."

"If your leg does tire, you know you can sleep in Asana's stable loft tonight. Gundin gave permission," Father said, his hand on Sloane's shoulder.

"I'll be fine." Sloane's cheeks grew hot. She didn't want to be a burden to anyone. The awareness that Father had surely asked Gundin made even her ears warm.

"I know you will, but..." Father trailed off as Ma had.

Sloane didn't wait to hear more. How many times had she heard the word *but* said to her? She bid them good-bye and gave Sherik a half-hug before turning to go.

She entered the stable through the back entrance into a tight space where Mohn's elder had allowed Father to establish his workshop. No sound came from the front. Lonn—the elder's young groom and valet—wasn't feeding the horse yet.

'Tis not like he'd notice you, anyway.

But mayhap tomorrow at the Prodigal Moon ritual, the other part of her hoped in vain.

When Lonn did speak to her, it was in short, awkward spurts, his eyes often downcast at her left leg, slightly smaller than the right and deformed since birth.

But mayhap tomorrow...

Sloane collected the stitching needle—long, metal, and much thicker than Ma's sewing ones—and was leaving when the elder's horse's neigh made her almost drop it.

She couldn't see Kenn, the enormous grey stallion was called, but guessed he was anxious for Lonn to come. But she couldn't wait. She needed to go.

Kenn fussed more as she closed the door behind her. She didn't like the elder's horse. Well, it wasn't that she didn't like it; she feared it, if she was being honest with herself. Lonn had had a good laugh the only time she'd attempted to pet it. Kenn had startled at her touch, and Sloane lost her balance and fell backward into the hay pile behind her. The elder's last horse, at least, had been a gentle, smaller mare. But the elder had purchased his new horse a year ago when he'd come back from a council meeting up north, Sloane couldn't remember where. When he'd come trotting into Mohn, the villagers gawked at the massive animal. *How much did that cost?* Some had whispered. No one else in the entire village could afford even an old nag. Sloane sometimes wondered about the elder, whom her parents said was adequate but unremarkable. How *did* he afford a stallion such as that? Nay, she didn't like the elder's horse.

As Sloane got closer to the entrance of Mohn—there was no gate —she set her eyes on the horizon in front of her, glad it was still early enough that no one was out yet.

No longer did anyone mention her leg, something Sloane rarely thought about on her own. After all, she'd turn eighteen on the next full moon—the Harvest Moon—and had lived in Mohn all her life. But she was aware of the looks. The half-smiles from the few girls in Mohn close to her age who'd never quite been able to include her. The kind words from some of the older women that felt a tad too forced. And the way others ignored her at times. When she'd been a child, Sloane had sometimes wondered why she'd even been born. Of course, her parents and other villagers, like Mistress Semla, the village tutor, had never treated her differently. Ma always said she was just like everyone else. And more often than not, Sloane knew it was true. But sometimes. Sometimes. Sloane still wondered when everyone else would see her. She didn't want to be special, like a village elder, one of Deogol's sovereign's scholars, or a hero in a song. She just wanted to be seen.

CHAPTER 2

Sloane

"Easy, Sloane. You have my word no one will steal your plate," said Nagel, Asana's pub owner, before giving a laugh.

A few patrons, who sat close to Sloane at the extended wooden bar, chuckled good-naturedly. Asana's pub, The Jolly Goat, with its carved wooden paneled walls, friendly bar stools, and sometimes, by chance, even a jongleur, was a marvel to Sloane. Mohn had no pub. Here, she could listen to travelers' stories, eat Nagel's delicious food—free of charge—and pretend she was someone. Mayhap it was because she was here only twice a moon, but Asana's villagers didn't seem to have time to be as awkward with her. Here, she was only the leatherworker's apprentice.

Sloane set her spoon on the bar and wiped her mouth on her sleeve, though she wasn't the least bit embarrassed, not even when a small burp escaped. The last time she'd had this much food in front of her was when she'd been here a fortnight ago. And with the fast of the Prodigal Moon tomorrow, she wanted her stomach *full*.

"You have success today?" Nagel asked, referring to Market Day, before he turned behind him for a pitcher that sat on the back counter.

"Aye," Sloane said with a grin. Had she ever. She peeked at the satchel next to her feet, which held Sherik's surprise. Four extra coins were tucked safely in the hidden pocket of her dress. Father's eyes were going to pop out of his head.

"So, your father let you come alone today?" Nagel asked, filling her goblet with cider.

"Aye." Her voice was muffled by the bite of roll she'd taken. *Finally!* she wanted to add but thought better. Nagel and Father were good friends. That remark could get back to him and hurt his feelings.

Father wants to protect you, the part of Sloane, who suddenly missed having this meal with him, thought. They'd shared this Market Day meal together every fortnight for the last eighteen moons. He'd have drooled over Nagel's stew today.

But... the other part of Sloane reasoned. She almost laughed. There was that word again. How was she ever going to be someone if there was a *but* at the end of every new idea she had? Every new responsibility she sought?

Still, both parts of Sloane couldn't deny that she should be content with her life in the hovel with her family. She loved being Father's apprentice—even if it did bring mixed emotions, what with Joah and all. She loved teaching little Sherik how to tie knots, search for pebbles, and practice reading. She loved her lingering evening talks with Ma while they darned socks.

She, like everyone else, knew to keep her loved ones close. The Befallen was out there somewhere.

But...she simply wanted to feel—

"You need a lift home, Sloane?" Nagel's wife, Sara asked, interrupting her thoughts. "Walbert said he was leaving in his wagon in about two hours and is going past Mohn." Her eyes flitted down. The bar blocked Sara's view of Sloane's left leg, but Sloane knew that glance.

She stuffed another roll into her mouth so she couldn't answer right away. Aye, she just wanted to feel capable.

"Nay, I'll walk."

"Well, if that suits you. But you'll need to leave soon to make it by sundown," Sara said, her fingers fidgeting together. "You don't want your ma to worry."

Stars, she was only fooling herself into thinking she was treated differently here.

"Aye, I know."

Sara wasn't wrong. And Sloane still had to drop off the stitching needle to Lewis, and he was quite the talker, but her stomach still had a little room. And it felt dazzling to be on no one else's timetable but her own for the first time in her life.

"Do you have any more rolls?"

THE NEXT MORNING, part of Sloane wanted to feel remorse for staying in Asana's stable loft last night, but when Gundin had also invited her to his family's supper, the decision had been easy.

Besides, Ma will be happy you're walking home in the morning light instead of past dark.

Sloane ambled along the road, enjoying the early sunshine on her face. The air had a stillness this morning and no birds had flown overhead, but Sloane didn't consider it. Sherik's surprise, the possibility of Lonn noticing her tonight, and showing off her coins to Father chased all else away. And with her belly properly filled last night, she'd make it through today's fast.

A cloud of dust came into view. The Ravyns? Cold dread stopped her.

Nay, it was only a single rider. He tore down the dirt road like the banshees of the Hoarfrost Moon were after him.

Stars be good, what happened to him?

Sloane stepped to the side of the road to let him pass.

"The Befallen!" the rider yelled to her as he sped by. "The Befallen's come."

The blood drained from Sloane's face. "Where?" she yelled back, but the rider didn't slow. She turned from watching his racing form grow fainter back toward where he'd come. Toward Mohn.

"No," whispered Sloane. "No, no, no, no, no."

Tears glossed over her eyes. Not Mohn. The Befallen couldn't have possibly hit Mohn. It was too small. Too insignificant. And her family was there.

Sloane readjusted her satchel. She had to get home. She tread on her right foot. The next step faltered as she forced weight onto her left foot, picking up her right again with haste. Step. Stumble. Step. Totter. Sloane quickened her pace, urging her left leg not to disobey her.

No, no, no, no... She thought the word over and over and over as she jogged, even when out of breath, and even when Mohn's surrounding rickety village wall—seeming as ordinary as could be— was in sight. If she repeated it enough times, her desperate wish for Mohn's safety would become true.

THE WORST PART was Sloane had been left alive.

The sick stench of death surrounding her, she could not process the knowledge her family lay motionless in their hovel, even little Sherik.

Aye, the worst part was she'd been left alive.

Sloane's leather satchel still hung from her slumped, slim shoulder. Hours ago, she'd dropped to the ground inside the entrance of Mohn. Every villager and animal lay on the ground, a corpse frozen where they'd been when it happened. There was no blood.

The Befallen did not work that way.

Some villagers' hands were stiffly holding their necks, their faces imprisoned in panicked expressions from the lack of air they'd died from. That was how it worked.

There were no survivors when the Befallen surrounded a village and choked the life from every living creature in its path like a piece of mutton lodged too far down someone's throat.

Or smothered? Suffocated? Sloane didn't know. No one did. Regardless, there were never survivors.

The Befallen had appeared in Deogol five years ago, soon after the end of the war in the Capella Realm across the sea, and it *still* remained largely a mystery. Only two things had been guessed at. It seemed to be an occurrence that happened around dusk, and it was believed it'd never transpired on the night of a full moon. But that was all that was known. There was no pattern, no tracking it, no defense. Not a soul knew if the Befallen was visible or cloaked in transparency; a multitude of men, women, and children simply sank to their knees, grasped at their throats, their eyes bulging with terror and confusion. Animals dropped where they stood: mules, mutts, swine, and chickens. 'Twas not until someone outside the befallen village stumbled upon the litter of corpses, both human and beast— sometimes fortnights later—that it was known the Befallen had swept across another village of Deogol.

Except this time, it wasn't an outsider. It was Sloane. Because she was that unlucky.

Sloane's hand absentmindedly twisted the strap of her satchel as she ignored the dried apple slices inside. Sherik's surprise. He'd never tasted them before. And now he never would.

Her eyes, blurred with tears, drew to the direction of the family's hovel down the pathway. She should be with them. Sloane whimpered. "I'm sorry."

The worst part was she'd been left alive.

It was sometime later, coming out of a stupor, Sloane realized the day had passed with her slumped on the ground, her legs aching, especially her left one, her stomach growling defiantly, her eyes stinging from the stench that'd only grown worse under the heat of the late summer sun.

A hot breeze blew across the back of her sweaty neck, her plaited hair laying across her shoulder. It seemed like years ago that she had braided it this morning thinking of seeing Lonn tonight. She hadn't seen his body. Most likely, he lay in the village stable, where he'd probably been mucking out Kenn's stall. The thought that his last moment had been shoveling manure renewed her tears. Or mayhap it wasn't Lonn. Mayhap it was everything.

Sloane peered around again, searching for signs of life to catch her attention, knowing there would be none.

If she curled up here in the dirt, closed her eyes, and ignored the incessant rattle of her stomach and the dryness of her throat, she could die, too. Then when someone happened upon Mohn, he would assume Sloane had died with her village. She'd be fully included with all the villagers for once.

Aye, that's what she'd do. She'd stay here on this spot until the sun or hunger or wild beasts stalking into the village overtook her. Aye, it would work.

Die without kissing your family goodbye? The thought wiggled out.

But the energy to enter the family's hovel didn't exist. Would the star gods forgive her? Images came to her. Sherik's freckled cheeks. Ma's warm embraces. Father's firm yet gentle instruction with an awl. Stars forgive her, but she couldn't bear to see them. If Joah was here, he'd march into the hovel and command Sloane to do the same, but...it was good her older brother wasn't in Mohn, or he'd be dead, too.

Mayhap you could find Joah.

Sloane sat up. It'd been two years since her older brother had left Mohn. It'd not been a pretty scene between Father and him. After all, Joah had been their father's first apprentice of his beloved trade. He'd said awful things. They both had. 'Twas the only time Sloane had ever witnessed Father *almost* strike one of his children. Instead, his choice phrases about Joah abandoning the family were stamped in her mind.

Sloane had replaced Joah, but his absence was keenly felt. She'd never find him. Deogol may be an island, but it was vast enough, and there were plenty of villages and towns, not to mention the capital city, Kestriel. Finding Joah would be impossible, especially given she had no horse and couldn't walk any great distance.

Nay, it'd have to be death, then. Sloane lay back on the firm ground before sitting to remove a small stone jabbing at her back. She willed herself to ignore the reek in the air. A fly buzzed around her face. She brushed it away.

Her eyes closed, thoughts drifting in and out, she was careful at first to avoid letting her mind wander into the hovel, but eventually, it all became too much. The stench of the unfairness overwhelmed her, and Sloane didn't stop her tears. She rolled onto her side and sobbed into the dirt.

IT WAS TIME TO STAND. Night had come. She rubbed away the remainder of her tears, smearing dirt onto her cheek, and spat grime out of her mouth.

Her left leg made it difficult to get off the ground, but she'd done it a hundred times before. She brushed dust off her long skirt, and noticed, even in the darkness, her leather shoes, the pair Father had made her, were filthy. Sloane used the hem of her skirt to clean them.

Once satisfied, Sloane straightened. The luminous, full Prodigal Moon caught her eye. The goddess of generosity. Gratitude. She stared at the perfect sphere hanging in the night sky, shaking her head. Her stomach growled. She wasn't supposed to eat until dawn.

Some generosity, part of Sloane thought in bitterness.

But...you're alive. Mayhap for a reason.

She pursed her lips in internal conflict. She wouldn't perform the Prodigal Moon ritual. But she supposed she could, at least, show gratitude by keeping her fast.

Now what? It was too late to consider a plan. She had a headache. But where to sleep? Certainly not the hovel.

I wonder what the elder's cottage is like inside?

After she entered and investigated the ground floor of the elder's cottage, grateful he and his stuffy, portly wife had apparently been upstairs when the Befallen happened, Sloane decided that the elder had not been adequate but greedy. The richness here was evident. While Sloane's family had slept on straw mattresses placed on the dirt floor of their small one-room hovel, the elder had no doubt slumbered in a real bed, judging by the comfortable chairs Sloane found in the parlor. She wouldn't see for herself, however. She'd had enough death for today.

Ignoring the excess of food she found in the scullery, Sloane opened the windows—real glass panes—found a spare blanket under the stairs, settled herself into one of the chairs in the parlor, and attempted to close her eyes.

The faces of the dead villagers swam before her.

"No," Sloane whispered. "Please, stars, make it stop."

It didn't stop right away, the gods in the stars didn't work like that, but eventually, Sloane did stop seeing the dead, and her mind gave way to a blank stillness so she could drift to sleep.

CHAPTER
3

Sloane

Something wasn't right.

Sloane, eyes wide open, mouth agape, sat frozen in the chair, listening. The wind rattled the open shutters, but it wasn't the wind that petrified her in the darkness of the elder's parlor. She could *feel* something.

Her back was to the cottage's entrance door. Had Sloane bolted it before bunkering down for the night? Nay, certainly not. Why would she?

Instead of imagining the faces of the dead, Sloane recollected the tales she'd overheard. Tales of the Ravyns. Rumors were the sovereign's army had given up on finding and capturing the infamous band of highwaymen.

Paralyzed with unease, Sloane eyed the shadowed silhouettes of objects in the elder's parlor. What could she use for a weapon? Two heavy-looking candlesticks sat on a table close to the hearth, but the six-foot distance might well as be six miles for all her fright.

A gust of wind banged something outside, and Sloane yelped, heaving the blanket over her head. She immediately uncovered herself: she'd never been afraid of the dark before. Father had taught her better.

A group of bandits preying on those who succumbed to the Befallen has never been waiting outside for you before, though. You should've stayed out there and died.

Heart pounding, Sloane turned in the chair to catch a peek out the window near the entrance door. The wind shifted shadows of what Sloane hoped were only tree branches against the moonlight. Mayhap she could pray to the goddess of the Prodigal Moon.

"Oh, moon goddess, hear an unworthy—" Another crack outside made Sloane give an involuntary yelp and clumsily leap from the chair. She stumbled through the parlor, tripping on the blanket.

A knife. The scullery would have a knife. Floundering in the unfamiliar darkened room, Sloane tripped again over an unseen stool before finding a butcher knife hanging from a leather strap on the wall next to the washbasin. Her panting blocked the whip of the wind. She wanted to tell herself to hush. There was a back door off the scullery, and Sloane moved faster than she knew she could to make certain it was bolted. Then she crouched between two wooden cabinets where she couldn't be seen from the window and where she could watch the door. The hilt of the knife in her hand felt so unlike holding Father's awls, sharp tools used in leatherwork. This handle was square and bulky in her small hands. She studied the glint of the blade's edge, cowering in the darkness. If someone burst through that door, would she be able to use this knife? Sloane had strangled and gutted a hen before, but this wasn't the same.

Nay, it's not. Hens aren't trying to kill you.

Sloane wasn't sure how long she crouched there, hunched against the cabinet, but eventually, the wind died and, in its wake, left a stillness that was almost eerier. She'd definitely felt something. Ravyns or ghosts in the wind or...the Befallen?

Steadying her breath, her legs aching unbearably for the second time in the last day, she dropped the knife and clenched and unclenched her white-knuckled fists.

The new light of dawn creeped through the window behind her, and she rubbed her tired face, wondering what next.

If she truly were to die, she should ram the knife through her stomach and get it over with.

It wasn't fair.

Between the Befallen, the Ravyns, or who knew what, a constant fear ran through Deogol, simply waiting for calamity.

This couldn't go on. At some point, through some bale, Deogol would be destroyed.

It wasn't fair.

"Someone needs to do something," Sloane found herself saying aloud. Not her, certainly, but someone had to stop this.

The part of Sloane, who was overtired, hungry, and grieving, laughed.

You mean the Unsung? You're going to find the supposed unsung hero who can bring all this to an end? Why not figure out when the Azure Moon rises, too, while you're at it?

The thought struck the other more determined and defiant part of Sloane as humorous also. That was a ridiculous and stupid notion indeed.

The Unsung was a hero foretold in an ancient prophecy called the Edan Lore, given to Deogol over a hundred years ago from the StarSeers of the Capella Realm. Everyone in Deogol knew the Edan Lore by heart—passed from generation to the next, carried through the country by peddlers, bards, even tax collectors—for it was said the StarSeers had forbidden it be written down. It foretold of the only chance that Deogol had against the Befallen: The Unsung.

But in five years, it was clear that the Edan Lore was becoming more a myth than a prophecy.

Nay, best to simply make her way back to Asana, sound the alarm, and hope Nagel and Sara or someone else in Asana would take in Mohn's leatherworker's daughter.

Crippled daughter.

Sloane instantly hated herself for the thought. She'd been taught better. Never had she let herself be branded by that word.

As if to be reminded the foolish thought wasn't her own, Sloane stood. She caught her blurred reflection in a clean pot hanging beside where the knife had hung. Her large brown eyes stared back at her.

Ma's pointed chin and Father's petite nose. There was still dirt smudged on it, and she wiped it off.

Stars, I look pitiful.

Sloane took the pot off the wall. It had a similar leather strap attached to it. She rubbed her fingers across the smooth surface of the thin piece of leather. Father's work. A simple strap, but even this held a tiny design, carefully pin-pricked by her father's expert hand. His was the most beautiful, ornate work. He could make anything; sheaths for knives, delicate shoes, things not all leatherworkers could make. Elaborate, yet functional.

He'd taught her well. Asana would take her in, and she would continue Father's trade and make a living for herself. She was no one's crippled daughter.

She made a list of items she'd need for Asana. There wasn't need for much food as it was only a half day's walk, although she'd need to take all she could carry so she wouldn't become a beggar before earning wages. She wouldn't accept Nagel and Sara's pity. She did know where Ma hid the family's coin in their hovel. She'd have to brave going in.

Now there was the matter of Father's tools. She must take those; they were her livelihood. But packing those would be heavy. Carrying that weight would mean trouble for both time and her legs.

"'Tis only nine miles," Sloane said to no one, scrunching her eyebrows together. It may take her a full day to reach Asana, but she'd make it. Aye, she *must* take the tools.

Then she had a thought. The elder must have coin hidden somewhere in this cottage.

That's stealing!

That greedy man has no use for them now, the other part of Sloane argued.

Moving through the scullery and parlor, Sloane made her way upstairs. The stench of the elder and his wife hit her nose halfway up the staircase. Threatening to gag, Sloane was glad she hadn't yet broken her fast.

Upstairs, there were two rooms. One contained a loom and had baskets of thread and yarn everywhere. The elder's wife had been quite the seamstress. Gingerly, Sloane lifted a bright blue shawl folded on a shelf. There was no need for a shawl in the summer, but Sloane had never had something so colorful—or silky smooth—touch her skin before.

She gazed at her own raggedy dress, a muslin shift covered by a brown, sleeveless woolen tunic tied at the waist with a leather belt. It was the only one she owned. Although Sloane had always been small, her recent growth made the sleeves of the shift and the hem of the tunic seem as though she were wearing a child's dress. Sloane toyed with a rip in her sleeve that she hadn't noticed before. She had the thought Ma would be irritated with her, but then bit her lip against thinking.

You need to move if you don't want to be caught on the road to Asana after dark.

Searching the elder's wife's sewing room, holding the blue shawl over her nose as she did so, Sloane found no coin in any box, drawer, or sack she searched. All she found, buried in the back of a chest's bottom drawer, were a few pieces of the wife's jewelry. It wasn't anything to get excited about: a shell bracelet and a pair of blue glass earrings the elder had probably brought back from his travels to the capital city, Kestriel, an iron broach in the shape of the Gale Moon's symbol, and a tarnished chain necklace with a misshaped and rough circular piece of what looked like onyx for its pendant. That might fetch a price; a stoneworker could possibly smooth the onyx and make real jewelry out of it. Sloane placed the chain around her neck, put the broach in her pocket, and disregarded the other two items.

Standing at the half-open door of the elder's chamber, the foul smell protruding from this room, Sloane took deep breaths into the shawl.

She couldn't do it. It was horrifying enough to think of entering the hovel, stepping over the bodies of her family, and packing their belongings. She couldn't take any more from the elder. The worthless jewelry would have to do.

Later, it took four attempts before Sloane finally had the courage to enter the hovel, and even when she did, she kept her eyes upward on the thatched ceiling.

She stepped over brown skirts tangled over Ma's green-hued skin and held back tears when she collected the six coins in the jar hidden in the false bottom of the trunk that lay next to the other items Ma treasured: a lock of baby hair from each of her children, a scrap of prized parchment with faded ink, the thank you letter to Father from the baron for his saddle, and a leather moon cuff—Ma's prayer wristlet worn specifically for prayers to the twelve full moon goddesses, the Azure Moon, the thirteenth goddess, too rare to count —inlaid with a pattern of delicate stamped symbols, each distinct to signify the different moons.

Sloane stroked the indentation of a husk of wheat encompassed by the perfect circle, which would be the next full moon, the Harvest Moon. Next to Ma's was another leather moon cuff, new and oiled. The patterns on the wristlet also depicted the full moons, their unique patterns easily discernible. Sloane put the new leather to her nose. The rich, earthy smell was an intoxicant to her.

It hit her. This moon cuff had been fashioned for *her*. Of course. Her eighteenth birthday was the next full moon, the day when all who were born under the Harvest Moon were celebrated. This gift she held—this last new thing created by Father's hands—was both a comfort and a gash to Sloane's heart.

Moon cuffs were only supposed to be worn on the night of the full moons, but Sloane figured there was little else that could befall her at this point, and so she shirked off superstition and slipped it on her right wrist as was the custom.

The Befallen had already taken everything.

CHAPTER
4

Sloane

It was time to go. The sun was high. Sloane would be lucky to make it to Asana before the stars etched the sky. She stood at the stable's back entrance door.

"Just go in," she prodded herself. "You must take Father's tools."

But Lonn's body is in there, the heartbroken side of her argued back.

She was being a sook, a coward. She'd been taught better. As the wooden door creaked open, Kenn's angry whinny startled her, and she fell backward, landing with a jarring *thump* in the dirt. Her heart pounded in her ears.

Stupid horse.

Wait! How?

How was it that she was hearing Kenn, who should be dead with the rest?

The wild neighing of the beast grew fiercer; she placed her hand on her chest, willing herself to steady.

Lonn's body forgotten, Sloane trod curiously to the front of the stable, where stamping in his stall, was Kenn. The grey stallion's water trough had been kicked over, and it was clear the horse was thirsty.

Sloane grabbed a bucket, pumped some water into it from the well outside the stable, and then, with satisfaction, watched the horse drink. While he drank his fill, Sloane pondered whether she dared pat him. He finished, prancing to the back of the stall, shaking his head wildly as if trying to remove his bridle. That was when Sloane noticed the saddle on his back.

"Oh, you must be so uncomfortable."

But a saddled horse meant no walking. If she could get on. And if she could ride.

How was Kenn alive? Sloane outstretched her hand and, making low, "whoa" sounds, gently touched the horse. Kenn's ears twitched back, but he accepted her hand on his shoulder. Sloane inched her hand up Kenn's reins until it was right below his muzzle. She drew the horse's head closer to her own.

"How are you alive?" Sloane whispered.

A gift from the morning star? A blessing of generosity from the Prodigal Moon? Sloane knew no stories of any living creature surviving the Befallen. It was impossible.

IMPOSSIBLE WAS HEFTING Sloane's father's heavy tools into the horse's saddlebags. Impossible was remembering everything she needed to take to Asana. Impossible was climbing onto Kenn. But most impossible was figuring out what to do when, hours later, Sloane was finally atop the horse outside the stable.

His reins held loosely in her hands, Kenn craned his head backward as if to ask, *well?*

"I suppose I just flick your reins and off we go," Sloane said, performing the action as she spoke.

The horse did not move but snorted as if mocking her.

She snapped the reins again. Nothing. She tried to recall the few riders she'd seen. When they wanted to go, it was as if the horse simply knew it was time.

Kick him, mayhap?

She did, and Kenn trotted toward the entrance leading out of the village. Sloane held the reins tighter. She trained her eyes ahead, avoiding any last looks at the villagers' bodies. When she was near the entrance, Sloane thought mayhap she should stop to take a last survey of Mohn. But she didn't know how to stop the beast, and she was far too nervous of what would happen should she turn in the saddle.

Nay. Best to remember Mohn alive, not stilled with death.

She kept her tears silent. Would the stars in the sky accept her people even though she hadn't given them a proper send-off? Were they already glints in the heavens gazing down on her? Sloane's lip quivered at the thought of little Sherik laughing and sparkling above.

Please, star gods. Take care of my family.

THE COUNTRYSIDE between Mohn and Asana was not beautiful this time of year. It was too far inland from the lushness of the Mehr Sea, and the vegetation that existed was dry and golden during the lapse between the Prodigal Moon and the Harvest Moon. Shade was nonexistent on this road. But Sloane did have a good vantage of the horizon and would be able to see any travelers coming her way.

Kenn slowed to a walk. She wished she were already in Asana and not on the open road, but she didn't know how to make him go faster.

You'd probably fall off if he hastened.

And so, they walked.

When the sun began sinking in the sky, Sloane spotted the large willow tree to the east of the road. She was about a mile away from Asana.

Good. Not even sunset yet.

That was when the rumble came from behind. The ground quivered as the sound grew closer, the clopping of many hooves against the earth became more distinct.

Sloane dared look and her breath caught in her throat.

At least a dozen riders were galloping toward her. And each one bore a black cloak that appeared as an inky streak behind him as they sprinted toward her. The Ravyns.

Sloane hysterically kicked at Kenn, flapping the reins in her panicked hands. But the horse, rather than bursting into a run, stopped altogether.

It wasn't a moment later Sloane found herself surrounded by the black-cloaked gang of Ravyns. One of them, a dark-bearded, young man and with an air of casualness as if he'd run into an old friend, reined his giant black stallion directly in front of her.

"Well, goddesses of the moon," he said, his voice as calm and steady as the expression on his face. "What have we here?" His eyes roved over Sloane—her cheeks burning—and along the stuffed-full saddlebags.

Sloane continued to sit straight atop the horse, wishing she appeared taller. She said nothing in return. Kenn stomped, unnerved by the crowd of horses and men surrounding them.

"What's in those bags, girl?" another of the Ravyns spoke. He, too, had a dark beard but with streaks of red that shined in the sunlight. His pink, sweaty face didn't take as kindly to being in the sun.

Sloane silently cursed herself for carrying no weapon, but what would she have been able to do against this infamous mob?

"No answer?" The first man gave a chuckle, the others following suit. "All right, get her down."

Six men dismounted and grabbed at Sloane, who whipped her arms around in defense. She was easily drawn down and dragged away from the stallion as she shouted, "Let me go!"

While the two men who'd spoken rummaged through the saddlebags, Sloane was forced to the ground, two men holding her hands behind her back as she sat in the dirt. She fought, but her arms were like twigs compared to their strong grip.

"What we got, Hux?" someone called to the dark-bearded leader.

"Tools, mostly, it seems," Hux returned, plucking a pair of large shears from the saddlebag.

That would have made a good weapon.

"Anything else, Brinley?" another said, striding to the reddish-bearded man. "Coins, anything?"

Brinley was digging through the other saddlebag. "Nothing but food." He hauled the bag of dried apples—Sherik's dried apples—out and held them above his head as someone would a prize. "Oh, not a complete loss." He laughed, stuffing one into his mouth.

The loaf of bread she'd so carefully wrapped in the blue shawl was flung onto the ground. One of the Ravyns stomped his foot onto the shawl and grinded it into the dirt. He cocked his head at Sloane and sneered as it became more and more filthy. A heat she'd never felt flushed through her body. She had had enough.

"Let me go, you cowards!" she yelled, a new fluttering sensation moving through her. Had her voice ever been so loud?

"Wha' ye call us?" An older man with a scruffy, blonde beard, which was split by a jagged scar running across his chin, unsheathed a knife and leaned down to her as he spoke. His breath smelled of moon mead, strong moon mead. The knife's blade pricked under her chin.

"You heard me," Sloane said, flinching before forcing herself to meet his eyes.

Hux laughed. "What spirit this one has. I say, girl, you're braver than most men we rob." He resumed searching the saddlebags in hopes, no doubt, he'd find better loot than leatherworking tools. But the coins were hidden in the inside pocket of her dress. They'd find nothing of value.

Did this Hux really think her brave?

The split-bearded man stood and began picking at his teeth with the blade of his knife. A piece of meat flicked out of his mouth and onto Sloane's cheek. A few Ravyns chuckled.

"You're disgusting!" Sloane said, using her shoulder to wipe her cheek.

"Yeah? How's this for disgusting?" He made a guttural, sucking noise deep in his throat and spat a large amount of mucus atop her head. This brought more jeers from the men watching, one of them yelling, "Good one, Rhiner!" Slimy coldness dribbled down the back of her head. She bit her lip to stop her tears.

"All right, that's enough," Hux said with the same casual tone he'd been using. "There's naught much here, but we may find a price for this lot." He nodded toward the pile of tools on the ground. "And, of course, this horse will fetch a price. This isn't a farmer's workhorse. Where'd you get it, girl? You steal it?"

Hux's question emboldened her further. "I stole nothing, but that may be difficult for thieves like yourselves to believe, shadow cats!"

Her words brought renewed peals of laughter.

"Search the girl," Brinley said.

"With pleasure," Rhiner said, eyeing her like a dew fruit to be skinned.

Dozens of hands roughly patted her body. It didn't matter where. Her hands still pinned behind her back, she kicked and writhed around. One fondled the lump of coins in her hidden pocket. A malicious grin appeared as he realized it was only accessible through the inside of Sloane's dress.

"Stop, stop!" Sloane cried, going clammy as her temporary bravery fled her body. "I'll give you what I have, leave me be!"

"All right, that's enough." Hux raised his voice. He was obeyed. "Lift her."

Sloane was hoisted onto her feet, but the haste in which they'd set her down did not give her time to steady herself on her good leg and she fell back onto the ground. Her skirts lifted in a tangled mess to reveal the curved deformity of her leg.

"She's a chuffin' cripple!" someone yelled. The laughter in Sloane's ears might as well have been a whip on her back. Her hands free now, she didn't bother to cover her leg.

"That's it, then." Hux's men instantly ceased. Sloane focused on his face, the afternoon sun creating shadows from the willow tree against his cheekbones. She could not cry. But staring into the leader's dark eyes, Sloane welled up, despite herself. For a split second, she thought mayhap she detected something like shame staring back at her, but—

"Hux!" Two new riders loped toward the group, who turned their attention to the newcomers. Through the mass of men's torsos and legs, Sloane glimpsed two more black-cloaked figures dismounting. "Sir," said one when they stood in front of the leader, "We caught sight of a caravan. Three wagons. Three! 'Bout four miles from here."

Of course. These were scouts scavenging for the Ravyns' next victims.

"Any guards traveling with them?" Brinley asked, hands on his hips.

"Four, sir. Nothin' we can't manage," one said, his back to Sloane.

"What we waiting for, then?" someone asked.

The question seemed to remind everyone of her presence, and she found everyone facing her once more, the two newcomers following suit. Then—

"Joah!" Sloane exclaimed, her eyes wide.

The tall, lean form of her brother stood there, his hazel eyes staring at her as if he'd seen a ghost. It took only one startled breath for him to recover himself and turn his expression into something harsh and alien.

"Joah?" Brinley's forehead wrinkled.

The black-cloaked figures regarded Joah. Hux, arms crossed over his chest, scrutinized Joah as if attempting to learn the secrets of the stars.

"Kerr?" Hux asked.

Joah gave a nonchalant shake of his head. "Aye, sir?"

"Joah!" Sloane's exclamation was forceful this time.

"This girl seems to know you, Kerr," Hux said, casually examining his nails.

"Joah, tell them I'm your sister," Sloane said, her open hands in front of her in a pleading motion.

"Sister?" Brinley asked. "I thought you had no family, Kerr? Or

Joah, is it?"

"She's obviously mad." Joah pointed at Sloane before snickering. "And desperate."

"You're certain you wouldn't lie to get yourself in with us?" Hux asked quietly.

"You know the rules, Kerr!" Brinley said, stepping closer to Joah. "We're phantoms. Phantoms with no ties to anything or anyone."

"Nay, sir. My family is dead."

"Your family *is* dead now, Joah!" Sloane yelled. She couldn't keep the high-pitched strain from her voice. "Everyone. Ma, Father, Sherik. The Befallen took Mohn. Everyone's dead."

Sloane could have sworn there was a flash-second of anguish in Joah's eyes before *Kerr* threw back a glare that was somewhere between indifference and malice.

"I don't know what she's ranting about," Joah returned coolly. "She's daft."

"How could you?" Sloane whispered, her eyes boring into his. "First, you abandon us, and now this? I might as well be dead, too."

Joah's act was a careful combination of relaxed posture and a pitying look meant for a stranger.

"Enough of this, Hux," Brinley said, moving to his horse. "Let's get on with it so we don't miss that caravan."

"Caravan, nothin'," Rhiner yelled. "I say we off to Mohn! If what this girl says is true, there's a whole trove waitin' for us there."

There were many shouts of agreement. Sloane dropped her head. Wasn't the Befallen enough? She had to be robbed and then left with the knowledge her village was to be ravaged?

"All right then." Hux held up his hand for silence, receiving it immediately. Sloane glared at Joah, whose eye contact was brief and hooded. Hux stood in front of Sloane. "Give us the coin you're hiding, girl, or I'll tear the clothes from your body and take it myself."

Without one thought of an argument, Sloane slipped her hand into the top of her dress, retrieved the bag containing her mother's coins and the elder's wife's iron broach, and stretched out her hand to

Hux. In the act, the onyx necklace, tucked under her collar, came into view.

"What's that?" Rhiner asked.

Sloane shrugged, finished speaking to these cowards.

Hux eyed it over the broach and the coins he was counting in his palm. "Give it to me."

"'Tis worthless," Sloane spouted, forgetting her oath of silence.

"Then you won't mind parting with it," Hux said.

The necklace was worthless. But as she watched Father's tools being loaded back into the saddlebags and Sherik's dried apples disappearing into their mouths, she had a desperate need to hang on to something.

"Hey, Kerr, Sy, you want one?" a short blonde man said to the two scouts, holding up the apples. Joah took one, the captive—his sister—forgotten.

"Those were Sherik's apples, Joah!" Sloane yelled then yelped in pain.

Rhiner stood on her left leg. Sloane's cries of agony rang out. Joah, in the background, was the only one who turned away from her.

"Give us the necklace, gimpy girl," Rhiner growled. "Before I hurt your other leg."

Sloane couldn't help but bawl. She tore the necklace's chain from her neck and flung it into the grass nearby.

"Enough, Rhiner." Sloane barely heard Hux over her own cries. "Let's go."

Rhiner's foot was forced off her. Hux gathered the necklace, making his way to his horse and leaving Sloane as a pitiful heap on the ground.

Through her blurred vision, Sloane watched the Ravyns mount their horses, Brinley holding Kenn's reins. Led by Hux, they cantered back down the road from which Sloane had come. Toward Mohn. Clouds of dirt covered their retreating forms.

"Joah! Stars curse you, Joah!" she screamed after them, before wiping saliva from her mouth and sobbing into her dirty hand.

CHAPTER 5

Sloane

Forgotten was the danger of traveling in the dark. Forgotten were the supplies so meticulously packed. Sloane placed one foot in front of the other.

The sun had set and the rising moon mocked her as the first tiny stars pierced the sky. Her normal, slow gait was hardly more than a hobble right now, her leg throbbing as though still being crushed. All cried out, her eyes stung, and she gave slight hiccups as she made her way.

Sloane stopped abruptly. *That's odd.*

Through the darkness, the view of Asana's rock village wall was visible, but the large gate leading into the village stood open, and the parapets that snaked atop the wall that normally held four or five sentinels stood in night's shadow. Unlit. Torches should be projecting light onto the darkened road.

Asana was still and unnatural-looking. Sloane's stomach dropped.

It couldn't be. Not two villages this close together. But then, why not? Sloane stood petrified, staring at the dim silhouette of Asana's outline.

Had the village fled?

But the answer, like autumn's cold rain, doused her in fear and knowledge. She remembered the eeriness she'd awakened to last night. But that made no sense. There were no tales of anyone sensing the Befallen from a distance.

With caution, Sloane strode two paces toward the open gate before stopping.

Wait! What if the Befallen is still here? No one knows what it looks like.

A breeze stirred the trees that lined the left side of the road, rustling the boughs. Sloane shivered. Was it hiding in the trees? She peered back the way she'd come. Behind her, mayhap?

"Cease your imagination!" she whisper-yelled to herself.

What was she afraid of at this point? Mayhap her pleas for her fate were to be answered after all, and Sloane could now die like the rest of her family—her blood quickened thinking of Joah, that traitor, riding off with the Ravyns—and be at peace.

She scanned the outline of the trees, looking for what? A face? A demon? A blackness swallowing everything?

A crack of thunder in the distance made her squeal. A storm was rolling in. She'd take cover in the gatehouse of Asana. She coaxed herself forward.

Once inside the archway of the gatehouse, Sloane's fears were confirmed. An old man, hair stark white, a spilled cup in front of him, and a crude spear beside him, sat frozen in death in a wooden chair. A jolt of lightning behind her showed his face. Frightened.

Unlike the villagers of Mohn, whom Sloane avoided examining, she found herself studying this elderly man's features. Even in the darkness, the wrinkles of his face stood out. In the flash of a new lightning burst, tiny silver whiskers protruded from his cheeks and chin.

Why was this man the guard on duty? He was a small man, not as small as Sloane, but she doubted he would pose a threat to any danger that approached these gates. It didn't matter. Had it been a young man, muscles wide, Sloane would have found him in the exact same position. Probably with the exact same expression on his slain face.

Sloane eyed others. A few lay outside the village stables near the gatehouse, two, who appeared to have toppled from the parapets of the wall, and another man slumped on the other side of the archway. This time, instead of growing despondent, she found something burning within her chest. The same sensation she'd felt earlier with the Ravyns.

How dare this curse!

The villagers of Asana were good people, friendly neighbors to Mohn. She thought of kind Nagel and Sara lying inside The Jolly Goat. Chatty Lewis. Gundin, who'd brought her an extra blanket two nights ago.

The thunder became distant, signaling the storm was moving away from Asana, mayhap toward Mohn.

Not Mohn. Those bastard Ravyns! Having dealt with both the Befallen and those ruthless cowards in the last day, Sloane wasn't certain which was worse. Joah's face swam in front of her. Her jaw clenched. The Befallen may be a nameless plague on Deogol, but those thieves were naught but the worst of men.

Entering the village stables in hopes her luck might be repeated twice, she found no animal save for a donkey, stiff on its side. Again, she wondered how Kenn had survived the Befallen.

Sloane slumped onto the straw in an empty stall, too tired to climb up to the hay loft. For a time, she simply stared at the dark wall in front of her, listening to the last of the thunder rolling. Could there be a second plan for her? It seemed impossible she'd be able to make it to another village, not on foot, anyway. And what of her trade? With the leatherworker tools, she was useful, but now...who would hire a lame girl from Mohn?

Eventually, the silence of the night took over, and Sloane, too exhausted to even remove her shoes, flopped onto the straw and fell asleep.

A stream of sunlight assaulted her through the open window. She awoke, squinted, and sat up, taking bits of straw stuck to her cheek with her. She brushed them away and took in her strange surroundings in the daylight. The stable was still an eerie sort of silent, but outside, a few birds chirped. Her stomach growled.

Well, there wasn't much else to do but find some food and search for any supplies she could use. Again.

With no leatherworker in Asana, there would be no tools to scavenge, only the stitching needle she could retrieve from Lewis's cottage. She couldn't think about that. It would only renew her rage with Joah and the Ravyns.

Was she any better than the Ravyns? Today, the thought of taking others' food and belongings—even if they were dead—made her chest tighten. The vision of Sherik's apples clutched by that nasty Brinley swam before her.

Would the goddess of the Prodigal Moon condemn her?

Sloane decided it'd be less scornful to take food from the bakery—Asana had a real baker's shoppe, not merely Eilia's bread stand in Mohn—rather than someone's dwelling.

She hobbled there, her left leg bruised from yesterday, and helped herself to almost an entire loaf of bread before noticing the metal tray of tarts scattered on the floor next to the oven—and the baker's body. Without anyone attending to it, the fire in the oven was only ashes. Sloane picked up a tart, which had landed on its bottom rather than overturned onto the top. She'd never tasted a pastry before. Sara's rolls were already a luxury. Sloane held the small pastry in her palm, transfixed by the thick, cherry-red liquid. The outlines of actual cherries were buried beneath the gooey surface.

She paused. *This would cost a moon's wages.*

You've already eaten the bread. Besides, you'll find a way to extend generosity of your own. Like the goddess would want.

Sloane's finger dipped into the sticky substance, and she stuck it to her tongue. It tasted exactly like what Sloane imagined the color red would taste like. The taste was bold and something between sweet and sour. She dove in.

With a renewed sense of resolve that she was helping herself out of necessity—and a bit of a stomachache, courtesy of eating four of the divine cherry tarts—Sloane left the bakery and spent the morning scavenging cottages for traveling supplies. In the tailor's cottage, she found a worn leather rucksack. Inspecting it, Sloane could tell it wasn't Father's work, far too sloppy. But it'd do. She filled it with as much dried food as she could find—better to not take anything that would spoil— along with a small knife and a wool shawl nowhere near as soft or beautiful as the elder's wife's.

The sack of silver coins she found in Asana's elder's cottage gave her pause. Sloane held one eye level to examine. Etched into the coin was the symbol of the Rapture Moon, the full moon in early spring.

"Stars, this is a fortune."

Sloane finished filling the rucksack with the heavy weight of apprehension sitting on her shoulders. Everything in her screamed she was stealing despite her earlier rationalizing with herself that she wasn't committing treason against the goddess of the Prodigal Moon.

You really are no better than the Ravyns, stealing like this. Sloane's stomach gurgled, thick with pastries and guilt.

"'Tis not the same," she reasoned with herself. "I'm only taking these supplies because the Ravyns stole everything from me."

Supplies that you stole from Mohn's elder.

"What choice do I have?" Sloane bit back tears. "Shall I use this knife to join my family?"

Sloane studied the knife she'd been toying with. The symbol of the last winter moon, the Hunger Moon glinted in the sunlight. The Hunger Moon represented a period of desperation. If one had prepared—and been given the blessings of the Harvest Moon—it was a span of days proudly testing the dregs of endurance. If the Harvest Moon had not been kind, well, there was a reason it was called the Hunger Moon.

Sloane dropped the knife as if it might sting her of its own accord.

"Ma, Father, I need you! This isn't fair." Tears covered her cheeks.

The worst part was she'd been left alive. She couldn't keep this thought at bay.

But she *was* alive. And, if she was going to stay alive, she needed to come to terms with taking the supplies.

'Tis not like the Ravyns at all, a voice inside uttered.

She wiped her nose and continued.

Digging through a chest in the cottage she stood in, Sloane came upon a set of flint and fire steel laying at the bottom of a drawer.

They were both common in their shape and size, but someone had clumsily chiseled something onto the steel. Sloane held it closer to her eye. It was a moon or was attempting to be. The circle was more of a wobbly, stretched-out square. But the accompanying symbol looked like a candle. The Prelude Moon. The first moon of the new year. A fitting symbol. The beginning.

Sloane rubbed her fingers along the jagged piece of flint, scanning the silent room.

Nay, she wasn't like the Ravyns at all.

Outside, Sloane stood with the rucksack on her back, the flint and steel held tight in her hands. Next to her was a handcart piled with hay. One of the farming villagers must have packed it to take to sell somewhere.

She'd not been able to stop the Ravyns from robbing her or ravaging Mohn, but if they came back this way, and she guessed they would, they'd not raze another village. Not when she could stop them.

Again, Sloane thought of Joah, his eyes darting away from hers.

Had Joah dared go into the hovel and see for himself their parents' corpses? She studied the moon cuff on her wrist. Though it was the time of the Prodigal Moon, both signs of the Hunger Moon and the Prelude Moon had found Sloane this morning. Desperation. And beginnings.

The steel slashed against the flint. A spark. Sloane rubbed them together again. Another spark. A third spark and Sloane lit a small piece of burlap cloth that would be her tinder. She blew on the tiny ember, watching the yellow and orange burn away the brown of the burlap. When the ember transformed into flame, Sloane scanned the village square and threw the piece of burning burlap onto the pile of hay. It made for excellent kindling.

The flames danced, the smoke making her give a small cough. She lifted a torch that lay next to her that she'd pulled from the gatehouse wall and lit it. With the torch, she set aflame the stable, bakery, the tailor's, and the cottages that lined the square. The only place she paused was The Jolly Goat.

"Farewell, Nagel and Sara."

The pub caught fire from her torch. She couldn't say more but kept a prayer going in her heart.

The fire rushed to devour Asana, including its poor fallen bodies.

At least they're getting a proper send-off.

It was the tradition in Deogol to cremate the dead. Sloane regretted that she hadn't burned Mohn, too.

Asana was swallowed. She covered her mouth with a handkerchief to not directly breathe in the smoke. The stench increased. Sloane walked outside the gatehouse, gagging on the smell of flesh.

The black smoke billowed into the blue sky. Eventually, the smoke would be easy to spot miles away. But she didn't care. Not at this moment. She'd been left alive, and she'd have no more disrespect of the Prodigal Moon's bounty.

As Sloane watched the fire, she continued her silent prayer to the veiled stars to accept all those of Asana whose ashes were drifting upward toward the heavens.

Finally, she started up the road leading north. She had no idea how far away the next village was. Asana was the farthest from home she'd ever been.

But she had nothing now, and that, she thought, was as good a beginning as any.

CHAPTER
6

In Kestriel, Capital City of Deogol: Tolvar

When Tolvar opened his bleary brown eyes, the morning's sunlight burning them, his first thought was of the cousin of King Rian, the sovereign of the Capella Realm. This was odd because he hadn't dreamed her, nor had he allowed himself to think specifically about her for several moons. Odd, indeed. Wondering how he'd stand, he rubbed his eyes and stuck his tongue out at the taste in his mouth. Had some mongrel defecated in his mouth after he passed out?

Tolvar groaned, the sun's irritation on his eyes catching up to his head. Stars, did it hurt!

Slowly, very slowly, Tolvar stood from the cot he'd collapsed upon last night after drinking himself into a stupor—again. He squinted against the bright light and realized he didn't recognize this room. Where was he? And what was that sour smell? It was a simple room, plaster walls with no decor and a worn wooden floor. The only other furniture was a wooden chair, which held a ceramic basin and pitcher. It appeared Tolvar had used it last night, and not to wash himself.

He had to leave this room immediately before he needed that basin again. Tolvar opened the door into a small corridor that led into what sounded like a kitchen, judging by the clangs of pots clattering, and leaned on the wall like it was a friend, getting his bearings.

Let's see...he'd found Ghlee...no, Ghlee had found him. Then they'd gone to the Silver's Edge, and they'd shared, what? Four? Five growlers together? Oh, Siria's skirt, his head hurt. Mayhap it was six?

"You up then?" A short, old woman appeared at the other end of the corridor. Her hands were on her plump hips, her dirty apron implying she'd been the one making the racket in the kitchen. "Right then. You can pay your two coppers and get out."

"Where am I?" Tolvar asked, hand to his forehead. Would his eyes ever open properly again?

In response, the woman gave an eyeroll and disappeared back into the kitchen.

Tolvar followed her, his first footfalls wobbly as if the floor shifted under him.

The smells in the kitchen would have been appetizing in normal circumstances, but upon entering the room, Tolvar's stomach threatened mutiny.

"I apologize about the, uh—mess in the basin, woman," he said. He fished through his coin purse, finding three coppers to hand her.

The woman's back was to him as she worked at whatever was cooking in the hearth.

"Hmmm," she muttered. "You can tell that no-good grandson of mine not to bring his stars-forsaken totty sots here again."

Grandson? Ah. Ghlee.

"Sot? Madam, I'm no sot. I just—" Tolvar started.

"Mm-hmm. Tell that to the smell of you. Ugh. You filthy drunkard. When was the last time you bathed?" She turned, eyes blazing, pointing her wooden spoon at him. "At least my grandson knows how to hold his liquor. Practically carried you in here, he did. Now, you paid. Out with you."

Tolvar swallowed any words he might return. Arguing with Ghlee's grandmother did not seem prudent.

"I am sorry again for your trouble. Good day to you." Tolvar made his way to the kitchen's backdoor.

"And don't forget that." Ghlee's grandmother nodded to Tolvar's sword standing in the corner. Ghlee must have pried it off Tolvar in his drunken state—he never took it off otherwise—and placed it there so that he wouldn't stab himself in his sleep.

The sword glinted in the light streaming through the open kitchen door. For a moment, Tolvar wondered if he should simply leave the accursed thing there, but instead, he snatched it by its leather belt, turned, and was out the door without another glance at Ghlee's grandmother.

"Stay away from my boy, sot!" were the last words she shouted from behind him.

Once Tolvar was through the alley and into the morning commotion of Kestriel, people walking with a purpose on the outskirts, horses and carriages striding down the middle, he realized he was on Morn Road. The row of book shoppes on the opposite side of the road confirmed it. The side nearest Tolvar was lined with four-story buildings, each holding dozens of rooms like the one he'd left. Ghlee failed to mention that his grandmother lived so close to the Silver's Edge.

Probably so you wouldn't know there was such an easy spot to pass out in.

There was a momentary pang of guilt.

He didn't remember being taken to Ghlee's grandmother's last night, but he could only imagine what an ass he'd been: Ghlee propping him up, pounding on the old woman's door in the middle of the night, Tolvar too drunk to stand or even slur two words together.

His head really did hurt so much.

"Oi! Wolf!" yelled a voice coming up the road.

Ghlee strode toward him, his blonde hair wet, his beard trimmed and combed, like always. He wore a fresh pair of hose and tunic, reminding Tolvar of the old woman's words about bathing. Ghlee's sword, too, hung from his side.

"Don't shout that name at me on the street," Tolvar managed to say, although he couldn't muster the proper tone of anger. All these surrounding city noises were making him feel as though he needed to sit. "Lest you should feel my bite."

Ghlee chuckled, clapping Tolvar on the back, causing him to lose balance for a second. Tolvar was taller than Ghlee, but both men were built similarly; broad-shouldered, and muscular from hours of training. Were it not for Ghlee's light features that contrasted Tolvar's dark ones, one might mistake the two twenty-five-year-old men as brothers. And in many ways, they were, having been close since boyhood when they'd first trained together, first as pages, then squires. "I'd like to see that, friend. Stars' shadow, you look awful."

Tolvar eyed him in warning.

"I see you met my gran?" Ghlee nodded toward the alley Tolvar had stepped from.

"Aye, lovely woman."

"Watch it." Ghlee's pale eyes cautioned. "Would you rather I'd left you slumped in the street? Could have let you be collected with the rest of the rubbish, I s'pose." He laughed before turning serious. "Div threw you out. Don't you remember?"

No, Tolvar did not remember the barkeep throwing him out of the Silver's Edge.

Was it for life? he wondered, then had another twinge of guilt, realizing his first worry was being barred from drinking in that tavern again. Thrown out? What had Tolvar done?

"Well," Ghlee supplied as if reading Tolvar's thoughts, "Let's just say, you should keep comments about your abilities with the sword to yourself when you can't actually *hold* your sword."

"Who did I fight?"

"Doesn't matter." Ghlee offered a pitiful look, patting him on the shoulder.

"Ghlee."

"Three men who were insulting the barkeep's son."

"Oh. Well, I stand by my defense of him." Tolvar's attempt at a grin pained his jaw.

"Aye, Wolf. But in the scuffle, you ended up punching Div's son."

Tolvar dropped his head in his hand.

"Aye. Banned for life this time, Div said. Mayhap 'tis time you took a night off from ale," Ghlee said.

"Don't start."

"Just looking out for you. Someone needs to, Wolf."

Tolvar shoved his friend aside with enough force to let him know what he thought of that idea.

"Suit yourself," Ghlee said. "Oi. It's already hot out here. Let's find some food."

At the mention of food, Tolvar's stomach lurched again. "You eat. I'll drink my breakfast."

Tolvar didn't wait for Ghlee's response but started walking down the street toward Fifth Street. There was an excellent pub on the corner. Of course, in Kestriel, there was an excellent pub on many corners.

CHAPTER
7

Tolvar

"By the way," Ghlee said later that evening as he and Tolvar made their way to their meeting at the Fox Hole. "Have you heard the Ravyns set an entire village on fire?"

Tolvar cocked an eye at Ghlee. That was odd. He'd been keeping himself informed on the bandits' actions over the past ten moons since he'd come to Deogol from the Capella Realm, and that seemed highly out of character for the group of highwaymen.

Chewing that information over, Tolvar and Ghlee turned down the crooked alleyway that cut to the back entrance of the pub. It was dusk now, and the lamplighters had begun igniting the torches that lined the street behind them, the flames casting tall, flickering shadows of the two men down the alleyway's entrance.

Their booted footsteps clomped in the deserted alleyway. Abruptly, Tolvar stopped and spun to survey behind them, drawing his sword. Ghlee instinctively followed his friend's actions, the two men peering down the alleyway, the torchlight in the distance like a trembling candle now.

After a few heartbeats, Ghlee asked, "You heard something?"

Tolvar strained his ears. It had been said the Wolf could hear better than the average man. In his past life, Tolvar had often laughed at the remark. He chalked it up to never letting his guard down.

He sheathed his sword. "Nay. I heard naught." His eyes were still trained on the jagged corners jutting out in the crooked passage of the alley. "Come. We're already late."

The two had not taken twenty paces when they saw it.

The whites of the eyes, appearing as if they glowed against the blackness of the alley, was what Tolvar noticed first.

Next to him, Ghlee swore and pulled his sword free again, scanning back down the alleyway.

Tolvar crouched to inspect the body. Five stab wounds in a circular pattern through the chest, soaking what had been a white tunic the color of blood. It smelled like rust. The man had a dark beard, and there was a leather hat next to him. He'd been stripped of any weapons or coins. His arms lay at his sides, one palm up, one palm down. Tolvar didn't need to roll up the man's sleeve to reveal the tattoo to know who this was. Ganifer.

"Curse the stars," Ghlee uttered from behind him. "There goes our meeting."

"Aye," Tolvar returned, glancing at the Fox Hole's back entrance not far from where they'd found Ganifer's body.

"Do we leave him? The sovereign did not exactly sanction this meeting," Ghlee said, crouching beside him.

Tolvar's response was to place his head in his hand. He needed a drink.

"Oi! What's this?"

Tolvar looked up; Ghlee pried a piece of parchment from Ganifer's hand that'd been palm down.

"*Stop seeking the Unsung. The Azure Moon comes, and you are too late.* Signed, *The Brones,*" Ghlee read aloud, holding up the parchment to squint in the weak light emanating from the back entrance of the Fox Hole. "The Azure Moon? Strange words. No idea who the Brones are. You?"

Tolvar shook his head before he snatched the parchment from Ghlee's hand, hurling it away from them. "Stars be damned, is more like," Tolvar said, silently counting the stab wounds on Ganifer's chest once more.

☾

Tolvar didn't drink so much that night that he couldn't stumble his way back to the inn. He'd rented a room for the last two moons ever since being banished by Captain Pharrell from Dara Keep, the stronghold of the Order of Siria, which was about six leagues from Kestriel. The room was not unlike his quarters there: simple and small, housing a bed, the mattress of which could use new stuffing, a desk without a chair, and a paned window where he could watch the comings and goings of the inn's entrance below on the ground level.

Ghlee had housed himself at another inn a few blocks away, larger with a few more extravagances. Tolvar didn't need a maid to make his bed or sweep the floor. To him, it was simply extra coin saved to buy more drinks.

After finding Ganifer's body, the two men had sneaked into the back entrance of the Fox Hole, taking the pub owner by surprise, and questioned him for any suspicious activity. Surely, he'd heard something happening in his own back alley? But the man had been useless; he hadn't heard anything as his assistant barkeep hadn't shown up this evening, and he'd been manning the whole of the pub on his own. They'd rattled a few patrons as well, but no one knew Ganifer, and, after searching, Tolvar and Ghlee hadn't found anything odd left around the pub either.

How? How had someone—these Brones—known Ganifer was to meet them tonight? Tolvar wondered again as he slipped off his boots. He'd been given specific instructions not to tell anyone about meeting them.

This was four now. Four almost-recruits to become the sovereign's Unsung who'd either died or disappeared. And frankly, Tolvar had had little hope for Ganifer as it was. Searching for the Unsung was one thing; recruiting an infamous gambler into the Order of Siria was another.

Pharrell, that idiot and his ideals of honors.

When Pharrell and two score Order of Siria knights had arrived from the Capella Realm, the sovereign had one command: find the

Unsung. Pharrell had insisted the Unsung become a member of Deogol's new branch of the Order of Siria.

What was the point of that? The Order of Siria had disbanded in Deogol almost one hundred years ago. Why reform it now? Who cared about the damned Order of Siria?

But the real question was who were these Brones to be watching them?

Tolvar stood and went to the window, his eyes searching the street below. Windows in the building on the opposite side of the street were shuttered, two hanging torches on the street giving off the only light. Tolvar kept his own room darkened, not lighting a candle. No one would see him standing there.

Was there a dim light of a candle in that window across the way? Tolvar squinted, the swirling in his head doing him no favors in focusing.

And what of it? Someone cannot have a candle lit this time of night?

Tolvar checked for the third time that the door was bolted and moved the desk in front of it as he did every night. He then unbuckled his sword belt, studying the weapon in his hand briefly before setting it next to the bed for easy access.

Cursèd weapon.

He fell onto his back in bed. None of this was going as it was supposed to. He was failing at this as he'd failed at Thorin Court. The pit of his stomach knotted up.

Don't think about that.

Tolvar's head continued to spin as he unsuccessfully warded off the dark thoughts seeping into his mind from his depths. The foul taste of bile threatened to come up. He sweated. Liquor was supposed to drown out thoughts, not make them pour out.

So much blood.

In the elapse of the Prodigal Moon's cycle, Tolvar had managed not to think about Thorin Court exactly one day, the day after the full moon. With Ghlee's prodding, Tolvar did something he'd never done. He prayed to a moon goddess, spending the entire night of the full moon on his knees in a field outside Kestriel's city walls, praying for penance.

So much blood.

But two days after the full moon, Tolvar awakened, face stained with tears, yelling out. His disturbance had brought the innkeeper's wife banging at his door. The goddess, fictitious though she was, had not forgiven him. But it didn't matter. It wouldn't matter even if she did. Tolvar would never forgive himself.

CHAPTER 8

Sloane

Traveling a great distance on foot would be a trial—that she knew. But after a week of gradually making her way up the road, stopping every few hours to rest her leg, feeling as though she were getting nowhere, Sloane was ready, once again, to lie down and join those of Mohn and Asana.

She'd met no one on the road thus far, though turned around every now and again for signs that the Ravyns might head this way. The road remained deserted.

The road to where? Sloane had no idea where she was going. She'd simply guessed which way to go when she'd come to a fork in the road yesterday.

The landscape had changed little. The fields on either side of the road remained dried golden brown. There wasn't even a small tree to shade her from the glaring sunlight. Sloane flapped the front of her dress collar to air out her sweaty front as she sat next to the road. She jiggled the water pouch. Not much left. She'd have to make her way the half-mile to the stream that ran parallel to the road. She wondered why the road hadn't been created closer to the stream. A half-mile away from the road and a half-mile back. By the time she got back on the road, the sun would be low in the sky. She wasn't getting anywhere. Not that she knew where anywhere was.

At the stream, she took off her shoes and soaked her feet in the cool water of the tiny stream that barely covered her ankles. Over her shoulder, she expected to see the Ravyns any moment. Mayhap she'd have a chance to use her knife on Joah. Joah! Her brother's betrayal stung fresh again.

How could he? How could Joah, only three years older than her, turn away from their parents' upbringing?

Sloane focused on her lap and realized she'd been tearing a hard slice of bread into pieces. She couldn't keep letting her mind wander back to Joah. It would ruin her.

The decision to spend the night by the stream wasn't difficult, although there were still hours of sunlight left. She wasn't in a hurry to get anywhere.

She stuffed the rest of the bread into her mouth, then fiddled with her moon cuff. Judging by last night's moon, it was growing closer to the moonless night of the Nay Moon—five nights, mayhap? —when the Prodigal Moon goddess would take her leave, darkening the sky to give the ancient stars one night without rivalry, and the new slivers of the moon would eventually stretch into the Harvest Moon. The Nay Moon was said to be a time when one could pray to the stars to See the future, but Sloane had never heard of anyone in Mohn Seeing visions from the stars. That was surely just a fable. Still, it'd be nice to think that in five nights, Sloane might be given some direction.

Because where am I going?

SLOANE LOST COUNT of the days, but her stomach hadn't lost count of how little food she had left. And it was hot, so hot, here on the deserted road.

The Nay Moon had come and gone, and Sloane received no fortune from the stars. Only sleepless nights terrified of strange nocturnal noises. Her imagination plagued her with thoughts of the Befallen and thieves and shadow cats—even though the felines supposedly haunted the forests, not the fields. Her hand grew tired of grasping her knife, her eyes weary of scanning the open road and the tall stalks of golden grasses.

"You're being a complete sook. Keep walking, coward," she uttered even as her eyes searched the horizon for movement.

It was close to another sunset, and she'd finally relaxed her shoulders a bit when, cresting over a small hill, Sloane spotted a wagon coming toward her.

Her heart in her throat, she scampered down the hill as fast as she dared on her leg. Mayhap she could duck in the weeds at the bottom and remain unseen.

I'll not be robbed again.

The eek of the wagon wheels and clopping of the horse's hooves grew closer. She quickened her pace. Her foot caught on a divot in the ground, and Sloane tumbled the rest of the way down the hill, her rucksack slamming into her back. Landing with a thud on her stomach, the approaching wagon's sound was all she concentrated on. She flattened herself on the ground, hoping the traveler's focus was on the road ahead and wouldn't notice her at the bottom of the hill.

She closed her eyes. At least it wasn't the Ravyns. Wait! What did that matter? Whoever this was could slit her throat and rob her just as easily.

Oh stars! Please protect me! Sloane prayed. *Hide me as you are hidden by the sun.*

The wagon stopped. Sloane didn't move. The traveler was resting. *At the top of a hill?*

"Eh, what you doin'?" a man's voice asked.

Oh stars!

Sloane opened her eyes and lifted her head. Sitting in the wagon, were two men; an old man with a thick, grey beard and a floppy leather hat who held the reins, and a young man with a long nose and pointed chin. Both were giving Sloane strange expressions somewhere between amused and bemused.

"You all right?" the younger man spoke. "You fall down?"

Sloane moved to her hands and knees before using all her effort to upright herself to a standing position.

"I'm fine." Her voice cracked. The men eyed each other.

"That looked like quite the tumble." The young man gave a low whistle. "What you runnin' down that hill for anyway? You think we gonna run you over?" His grin revealed a silver tooth. The old man snickered.

"I was—getting out of the way," Sloane said, placing a hand on her hip.

"Fact o'matter, I think you accomplished that. Where you headed?" the young man asked.

She opened her mouth to speak, closed it again, and then said, "That way," gesturing in the direction they'd come.

"You goin' to Vithal?"

Vithal? She'd never heard of it.

"Aye," Sloane said with what she hoped was a convincing tone.

"Ain't no work for you there. We just come from there." The young man rubbed sweat off his forehead.

"How do you know I'm looking for work?" Sloane asked.

"Well, ain't you?" he asked.

"I'm—I suppose I am," Sloane said. *These two must think I'm a halfwit.*

"We're headed back to Branwell. You want to come along? Might be safer than travelin' alone." The young man threw out his hand. "Not that I'm sayin' a girl can't travel on her own. It's just we've heard rumor the Ravyns are in these parts. Safety in numbers, I say."

Sloane made a swift decision to say nothing about the Ravyns. "That so? Well, I'm not certain what we three would be able to do against them. At any rate, I think I'll continue to Vithal."

She started walking through the field below the road. Hopefully, they'd get the hint to be on their way. She'd walked five paces before checking if the two still watched her.

"You a cripple?" the young man said.

"You a bastard?" Sloane shot back before she could stop herself.

He raised his eyebrows before giving another whistle and turning to the old man to say something she couldn't hear. Sloane turned away again, her cheeks hot. She expected to hear laughter but instead heard someone hop from the wagon.

The young man stood beside the wagon now, wiggling his leg at her. What Sloane hadn't noticed about him was where his right leg should have been was a peg leg in its place.

"Lost it when I was a boy. Had the cors fever, I did." He still wagged his leg in a playful manner, a mischievous grin on his face.

Sloane glanced from the peg leg to the old man's half-smile.

"Sorry 'bout my mouth," the young man said. "Fact o'matter, didn't mean nothin' by it. Not every day you meet someone like you. A good omen, I say."

"'Someone like you?'" Sloane returned.

"Aye. We can't be that different. You're lookin' for work. We're lookin' for work."

"*You're* lookin' for work, I ain't," the old man interrupted.

"Fine. I'm lookin' for work. Come to Branwell! We got room and board and everythin'." He took in her leg. "It's a long walk to Vithal."

"I'd have to pay you." Father had taught her better than to accept charity. "But I'm afraid I don't have any food."

"We don't need your coin and got plenty o'food," he said, gesturing to the wagon. "I'm Alvie." The young man pointed to himself. "And this here is Lauge." Alvie's thumb indicated to the old man eyeing Sloane from the wagon's seat. "He don't say much."

"That's because you ne'er stop talking!" Lauge said from the wagon.

"That so?" Alvie turned back to him, hands on his hips, feigning indignation.

"Aye. Now help that girl up here so we can get goin'."

"Ah, Lauge, you always get nervous at dusk. I tell you, what's goin' to happen is goin' to happen," Alvie said before turning back to Sloane. "What d'ya say?"

Sitting in a wagon did sound like the very stuff dreams were made from. Mayhap she should take it as a gift from the crescent Harvest Moon that would rise tonight. Sloane began her way up the hill. Alvie met her halfway, and, despite his leg, was quite agile on the slant of the hill. They grasped hands, and he helped Sloane steady herself up the hill. Normally, she would have felt as if she'd sooner crawl into a field eel's hole than receive help, but instead, Alvie's smile—the silver tooth glinting in the sunset—put Sloane at ease, and she returned a slight one of her own.

When they were all seated on the wagon's bench, Alvie squeezed in the middle, Lauge flicked the reins of the nag towing the wagon.

"I'm Sloane, by the way," she said.

"Sloane?" Alvie said as if deciding whether he believed her. "I like it. Where you from?"

A lump caught in Sloane's throat. "Mohn," she replied softly.

"Never heard of Mohn," Alvie said. "Lauge, you heard of it?"

"Aye, 'tis south of here, I believe. Am I right?" The old man eyed Sloane again.

"Aye." Sloane wanted to say that it was gone now—gone to the Befallen. But couldn't get that out.

"Me and Lauge, we're from Kestriel."

"Kestriel?" Sloane said. Though a few tales of the capital city of the sovereign had been handed down and passed around the village from the elder's travels, she'd never met anyone *from* Kestriel. "What's it like?"

"Big." Alvie started, and Sloane sensed his delight at being asked. She had a feeling she was in for the first of many stories.

CHAPTER
9

Sloane

S loane didn't want to spit out the bite of stew she'd placed in her mouth—apart from it being terribly rude, she was certain the rumble of her stomach was quite audible—but her taste buds did not agree. Still, she swallowed the spicy substance, opening her mouth to stick out her burning tongue. Sloane's eyes watered. How could they eat this?

Alvie and Lauge shoveled bite after bite of stew into their mouths, Lauge getting a few splattering drops on his beard, never stopping to pause from the spiciness of the flavor.

This was really what they ate in Kestriel? How could anyone stand to eat an entire bowl of this?

They'd traveled for three days, and, after hearing all the stories about the capital city, Lauge mentioned he had some leftover spices from Kestriel he'd been saving if Sloane wanted to try a traditional Solstice Stew. Eyeing him warily, Sloane asked if it was blasphemous to eat outside of the time of the Solstice Moon? The two men assured her it wasn't, that it was simply called that because of the strong, festive flavoring. With cautious excitement, Sloane had been eager to taste something made for the dignified citizens of the capital city.

Now as they sat around their campfire, she studied the thick red-orange liquid with bits of root sticking out, the smell tickling her nose, and wished for the simple taste of Ma's cooking. She brought another bite to her mouth, the spice offending her tongue once again.

"Excellent stew, Lauge," Alvie said, licking his bowl. He'd already finished.

Lauge grunted in response, his attention also on his food.

"You going to eat all that?" Alvie said, pointing at Sloane's mostly full bowl.

"Nay," Sloane said, "Please." She handed it to Alvie.

Alvie dug into Sloane's helping, eating as fast as he had his own.

"Not for you?" Lauge said, winking at Sloane.

"It was delicious," Sloane said. "I find I'm not hungry, I s'pose."

"There's one more piece of bread," Lauge said, taking another bite.

Sloane pursed her lips. To take the last piece of bread at a meal was bad luck, tempting the goddess of the Harvest Moon. But she was hungry. Her eyes went to the basket of bread.

"I think that's only ill-luck during the Hunger Moon," Lauge said as if reading her thoughts. That was odd. She'd never heard of this tradition being only for the Hunger Moon. "Though I never understood why. Why during the time people are most hungry would you let a piece of bread go to waste?"

"I always eat the last piece of bread during the Hunger Moon," Alvie remarked, giving Sloane's bowl a lick. "That bit of ill-luck is rubbish, I say."

"Don't say that." Sloane grimaced.

"Why not?" Alvie wiped his face with his sleeve. "Let me ask you this: Why would the goddess demand that? And anyways, I never heard of anyone getting ill-luck from eating the last piece of bread. Unless you count starving, but I guess they were already doing that.

"Fact o'matter is," Alvie leaned in, "the goddesses are silent now, aren't they? Have been for years. And the Befallen ragin' around proves it. Fact o'matter is no goddesses are listenin'."

Never had Sloane heard anyone speak blasphemy of the moon goddesses. She stared wide-eyed at Alvie across the flame. She'd need to get away from these two as soon as they got to Branwell and pray for forgiveness during the Harvest Full Moon for being in their company.

Alvie noticed Sloane's expression and lifted an eyebrow in confusion.

"Wait a minute...you really a believer? Thought everyone was givin' up on that rubbish."

"Stop calling it rubbish."

What about the Edan Lore? One couldn't believe in the Edan Lore and not believe in the moon goddesses. 'Twas not possible. And *everyone* believed in the Edan Lore.

She was about to ask Alvie this very question when he said, "What they ever done for you?"

"That's not the point," Sloane started. "They bring the rain, the crops. They create the waves of the sea; they turn the colors of the leaves on the trees."

Alvie shrugged then rubbed a finger across the bottom of the bowl to mop up the remains of the stew. "Then how do you explain the Befallen? Or the...uh," he waved his spoon around as he thought, "what's it called? Oh aye, the Unsung."

Lauge, who'd said nothing, handed Sloane the piece of bread he'd nabbed from the basket in the wagon. His eyes fell on the moon cuff she still wore as he sat next to her, taking a spearmint leaf out of his pocket to chew on.

"Fact o'matter is the Edan Lore is rubbish, too, I say. I don't even remember most of it anymore. It's like ill-luck following you when you eat the last piece of bread. Rubbish."

"All right, Alvie! The girl's entitled to her own thoughts, you duffer," Lauge shouted. "Stars almighty."

Sloane hesitated to lift the spongy bread to her mouth. *What have they ever done for you?* She still hadn't told Alvie and Lauge about Mohn or Asana. They didn't know the reason she sought out work was because it was literally her only option.

She ripped off a fraction of the bread and stuffed it into her mouth. It had an herby taste to it—stars, those two liked their flavors—

but it wasn't spicy, and it certainly didn't taste like bad luck. She beheld the partial moon rising in the grey-blue evening sky. Ten nights to the Harvest Full Moon now?

"Do you really not know the Edan Lore?" Sloane asked.

"Nah. I don't mean to hurt your feelings, Sloane, but what for?"

Alvie was wrong. He was a bit of a heretic, that's all. Still. How could you believe the goddesses offered prosperity and protection when you'd found your entire village dead? Her eyes stung with tears, and she was glad it was dark.

But she had to admit Alvie was right about one thing. Where was the Unsung?

It is rubbish, the still-hungry part of Sloane suspected. *You've had enough ill-luck for five lifetimes.*

Alvie muttered something about seeing to the nag and left Lauge and Sloane staring at the fire.

"Bah. Don't mind Alvie. He has his reasons for being a hard-nosed mule," Lauge said.

Sloane nodded but kept quiet.

"You wear your moon cuff outside the full moon," Lauge said, nodding at her wrist.

Sloane wanted to cover it with her sleeve, but that seemed foolish.

"I thought moon cuffs were only for prayers to the full moon, and it was tempting the goddesses' ill-humor to wear them otherwise."

Her face flushed. Sloane slipped the cuff off her wrist. Was Lauge a heretic, too?

"May I?" Lauge asked, extending a hand to inspect the leather wristlet. Sloane gave it over, her lips pursed. She made a close-lipped smile when Lauge placed it to his nose to sniff.

"Why this is new, isn't it?" Lauge brought the moon cuff close to the firelight to examine the different embossed symbols. "Beautiful work."

"My father made it," Sloane said, feeling as though the phrase might choke her.

"Expert hand he has." Lauge was slowly spinning it to see the different patterns. Sloane focused on the flames so she didn't cry. Father *had* been an expert hand, indeed. "Oh ho!" Lauge exclaimed, rubbing his fingertip over one of the symbols. "The Azure Moon."

The Azure Moon?

Slone snatched the moon cuff and inspected the circular symbol Lauge had been focusing on. There it was: a thirteenth symbol on Sloane's moon cuff. She counted again. Aye, thirteen. How had she not noticed? And why had Father added that moon to her cuff? It wasn't unheard of, but certainly rare.

The thirteenth symbol was no more than a circle with a bold embossed outline. The Azure Moon.

"I haven't seen an Azure Moon symbol for an age," Lauge said, taking another spearmint leaf from his pocket and focusing on the flames of the fire. "Stars, the Azure Moons are glorious. Have you ever seen one?"

"Nay," Sloane said.

The Azure Moon was extraordinarily rare. It appeared only every ten years, and the only one that'd risen in her lifetime had been on a rainy night when she was eight. She hadn't seen it. Priestesses all over Tasia endeavored to predict exactly *when* the Azure Moon would rise, but it didn't work that way. There was a bedtime tale about a diviner, the Cibil of the Nay Moon, who'd been the only one able to predict exactly what night it rose, but that tale was almost as old as the Edan Lore.

It was then Sloane realized something. The Azure Moon would supposedly rise *this* year. But when? That was important. More so now than ever as the Befallen ravaged this land. The Azure Moon was a key part of the Edan Lore and Unsung's success defeating the Befallen.

Sloane bit her lip, then recited— like she'd practiced with Ma and Father as a child—the last two lines of the Edan Lore. "Beware, the night of the Azure Moon comes every years ten, the Unsung has one chance aflame, else all must begin again."

Lauge paled. "Stars, girl. I haven't heard those lines since I was a lad."

"How can that be? Everyone knows the Edan Lore."

"It's like Alvie said. Many have forgotten lines from the Edan Lore. I been all over this stars-forsaken island, and most only know the first lines."

As if to test herself like when she was young, though she didn't need to, Sloane recited the entirety of the Edan Lore:

> Woe is that time when the lee of the island befalls
> When havens are vanquished, and the threat of death
>   calls
> For none shall be spared when cursèd shadows arise
> If not for the Unsung, 'twill be the whole of demise
> Powers of both temperance and that of great strength
> Yea, a hero Unsung, bearing the fortitude of faith
> 'Tis the Unsung's winding and shadowy path to
>   the end
> That will cease the Befallen, confronting death to
>   transcend
> And to conquest over this curse lest it strike land
>   anew?
> The secret is held with the goddess of the moon
>   Azure blue
> At Ayla, a weapon she'll give the Unsung on her sole,
>   obscure night
> Its power will bury the curse and restore the world
>   aright
> Beware, the night of the Azure Moon comes every
>   years ten
> The Unsung has one chance aflame, else all must
>   begin again.

Silence between them followed.

"Why have people forgotten the Edan Lore?" Sloane wondered.

"Who knows?" Lauge returned. "I take it that Mohn is a devout place? To the moon goddesses, I mean."

"Of course," Sloane said, staring at him puzzled. What did that mean? Surely all of Deogol was devout.

"I think you'll find more people in Branwell are like Alvie," he gestured to Alvie in the background grooming the nag. "Especially with the Befallen. Scares everyone too much. People lose their faith. When I was a boy, I remember learning the words of the Edan Lore and thinking it strange learning that an unknown hero would stop a mythical destruction. The Befallen didn't exist back then, 'course. People didn't know why they needed to know a prophecy that was a hundred years old. Didn't seem important.

"As I grew older, I found less and less people in my travels who knew the entirety of the Edan Lore. There were no dark dangers, so people didn't trouble themselves. But now, dangers are here, stars almighty, and Deogol is waiting for the Unsung. Ha! *That* part they remember. I've even heard rumors that the sovereign is actually searching for people to be the Unsung. But there's no faith behind it. We want the hero but aren't willing to give devotion."

Sloane wasn't sure what to say. The Edan Lore had always been sacred to her—everyone in Mohn. "But there *must* be many in Deogol who still know the Edan Lore includes the Azure Moon? The Scholars of Kestriel? Priestesses? The Cibil of the Nay Moon? Someone?"

"Mayhap. Though, there aren't many priestesses left, I think. Less and less, says I. And as far as the Cibil is concerned, I ne'er heard of anyone finding him. 'Course, he'd be over a hundred years old." Lauge's sigh showed his age. "But if you believe the Azure Moon rises every ten years," he raised an eyebrow for meaning, "when it comes, ain't no one in Deogol going to be in Ayla ready to accept any weapon. The Befallen surely won't be defeated in my lifetime."

CHAPTER
10

Sloane

Sloane was convinced the sun had never been hotter. Beads of sweat rolled down her back as she fanned herself next to Lauge in the wagon. Alvie was in the back of the wagon bed, shifting the men's supplies around, searching for something. He hadn't told them what. By nightfall they would reach Rock-and-Tree, which wasn't a village exactly but more like a small, permanent encampment, Lauge had said. They'd be able to buy a meal there. Lauge winked at Sloane when he said this part, making her blush again that she hadn't been able to stomach the Solstice Stew. Sloane had never heard of Rock-and-Tree, but from Lauge's description, it sounded as though it was aptly named.

She smiled to herself. She was going to buy their meal tonight. She'd decided that even though Alvie seemed to be a heretic, these were indeed friends. And as far as Alvie's remarks about the moon goddesses? Well, that was just Alvie being Alvie, she'd decided. Stars, that man was always saying something about something. It was kind of odd to have him not telling a story right now.

The wagon rumbled back and forth, and though Sloane was glad to not be walking under this sun, she found the movement combined with the heat was giving her a headache. Ma would have offered her some of her special tea she made for ailments, and the scent of sweet cloves was a memory on her tongue.

"A copper for your thoughts," Lauge said, his eyes never leaving the road in front of them.

Sloane shook her head, "'Tis nothing."

"You're thinking of home." Lauge drew out the words as if in song.

"How did you know?" Sloane pulled at her collar. Lauge winked at her and began singing, his voice pleasant and deep.

"Oh, call me back to the place called home
Call me back again
Where the air is scented with honey's touch
Call me back again
And n'er again will I leave ye behind
Call me back again
I'll kiss the face I have missed so much
Call me back again"

When Lauge finished, Sloane's eyes were glassed with tears.

"My father used to sing that song," she said, her voice barely audible.

"Did he sound as good as I?" Lauge said, making Sloane chuckle. He snorted, too. How long had it been since she'd heard her own laughter? Since the Rainless Moon, mayhap? It felt wonderful.

"Nay, you're a far superior singer. As a child, I sometimes wondered if my father couldn't sing the skin off a toad."

They laughed again.

"Still," Lauge said, his playful expression disappearing, "I dare say you would have me trade places with him now, and rather it was he who was singin' to you?"

Sloane sobered, too. "That'd be difficult. My father's dead."

"Ah," Lauge said as if he'd just discovered a new pattern of stars in the sky. "I see. And may I ask...your mother?"

Sloane merely nodded.

"Young to lose parents. Is that why you seek work?"

"It is." Sloane fidgeted with her torn sleeve so she wouldn't have to focus elsewhere.

"When did—" Lauge started but was cut off by Alvie hanging over the seat between them, a giant floppy hat on his head that hadn't been there before.

"Oi, Lauge, I haven't heard you sing for a moon of nights. What'd you pick that mopey-lopey song for?"

"Will you take that infernal thing off your head!" Lauge shouted. "That's for Carrin, you dolt!"

"But don't you think it's nice? It looks rather fetching, I'd say," Alvie said, his hands pulling on the brim, his face tugged into a silly expression.

"You look like a fool. Take it off. I don't want your grubby prints all over it when I give it to Carrin."

"Who's Carrin?" Sloane asked.

"She's Lauge's girl," Alvie laughed, batting his eyes mockingly.

Sloane raised an eyebrow. "Oh?"

"Hmph. She's a woman, something Alvie would know nothing about, and a fine one, too." Lauge's back straightened at these words.

"That's why it's so hard to believe she'd take up with the likes of you," Alvie said, removing the hat. "She's not going blind, is she?"

"Better blind than stupid, you rag-tag! The girl you take up with would need to be both. I don't know why I put up with you. When we get to Rock-and-Tree, I'm leaving you there."

"Bah," Alvie said. "That's what you said in Kestriel, and Pine..." He enumerated the names of the places on his fingers. "...and Asana, and Vithal—"

"Asana? You've been to Asana?" Sloane asked.

"Aye. Lil' place. Barely nothin' at all."

"'Tis the village nearest to Mohn, my home," Sloane said before thinking.

"That o'fact?" Alvie said. "I mean, 'tis a nice place, that."

"It's all right, Alvie," Sloane said, "It was small. But it was bigger than Mohn if you can believe."

"'Was'?" Lauge said.

"I mean..." Sloane trailed off. "I didn't mean to say that."

The only sound was the wagon wheels rolling on the road and the clip-clop of the nag trotting along. Sloane was only too aware of the sun's rays beating down on them again.

"Sloane, I don't mean to pry," Alvie broached, "but fact o'matter is I think you did mean to say, 'was.'"

"Was it the Befallen?" Lauge's voice was filled with dread as if her next words could strike him down.

"Aye," Sloane whispered before clearing the scratchy lump in her throat. "It took Mohn. And Asana. They're all dead. Everyone."

Again, there was a pause. Sloane listened to the rhythm of the wagon and horse's hooves.

"'Cept you," Lauge said. He'd brought a hand up to play with his beard. His eyes were straight on the road again and his shoulders, straightened moments ago, bowed.

"'Cept you," Alvie repeated, his eyes bulging. "Stars, Sloane, you survived the Befallen?"

"Nay." She shook her head vigorously. "'Course not. I was in Asana the night the Befallen overtook Mohn. Then the next night, it must have taken Asana because when I got there to seek refuge, everyone there was dead."

"The next night?" Lauge's voice rang with alarm.

"Aye," Sloane answered.

"There aren't any accounts of the Befallen striking two nights in a row." Lauge took another spearmint leaf out of his pocket and chewed on it like it was a rock. He clenched his teeth over and over. "When did this happen?"

"The night of the Prodigal Full Moon," Sloane added.

"Stars almighty," Lauge said. "The Full Moon? What's next?"

Sloane had forgotten the Befallen supposedly didn't come on a full moon.

Stars.

"Fact o'matter, Sloane, you survived the Befallen twice." Alvie held up two fingers. "That's gotta be some kind of trick or somethin'."

His words were gentle and full of awe. "You're good luck!" He snapped his fingers at these words.

"Trust me, Alvie, I am not good luck," Sloane said. Alvie did not reply but sat back and leaned against the side of the wagon bed. Sloane glanced back. In the days she'd known him, she'd never witnessed him this quiet or this still.

"My, my," Lauge whispered to himself, drawing her attention.

Yet again, there was nothing to listen to save for the sound of them rolling along the road. One of the wheels began to squeak. Lauge made a face at the sound but stayed quiet, chewing on his leaf. Sloane gripped her thick plait of hair and fidgeted with the braid.

The wheel squeaked again, this time louder, and then there was a rattle followed by a jolt, and her teeth jarred together as the wagon jounced and collapsed on one side. Sloane bumped her knees and elbows against the wagon's frame. Lauge nearly fell off his side, which was now higher than hers. In the back, Alvie gave a loud "oof." The old mare whinnied at the sudden stop and looked like she might lose her footing.

The three got out of the wagon to see one of the back wheels cracked and broken.

"Curse everything to the moon and back again," Lauge shouted, stomping his foot, pacing away.

Alvie bent down, steadying himself on his good leg, and inspected the snapped wheel.

"And we was almost there," Alvie said.

Sloane fanned herself again, surveying the terrain. Like all the landscape they'd passed for days, there were no trees at all, just tall golden grasses.

"I told you I wasn't good luck."

CHAPTER
11

Tolvar

Tolvar couldn't decide if the man standing in front of him and Ghlee was the ugliest man he'd ever seen, or the dumbest. Mayhap both.

They were in one of the private training yards positioned in the outer bailey of the sovereign's castle. The Order of Siria had been granted permission to use it as long as they were discreet and came in through the west entrance, which was always guarded by six soldiers. Six. Tolvar shook his head, sparing them a glance. Two the size of taller children, one who appeared to be on death's door, one who kept sneezing, his red eyes flinching every time a fly flew past, and two women, who actually seemed to be the most skilled of the lot. Ghlee and Tolvar would be able to down these six in approximately three sneezes. Pitiful. From what Tolvar observed, most of the sovereign's soldiers were of that caliber. How could Tolvar think he would find more success finding the Unsung in Kestriel?

Which brought Tolvar to the ugly, pocked man in front of them, one eye noticeably bigger than the other, brown hair in a greasy mess, standing in a battle stance, holding his sword in the *wrong* hand. And it wasn't that there was a right or wrong hand necessarily. Tolvar accepted people could favor either, but this man was lefthanded. The ugly man had swaggered into the Cat-and-Geese Pub the night before, roughly tapped Ghlee on the shoulder—with his left hand— and demanded a chance with the Order of Siria.

Ghlee had given Tolvar an expression that said, this one certainly *is* unsung.

Unsung was right. Unbathed was true, too. Not that Tolvar had any standing on that particular subject, he supposed. The man—Hanold, Tolvar just remembered his name—had bought Tolvar and Ghlee several pints of ale for an hour, boasting of his skill with the sword, so the two had begrudgingly offered him a chance.

And now the fool stood before them, holding his sword in the wrong hand.

Skilled, my eye.

Ghlee gave Tolvar a knowing smirk, then said, "Right then, show us your shield stance." Ghlee tossed a wooden shield to Hanold, who fumbled catching it, the sword falling out of his hand in the process.

"Stars almighty," Tolvar whispered under his breath, pinching the bridge of his nose between two fingers. "Pick up your sword, man."

Hanold, red-faced, picked up the sword, this time holding it in the proper hand, and faced Tolvar, who walked up to him. With a quick strike, Tolvar simply swung his sword into Hanold's blade. Hanold's sword dropped to the dirt again.

"Oh no," Ghlee said behind him.

"I'm sorry, sir," Hanold said, bending to retrieve the sword.

As he bent down, Tolvar pointed the sword's tip below Hanold's chin.

"You're dead." Tolvar said, his brown eyes piercing the man's. Hanold's flushed face turned a deeper red. "Skilled in the sword? I think not. But you've had your chance, and now you've a tale to tell as well. Would that I could be there to hear your version. Now off with you."

He nodded to the two women guards standing by the entrance, who trotted up and led Hanold out, the man too sheepish to utter another word.

Tolvar slashed his sword through the morning air before sweeping it from one side to another, pivoting his feet instinctively as he did so. After a few routine swings and stances, he ceased, thrusting his sword forward as if straight into an enemy's heart. He huffed a sigh, his eyes fixed on the blade.

Clapping sounded behind him.

"You amaze yourself with that little dance, Wolf?" Ghlee said. There was laughter in his voice.

"What a waste," Tolvar said, bringing the sword close to examine the hilt.

"Do you think you gave him a proper chance?" Ghlee asked, nodding toward the gate from where Hanold had left.

"A proper chance? Your gran could hold a sword better."

"I've no doubt about that." Ghlee raised his eyebrows. "She wouldn't need one, though. She'd just tell the Befallen to douse out, she would."

"This is all a waste of time." Tolvar frowned at the guards again. It'd been almost a full *year* since they'd been seeking the Unsung. How many in Deogol had died in that time? And the last twelve recruits they'd found had either disappeared, or been murdered, or been too idiotic to know which side of the sword to hold. "We need a new plan. Surely the Order will take us back now. I cannot stand any more of this."

Ghlee stood quietly through Tolvar's outburst, his arms folded.

"You forget, I *am* welcome back at Dara Keep. 'Tis you who still needs to make amends. You know Pharrell isn't going to let you set foot through those gates yet."

"Bah." Tolvar paced away. Pharrell had been the bane of his time in Deogol, reminding Tolvar at every turn that he wasn't part of the Order of Siria, but here at the bequest of the sovereign. He ran his fingers through his mop of hair. He could get himself under control. He just needed to breathe. And why did a mug of ale suddenly sound like just the thing?

"Wolf," Ghlee said, striding to stand next to him. The sovereign's keep towered over them, the shadows of which made the summer air feel cooler. "We've been tasked."

Tolvar audibly growled at his friend.

"You don't think the Unsung is out there, do you?" Ghlee said. "After all this time searching, I've just realized you don't even believe in the Edan Lore."

Tolvar flexed and unflexed his jaw. "What's there to believe?"

"Don't forget it was your Capella Realm's StarSeers who gave Deogol the Edan Lore a hundred years ago. Do you deny them?"

Tolvar wasn't going to answer that. "Do *you* believe it? Some Unsung hero really walks the earth, Ghlee? I've overheard enough talk at the pubs. Most even doubt your moon goddesses now."

"Careful."

"Meanwhile, when the Befallen is not wreaking havoc, there's a band of criminals stalking Deogol that your sovereign won't round up with his own soldiers or allow the Order of Siria to. And I'm to believe some nobody is what Deogol needs?"

"Are you finished?" Ghlee asked.

"Almost. The Befallen cannot find a way off this stars-forsaken island. The Capella Realm may be the illuminated empire, but no one knows what power the StarSeers will have against it, if any. A hero is needed now. And 'tis growing difficult to believe that hero will be some nameless dolt, and we are simply shepherds."

"Now are you finished?" Ghlee asked.

"Aye."

Ghlee scratched his chin, toying with his own sword in his other hand. "Wolves don't make good shepherds, 'tis true. But as your friend, I would remind you there is more than one reason you took this task."

Tolvar snorted, "Oh, aye, I forgot. Redemption."

Ghlee gave Tolvar a knowing look. "And to answer your question, Wolf. Aye, I do believe. We will find our Unsung yet."

GHLEE CONVINCED Tolvar to train for a few hours, but when the sun was hottest in the sky, and Tolvar thought he'd fully sweated every last drop of liquor out of his being, he plunged his sword into the nearest practice dummy's stuffed chest and declared it was time for a drink.

By this time, several of the sovereign's soldiers, castle retainers, and even the sovereign's niece, Princess Benetha, and her three ladies-in-waiting had formed an audience along the perimeter of the yard surrounding the two and a dozen or so other sovereign's soldiers who'd joined them. It wasn't every day one could see the Wolf at sword practice. Tolvar didn't particularly like the crowd that'd built around him, but was always taken aback that Ghlee performed better in front of an audience. He also sobered at the idea that Ghlee never seemed to mind that it was the Wolf and his knight's reputation that drew the crowd; Ghlee's good humor was intact always. He almost wanted to apologize for his earlier outburst. Almost.

Dozens of people clapped, and even a few whooping cheers echoed off the yard's thick stone walls. Tolvar rolled his eyes as he took off his tunic to wipe his drenched face. This was no exhibition.

Siria's skirt, what would Leon, his former commander, say to Tolvar showing off and parading his skills around like a high-priced stallion ready to stud? He really did need a drink.

"M'lord?" said a delicate voice behind him.

He turned to find the sovereign's short niece standing before him, flanked by her taller ladies-in-waiting, all four of them looking as if a breeze might topple them over. Stars, he hoped there would be no swooning. He'd hate to watch one of them fall to the ground.

"I'm not a lord, Your Highness," Tolvar said through gritted teeth that he hoped resembled a smile, "but I am at your service all the same."

The princess blushed up at him. Stars, she was short. Her pale blue eyes matched the silk of her gown, but it made her washed-out in Tolvar's opinion. And normally, he liked blue eyes. It was said she was pretty. Mayhap Tolvar didn't have time to think about pretty girls.

"My apologies for any offense, m'l—Sir Tolvar," Princess Benetha said. "I only assumed the Wolf had land in addition to title." Her teeth *were* straight, he supposed. That was a plus.

"Forfeited."

"Oh." Princess Benetha looked genuinely sorry. "I did not know."

Tolvar leaned down to speak more closely to her ear. "'Tis not a subject I generally shout from the battlements, Your Highness, being that it marks me as a failure and outcast and all."

The princess's pale eyes darkened. "Sir Tolvar, are you mocking me?"

"Nay, Your Highness." Tolvar stood straight again. "I love the reminder of being stripped of my titles and land. I love the reminder of my failure to protect—"

"All right." Ghlee came next to Tolvar, shoving his shoulder, forcing him to take a step back from the princess. "That's enough history lessons for this afternoon. Your Highness." Ghlee's bow was quite exaggerated. "Please thank your uncle once again for allowing the Order of Siria to utilize his training yard. His contributions and patronage to our great cause show his keen nature, and when we stop the Befallen, the spoils shall be his."

Siria's skirt, Ghlee.

The princess stared icily at Tolvar. Finally, she acknowledged Ghlee with a nod.

"You should keep your Wolf better trained. The glories of his own past reputation will not serve him well if he's put down like a dog." Princess Benetha and her ladies turned and sauntered away.

A few comments made by those who'd been listening were thrown at Tolvar as the crowd dispersed, and he was left watching the retreating form of the princess, feeling Ghlee's glare on him. She did have a cunning tongue, that one. Mayhap she wasn't too short.

"Have you gone completely mad?" Ghlee's calm tone did not match his expression.

"Not completely," Tolvar replied.

"You damned fool. How long until the sovereign hears that story, eh? Tolvar, listen to me for the last time. You have nowhere else to go. You've been banished by your own sovereign. You've been banished by Pharrell. The sovereign of Deogol has offered you refuge here only because you are the Wolf. Who, by the way, would never speak to royalty like that." Ghlee paced away. "Stars, man, I have my own reputation, too. I may not be the great Wolf who earned his spurs at fifteen and won the Battle of Cassia in the War of a Hundred Nights, but soon that's not going to account for much. Why did you have to say that to her anyway? Do you think she was baiting you? The niece of the sovereign? I daresay she doesn't even know where Askella is in the Capella Realm."

"All right," Tolvar's voice was harsher than he'd intended. "You've made your point."

"I'm certain." Ghlee snorted.

"You think it's easy being the Wolf and not the Earl of Askella? Do you think it's easy living with the knowledge of why, Ghlee?"

"Siria's skirt, how long are you going to wallow in your own self-pity?"

"They're dead!" Tolvar shouted, gripping Ghlee's tunic in his fists. "They're dead. All of them. And 'tis my fault."

Ghlee kept his voice soft. "You didn't kill them." He met Tolvar's eyes, not appearing the least bit bothered that he was still being held by his collar.

"Nay, but I didn't save them either." He shoved Ghlee away, pulled on his tunic, grabbed his sword, and stomped toward the gate.

"Tolvar!" Ghlee called after him.

"Douse out, Ghlee," Tolvar called back over his shoulder.

Tolvar could barely walk in a straight line. His heart pounded in his chest, and his vision blurred. Absent-mindedly, he jangled the coin purse that hung at his side. Good. There was enough to get properly drunk this time.

CHAPTER
12

Tolvar

Tolvar thought he hadn't been able to see straight walking to the tavern. But staggering back to the inn well after the waxing moon was high in the sky after spending all his coin at the tavern, the torches along the street appeared to dance in circles before him. At one point, he stumbled into an empty cart left on the side of the road. He barely felt his shin, which he had a notion should be stinging in pain.

Squatting, thinking he should inspect it, Tolvar wobbled and found himself on the ground gazing up at the night. The stars, like the torches, swayed in circles.

Once, Tolvar had met with a StarSeer, one of the Five with the ability gifted from Siria, the brightest star, to peer into the stars and See the future. Lady Tara of Ashwin, the Capella Realm's most southern region, had appeared ageless, her golden hair flowing as if caught in a summer's breeze even though they were indoors. Tolvar closed his eyes, remembering kneeling at the dais where she stood. When she'd descended the stairs, she'd gestured to him to stand, her eyes bright as if the stars themselves hid there, and serenely greeted him like he was the most important person on the continent. The meeting was naught more than a fleeting moment, Tolvar's father anxious to begin the private audience he'd secured with her and her council.

Lady Tara uttered only seven words to Tolvar before exiting the

Hall with Tolvar's father and her entourage: "You shall require forbearance in your future."

Tolvar's bemused eyes followed the StarSeer, Lady Tara, out of the room. She walked as if she floated. He'd wanted to ask her what she meant later, but he didn't see her again before he'd left Ashwin the next morning. *Forbearance?* That'd been part of his training to become a knight, to become the Wolf. Why would Lady Tara say that to him, he'd wondered over and over.

Now as he lay in the street, the contents of his stomach sloshing about, Tolvar wondered if he still possessed forbearance at all. Could a man lying in the street profess such a thing? A sot, Ghlee's gran had said.

You shall require forbearance in your future.

And how would that have helped you? Tolvar wondered. His heartbeat quickened. He could feel the anger take hold of him, intoxicating him with a mixture of rage and guilt and grief.

Why hadn't that blasted woman said, *Watch Crevan, he's not what he seems.* Or *The dawn after the Hoarfrost Moon will bring the attack you have worked so tirelessly to stave off.* Or even, *Your family shall be betrayed and slaughtered by your own brother, and you will not be able to stop it because you are blinded by your own arrogance.*

Nay, Tolvar was given none of those warnings into the future. Lady Tara told him—and his father—nothing of use. And now, because of him, his father and the others were dead, and in the incident, Tolvar's reputation, title, and lands had all been stripped from him. All he had left was his father's blasted sword, a revenge pact, and an impossible task to find a nonexistent person in Deogol as a means to find redemption.

"You must be the greatest fool who has ever lived," Tolvar said, the words slurring on his tongue.

"I couldn't agree more," a voice said.

It was difficult to manage, but Tolvar craned his neck to see who stood there. It was five someones, if his drunken mind was counting right upside down. Five men, all armed with—was that a wooden club the speaker held?

His attention focused on the club, Tolvar was not ready for the impact of the boot to his stomach. He cringed from the kick, an involuntary "oomph" escaping his lips. He had no time to get his bearings before another boot kicked into him, this time his back. Tolvar struggled to kneel so as to transfer himself to a standing position, but this time, a fist drove into his face. He tumbled back. Another blow. In the darkened mix of boots and fists, Tolvar's world spun.

His training should have taken over. His instincts should have kicked in. But Tolvar was too inebriated to crawl away from the men striking blow after blow into his face, his head, and his sides. The next jab came at his kidneys, and Tolvar vomited onto the cobblestone street.

"Get him up," the same voice commanded.

Tolvar was lifted and held by arms, vomit still dripping from his beard and onto his stomach. The stench made his good eye water. The other eye was already swelling, as was the cheek below that. The speaker, the man with the club, was about Tolvar's height, older in appearance. He wore a red tunic, though in the dark and with the world still whirling, it was difficult to be certain. The man sneered. The obvious leader.

"What a disappointment that was," he said. "I'd heard the great Wolf was a soldier and knight. But, uh, I suppose those days are behind you."

Tolvar spit at the leader's feet but missed his boot. In return, the leader drove his club into Tolvar's stomach. He doubled over in pain, his knees buckling, and his weight being fully supported by the men who held him.

The leader leaned down so he and Tolvar were at eye level. He whispered something, but Tolvar could only hear his own heavy breathing and his heartbeat thumping in his ear. The world was going black in front of him. There was more pain as the leader grabbed a fist full of Tolvar's hair and held up his head.

"I said I thought I told you to stop searching," the leader said. His words sounded far away.

"Stop search..." Tolvar slurred, his eyes closing, his head hanging at his chest as the leader let go of his hair.

Laughter surrounded him. Why did the left side of his face hurt so much? The faint idea came that he should be fighting someone right now, but his body started to feel numb. He opened his good eye again, the men still laughing. And where was Ghlee?

He sensed his sword belt being unbuckled. His sword!

Tolvar's movement, certainly unprepared for by the men who held him, was impossibly nimble and only achieved through years of practice. Tolvar's muscle memory took over.

He jerked his arms up, elbows pointed out, and freed himself from the two men. Catching them by surprise, Tolvar grabbed the back of each of their heads, slamming their faces into one another. There was a cracking sound. The two sunk to the street unconscious.

In this motion, the man who'd been loosening Tolvar's sword belt was knocked off balance. Tolvar used that instant to drive his elbow into the man's face. He staggered back.

Tolvar shifted but was struck in the back by something solid. He faced the new opponent, but these circling movements were catching up with him.

He steadied himself. The new opponent swung a dagger. Tolvar dodged back, the blade barely missing him. In the meantime, the other man who'd regained his balance charged into Tolvar, sending both to the ground.

Tolvar unsheathed his sword and it found its mark as he thrust it behind him into the man's chest. The man shuddered, then went limp on top of Tolvar.

Coughing and spitting, his rattled brain ordered him not to vomit again. He shoved the body off him, heaving himself up to face the man wielding the dagger. But rather than jumping to his feet,

Tolvar's state made the action awkward. He forced himself to stand but wasn't entirely certain he wasn't still slouching a bit. He was winded, even though he'd trained that afternoon. His drunkenness was catching up with him once more. Still, Tolvar huffed out an exhale and regripped his sword, readying himself. The daggered man stood next to the leader, who was tapping his club into his palm.

"Now that's more like it. You might be the Wolf after all." The leader's eyes darted from Tolvar back to the club in his hand. "However, I must insist this time you listen to reason. Stop seeking the Unsung."

"Are you one of the Brones? How do you know I search for the Unsung?" Tolvar managed to get out before he coughed again. "Did you kill Ganifer?"

The leader quirked an eyebrow.

"Why do you seek to stop me? The Befallen has claimed hundreds of lives in Deogol and will continue to do so."

"Mayhap not."

Tolvar sobered. "What do you mean?"

"The Befallen ravages here, but Deogol could simply send it elsewhere." The leader of the Brones stopped tapping his club and held it loose at his side, giving the appearance of nonchalance. But Tolvar didn't miss his firm grip on it.

"Elsewhere? There's no controlling it."

"The Capella Realm really should educate its citizens better in the goddesses of the moon. You've far too much stock in the stars."

Tolvar snorted. He shifted his stance to seem relaxed. However, his feet were ready to pivot into action. "Moon goddesses. We need not pray to bygone myths. The StarSeers have reigned in the Capella Realm for a thousand years. The gods of the stars shield us from darkness."

"And what of the Curse of Adrienne?" The leader said, tilting his head, clearly amused by Tolvar's wince.

Tolvar studied the hilt of his sword, letting the assault of the word

Adrienne pass over him. He wasn't about to recoil. A few more breaths, and he'd be ready to strike again.

"To speak of the Curse of Adrienne is to speak impiety. In all lands. Careful."

"Do you wonder how the Capella Realm can hold itself so mighty in its own eyes? You do not believe in the goddesses of the moon, yet believe the stars speak to prophetesses—whose wisdom the Capella Realm will not share with other kingdoms—and gift you fortune and safety from darkness. You do not believe in the goddesses of the moon, yet here you are from the Capella Realm following nonsense written in the Edan Lore that directly intertwines with the goddesses, the Azure Moon specifically."

"The Azure Moon? There's naught in the Edan Lore detailing anything about any moon."

"Ah, I see. Yet another who does not know *all* the words of the Edan Lore. Don't feel bad. Even though it is going to cost you."

Tolvar briefly scowled in confusion. What was this madman talking about? He'd attacked Tolvar and now stalled so he could finish him. "Besides, I don't need to believe in the moon goddesses. I'm in Deogol to fulfill a task."

"Aye, a knight's quest. Like the ancient tales." The Brones leader chuckled. "But you shall fail in your quest. Stop seeking the Unsung. Not only does that person not exist, but we've found another way to rid Deogol of the Befallen. 'Tis a pity the Capella Realm and lands beyond its borders shall have their turn. But your realm abandoned us when the Befallen came five years ago. Your friends, your allies."

Tolvar had naught to retort. The Capella Realm and other kingdoms *had* abandoned Deogol. Left the island to its own devices to contend with an unbeatable and dark force.

"I see my words strike close. 'Tis no matter. As soon as the Azure Moon rises, Deogol shall be saved. And the Capella Realm's troubles will begin."

The leader didn't wait for Tolvar to respond. With three strides, he'd bashed his club into Tolvar's blade. There was a *clang!* Tolvar parried, but the force of the blow was none like he'd ever encountered. The club wasn't wooden. What was it? Tolvar changed his stance, slashing his sword at the leader. The other man came from behind and attacked. In another fight, why, just one this afternoon, Tolvar could easily take two opponents at once. But he was still dizzy, had one good eye, and the gravity of the leader's words distracted him.

Think about that later, you sot!

Tolvar lunged at the daggered man, pivoted, and blocked the leader's club. He then turned and swung his sword back to block the next attack, reversed, and bashed a strike at the leader. Again and again. Again and again.

Finally, Tolvar's sword flicked the dagger out of his opponent's hand. He wasted no time. His pommel found the man's temple and, like the others, he went slack and fell to the ground.

But Tolvar left himself too open. A mistake the Wolf had never committed before. The leader's club impacted with Tolvar's own temple.

He saw stars as a burst of pain howled through his head. This time when the world blackened before him, Tolvar fell. And he did not get up.

CHAPTER
13

Sloane

There were worse things than a broken wagon wheel. There were worse things than spending a drenched night in a sudden downpour, huddled together under the wagon as the only shelter. There were worse things than determining the next morning that the wheel was unrepairable and deciding to heft what supplies they could tie to the nag and on their backs. Lauge looking sadly back at Carrin's hat, Alvie looking longingly back at a sack of potatoes, Sloane looking guiltily back at the wagon, wondering if somehow it was her extra weight that caused the wheel to break.

But Sloane knew what was worse. Because she'd faced it twice.

The Befallen.

The three stood at the edge of Rock-and-Tree's encampment, Lauge dropping the nag's halter, staring.

Dead.

Everyone in Rock-and-Tree lay on the ground dead. Mostly men, it seemed, the encampment being a passing-through sort of place. It was still morning, and the stench—the smell of death—hadn't set in yet. The smell that Sloane viewed as something that now followed her, or preceded her, rather. A row of fallen horses lay half-stacked on one another as if they were a sequence of fence posts that had each fallen onto one another. There was even a dead owl laying splattered on the ground as if it had fallen mid-flight. How unlucky.

It didn't appear the rain had been as hard-hitting in Rock-and-Tree as it had for Sloane and her companions. Droplets covered everything, but there weren't collections of muddy puddles here. Sloane found it a cruel trick of nature the way the droplets gave everything a sparkling effect in the morning light. She wanted to vomit.

"Stars almighty," Alvie uttered, brushing his fingers through his hair, his face contorted in shock and fear.

Lauge walked forward gently as if in reverence, taking off his hat as he did so. "I've never seen it for myself." His voice was shaky, and he withdrew a kerchief from his tunic's pocket and wiped his eyes.

Sloane stood there, her eyes working to avoid the man with the lute next to the man with the music pipes. Music. Their last moment had been making music. Close to them was a cookfire still smoldering a bit, the last remnants of smoke drifting into the morning air, a small fallen group of men encircling it, plates of a dinner they never got to taste spilled around them.

In a nearby area, a group lay still clutching playing cards, Give-and-Go, by the looks of it—Joah's favorite game. Worst was a tiny figure laying on the ground face down. Beside the tiny one was a woman, arm outstretched as if in protection.

Sloane's eyes welled, and she found the sky so she wouldn't see more. This had been a happy place in its last moments. A place where travelers were simply relaxing and enjoying friendly company after a long day's journey.

Someone needs to do something.

Blast, this was too much. Much too much. Alvie came to stand next to her. For a moment it seemed he might put an arm around her shoulder, but instead he sighed, also studying the partly cloudy sky.

"You found your family like this?" Alvie asked.

Sloane nodded.

"This is...this is awful. No one should die like this. I'm so sorry, Sloane."

Sloane found herself patting Alvie gently on the back. His face appeared as though the happiness would never return to that silver-toothed smile.

"Someone should do something," Alvie said.

Sloane cocked her head at him. "Aye. Someone should."

"You can," Alvie said, his eyes becoming alight.

"What?" Sloane spluttered.

"You've survived the Befallen three times!"

"What? I have not."

"You're good luck. Fact o'matter is if our wheel hadn't broke, we'd have been here. We'd have been here!"

Sloane put her head in her hand, shifting her stance onto her good leg. "That's not a sign of good luck, Alvie." Stars, she was exhausted. This was much too much. "Besides, I thought you didn't believe in the Unsung? Not that you should. Look around."

Alvie studied Sloane, tapping a finger against his silver tooth. "I see it, Sloane. You're good luck."

"Alvie! Hear me. I'm not good luck. My family is dead; my village is dead. I was robbed by the Ravyns..."

"The Ravyns?" Lauge said in the background.

"...Curses! Look at me!" She pointed to her leg.

"Ah, don't be going and giving me that." He pointed at his own leg.

Sloane trembled. Ma's skirts. Joah's horrible expression. The smell of Asana going up in flames. She knelt. Whimpers turned into sobs. Her very core shook with the wounds of unfairness. Wounds that would never heal, for they reopened scars that'd been added to Sloane's soul her entire life.

She cried out, the sound echoing through her entire essence. "I should've died! I should've died with my family!"

Lauge and Alvie enveloped her in an embrace. She continued to shudder for a few moments until finally, she melted into their strength, her heartbeat steadying.

Judging by Lauge's face when she looked up, Sloane knew she must be a pitiful mess. She wiped away tears, her breath coming in staggered hiccups. Without meaning to, Sloane caught another glimpse of the child and mother laying on the ground. Again, she wanted to vomit, but she'd expelled enough fluid. Her insides, so cold moments ago, turned hot with the injustice of what she saw. It wasn't fair.

Someone needs to do something.

"Come on, you two," Lauge said, eyeing a wagon that stood empty near the line of fallen horses. "There's nothin' we can do for this lot. Best thing to do is get to Branwell and sound the alarm."

THE TOWN of Branwell stood before them, walled off and gated, the entrance guarded by soldiers. The wall was made of huge stones, and Sloane wondered how piling such enormous stones on top of each other was possible. The gate was big enough to fit two wagons through it at once, though right now, it was only open a few feet to let outsiders in after inspection.

Sloane's palms went clammy. She eyed Alvie and Lauge beside her on the wagon, but neither seemed the least bit concerned about going through Branwell's checkpoint.

It was late afternoon now, and most of the ride had been silent, each of the travelers lost in their own thoughts. Lauge, especially, looked like he would bite through his lip, chewing on his spearmint leaf with so much force. Sloane's eyes stung, and she half-worried whether she should be ashamed of how she'd behaved. After all, she *was* alive. Alvie was right. If their wheel had not broken, they would have been right there in Rock-and-Tree, laughing and singing until...

Sloane was numb. Her fortitude about someone taking action had long since dissipated. What could anyone do, really? Nothing.

About an hour from Branwell, Alvie had perked up and began telling stories about being a pickpocket in his youth. Or rather, attempting to be one. Having a peg leg was not quite convenient for stealth, he'd laughed. As his stories went on, Alvie spoke of being hoisted up and thrown into a pig pen after being caught pickpocketing. Being starved, he said he'd simply helped himself to the pig's trough, eating himself full for the first time in his life. Alvie patted his stomach for effect. His indifference to eating in a pig pen, describing the pigs there as if they were friends, made Sloane crack a smile.

But now, scanning the wall, thinking about the loss of Father's leatherworking tools, wondering if anyone would hire a girl like her, Sloane felt a new kind of dread.

"You'll get used to the smell." Alvie smiled his silver-toothed grin, nudging her shoulder with his.

The stench hit Sloane's nose right as Alvie said the words. It was like the faint smell of burning accompanied by the odor of rotten eggs. But from her viewpoint atop the "borrowed" wagon, she certainly couldn't see anything that would create such a pungent odor. Branwell appeared to be the size of seven Mohns. But that smell. Sloane's eyes watered.

"What is it?" she asked.

"The bog," Lauge said, his eyes fixed on the travelers in line in front of them waiting to gain entrance.

"Bog?"

"Aye, there's a bog on the other side of that hill o'er there," Lauge said. He pointed but remained focused on the cart in front of them.

Why would anyone build a town next to a bog?

As if reading her mind, Lauge said, "Aye, 'tis unpleasant. But my pa used to say long ago it was crystal clear. Not a bog at all. Once, all bodies of water on Deogol were connected—even that bog—a network of rivers, streams, and lakes stretching all the way from the hills of Neomah to the swamps of Kage Duna. You might be interested to know there's even a legend, the Tale of Adria, if I remember correctly, that talks of the waters being a gift from the goddesses of the moons." Lauge gave Sloane a wink. "But," he paused. "Time has changed all that now."

Sloane had questions, but they'd reached the gate. An aged, portly man in a brown uniform that barely covered his stomach stopped them.

"So, you're back, Lauge," he said, his round face studying each of them carefully.

"Aye, couldn't get rid of Alvie this time."

The soldier did not laugh at the joke but wrote in the leatherbound logbook he carried. "There'll be no room in the inns what with the upcoming festival in a few days. Too many comin' early this year. And probably no work." The way he eyed Alvie's peg leg over his logbook made Sloane want to throw something. He shifted his attention to Sloane. "Branwell don't have room for outsiders right now."

"What's that supposed to mean, eh? You just said people already comin' for the festival. Besides, she's with us," Lauge said. "Carrin will vouch for her."

"Where you from, girl?"

"Mohn," Sloane said quietly.

"That's impossible. Whole village dead." The soldier frowned.

"Obviously not," said Alvie. "Clearly. As she's sittin' right here."

"Don't get cheeky. The elder's given strict instructions. A fortnight ago, some Ravyns sneaked in here. Still haven't found three of them. Where you really from?"

"She's from Mohn," Lauge sounded exasperated.

"You been gone from your home a while?"

"Only a few weeks."

The soldier's frown turned to a scowl. "Where were you the night of the Befallen?"

"Asana."

"Asana? That place burned to the ground almost a moon ago."

"Burned?" Lauge repeated. He threw Sloane a glance.

"Aye." The soldier crossed his arms over his massive chest. "Nothing but charred corpses found, they say. Funny that. Some people think it were the Ravyns who set Asana on fire, but in the ashes was found coins. Ravyns not likely to burn a village they ain't pillaged first. But no one knows who might've done it otherwise. No one can find anyone from Asana still alive. And right after Asana was discovered, Mohn was discovered. You know anything about that?"

"Nay," Sloane said, certain he would find the lie in her eyes.

"What would she know about it?" Lauge said. "She look dangerous to you?"

Alvie laughed. "I don't know. She's so short, when she punches, she'd have right good aim for—"

"Alvie!" Sloane said.

"All right, that's enough." The soldier wiped his brow. "Oi! I've a mind to turn you around and send you into the bog."

Alvie chuckled. "Maybe it would help its smell."

"Quiet, boy!" Lauge whacked Alvie on the shoulder before turning back to the soldier.

The soldier would not take his eyes off Sloane as if in the middle of the decision. "All right. Enter. But be sure not to cause trouble."

The wagon rolled under the gate and along the main road into the town. So many people in one place! There seemed to be commotion everywhere. There were people entering and exiting real shoppes. Shoppes for buying meat, cloth, shoes, and books. Sloane had only ever seen one book, and here was a shoppe full of them. Stars! What did they cost? The town was full of smells, too, although the stench of the bog was interlaced with all of them. She caught a whiff of some spice, smoke from chimneys, and many sour smells that made her nose wrinkle. Despite all the excitement of being in a town, Sloane peered back at the gate entrance, worried that soldiers were coming to stop them.

"Lauge?"

"Aye?"

"Why didn't you tell that soldier about Rock-and-Tree?"

"I wasn't about to feed his fire. That one was lookin' for trouble," Lauge said, slowing the wagon so some townspeople could cross the road in front of them. "Don't worry, girl. Carrin is friends with the elder's wife. We're not going to let Rock-and-Tree be left to ravagers."

CARRIN'S COTTAGE smelled like cinnamon sticks. Sloane had no idea where the woman had procured such a luxury—mayhap from the elder's wife? —but was glad to be smelling them and not the odor of the bog or other smells of the town.

"It's bad enough I must smell it when I go to market. I can't stand it. I swear I must sniff my clothes all day long," Carrin said after returning from giving the news of Rock-and-Tree to the elder's wife.

Sloane wondered why Carrin lived here if she hated the stench so much, but supposed the answer was she lived here because she lived here, the same as her parents lived in Mohn. She sipped her tea, scanning the room. Other than trespassing in the elder's cottage, she'd never sat in a place like this. Carrin's cottage was simpler than the elder of Mohn's, of course, but it certainly was grander than any common home in Mohn, or in Asana. The chair Sloane sat upon was cushioned and hanging from the windows in the parlor were real curtains made from white muslin. Sloane's family hovel had a single window with only a shutter. In fact, she couldn't think of a single place she'd been to before with curtains, even the elder of Mohn. Was Carrin wealthy, or was Mohn that poor?

Alvie entered the cottage with the last bundle from the wagon, his peg leg clopping on the wooden floor as he crossed the room.

"That's all of it," Alvie said to Lauge, who sat next to Carrin, holding her hand, grinning like a kitten that'd found spilled milk.

"M'thanks, boy," Lauge said, though his eyes were still on Carrin. The woman's frizzy blonde hair revealed strands of white in the light of the sun coming through the window. Her face, boasting a few wrinkles here and there, was a kind one. She was so obviously at ease, getting everyone tea, asking Alvie after his leg, listening to the story of the wagon wheel breaking, giving genuine concern for their ordeal in Rock-and-Tree. Sloane decided she liked Carrin, even though the woman had, like Alvie, proclaimed it lucky in the end that the wheel had broken.

"And what will you be doin' for work this time, Alvie? The man who seems able to learn any skill," Carrin asked later after she'd fed them a satisfying meal of mutton and beans.

"Don't know, maybe juggle." Alvie stood, picking up three pieces of dew fruit sitting in a bowl on Carrin's table. Sloane laughed with the others as she watched Alvie juggle the fruit. "Might get a few coppers, eh?"

"Not bad, for a duffer." Lauge laughed, settling himself further in his chair, chewing on a spearmint leaf. His brow creased, and Sloane somehow sensed he was trying to put the ordeal of Rock-and-Tree behind him. How did one do that exactly?

You don't. You learn to bury it inside yourself.

Sloane took in the scene, noting the tender way in which Carrin and Lauge gazed at one another, the way Alvie excitedly told stories, his face expressive and earnest. It was difficult thinking about leaving the only two people she knew in the world now, if she didn't count Joah, which she didn't. She scrutinized the door, sighed, and then stood. She needed to find an inn.

"I hope you don't think you're leaving," Carrin said.

Before Sloane could speak, Lauge winked and said, "Don't be stubborn, girl. You've earned a nice place to sleep. Especially after today."

"I couldn't ask that," Sloane said.

"Sure, you could," Alvie said. "I do it every time we come here."

"Besides, with the Harvest Moon Celebration comin' there won't be rooms anyway." Carrin took Sloane's rucksack from her. "You're staying here, and that's final."

Sloane wanted to argue, well; actually, she didn't want to argue. She wanted to stay. But taking up others' generosity? She'd been taught better. Still, where would she go? And after today, why did she want to go? Wouldn't it be better to hang on to her friendships for as long as she could?

She found herself yawning and rubbing her aching leg. "All right, but only until I've made enough coin to support myself."

CHAPTER
14

Sloane

T here was something strange about seeing flowers sold in a place that stank of bog. After four days in Branwell, Sloane had still not grown accustomed to the smell, nor could hardly believe Lauge's words that it had once been clear water. The orange, white, and yellow blooms of the Moonbeam flowers on the cart that she and Alvie passed as they walked along Straight Road were perfect colors for tomorrow's Harvest Moon Festival. But for as many Moonbeams were on the cart, Sloane certainly could not catch a whiff of their fragrance.

They were headed to a launderer, a lead given to them from Carrin. Sloane had never heard of someone whose trade it was to clean others' clothes, bedding, and other linens, but the others told her that in Kestriel, there were several. Evidently, the launderer's apprentice had run off with a traveling musician, and he was seeking help. Sloane hoped so. She'd been to the two leatherworkers in Branwell, and neither gave her a chance. The first told her there was no such thing as a female leatherworker. She'd explained her two years of apprenticeship, and, at first, it seemed as though he might test her skill. But when she strode forward on her left leg, she'd slipped on an oil spot on the floor and fallen. The leatherworker, brows crossed, scrutinized Sloane's leg, then shook his head. The second took one look at her and said he didn't hire cripples. A block away from his shoppe, Sloane slumped on a barrel set next to an alleyway to get control of her tears. One didn't need perfect legs to do leatherwork.

Since then, she'd been turned away from an inn wanting a housekeeper, a pub asking for a barmaid, and a butcher shoppe seeking an apprentice. All of them gave the same reason for not trying her out, even the grey-haired, kind-faced woman in the pub. No one wanted to hire a "cripple."

Rounding the corner to the launderer's, Sloane braced herself for rejection once again. Alvie chattered in her ear, this time about how, a few years ago, he'd learned how to press flower petals to create a picture.

"Why would you do that?" Sloane asked, wrinkling her nose.

"'Tis pretty. We need more pretty things, I say," Alvie rebuffed. Sloane pined for Alvie's outlook. He'd been denied *seven* positions of apprenticeship or hire—all for the same reason—but remained chipper.

If Sloane thought she'd ever been treated unfairly in Mohn, here she was learning that cruelty knew no boundaries. She pursed her lips in memory of being turned away from the leatherworkers, then tightened her fists. If they'd just given her a chance, they would know what she could do.

Her stomach burned again, thinking of the Ravyns robbing her of Father's tools. If she had those now...but then, at this moment, what she wanted was Father. She wanted him to enfold her in an embrace and tell her everything would be fine. That she was no one's crippled daughter.

Sloane brushed a hand against her cheek to wipe her tears.

Damn the Befallen.

Branwell's elder had gone to Rock-and-Tree with a group of the higher members of the town and soldiers to give the lost souls there a proper farewell. In the distance, Sloane saw a tiny billowing of smoke from the pyre before it got dark. All the belongings of those who'd succumbed to the Befallen would have been burned as well, it being ill luck to rob from them. Sloane grimaced, thinking of taking supplies and food from Mohn's elder and those in Asana. Mayhap that's why she could find no luck of her own. She'd lost it when she'd decided to steal.

"I say, Sloane, you listenin'?" Alvie said, bringing Sloane back to where they now stood in front of a dilapidated one-story stone building. It had no windows.

"Um, nay," Sloane said, eyeing the launderer's place.

"I was only telling you the secret to making the best honey bread you ever had."

"I've never had it," Sloane answered, her eyes plastered on the depressing place in front of them. The wooden door was wide open, and dank, warm air wafted out.

"Well, fact o'matter—hey, you crying?" Alvie's finger brushed off a tear from her cheek.

"Nay, I'm fine." She rubbed her palms against both cheeks.

"What is it?"

"Nothing. Come on. The sooner we get refused, the sooner we can go back to Carrin's, and you can see if she has the ingredients for honey bread."

LIMP. *Clunk. Limp. Clunk.*

Walking back from the launderer's, their footsteps on the cobblestones of the road was all Sloane could focus on: *Limp. Clunk. Limp. Clunk.*

She'd wanted to be wrong. The launderer had, at least, asked them how much weight they could carry. Alvie picked up a massive bundle near them and hefted it above his shoulders. Sloane knew the bundle must weigh more than she did. She'd simply shaken her head, gaping at the ground, feeling as though she were disappointing Ma somewhere in the stars. The launderer turned them both away.

"Ah, don't worry, Sloane," Alvie said over the *limp. Clunk. Limp.*

Clunk. "We didn't want to work there. That place smelled like dirty soup."

"Don't tell me you've had that, too?" Sloane said, willing herself to match Alvie's upbeat tone.

"Nah, but I have eaten mill mice before," he said.

Sloane wrinkled her nose. "You're joking?"

He shrugged. "Sometimes you gotta eat what you can catch, I say. I think I could catch one of them. They're not too fast. Probably wouldn't have much luck catching a shadow cat, though."

Sloane snorted, picturing Alvie chasing a great black cat the size of a donkey.

"How much farther?" she said.

"Your leg hurt?" Alvie asked. The words were casual, like asking someone if they'd slept well. The truth was Sloane's leg did hurt. But she wouldn't admit it. She'd spent days contending with others looking at it like a weakness. She'd been taught better.

"I'm fine."

"No, you're not. Come on. I know a shortcut."

Alvie turned into the alley between a silversmith's shoppe and an apothecary. The alleyway curved, cutting off her view to the other side. But here in the daylight, it was only slightly dimmed by the shadow of the buildings. She wasn't sure she wanted any part of Alvie's shortcut.

"I don't know about this."

"It's fine. Fact o'matter is, I can see your leg's bothering you. Come on. 'Tis only a little ways, and then we'll be on Spell Road. No need to take the long road, I say." Alvie began making his way down the alley, his leg's *clunk* giving off a slight echo.

Sloane couldn't describe why taking the shortcut was a bad idea, but Alvie was right; it wasn't dark, and it'd be pleasant to cut time off their walk. She was nervous for no reason. Mayhap that was an aftereffect of encountering the Befallen. Thrice. Sloane followed Alvie. He disappeared around the curve of the alleyway.

Abruptly, Sloane couldn't hear the *clunk* of Alvie footsteps in front of her.

"Alvie?" she called as she stopped.

Why is my heart beating so fast?

He's probably just waiting for you. Don't be a sook!

But why hadn't he answered back? Was he playing a trick on her? If so, it wasn't funny.

"Alvie!" Sloane shouted and limped faster to where Alvie had disappeared.

Four men stood there, all of them at least a head taller than Alvie. Two of them twice the size of Sloane. Three of them bore dark, scraggly beards. The fourth's beard was a sandy color, and a scar drove down his chin, splitting it in two. Why did he seem familiar? A couple had holes in the knees of their hose. One man held Alvie in a headlock in front of him. Alvie's face was pale, sweat dripping from his forehead, his eyes bugged out as if he were on the verge of passing out. The other three men held large knives, all of them poised to attack. Four pairs of eyes bore down at her.

What am I going to do?

You never have a weapon! She thought of her Hunger Moon knife she'd taken from Asana tucked away in her rucksack at Carrin's.

Other than Alvie's flailing, no one moved.

"Let him go," Sloane said, meeting the men's dark eyes.

The blonde man, who stood next to the man holding Alvie, snorted. His companions did not join him but kept still as if they were shadow cats studying prey.

"And what you goin' to do if we don't? Lil' miss?" another man said.

"We found nothin' on this gimp. What you got for us?"

Sloane's shoulders were already tense, every muscle in her back tightened. She was so tired of being scoffed at, turned away, laughed at. She'd seen death. She'd been robbed. She lived with the knowledge that somewhere Joah ran with savage thieves. It was too much.

Someone needs to do something.

She was small. She wasn't fast. And she was scared. More so now than when the Ravyns robbed her. But she'd had enough.

With every ounce of agility Sloane could force into her left leg, she hobble-charged at the man holding Alvie, growing whiter by the second. She had no plan. Only to knock the man off his balance and make him lose his hold on her friend.

Sloane held out her arms, hands formed into fists. She was close. She was going to save Alvie.

Abruptly, Sloane felt as though her arm was being separated from its socket. The tallest man sheathed his knife, snagged her wrist, and yanked her to him. He dragged her wrist into her back and then jerked up, making it feel as though her arm might break.

She cried out in pain. Any moment now, her shoulder was going to be ripped in two.

"Alvie!" Sloane yelled, watching his eyes close. The man holding Alvie grunted and he let go, Alvie's body slamming against the stone of the ground. "Alvie!"

One sniggered. The sound was guttural and as foul as his companion's laugh. "I cannot believe it. Two. Two cripples. What? You two join an order or somethin'? Ooh-y. What a pair!"

All four laughed, surrounding Sloane in humiliation. The ugliness of the laughter filled her with dread as the man's hot breath came close to her. He twisted upward on her wrist again, and renewed cries of pain escaped her.

Her other arm was free. She'd been such a nonthreat, it dangled beside her while the other screamed in agony. But her other arm was free. And Sloane was quite small compared to the man. Ignoring the pain of her trapped arm, Sloane pulled back her free arm and lunged it backward as hard as she could.

Please be hard enough, she begged herself.

Her elbow found its mark in the man's groin and instantly he let go and doubled over, moaning. His companions stood startled. Sloane didn't know what overtook her, but she grabbed his knife the instant before they recovered. She held it in front of her, feeling its weight in her hand.

If you can cut leather, you can cut a man. Don't be a sook.

She knew she seemed pathetic. The expressions of the three men did not, for a moment, let Sloane fool herself into thinking she appeared the least bit threatening. But she wasn't going to do nothing. She'd had enough.

"What you think is going to happen? You going to chop us into a salad, lil' miss?"

The blonde moved to take the knife from her, but she swiped the blade away and drew blood. She stared at the gash she'd made along his palm. He, too, seemed surprised to find his hand bleeding.

"All right, that's enough of this rubbish," another said, moving toward Sloane.

"Fire!" Sloane screamed from the bottom of her being. "Fire! Fire! Fire! Someone come quick! Fire!"

The men's rage was more than obvious—their companion staggering up from the ground—but it was a few heartbeats before they advanced. Sloane yelled "fire" over and over and over, staring into their dark eyes.

Already, footsteps approached. Fires in a village or town were an emergency. A small fire caught in one building could easily spread to others. It could devastate a place. Father had once said an entire five-block radius of Kestriel burned down long ago because a girl hadn't doused out her candle before falling asleep. No one ignored the word "fire" being yelled.

Two of the men took off down the opposite side of the alleyway. The man who'd been elbowed in the groin followed them, throwing curses at Sloane as he did so. Dripping blood from his hand, the sandy-bearded man, his ugly scar reminding Sloane of something, traveled his eyes from her to Alvie, who'd begun to move and moan, to where his companions had fled.

"Bet you think you're mighty clever, gimpy girl." Without another word, he kicked Alvie in the stomach, then punched Sloane square in the face.

She staggered back, broke off her yelling and fell against the wall. She slumped, her cheekbone bursting with white-hot pain, and closed her eyes against the throbbing. When she opened her eyes, three confused men holding buckets of water stood above her. Alvie sat holding his side.

She remembered who the blonde man was: Rhiner, one of the Ravyns.

CHAPTER
15

Sloane

"Fact o'matter is, those blokes simply took me by surprise," Alvie said, propped up on his makeshift bed in Carrin's parlor.

Lauge, Carrin, and Sloane surrounded him. One of Sloane's hands clutched Alvie's hand while the other had a cold compress Carrin had given her pressed to her bruised cheek. Alvie's voice was raspy and weak, but his grin was ever-present. But as he shifted uncomfortably on the pile of blankets, his teeth clenched.

"Alvie," Lauge said, his voice somewhere between a plea and consoling. "You're lucky you're alive, 'specially since one was a Ravyn. You gotta be more careful."

Alvie frowned. "Ah, Lauge. I just..."

Sloane could see her own thoughts mirrored in Alvie's solemn eyes. He just wanted to walk down the alleyway like anyone else.

They would have robbed us no matter who we were. Were those other three Ravyns, too?

She hadn't recognized them. She pictured Rhiner spitting on her, and her head momentarily felt wet and cold.

"I'm just grateful you're both safe," Carrin said. "Sloane, that was a clever thing you did, calling 'fire.'"

She blushed. Alvie lowered his chin.

"I should've been the one to save her," Alvie said quietly.

"Don't think about it anymore," Sloane said. "'Tis over now." She squeezed his hand.

Rhiner. Here in Branwell. Did he recognize me?

"You've got your color back anyway, Alvie," Carrin said. "Right. I'm going to go to the constable's headquarters. See if they've found them yet. They were glad to have the description of that Ravyn, Sloane." She stood.

"I'll go with you," Lauge said, following Carrin. Sloane set the compress on a table and patted her stinging cheek before picking up Alvie's hand again.

"I tell you, Sloane," he started again once they were alone, "if I hadn't been caught off guard, that Rhiner wouldn't have known what hit him."

"I know."

They sat in silence.

"I was eight the first time I got robbed," Alvie finally said. "All I had on me was a half o' apple I was savin' for later. It'd gone all brown and everything. I think there was even a worm in it. But it was mine, you know? These bigger children cornered me—in the middle of the stars-forsaken street—and took my half o' apple. No one passing by even glanced at me. Guess I can't say I blame 'em. What would anyone want with a dirty lil' street mouse?

"I threw a couple good kicks and punches, though. Caught one in the nose and," Alvie snickered, "he was covered in blood in a few heartbeats. That was somethin'." He paused. "After that, I made sure it was harder to rob me. I got a job at the docks in Kestriel haulin' cargo. No one wanted to hire me at first, but I finally convinced this old man who didn't want to lift anythin' anymore, on the count of him being so old and everything. I made sure the muscles I had were strong, that I *could* throw a punch. Ha! Used to practice punching the bags of cargo. I'm sure I looked mad, me this scrawny orphan with a peg leg punching bags of barley for no reason." He laughed some more.

Sloane remained quiet throughout Alvie's story, her eyes fixed on the scars that covered Alvie's hand she held.

"You didn't tell me you were an orphan."

"Oh. Yeah. My parents died from the cors fever. My uncle had my leg cut off, so the plague didn't spread to the rest o' me. But then, after a couple moons, he died, too. He was the last family I had. After that, I lived on the streets for a while. 'Til I met Lauge. Guess he's my family now, that ol' goat."

"I'm sorry you lost your parents at such a young age," Sloane said. The thought of Alvie as a street urchin, roaming around Kestriel while relearning how to walk...her own heartbreak surfaced again. So much death. It wasn't fair.

"Bah." Alvie took his hand away. "Things have turned all right for me. You gotta look on the full side of the moon, I say."

Sloane quirked a smile. "I thought you didn't take in with the moon goddesses?"

Alvie was quiet.

It occurred to Sloane that mayhap Alvie wasn't always as cheerful as he appeared. "What is it?"

"Fact o'matter is I *want* to believe, but it's difficult to believe that tomorrow night, the Harvest Moon goddess is goin' to hand out blessings, isn't it? Where are the goddesses the other nights of the year? Where are they when the Befallen strikes upon villages? When your whole family gets takin' in? Whether by fever or some dark magic no one knows about."

Again, Sloane had no answer. She glanced at her right wrist; she'd taken her moon cuff off and placed it in her rucksack when they'd arrived here. She'd wear it tomorrow night, though, despite Alvie's words and the weight on her shoulders this last moon. Her first time wearing it on the full moon. She wouldn't let her parents down.

Alvie sucked in his breath loudly, bringing Sloane back from her thoughts.

"What is it?"

"Ah, this wretched thing," Alvie said, his hands going to his peg leg. Here in Carrin's parlor, they'd shared a sleeping space for almost a week, so Sloane knew Alvie slept with his peg leg unattached to the stump of his leg, but he always waited to take it off until he thought Sloane was asleep.

"Let me help." Sloane went to pull up his hose.

"No!" He moved to stop her.

Sloane froze. She saw the frayed rope strapping the wooden leg to Alvie's thigh, and, even in the dim late-afternoon light, she'd seen the welts under the rope that marked his skin.

"I'm sorry, Alvie. I—I was just trying to help you."

"I know. Just don't, all right?" He held his palms up defensively before fixing the hose back in place.

Sloane nodded. "I'm going to get some air. Will you be fine here?"

Alvie's grimace faded. "'Course. I'm always fine."

MAYHAP SLOANE SHOULD HAVE BEEN MORE fearful of walking the street alone after today's frightening episode, but with each incident she'd faced over the last moon—each one like an added stone she must carry, getting heavier and heavier—Sloane also felt something else. A small flicker of hot anger burned in her. First her family, then Joah and the Ravyns, then—Nay! She could not, would not keep cataloging all these incidents as if she were a victim counting scars.

She entered the main square of Branwell, noting the lanterns being strung for tomorrow's festivities. A few people were arranging a floral figure of the Harvest Moon goddess out of Moonbeams. As Sloane passed, their fragrance momentarily blocked out the sour smell of the bog.

Sloane stopped and watched a group of children kicking a leather ball in the field outside the town gate, which had not yet closed for the evening. Beyond the field was the small hill blocking the view of the bog.

With naught else to explore and a sudden desire to be alone, Sloane shuffled out of the gate, passed the group of children, and began mounting the small hill. She heard laughter behind her and wondered if one of them had made a comment about her gait. The hopeful side of her tried to banish that notion, but the hopeful side was also the naive side.

It was a pitifully small hill, but Sloane still found herself perspiring and her leg aching when she reached the top and gazed below at the green-and-brown water of the bog.

Up close on the other side of the hill it smelled much worse, but Sloane, nose scrunched, cheek tender, stood alone at last. The water could have been ten inches or ten feet deep. There was no telling. Much of the bog was covered in bright green patches of algae, and tall reeds grew out of it. The reeds blocked the length of the bog, but Sloane would have been amazed to see it connected to a stream or river as Lauge had told her. It was much too stagnant.

Could this really have been a clean pond once?

She'd never heard the Tale of Adria and she had a moment's ache in her chest knowing she'd never be able to ask Father and Ma if they knew the legend.

She sat at the base of the hill, grateful the sound of the children was muffled in the background, and the hill blocked her from sight. Sloane searched the sky to gauge the time. She would need to be inside the gates before they closed at dark.

It hit her then, what she'd faced today. Stars almighty, she should be dead. How many times could she say that now? She put her face in her hands, then clenched her teeth from the pain under her eye where Rhiner had punched her. She should be dead. Her breath caught as she choked back the tears.

"Ma, I wish you were here."

The thought of her mother made her mind turn to Alvie. Oh, Alvie! What had his childhood been like? Remembering Ma's Harvest Moon tarts—which she now knew weren't tarts at all since she'd tasted real sugared tarts—made it feel as though another stone had been added to her being, but at least she'd had a childhood with parents. And aye, Sloane had been taunted or ignored, but she'd never had to defend a rotten half-apple before.

"Bless the moon, my thoughts are as scattered as the stars themselves," Sloane whispered.

A breeze began to blow. The reeds in the bog swayed back and forth, sounding like sand being sifted through a sieve. For all its horrible smell, the bog grew peaceful. Twilight was near.

Even though it was a suspicious time—now associated with the Befallen—if Sloane could pick a dress of any color, she would pick this muted purple, the color of dusk faintly seeping into the sky, like a pastel paintbrush stroking it pale before coating it black.

She searched for the rising of the moon, the last moon of the Prodigal Moon cycle. Could that goddess offer any more generous gifts? How did one pray to a goddess who was about to take her leave for the year? Did Sloane feel like praising or cursing her? She should be dead.

The breeze caressed Sloane's wet cheeks.

"Ssssslllooooo..."

Sloane gaped behind her. Nothing. She focused. Aye, the voices of the children were still in the distance.

"Sloooooooannnne."

Her eyes darted this way and that, straining to see movement. Curse her anyway; did she really have no weapon again? Moreover, had she heard her name? It was as if the breeze itself whispered to her.

"Hello?" Sloane's voice was so quiet she doubted anyone sitting beside her would have heard.

Nothing. There was only the breeze and the children playing in the background.

Then, Sloane dared to believe that something twinkled under the water of the bog. Some light?

"I must be going mad." Sloane stood, ignoring the goose pimples on her arms. Her heart pounded in her ears; her eyes could not tear away.

The night watch's bell rang. The gate would close soon.

Sloane forced her eyes from whatever glowed underneath the bog's water and scrambled up the hill with as much speed as her leg allowed.

Although the terrified part of her wanted to put as much distance between her and that detestable bog as possible, the other part of Sloane, the part that kept the anger alight, wanted to go back and see if the Prodigal Moon really had left a last gift.

CHAPTER 16

Sloane

Lauge's cheeks were rosy from all the moon mead he'd drunk. He laughed again into his mug, Carrin next to him, doing the same as she lifted hers in unison.

Sloane chuckled along, though she didn't have a clue what Lauge had said. The crowds were too noisy.

It was after dusk, and the main square of Branwell was filled to the brim with people. Lanterns gleamed upon the celebration. For once, the bog's smell wasn't so stark. Sloane caught whiffs of Harvest tarts, grilled candied walnuts—she'd wanted to cry upon tasting them, they were so delicious—meat pies, and even racks of boar. Music played on a raised stage that'd been erected in the middle of the square, townsfolk dancing and swaying in the end-of-summer evening air. Children scurried about, carrying bouquets of Moonbeams arranged in a perfect circle to signify the full moon. What a celebration! In Mohn, there was a Harvest Full Moon Festival, of course, but nothing this extravagant. She ached to think of how Sherik would've loved this music and the taste of sugared dew fruit.

Mayhap he shined on her now, reveling in the festival from his place among the stars.

"Where's Alvie?" Carrin asked, surveying the crowd.

"He went in search of honey bread," Sloane said. She couldn't believe he had room in his belly for more food. She scanned the crowd. There was no finding anyone in this sea of faces.

Three of the men who'd accosted Sloane and Alvie in the alleyway yesterday had been arrested, while, of all things, robbing someone else. But Rhiner hadn't been caught. Sloane ignored the black-and-blue bruise under her eye. Mayhap he'd fled Branwell.

Or he could be in this very crowd.

"I think I'll find Alvie," Sloane said.

Casually, she squeezed through the mass of people, doing her best to not to get trampled. She wasn't worried. It'd be foolish for Rhiner to be in this crowd. Still.

"Sloane!" She heard her name and turned around, her toes smashed by a loose footstep in the process. Alvie was making his way to her, a giant mug in one hand and what appeared to be an entire loaf of honey bread in the other. "Told you I'd find some. Wait 'til you try this. It tastes like—"

"Honey?" Sloane supplied. They were practically yelling even though they stood right next to each other. "Come on." She shuffled through the crowd toward the town's gate—open late for the festival— leading to the field she'd found yesterday, where there was only a slightly less gathering of people. She didn't necessarily want to be close to the bog again, but at least out here, she wouldn't get stepped on.

On the field, Sloane and Alvie no longer shouted over the music and rabble of festivalgoers. Alvie rambled on about a dancing dog act he'd seen while searching for the honey bread, boasting he could join them if he had an inkling to do so. He appeared to be back to his usual demeanor.

Out here, a few had set out blankets, having picnics, celebrating in a quieter way. Waiting for the full moon to rise, and with that, the welcoming of the goddess of the Harvest, who would gather all prayers of the faithful. But far more townsfolk reveled in the square than were waiting for the rising of the moon. In Mohn, the entire village would be waiting together by now, the festivities giving pause for devotion.

A lute player strummed music at the other end of the field. A corner of her mouth lifted when Sloane recognized the old folk song he played, "The Peasant and the Princess." She spun her moon cuff around her wrist. Her first full moon wearing it. She offered a silent thank you to Father, holding back tears at the same time.

She noticed a few others wore moon cuffs as well. But not everyone. At Harvest, souls were supposed to give thanks for the fruits of a summer well-labored, and offer gratitude for bounties, preparing for the next phase of the year: autumn. What would Sloane offer thanks for?

"What is it?" Alvie asked as they sat on the grass.

"Just thinking about what I shall pray for."

Alvie snorted. He was not wearing a moon cuff.

"I thought you said yesterday you *do* believe?" Her brows knitted together in confusion.

"Well, that was yesterday, wasn't it? Anyway, we'll see," Alvie said. "I don't need to say words out loud, mind you. Fact o'matter is the goddess knows what I pray for. If she wants to answer it, she can. If not, I'm no better or worse off than I were yesterday. Am I to believe somethin' magical will happen?"

Sloane didn't want to argue.

They were quiet, Alvie having stuffed his mouth with honey bread, and Sloane continuing to consider her own gratitude. Honey bread *was* delicious. She supposed that was worth a small prayer of thanks. She'd met Alvie and Lauge. And Carrin, of course. That could warrant another. These friends might feel like family someday.

But what about Sherik and Ma and Father?

And stupid, deceitful, Joah? The darker side of Sloane wormed the thought into her heart.

Aye, but I'm alive, and I cannot begrudge the goddess that. I should be thankful, the side of Sloane peering at the evening's first star responded. *I should be dead. But I'm not. I—*

Her thoughts were interrupted by three trumpets blaring. Everyone was quiet as scores of townsfolk entered the field from the town gate. On the other end of the field stood an older man with wisps of white hair on the sides of his head. He wore lengthy ivory robes. This must be Branwell's elder.

"People of Branwell." His voice was louder than Sloane would expect from one his age. "Despite the hardships of losing eleven of our brothers to the Befallen this summer in a tragedy they suffered hunting in the woods, we are blessed. We've a good crop, our storehouses are full, and we're prepared for what comes next. We are also blessed this night as it is the full moon, which means Deogol need not worry about the Befallen this night."

Cheers erupted from the townsfolk.

Except the Befallen did hit Asana on the full moon.

"I would ask you whether you pray to the Harvest moon or not, that you keep some thought of thanks in your heart tonight. Embrace your brothers. Feast on our bounties. Gladden the streets with the goodness of your souls."

More cheers from the crowd. It was then Sloane caught a nearby mother embracing her two children. There was much to be thankful for.

"Slooooooannnne."

"Alvie! Did you hear that?" Sloane surveyed the hill. In her mind, she saw the glowing...something under the murky water.

"Hear what?"

"That voice."

"The elder? Sloane, he ain't hard to miss."

"Nay, not the elder. Like a..." She trailed off. Like a breeze? Like an echo? Like magic? "Never mind."

"Last," the elder quieted the crowd. "I am certain you, too, have heard the rumors. 'Tis true. The Order of Siria is here in Deogol."

Murmurs rippled through the crowd.

"Whoa! The Order of Siria." Alvie's eyes bugged out. "They's the most famous knights in all of Tasia!"

The elder held up a hand so he could continue. "The Order of Siria seeks the Unsung hero. The sovereign himself has sent a message from Kestriel to let all of Deogol know the Unsung *will* be found."

The stir of sounds from the crowd was a jumble of cheers, laughter, and some not too friendly comments thrown in the mix.

"Come now! I know some of you may not believe in the Unsung of the Edan Lore, but I'll remind you 'tis all we have. The Befallen *is* real, and even if little is known about it still, its victims grow in number. Rock-and-Tree is only the latest incident of unfathomable death. Therefore, 'tis the sovereign's intention to find the Unsung by the Solstice. Mayhap among us here tonight is the Unsung."

The crowd was quiet after these last words. Sloane scowled at the elder. By the Solstice? That was a mere three moons away. And what of the Azure Moon? She went over the words of the Edan Lore in her head. It seemed far too simple that the sovereign could make a grand announcement, and suddenly the Unsung would appear. She wondered if the elder was one who knew the entire Edan Lore or merely an abridged version Lauge said only most knew now.

"The moon rises soon," the elder said. "Bless you all, and do not forget to offer your thanks."

The townsfolk offered cheers and applause, but it wasn't as enthusiastic as it'd been before his relay of the sovereign's announcement.

"Sloooooooannnne."

This time, Sloane turned around. It came from the bog again. Curse or gift? What should Sloane believe?

"Alvie, come on." She stood and began treading up the hill.

"Where you goin'?"

"Just come on," Sloane called behind her.

At the top, Sloane watched many townsfolk returning to the square. They weren't even going to wait for the moon to rise? Not even offer a short prayer of thanks?

Alvie came up behind her.

"What we doin'?" he asked, taking a swig of his mug. "Would you look at that ugly bog? Oi. That smell could drive you to live with pigs, I say. Hey, where you goin'?"

Sloane made her way down, her eyes scanning for the glow beneath the stagnant water. Her nose wrinkled. So much for the sweet taste of honey bread. All the food in her belly churned. Still. She had to see. The reeds were motionless. There wasn't a breeze this evening. Where had that voice come from?

"Well, 'cept for the smell, I suppose it's nice here," Alvie said, plopping onto the grass beside her and emptying the contents of his mug.

Nothing. Sloane sat next to Alvie, half disappointed, half relieved.

"What we come here for?"

"Nothing."

They sat in companionable silence for a time, Sloane still scouring the bog's water.

The moon rose in the sky, peeking from behind the reeds. A beaming, perfect circle. Because it wasn't completely dark yet, it did not shine pale, but projected radiance as if all the stars in the sky had been reaped together to gather a harvest of light. It was brilliant.

On the night of the full moon, one could pray to the goddess at any point before morning, but Sloane had always liked the idea of offering her prayer at first sight of the moon. Nervous that this was her very first prayer with a moon cuff, she took a deep breath. She knew what to do. She'd watched her parents and others in the village.

Sloane placed her left hand over her moon cuff on her right wrist and then brought both hands up, her right hand made into a fist to rest below her collar bone at the center of her chest. Her head bowed so that her chin touched her right hand. Hands. Heart. Head. All connected. She closed her eyes, quieting her mind, tried to block out the rabble behind her on the field, tried to block out Alvie picking at the grass beside her. And she still wasn't certain what to pray for.

The warm faces of her family swam in front of her. Then the cold, blank eyes of Mistress Semla. The poor villagers of Asana. The travelers of Rock-and-Tree. No more. She couldn't see anymore. Had people really forgotten the Edan Lore? Did this Order of Siria know all of it? They must.

But what if they don't know it?

What does it matter? You're not the Unsung, thought the side of Sloane prone to scoffing.

I know. But I could help. Someone needs to do something, answered the side of Sloane gripping her prayer wristlet. For what seemed hours, Sloane remained in her prayer position with her eyes closed.

"Oh, goddess of the Harvest," Sloane whispered, hoping Alvie couldn't hear. "I offer thanks for my miserable, unimportant life." Because it was true. She was no one, but that didn't mean she couldn't do something. "I wish to—"

"Slooooooannnne."

Her eyes popped open. She saw it. In the murky water was a small glow. And it seemed to be drifting toward her. Crouching, Sloane got close to the water.

"What you doin'?" Alvie said behind her.

"Sshhh."

What glowed underneath this stagnant, dank water? And then, the green-brown water—that there was no telling where the bottom was—rippled. As if a breeze blew away the algae and muck and even the stench. Sloane saw what glowed under the water, close to the bank now, was naught more than what was a small reflection of the moon.

Disappointment flowed through her. For a moment, she'd thought—

"What *is* that?" Alvie's voice was quiet next to her. He, too, knelt beside the bog, staring at the small glowing circle. "Did you see? Did you see the water? It moved! Sloane, there's no way that should've moved."

"It's only the moon's reflection," Sloane said, keeping her tone light.

"Nah. That's not the moon's reflection. Look where the moon is. There ain't no way that's comin' from the moon. It moved! Besides, if it were the moon's reflection, it would look like it's on top of the water, but that is *under* the water." He sat up and crossed his arms over his chest for good measure.

He was right.

"What do you think it is?"

"I dunno, but, blimey. Somethin', eh?"

Sloane leaned closer. Below the surface, the glowing circle appeared close enough that Sloane could reach into the water and touch it if she wanted. It mesmerized her.

And then, the glowing circle began to transfer shape, transforming into an ovalish circle. What was more, the shape ceased glowing and turned a greyish hue the color of smoke, a weak light dimly radiating from it.

Sloane took the moon cuff off her wrist, rolled up her sleeve, and dipped her arm into the water. As she attempted to clutch the grey shape, her fingertips felt something smooth. One instant, she had her fingers wrapped around it, slick, not perfectly circular, thin. The next instant, it vanished. Her hand was an empty fist when she brought it above the water's surface.

Had she dropped it? No, when Sloane focused on the water, there was nothing there but murk, algae, and gunk resting on the surface as if it had never parted or Sloane had never disturbed its surface. It was completely still.

She tried to make out a glow or the grey hue, gazing from the bog to her arm, still wet, the remnants of algae clinging to it. Alvie stared dumbfounded at her.

Sloane's eyes drew to the moon, fully risen now.

What just happened?

Something familiar, something she should know, prodded the back of Sloane's mind, but it, like the shape in the water, disappeared as soon as she tried to grasp it.

Back amongst the throngs of people, Sloane and Alvie made their way back to find Lauge and Carrin, bumping into person after person as they went.

Sloane froze. "Alvie, it's Rhiner."

He was several scores of people away from them. As he walked alone, his eyes shifted. He was searching for someone. Her.

"Come on," Alvie said, pulling Sloane's arm and striding with more determination.

The gate was nearby. Sloane glanced back. As soon as she turned, she wished she hadn't. There was still a crowd between them, but Rhiner's dark eyes were transfixed on her. And it wasn't that he recognized the girl from the alley, he recognized *her*.

"Hurry," Sloane said, tripping over someone's foot.

"Oi! Watch it," a voice snapped from behind her. They were almost to the gate. She wasn't sure why that meant something to her. Mayhap because there were town guards stationed around the square. She felt Rhiner inching closer to them, no doubt taking large strides and chucking people out of his way.

They were at the gate when the town square bell—only rung in warning or disaster—began to chime.

Voices exclaimed in unease, and in the square in front of them, shouts came. It sounded as though an argument was happening.

"People of Branwell, the Befallen attacked the village of Slough Groth!" a man in a green uniform shouted. Green. Not from Branwell.

Sloane went rigid. *On the night of a full moon? Not again.*

"What's more is there's a witness..."

"A witness?" Alvie's whisper echoed Sloane's thoughts.

To date no one had *ever* been witness to the Befallen. No one. For Sloane, the mysteriousness behind the Befallen was what frightened her the most.

Sloane strained her ears.

"...a hunter, who was late returning to the village, has sworn he saw what looked like a cloud, dark as coal, covering the entire village." The green uniformed man had trouble keeping the emotion out of his voice. "He couldn't see anything. Then it vanished, he said. When he got there, everyone was dead!"

"Where's this witness?" someone in the crowd shouted.

"Been taken to Kestriel to inform the sovereign."

Everyone began speaking at once and whatever else the soldier said was heard no more. Sloane focused on the moon before eyeing behind her. Rhiner was gone.

SLOANE PLACED the last item in her rucksack. It was heavy, but she'd only have to carry it to the main gate. Last night, after the announcement, she'd overheard a group who planned to caravan to Kestriel at dawn. It seemed the elder's words mixed with the soldier's news had prompted action. If the Order of Siria was searching for the Unsung, it was time they found one, she'd heard a tall man say. When Sloane asked one of the men if anyone could come, he answered, "anyone who can pay their own way." Sloane was glad her skirts covered her leg, but the man had been so distracted, she doubted he would've noticed. She couldn't fully explain why she needed to go; there would certainly be little for her to do once there, but she could at least make certain the Order of Siria knew the entire Edan Lore. She felt foolish. Of course, they would know it. They were closely connected to the StarSeers of the Capella Realm.

But what was keeping her here in Branwell?

She hadn't slept. Instead, she'd spent one half of the night packing—fretting about her decision while she did so—and the other half explaining to Lauge and Carrin over and over why she had to go while trying to convince Alvie to come with her. Lauge and Carrin relinquished, but Alvie refused, saying something about rubbish.

Dawn was coming. Time to go.

Lauge and Carrin hugged her goodbye.

"Wish I could talk you out of this," Lauge said, his embrace fatherly.

Sloane whispered in his ear, "The Azure Moon comes."

He nodded, lips pursed.

"All right, we better get goin'." Alvie came out of the scullery, a rucksack of his own slung on his back.

"You're coming?"

"Aye," Alvie said. "I'm startin' to wonder if I should've given you a ride in my wagon."

"*My* wagon, you mean, boy," Lauge said.

"Whatever. Fact o'matter, we have no idea what we're doing, why we're going, and we're surely going to find trouble, but life is the grand adventure, I say. Let's be off."

"Thank you, Alvie," Sloane said, opening the door to the cottage and starting out into the early morning air.

CHAPTER 17

Tolvar

"If this doesn't offer an incentive to cease your endless attachment with liquor, I know not what will," Ghlee said, standing above Tolvar with less than a friendly expression on his face.

Tolvar squinted, or, rather, tried to squint. Only one eye would open.

"Don't speak," Ghlee said. "Hear me, once and for all. I don't know what happened to make you a punching bag two nights ago, but the Wolf should have easily beaten them. Even if it was five against one. Stars almighty, you're lucky you aren't dead."

"Why aren't I?"

"Someone saved you." Ghlee smirked. "Luckily, I'd narrowed my search to that block."

"My thanks. Although I'm uncertain it was a life worth saving," Tolvar said, sitting. His head, ribs, shoulder—even his hair—hurt.

"Just barely," Ghlee said, eyebrows raised. "While you've slumbered, I've waited with breath that is bated for two days to hear what happened."

"Did you kill the last one standing?"

"Nay. Ran off as soon as he saw me. I don't think he wanted to end up like his companions."

"I was attacked. 'Twas strategic. They must have been watching me. These are the Brones who left the note about the Azure Moon."

Ghlee nodded.

"The leader said something about..." Tolvar was having trouble remembering, "about finding a way to make the Befallen leave Deogol, or something of that nature."

Then he remembered. The Curse of Adrienne.

"Ghlee, are you certain we have all the words of the Edan Lore? There's naught about the Azure Moon that we are missing?"

"I wouldn't think so. I grew up reciting it as a boy like everyone else in Deogol. We could try the sovereign's library. That is, after you've had a bath."

ANOTHER TRICKLE of melted wax dripped onto the gold candle holder that stood on the marble table. Tolvar eyed it in annoyance. Soon he'd have to again call one of the useless scholars over to fetch him another candle.

He'd been hunched over stacks of tomes for two days. The Wolf had never been known for reading.

"Why in Siria's skirt is it that libraries never have enough light?" Tolvar growled at Ghlee, who was sitting across the table from him, bent over a piece of parchment. "They're always these underground, dark tombs. No windows. It makes as much sense as going to battle with a kitchen knife."

Ghlee grunted in response but did not look up. Tolvar stood and stretched his back, careful not to extend too far lest he should pain his ribs. He scanned the vast hall, or, rather, tunnel, as it seemed more accurate to name. In the dim candlelit space, one could hardly make out the high ceiling above. Tall shelves of books, parchments, and even several leather boxes, holding stars knew what, bordered the walls. Reading tables lined the center of the hall. Tolvar felt claustrophobic.

"Aye, I tell you, the only library I've ever been in that was properly lit was in Blagdon, Lenfore's largest city. Now there's a library. Windows ceiling to floor. Plush chairs that could fit two of me."

Ghlee leaned back in his chair. "I wasn't aware that you even knew what a library was, Wolf. Stars, I can't believe you've kept us cooped up in here this long."

Tolvar regarded the books and rolled-up parchment on the table waiting to be perused. He really did hate to read. And his eye, although no longer swollen, was shiny black, bruised, and not making it easy. "'Tis the only thing keeping me from the taverns, I must admit to you."

"Ah, so you're a reformed man."

"Stars, no. But it hurts to blink, no less swallow ale." Ghlee snickered at Tolvar's words. "Besides, if the Brones are foolish enough to attack me over this Azure Moon and brazen enough to speak of the Curse of—" he stopped himself from saying the word Adrienne, "then the Order is most assuredly missing something."

"The scholars said the Chief Scholar returns tomorrow morning. If anyone can help us with the missing piece of the Edan Lore, she can."

"*She?*"

Ghlee leaned forward. "Aye. Shouldn't a reformed man be open to the idea of the Chief Scholar being a woman? After all, your StarSeers are all women."

"I told you, I'm not reformed. And there's no comparison between those ordained by the heavens and one who simply found she could out-read everyone."

Ghlee's quiet expression, under the candlelight, appeared foreboding.

"What?"

"I get the impression that before all this is over, you *will* be a reformed man."

"Ha! Redemption and reform are not the same."

"We shall see."

Tolvar did not appreciate the expression Ghlee gave him. It reminded him too much of the glares his commander, Leon, gave.

"Let's get back to it," Tolvar said, sitting with a sigh, the candle next to him flickering as if in protest.

"M'lords, m'lords!" A frantic man's voice called from the doorway.

"I'm not a lor—"

"Cease," Ghlee warned Tolvar. He closed his mouth.

One of the sovereign's scholars approached, his stupid hat bouncing on his head. Scholars wore robes of a silvery-grey material, and on their heads wore small caps, different colors symbolizing status and expertise. Tolvar had no idea what a dark purple cap meant but found the cap's appearance ridiculous. The man was barely more than a youth, face as clean-shaven as the day he was born.

Scholars in the Capella Realm need not set themselves apart by attire. Anyone could be considered a scholar. It was the same as addressing those in Deogol as "scholar," just like "elder" or "sovereign" rather than by name. Once elevated to a certain position —and Tolvar always had trouble remembering what the specific positions were—those in that station forwent their birth names for the rest of their days. Sometimes Tolvar wondered that knights were not simply referred to as "knight." He found it amusing thinking of calling Ghlee "knight."

I wager King Rian wouldn't take kindly to being called "sovereign," though. Tolvar visualized the imposing form of the Capella Realm's serious-minded sovereign.

"M'lords, the sovereign approaches," the scholar said.

"The sovereign?" Ghlee stood, straightening his doublet. Tolvar also stood, his hands clasped behind his back. Both men's eyes were drawn to the entrance, which was barely visible.

Now what? Tolvar rocked side to side, determining whether the sovereign's visit was a good or bad incident. He supposed he still needed to grovel about offending spoiled Princess Benetha.

"My liege," Ghlee said, bowing to the slinky figure who emerged into sight.

The sovereign wasn't as short as his niece, but height was certainly not a trait of the family. No matter how many times Tolvar had an audience with the sovereign, he couldn't get over how crooked the man's nose was. It would go without saying the sovereign would never have suffered a broken nose; it was an oddity. His beady eyes were pale blue like Benetha's but lacked any warmth behind them. Nay, the sovereign's eyes were of a man who'd spent over half a decade of his rule waging war against an invisible monster—and was losing.

"Your Majesty." Tolvar bowed his head likewise.

"Peace," the sovereign said, holding up a palm. "You may save your kowtowing. I'm uncertain of its sincerity anyway."

Tolvar cleared his throat and found a spot on the stone floor to focus on.

"I haven't much time, and rather than commanding a summons and waiting for you for a duration unsuitable for a sovereign...again —" The sovereign's beady eyes landed on Tolvar as Ghlee paled in the background. "I've come as a courtesy to the relationship I have with the Order of Siria, to let you know I've sent a decree notifying the citizens of Deogol that the Order is being reestablished here and seeks the Unsung. My council and I feel it will only be a matter of time before those who feel they might best the Befallen flood Kestriel with offers of aid."

"My liege—" Ghlee began at the same time Tolvar yelled, "Are you out of your mind?"

"I beg your pardon, Sir Tolvar?" The sovereign's voice was quiet but threatening. "Choose your next words with care."

Ghlee shook his head vigorously.

"My apologies, Your Majesty. But we cannot accept a gaggle of numpty fools into the Order. The Order isn't some band that one can join by signing a bit of parchment." His voice was rising, but he didn't care. "And how in Siria's skirt do you think the Edan Lore even works? If a volunteer was all I needed, I would have defeated the Befallen myself ten moons ago when I got here. Your

Majesty is hawking an idea of hope like it's this season's barley crop."

"Sir Tolvar—"

But Tolvar continued. "The Order has been here inconspicuously for a year. What in stars' shadow do you think will happen now that your people are aware of it? You think your volunteers are going to seek the role of the Unsung out of loyal duty or a chance to glimpse the famed guard?" He ran his fingers through his hair. He could feel his pulse in his neck.

"Are you quite finished?" the sovereign asked. Behind him, Ghlee sunk to his chair, his head buried in his hands.

"Aye."

"Let me remind you, though your reputation for many things, insolence being one of them, precedes you, you are here in Deogol because of my incredibly good will. Mayhap you'd like to set sail and take your chances back in the Capella Realm. I hear the bounty on your head is quite high now."

Tolvar stared back at the floor.

"Let me also remind you it is I, not you, who is sovereign here. Though I welcome the restoration of the Order of Siria and their help, the Befallen and its impact on my people are my concern. The Edan Lore does not state one cannot voluntarily become the Unsung—"

"Your Maj—"

"Cease. This curse has plagued my country enough. Extreme measures must now be taken. A new tactic tried. Have you no experience in these matters, *Sir* Tolvar?"

Tolvar remained silent.

"'Tis good you have unrattled your tongue." The sovereign's nostrils flared. "Hear me. The two of you will see and test *anyone* who wishes to aid in the fight against the Befallen. Or so help me, I care not for the Order's influence, I'll see you both hanged from the rafters and have your bodies thrown into the sea. Is that clear?"

"Aye, Your Majesty," Tolvar said after a moment's hesitation.

"Excellent," the sovereign said. "Now, I'll leave you to whatever it is you were doing."

He strode away, but Tolvar called out, causing the sovereign to sigh and turn back. "Your Majesty. What do you know of the Azure Moon being connected to the Edan Lore?"

In the shadows of the poorly lit hall, the sovereign seemed to be pondering, searching his own knowledge. It occurred to Tolvar that here was a man desperate to save his people.

"I'm afraid I have no knowledge of what you're speaking about. Why?" the sovereign finally said.

"'Tis no matter, Your Majesty." Tolvar wondered if the sovereign had been informed about the Brones' attempt to kill him in the street, but he didn't want to burden him further. "And I apologize for my outburst. I am at your service."

The sovereign nodded and left.

CHAPTER 18

Tolvar

Tolvar concluded that the gods of the stars, which he only sort of believed in, must hate him. Or mayhap the goddesses of the moon, which he didn't believe in, were working against him.

He and Ghlee sat behind a rickety table that wobbled so much there was no way of setting anything on Tolvar's side of it. It didn't matter. The table was there as more of a barrier between them and the scores of men, and even a few women, who lined up in the training courtyard waiting to meet with the great Wolf and his Order of Siria comrade for a chance to join the cause against the Befallen. The sovereign's declaration coupled with the news of Slough Groth apparently propelled the hero in people.

The interviews had been taking place since dawn, and a half-dozen men and one woman had been advanced to a later sparring round in which their propensity toward combat skills could be tested. They'd just turned away a lad who couldn't have been older than nine. The boy beamed up at Tolvar, asking if he could see the scar on Tolvar's arm he'd received from a battle with a shadow cat.

"Don't you have better things to be doing?" Tolvar grumped, but Ghlee, eyeing the balcony where the sovereign stood watching them, tugged Tolvar's sleeve to reveal the marks. The boy gave a "wow" at the indentations that were clearly teeth marks. Tolvar pulled his sleeve back, shaking his head about being given undue attention for scars he'd received eight years ago. He had a mind to lift his tunic and ask the boy if he wanted to see his other scars. Two in his shoulder from arrows in a battle against the forces of the Earl of Namid. A long slice running across his stomach from the War of a Hundred Nights. Or there was always the scar right below his heart that his own brother, Crevan, had given him. Tolvar clenched his jaw in memory.

So much blood.

Nay, best not to draw attention to his other scars.

And what of the scars in his mind? The sound his father made being stabbed by his own son? The sound, which could never be described as a cry, for it was something made of deeper stuff, was imprinted on Tolvar. Snow turning crimson, he'd lain there in the courtyard, unable to move from his own wounds. Not able to stop Crevan. Not able to cease the sound penetrating his ears.

"Wolf?"

Ghlee was staring at him, an eyebrow raised. There was no way for Ghlee to know what Tolvar had been thinking about, but he was like family; his expression reminded Tolvar that Ghlee understood him.

"All right," Ghlee stood, shouting at the mass of people. "We are most glad so many of you have responded to the sovereign. For now, we shall pause for the midday meal. You may come back in one hour's time."

"You all right?" Ghlee asked when they were seated alone at one of the long tables in the castle's secondary hall, called the Crescent Hall. It was half the size of the Great Hall, with two tables instead of five and one fireplace instead of four. There was no dais in this hall, but a sovereign's table presided at the front. A long, stained-glass window covered almost the entire wall on the opposite side of the hall, illustrations of the twelve moon goddesses depicted in it. A few servants walked in and out of the room, carrying trays of food for the sovereign's lesser guests and high-ranking retainers and officers. Only one other group of men were in the Crescent Hall, stuffing their rowdy midday meal into open mouths.

"Aye, I'm fine." Tolvar shoveled a spoonful of beans around his plate.

"At least in the training yard, we can see the sun and don't have that ghastly smell of dusty books surrounding us."

Tolvar nodded, focusing on his food.

"Do you think she was telling the truth?" Ghlee leaned in.

Tolvar put down his spoon, wiped his mouth on his sleeve, and scratched his beard. "Do you?" Despite the men at the other end of the hall being too loud to hear them, Tolvar, too, quieted his voice.

"I want to trust her. Stars know the Chief Scholar, of all people, should be able to be trusted. But..." Ghlee trailed off.

So Ghlee *was* having the same concern as Tolvar.

Upon her arrival yesterday morning, they two had sought the Chief Scholar in her private antechamber attached to the library. A tall, willowy woman, her silver robes seemed to drown her. The scholar's cap she wore, by right, was cobalt blue, matching the sovereign's banner. Under her cap, her raven-black hair was pulled into a tight knot at the nape of her neck. Tolvar had never seen such stern-looking eyebrows on a woman—or man, come to think of it. Despite her dour expression, her voice was smoothed over with a kind, calm tone. So much so that when the men asked her about the Azure Moon's role in the Edan Lore, her voice kept its steady timbre. Her only reaction had been to draw her palms together and place them under her chin.

"The Azure Moon is wrapped in mystery," the Chief Scholar said. She'd then turned to some letters on her desk as if that were the end of it.

"So, you've never heard of the Edan Lore missing lines having to do with the Azure Moon?" Tolvar pressed again.

The shake of her head was so subtle that if Tolvar's focus had not been so fixed on her, he wondered that he might have missed it.

"Your grace," Ghlee tried again. "We have reason to believe that a piece of the Edan Lore has been lost. Might you, in your esteemed position, research this for us? Help us?" There was no missing the sincere plea in Ghlee's voice.

The Chief Scholar's lingering stare drove chills up Tolvar's spine.

"I will see what I can find. But I feel certain I cannot help you. My apologies, sirs."

With that, they'd been dismissed. And now, sitting at the midday meal, Ghlee mirroring his thoughts about whether the Chief Scholar withheld something, and more to the point, if she had, *why* she would withhold something, Tolvar suspected all these muddled events of late were drawing him further from finding the Unsung, not closer.

"Are there really no copies of the Edan Lore? In writing, I mean," Tolvar asked.

"According to legend, your StarSeers forbade it when they gave it to Deogol one hundred and fifteen years ago," Ghlee said. "Though why that would be is beyond me. 'Tis only been handed down orally, children learning it in their earliest years. Tolvar, I know you might not want to hear this, but it might be possible—"

"Cease. I know what you would say, but I know what that man said, same as the note in Ganifer's hand."

"But if the Chief Scholar doesn't know about the Azure Moon, then..." Ghlee trailed off, lifted his spoon again to jab at his plate.

Tolvar shook his head. In the Capella Realm, prophecies, fortunes, even predictions of weather were written down. Why would the StarSeers command such a thing? It had to be written somewhere. Unease prickled at the back of his neck.

Later that afternoon, Tolvar had been tempted to smash their wobbly table at least a dozen times. He and Ghlee had agreed it was in everyone's best interest for Ghlee to do the talking.

"And that's all you know of the Edan Lore?" Ghlee kept his voice pleasant, but the scowl Tolvar gave to the young man with a small patch of hair on his chin was threatening. It was an expression usually reserved for battle. His back hurt from sitting. His head ached for ale. And he and Ghlee had now seen over six scores of people. None of them were the Unsung. They just...couldn't be.

"Aye, m'lord." The young man's voice cracked. "That *is* the Edan Lore. Learned it when I was a boy, I did. Know it like the back of my hands."

"Hmmm, which are filthy, I might add," Ghlee said. "Right, off you go." He waved a hand toward the gate for him to exit. "Well, that's the last of them. Not a single person knew anything about the Azure Moon. Wolf, I don't want to start yet another argument, but is it possible you remember it wrong? That night. You were drunk, after all."

Tolvar didn't even glance at Ghlee. "Do not start that again. Come. I've abstained long enough. To the King's Pub."

It felt good to stretch his legs. Tomorrow, he vowed, they would train in the morning before seeing any more fools hoping for glory. Tolvar tightened his grip on his sword. Aye, too long. Ghlee was abnormally quiet beside him. Ghlee did not want to believe there were missing pieces of the Edan Lore. It was a source of pride. And what to make of the Chief Scholar? If she'd never learned it as a girl, then it would stand to reason that she might be unaware of it as well. He could not believe, like Ghlee, that these Brones—such a stupid name—would attack him and speak of the Curse of Adrienne of all things if they did not know something about the Edan Lore. They'd been much too earnest in their efforts.

They entered the pub, and Tolvar salivated at the scent of liquor in the air. A twinge of shame followed. Had he not been drunk, Tolvar would have easily been able to capture the leader and gotten some answers. This would be a moment to make amends.

"Don't let me drink into a stupor, Ghlee," Tolvar said, flicking a coin out of his purse and heading to the counter.

CHAPTER
19

Sloane

S loane considered Branwell huge. Kestriel was monstrous. Alvie
nudged her and she closed her gaping mouth. The forbidding
thick stone walls of the sovereign city towered over their caravan as
they waited their turn to gain entrance.

The four-day journey had been an ordeal. The rocking to and fro
in the back of a wagon gave Sloane a constant headache, but that was
nothing compared to the chase the Ravyns had given them two days
ago, which was a nightmare Sloane could still not believe in her
wildest dreams that they'd escaped. Seeing those black cloaks
flapping in the wind again in the distance reopened the wounds of
Joah's betrayal. This time, though, she'd been ready. On the night of
the Harvest Moon, she'd purchased a scrap of leather to make a
sheath for her Hunger Moon knife. The leather cost a third of what
was left of her coin, but she would never again be weaponless.
Though the sheath was rough and not her best work, making it had
helped pass the time in the wagon. More importantly, she could now
carry the small knife in the pocket of her dress.

Sloane still couldn't imagine what'd made the Ravyns eventually
turn away from their chase. The six-wagon caravan was large but
certainly no match for them, even with the eight Branwell soldiers
who accompanied them on horseback. One moment the Ravyns were
gaining, gaining, gaining on them, and then, they'd splintered off their
ranks, and each clump simply rode away in opposite directions.
Sloane's eyes strained to find Joah among them, but she couldn't pick

him out. She hated herself for being disappointed that she couldn't spot him—and that the reason she'd wanted to see him wasn't so she could stab him. Had Rhiner rejoined them? Her black eye wasn't as visible, but still hurt.

Since that chase, Sloane hadn't slept. Judging from the other travelers' red-eyed, exhausted faces, it seemed no one had. How could they? Everyone gave a cheer upon the Ravyns' retreat, but when night fell, Sloane caught plenty of weapons, or what could be used as weapons, nestled beside her sleepless companions.

But the gigantic walls of Kestriel had snapped her out of her tired stupor. That a wall could be that high? Taller than the tallest tree Sloane had ever seen.

The guards at the city gate weren't as gruff as the one in Branwell, but matter-of-factly commanded everyone to stand on the side of the road while they inspected everyone's baggage, boxes, and packs. Sloane was surprised they were allowed to hang onto knives and swords—a crossbow the only weapon confiscated—and the travelers were waved through, no guard bothering to ask about anyone's business in Kestriel.

The city was as Alvie described. Blocks upon blocks of buildings: shoppes, stacks of housing structures, pubs, taverns, even a theater. The wide streets allowed for carriages and carts to pass in either direction with plenty of space for both horses and pedestrians. In the distance, Sloane saw the castle of the sovereign, a massive fortress with—she counted—eight towers. Soldiers in cobalt uniforms seemed to stand on every corner or were patrolling the streets on horseback. People were everywhere. There were smells, too. Nothing like the bog, but the stench of sewer and garbage intermixed with a spice dealer's shoppe or a brewery nearby.

With their rucksacks slung on their backs and walking at a pace that suited them both, Sloane and Alvie made their way through the main road, High Road, Alvie said it was called. Sloane peered in awe at the perpendicular roads. The city went on forever. After walking a few blocks, Sloane glimpsed the road to her right and gasped. It was merely a sliver of the blue water, but Sloane's excitement couldn't be contained. The Mehr Sea.

"Alvie! Let's go to the docks!"

At first, Alvie complained, but after a few minutes, the two found themselves standing on the docks, Sloane gazing at the blue-green water of the Mehr Sea in wonder. She inhaled the salty air deeply as gliding gulls squawked overhead. Sloane and her brothers had always dreamed of coming to the sea. A vision of Ma filled her mind: the children fantasizing of the sea while she sewed, her eyes twinkling in their direction.

It was midday, the stars were veiled, but Sloane peered up to the heavens.

"Here it is, Sherik. The sea." Her lip trembled, but she huffed out an exhale instead, resisting tears. Had Joah seen the sea? What *had* made him join the Ravyns? The Joah who daydreamed of the sea would never have done such a thing. She strained to see the edge of the horizon, hoping to catch a glimpse of Seabeckon, the port city of the Capella Realm on the other side. It was impossible, much too far away, but to survey the faraway line of the water's horizon made Sloane feel both small and awakened. This world was a grand place, indeed. Sailors and workmen scurried along the docks, some moving back and forth from planks onto ships, which were nearly as tall as the buildings they'd passed. She turned to where the rear of the city block faced them. Aye, grand indeed. This was why she was here.

The two found an inn a few blocks away. Alvie liked it because it was close to a bakery, the scent of yeast and roasted sugar wafting out of the open door. Sloane liked it because she'd never been inside an inn and found the whole arrangement fascinating, a large common dining room downstairs, the innkeeper and a few servants dashing to and fro to men and women alike eating their midday meal. Three men sat on stools at the wooden bar, drinking ale and laughing.

Upstairs, a corridor of doors greeted them. Sloane wondered what sort of interesting people were behind each one. Their quarters, shared to save coin so they could eat, were meager. A large bed stood in the middle of the room, two small tables on either side. Alvie joked that he hoped he didn't roll over onto Sloane and knock her off the bed in the middle of the night, but Sloane only smiled. They'd shared sleeping space for long enough. Sharing a bed would be no different. Besides, she couldn't stop staring at it. She'd never slept on an actual bed before. Straw mattresses, makeshift blanket beds, the hard ground, chairs, even the bed of a wagon now, but never a *real* bed. She half-wished it was nightfall already. But then she saw the window.

"Alvie, look! You can see the sea!"

Alvie chuckled, coming to stand next to her. "Stars almighty, Sloane. It's just water. You can't even drink it."

The gentle waves held Sloane's attention before she eyed the mass of people hurrying along the road below. They weren't here for the sea. They needed to find this Order of Siria somehow. Getting here had more or less been the plan, and Sloane blushed to think that she had no idea what to do next.

EXCEPT FOR TRAVELING to Asana to barter on market days, Sloane's entire world had been restricted to Mohn. But since the Befallen, she felt as though she'd traveled across the entire continent of Tasia and back. And she'd learned there wasn't much difference between the way her own villagers had stared at her and the way strangers she'd met on her travels eyed her leg or her distinct gait until now. Mayhap Kestriel was too big a place for strangers to gawk at a crippled girl and a man with a peg leg walking down the street. Certainly, there was the familiar lingering of a few pairs of eyes, but by and large, no one paid them any heed that late afternoon as they made their way from the sovereign's castle to a nearby pub.

Despite his protests, Alvie had made inquiries and found that the Order of Siria was conducting interviews at the castle. By the time they'd arrived, however, the gates were closed. Sloane, frustrated and tired, and Alvie, unemotional and hungry, agreed it was time for a meal.

They entered The King's Pub, though Sloane found little about the establishment to be kingly. It may have been at one point, but the dingy, faded red velvet chairs and matching curtains made the place smell musty as though all good days were of the past. Despite the pub's rundown appearance, the place was crowded and noisy. By chance only, Alvie and Sloane secured a small table in a corner as someone was leaving. Alvie settled in immediately, yelling to the barkeep to bring two ales and a plate of spiced nuts. Sloane frowned, wondering if spiced meant anything like the Solstice Stew.

Their ales in front of them, Alvie raised his glass.

"To the water and sand! To the sky and the land! I'm a fool and a sinner, and I ain't gettin' thinner, but I've got a drink in my hand!" He saluted and drank.

Sloane brightened to hear the traditional toast.

She scanned the pub, watching the various groups of men: merchants, soldiers, tradesmen, with a few women sprinkled in the bunch. Mohn had no pub; there'd been a few tables set up in the back of the grocer's shoppe. Her parents had enjoyed occasional nights there with other villagers, laughing, telling stories, and playing cards. If Sloane focused, this pub in Kestriel didn't seem so far removed from the leisure time relished by those in Mohn. She took a sip and tried to let the wetness soothe her rather than burn its way down. If her parents were still alive, mayhap she'd be with them now at the grocer's instead of this faraway place where everyone seemed big and loud.

Alvie ended up eating the bowl of spiced nuts that a barmaid carelessly placed on their table, but Sloane did find the charred fish and bread she was served to be delicious. Mayhap she could pretend she was at The Jolly Goat. The ale relaxed her, and it seemed like such an oddity to feel both apprehensive about finding the Order of Siria tomorrow and exhilarated at finding herself in a real Kestriel pub. Alvie had begun telling jokes and laughing with some tradesmen sitting near them. Sloane marveled at the ease in which Alvie made friends.

Knowing when someone was watching her had become something of a talent for Sloane. She glanced toward the entrance, where she'd felt eyes solidly rest on her. But, dark outside now, the pub had become even more crowded. In the jumble of faces, Sloane didn't catch anyone's eye. Her gaze paused at a table near the window where there sat two well-built men, one dark-haired, one blonde, with four men standing around them holding their attention. Mayhap she'd imagined it.

But she hadn't yet finished her second glass of ale when she felt someone's attention linger on her. This time, Sloane slowly surveyed the crowd. The two men she'd studied earlier were still at their table, surrounded by others. She caught the expression of the dark-haired man, who seemed to Sloane as if he wished he were being left alone. But nay, he wasn't looking at her. No one was.

Sloane started when a woman and two men—who she guessed were sailors, for they smelled like sea salt—cackled next to Alvie.

You're being absurd, thought the part of Sloane who half-swayed to the lute music.

I am being absurd, agreed the other part of Sloane, who wanted to be convinced she was being paranoid.

Still.

Sloane took one last sip of her ale then pushed the glass away. There was naught to fear, aye, but better to not leave *everything* to chance. The ale had loosened enough of her mind. She laughed along with the others at Alvie's joke, even though she didn't have a clue what he'd said.

CHAPTER
20

Tolvar

W hen you were the Wolf, and not in a completely drunken state, it was nearly impossible to *not* be aware of everything going on in your surroundings, stars help you.

The table for two that Tolvar and Ghlee were seated at did naught to dissuade the small group crowded around them. Now that they were holding interviews of all blasted things, it was challenging to have a quiet drink without being noticed. Being the Wolf seemed to have all the disadvantages this eve. It was noisy beyond belief in the pub tonight. Was it always this loud, or had Tolvar just not drank enough?

Despite being offered many drinks, true to his words, Tolvar refrained from drowning himself in ale. But that didn't give him cause for celebration. Rather, every man who stood around them with a story, joke, or request of Tolvar's tales was only causing immense irritation. It was lucky Ghlee was there to cut men off or entertain them with a story or two of his own. Stars, Ghlee seemed to be having a good time. He'd even managed to say a few words to the barmaid who he'd gawked at the last few times they'd come into the King's Pub.

So, while Ghlee and the swarm of new friends laughed, Tolvar sipped his ale, instinctively scanning the pub as he did so. He counted eleven groups in all who were each engaged in their own merrymaking, three of which were playing and gambling on rounds of Give-and-Go, a fruitless card game Tolvar despised. Four tables were occupied by pairs, two of which appeared as if they were having a dreadful time, six men sat at the bar, two speaking but obviously not familiar with one another. The lute player in the corner played another verse of "Oh, If I Had the Ransom of a King," a tune often played in this pub, and the barkeep and his three barmaids were scattered around the pub refilling cups. Nothing of note.

At times, Tolvar couldn't help but wonder about the attitudes of the people of Kestriel. True, the Befallen had never infiltrated the sovereign's city, but what was to say it wouldn't eventually? It was as if Kestriel simply regarded itself as a haven. No one ever mentioned concern that the Befallen might plague this city one day. The soused patrons here proved it.

Stars, it was boring sitting here without being lost in ale's intoxication. Tolvar glanced at Ghlee to read whether his friend was ready to leave, but Ghlee's eyes were on that red-headed barmaid again. It appeared Ghlee was trying to will her to their table, even though the four men standing around them were blocking Ghlee from her view. He shook his head. Mayhap it was time to order another drink. Tolvar downed the remains of his ale.

He was about to call the barkeep to their table when a small woman at a table across the pub caught his eye. She was part of one of the groups not playing cards. Instead, the group seemed to be enamored with the pointed-chinned man who sat across from her. It was much too loud to hear what the man said, but every time he opened his mouth, the group erupted in laughter. The woman laughed, too, although it didn't appear genuine. She had the biggest eyes he'd ever seen. Brown. So brown, they appeared almost black, like the moonless sky. He studied her, trying to decide why exactly he was doing so. She was pretty enough, he supposed, but certainly no great beauty. It was those eyes, he resolved. They were a combination of innocence and hope and...something else. But young, certainly. Just coming into her womanhood? Nay, she must be older, evidenced by the way she sat with her shoulders straightened. Those eyes betrayed something about her.

Grief. Tolvar saw it now because he imagined that's what his own eyes reflected. This woman had suffered grief. And it was still fresh.

Not wanting to be caught staring at her—it was said that the Wolf had an intensity to his gaze—Tolvar again searched for the barkeep. But someone else snatched his attention. A man at the bar. He was big in size, though Tolvar suspected he couldn't be taller than himself. The man with his sandy, untrimmed beard and broad shoulders tense, held his pint stationary in a bandaged hand. And he was focused on the small woman. But he did not gaze at her. Nay, this man surveyed her like a hunter studied prey.

Tolvar leaned back and folded his arms. What was this man's angle? His plan? The severity of his stare did not leave much open for interpretation. Tolvar noticed that every so often, the woman scanned the room as if searching for someone. When she did, the man at the bar was careful to avert his attention and slink behind the man he sat next to. Tolvar, too, turned so the woman wouldn't see him watching her.

"What are you doing?" Ghlee asked, holding his ale midair.

"Nothing," Tolvar said, picking up his cup again. It was none of his business. His attention turned to the old man in the middle of a lengthy sea story whom Ghlee was humoring. Ghlee's barmaid finally approached with a tray of freshly filled cups, the amber liquid sloshing seductively in the lantern light on the wall. Tolvar picked up his fresh pint and raised his cup absentmindedly as someone toasted the Order of Siria. Behind them, the splitting sound of a cup clanging onto the floor made everyone turn. Tolvar used that as an opportunity to peer back at the woman and then at the man at the bar.

He was gone.

Tolvar did a brief scan to make certain. Aye, gone. He'd probably grown bored and left. The woman with those big brown eyes laughed, and Tolvar's grip that he hadn't realized was so tight loosened. Good riddance to whoever that man was.

A shuffle of newcomers entered the pub, and Tolvar was surprised it could become more crowded. Ghlee still didn't appear to be ready to leave. Tolvar thumbed the hilt of his sword, wondering if he should leave without him.

"Sirs, sirs," a voice came from the entrance. There stood a young scholar dressed in his grey robes and silly hat. He made his way through the mass to their table. "Sir Ghlee," the boy started before whispering in Ghlee's ear. Ghlee raised an eyebrow and scratched his beard.

"You're certain of this?" Ghlee asked the boy.

"Aye, sir." And then, without another word, the scholar walked straight back out of the pub without glancing back.

"What was that?"

Ghlee discreetly lifted his hand and shook his head slightly. Evidently, this was not the time to ask.

Tolvar watched impatiently as Ghlee started up his conversation with the men surrounding the table, fidgeting with his cup.

"Shall we order another," Ghlee said after a while.

"Let's depart, Ghlee. I can't hear myself think."

"I think we should stay," Ghlee returned. His voice was even, but Tolvar caught an undertone. Ghlee was waiting for something. Or someone?

"Fine, but I need the privy." Tolvar stood, turning toward the back of the pub.

The woman and the man she'd sat next to were gone.

The hair on the back of Tolvar's neck raised, seeing their seats, which now held two others. He reminded himself that the man at the bar had long since left. But...

He couldn't explain the instinct. Stars, he couldn't explain his interest. But Tolvar pivoted and made for the entrance of the pub.

"Wolf! Where are you going?" Ghlee shouted from behind him.

"I'll be back," Tolvar said, making his way into the night.

CHAPTER 21

Sloane

Despite Sloane's determination to enjoy herself, she and Alvie still left the pub much later than she liked. It wasn't that the streets were empty. There were plenty of people on the streets who'd spilled out from the many pubs, taverns, and inns. The torches from within and those lining the streets certainly didn't give off a foreboding quality; rather, the road was full of boisterous voices. Sloane didn't know a place could be so alive at night. However, she found herself turning around to peer over her shoulder, feeling the sheath securing the knife in her pocket, as she and Alvie, who careened and swerved in his drunken stumbles, made their way to their inn.

"Oi, we almost there?" Alvie slurred.

"Aye, close," Sloane said, squinting to see the corner where they needed to turn.

She could barely make out the inn's wrought-iron sign hanging in the distance when she felt someone directly behind her.

"Well, well. Look who it is? Two cripples."

Sloane spun and felt her legs go weak beneath her. There stood Rhiner, who'd evidently followed them all the way to Kestriel. His cold glare had a wild quality.

Sloane started to feel for her knife but stopped herself.

"Thought you'd escape me, gimpy girl? Imagine my surprise when I remembered where I'd seen you last," Rhiner said, drawing a large dagger with his bandaged hand and pointing it into Sloane's stomach. Beside her, Alvie was as white as alabaster.

"All right, now. Don't do anythin' foolish. There's people everywhere," Alvie stuttered, his voice strained. If only his words were true, no one was in the immediate vicinity. From a distance, the three of them could very well appear as though they were having naught more than a pleasant conversation.

"True. Let's take a walk."

"Nay," Sloane said.

Rhiner's dagger was so fast, Sloane barely believed her eyes. He slashed across Alvie's arm, slitting the sleeve, soaking it with blood. Alvie gave a cry, but Rhiner brought one hand to Alvie's mouth, the other holding the dagger below his neck.

"Walk. Before I find somewhere else to put this."

Rather than turning the corner onto the street, Rhiner directed them into the alley nearby. Another alley. She was going to be sick. The noise of the street behind them faded away, and the echo of Alvie's peg leg hitting the stone ground became Sloane's focus.

Think, both parts of her commanded. The knife was heavy in her pocket.

The alley was void of anything helpful. No boxes. No debris to use as a weapon. No doors to pound on.

"And don't even think about your little 'fire' ploy again, gimpy girl. One word, and your friend dies."

"What do you want?" Sloane asked. "We have nothing. Here. I have these few coins. They're yours. Just take them and leave."

"Ah, no. I'm going to show you what happens to dirty lil' cripples who think they're better than they are. Yeah, when Hux and Brinley —those chuffin' bastards—banished me from the Ravyns, I knew *you* was to blame."

Sloane's face burned. Did she dare pull out her knife? She glanced at Rhiner's dagger so close to Alvie's back it seemed like a sneeze would thrust the blade into him.

When they were at the alley's dead end, Rhiner told them to turn around.

"Right then. Take off your leg, lil' gimp."

The dread, bubbling inside, boiled over.

"You can't be serious," Alvie said, his hand clutching his other forearm to stanch the bleeding.

"Do it!" Rhiner shouted. The whites of his eyes bulged; the blade of the dagger waved around.

Alvie sat on the ground, lifted his hose, and methodically untied the rope that held the peg leg onto his stump. He caught his breath, and she forced her eyes to the shadowed wall of the alley. Alvie tried not to cry.

The wooden leg was handed to Rhiner, who examined it for a moment. "My own brother was a no-good cripple. My folks spent every last coin they had on him. Every last coin. Healers. Herbs. Then tryin' to get him one of these. And I spent nights starved. Wore out m'only shoes clean through. And then what happens? My folks died. My brother gets an apprenticeship with a tailor. Makes good coin, too. And what did I get? Nothin'. Then finally, I join up with the Ravyns and have everything. Until *you* come along."

Sloane and Alvie eyed each other.

"You needs to pay." The man sheathed his dagger, lifted the wooden leg over his head, and brought it down on Alvie's head. The *thwack* noise made both Alvie and Sloane cry out. Alvie's head swayed as he brought his arms up to shield himself.

Sloane screamed, and without thinking, drew her knife and drove its blade between Rhiner's ribs as he raised his arms again to strike Alvie. Sloane was distantly aware she was still screaming. One echoing, piercing scream.

Rhiner focused on the knife in his side, oozing with blood. Forgetting Alvie, who looked as if he might fall unconscious, the man yanked the knife from his side and flung it down the alley.

Sloane stopped screaming.

"You just sentenced yourself to death," he said, spitting.

Sloane stepped back, finding the wall against her back. "Do it then. I meant it that day on the road when I said you were a coward." She dared herself to not look away. Rhiner brought the wooden leg down, aiming for Sloane. She ducked and rolled out of the way in the opposite direction of Alvie. It was a stupid move. Once she was on the ground, her movement would be limited. Another swipe. Another roll.

"Stop moving!" Rhiner yelled.

Sloane rolled again, but this time, Rhiner was ready for her. Wood smacked into the side of her head. She sprawled onto the stone ground.

Everything became muffled except the ringing in Sloane's ears and a dripping of water coming from a nearby spigot. Through blurry vision, Rhiner stood over her. He said something, but Sloane couldn't make out his words.

"What?"

"I said, say your last prayers."

Something behind the man caught her eye. An enormous shadow. A shadow that swallowed the man, the alley, everything.

"I hope you've said yours," the shadow growled.

A long blade of a sword punctured Rhiner's middle, spraying her with blood. She screamed, covered her face, and tucked her legs into a ball. There was a thump of something—or someone—heavy hitting the ground, and then all she could hear was her own panting.

"You all right?" The same growling voice held less edge. Sloane uncovered her face to find the massive form of a man crouched in front of Alvie.

"Aye," Alvie breathed, turning his head toward where Sloane lay on the ground. "Blimey. Fact o'matter is, your timing couldn't have been better."

A deep chuckle resonated from the man. Still crouching, the man picked up Alvie's peg leg, which Sloane noticed lay next to Rhiner's still form, and handed it to Alvie. Alvie clutched it, and the man moved. Sloane found dark eyes gazing at her.

The fierceness in those dark eyes gave way to a gaze of warmth and...what? Protectiveness? His mouth was drawn in a firm line that gave Sloane the impression he'd like to kill that man thrice over.

"That was quite the pummel you took to the head. Do you hear me clearly?" His voice was wrapped in a gravelly softness. How did he do that?

"Sloane, you all right?" Alvie said beside the man.

Sloane cleared her throat. "Aye." She forced herself to a sitting position. Her head was ringing. She rubbed her temple to find a large bump forming there. She looked past them to Rhiner.

She'd seen and been close to death before. Why did Rhiner's still form feel different? Quick, short breaths escaped her.

"Sloane?" Alvie said, alarmed.

"I'm okay," she managed.

"Here." The man held out a kerchief to her. "You can wipe off the blood."

Sloane took it, his calloused finger grazing hers as she did so.

"Can you both stand?" he asked Alvie before he stood, handing another kerchief to Alvie. "We'll need to wrap that arm of yours."

"Thankee," Alvie said, standing and pressing the cloth to his arm. "I'm good. Sloane?"

She merely nodded, gaining control of her breath, and moving to her hands and knees to pick herself up.

"Let me help you." The man stretched out a hand. Sloane did not take it.

After she stood, her head hurt worse. She found the man closely inspecting her eyes again. A chill ran down her spine.

"Doesn't appear as though you'll have lasting effects," he said, then turned to the alley's entrance. "Where are you staying? I'll escort you to your inn."

"How do you know we don't live here?" Sloane asked. She was met by an expression that said, *please.* "And are we just leaving him?" She did not look at the body she pointed to.

"I'll alert the sovereign's guard. But one less lowlife in the city is not my greatest concern."

"Oh," Sloane said. Was this man part of the sovereign's guard himself? He certainly gave the impression he could be.

Alvie told him where they were lodged, and the three made their way up the road. The man slowed his pace to match theirs but did so without comment or even acknowledging it.

"I s'pose a thanks is in order," Alvie said, checking the kerchief Sloane wrapped around his arm. "Can we buy you a pint when we get to the inn?"

"My thanks, but nay. I must get back to the King's Pub."

"The King's Pub? That's where we were," Alvie said.

"Aye, I know. I saw you leave after I observed that man watching the two of you all evening."

"That's why you look familiar," Sloane said. "You saw him *watching* us?" She felt chilled.

"Aye. What? You owe him coin?"

"Nay. More like he thought he would teach us a lesson, it seems," Sloane said. She told herself they were safe now, but her eyes darted to and fro. The streets were now much more deserted.

"Lesson? For what?"

"For being us, I s'pose." Sloane said, adding an edge to her voice. The part of Sloane, who'd been through more than enough for one night, dared him to comment on the pair of them.

The man made no comment but nodded as if he understood.

"So what? You go 'round saving people for a livin'?" Alvie asked.

"Only in my off-time." There was something about the way he said it that made Sloane wonder if it was true.

"You a knight?" Alvie asked, pointing at his sword.

The man sighed first. "Aye. From the Capella Realm."

"Oi! That so?" Alvie couldn't hide the excitement from his voice. "You with the Order of Siria?"

"Alvie!" Sloane chided. She reeled that this knight had been watching them in the pub.

The man paused in the street. "Certain it wasn't that mouth of yours that drew your attacker's attention?"

Alvie grinned. "You *are* from the Order of Siria! Blimey! I knew it. 'Tis your lucky night. Sloane and me, we's here to find you."

The man snorted. "I doubt that very much."

"And why wouldn't we be?" Sloane asked, her arms crossing her chest. "As a matter of fact, we *are* here to help. I have information about the Edan Lore that will help you."

"That so?"

Oh, she wanted to wipe that smirk off his face. "Aye. You're missing a portion of it."

Had Sloane known her words would make the man's face drop as immediately as it did, she would have slowed them.

"About the Azure Moon?" For the first time, his face lost its arrogance.

"Mayhap," she said, but when he furrowed his brow, she added, "Aye. About the Azure Moon."

The inn's sign was ahead. "Well, then. I think I will take you up on that drink."

CHAPTER
22

Sloane

S loane made her way back to the table from the privy where she'd washed the blood off her face to find Alvie and the knight seated in the quiet common dining room of the inn. Alvie chattered away, pint completely full. The knight quietly sipped his ale, half gone. Sloane suspected the knight had not gotten a word in, though he appeared content to listen.

"Anyway, that's how I ended up havin' a drink with the duke's son's tutor's nephew," Alvie was saying as Sloane sat. "Said I'd make a right fine knight myself."

"Meet Alvie." She chuckled and took a swig of her ale, hoping it'd help her headache.

She set her cup on the table, raising her eyebrows at the knight. He was studying them. Like he could find out anything he wanted if he observed them long enough. He was thirsty for the information she had. But what could this knight give her in return? Sloane's plans over the last moon had consisted of short goals. After she gave over this information, then what? What was the apprentice-daughter of a leatherworker supposed to do then? Sloane wanted to be of real help to the Order of Siria. If she simply recited the entire Edan Lore to his man, she suspected he'd part ways with them before finishing that cup he'd almost *emptied.*

"I suppose we should ask your name, sir knight."

"Tolvar." Then pointed and nodded at them. "Alvie. Sloane."

"Aye, from Mohn."

He paused before saying, "I heard your village succumbed to the Befallen."

"It did. I wasn't there that night."

Tolvar cocked an eyebrow. "Lucky."

"Lucky, nothing. My family perished. Everyone I knew. That man in the alley was one of the Ravyns. They robbed me of everything. I have nothing now. That's why I want to help. Someone needs to do something."

"I am sorry for your loss," Tolvar said, snapping his fingers to the innkeeper to bring a new cup. "I'm here in Kestriel for that very reason."

"What you holdin' interviews for?" Alvie asked, glancing at his newly bandaged arm.

Tolvar's face tightened. "The sovereign wants the Unsung found sooner than later."

Sloane snorted. "You think interviews are the way to find the Unsung?"

Tolvar's tilted his head, those dark eyes dancing in amusement. "Do you?"

"Nay," Sloane said. "The Unsung won't be a soul who answers queries correctly. The Unsung will be—"

"Aye?" He leaned across the table toward her, those fierce eyes not missing anything.

"Mayhap there is no Unsung. Someone just needs to act. Not interview."

Tolvar flexed his jaw. Did he have the same notion? As much as this man appeared to be reading every gesture and word from them like he was mastering their secrets, Sloane was having difficulty reading him in return. She needed to think quickly. Somehow, she knew this was her only chance to make the next step in her path.

An idea occurred to her.

"Mayhap." Tolvar downed half his new cup and glanced toward the door. "But what I need is for you to tell me what you know of the Azure Moon." Stars in heaven, this man could put away his liquor.

"What questions are you asking those you interview? If I can answer them, what happens next?" Sloane studied her cup.

"Sloane, what you doing? Tell him the Edan Lore. That's why we're here," Alvie said, choking on his ale.

Tolvar set his cup down and crossed his arms. "I thought you wanted to help?"

"I do." Sloane crossed her arms, too. "What happens?"

Tolvar chuckled as if he were appeasing a child. "Those who pass *all* tests are invited to Dara Keep, the newly reinstated Deogol fortress of the Order of the Siria, for trial to be enlisted. The commander there is hopeful that one of them may be trained to be the Unsung."

"You serious? Enlisted into the Order of Siria?" Alvie grabbed her arm excitedly. "Sloane, don't tell him anything. She'll answer your questions."

"Nay." Sloane said at the same time Tolvar said, "You're not going to Dara Keep."

"Why not?" Alvie's voice rang with indignation. "This Azure Moon sounds pretty important to you."

The knight put his head in his hands. "I'm losing patience. Are you going to help or not?"

"Are you going to reward me or not?" She was finished being cast aside.

"Saving your life doesn't count?" Tolvar sat up, his voice growing loud.

"I'm grateful for that," Sloane said, her eyes meeting his. "Truly. But I can be of help to the Order. I know the Edan Lore. Does anyone else you've encountered?" What else could she say? "Also, I'm a leatherworker. I'll earn my keep. Please, Sir Tolvar. The Befallen has taken everything from me. Let me help."

"And me," Alvie added.

"You? And what can you possibly do?"

"Most anythin'. Scrub. Polish. Lift things. Muck out stalls. Juggle.

And I tell the greatest tales you ever heard. Don't the Order of Siria need a bit of entertainment?" Alvie said.

"Stars be damned," Tolvar said. "The Order of Siria isn't searching for...ones such as yourselves."

Sloane narrowed her eyes. "Such as ourselves? Ones who've traveled all this way to help you? Ones who've exactly what you're searching for? Ones who, despite losing everything, are still carrying hope?"

"Cease." Tolvar held up his hand. "The Edan Lore is important, but who's going to fulfill it? It needs to be someone who is up for it. Just now in the alley—"

"I got a good slice of him before you showed up!" Sloane stood, cursing herself when she corrected her balance momentarily. "Good luck with your Edan Lore. Since I know it and you don't, I'll tell you this much. You're on borrowed time."

Sloane rammed her stool into the table and made her way to the stairs of the inn, too aware those dark eyes followed her.

"Wait!" Tolvar called. Sloane didn't turn around but did stop. She waited for him to go on, but the only sound was footsteps from behind. Tolvar stood in front of her. "I do not mean to insult you. I'm certain you've had plenty of that in your short years but fighting the Befallen is a matter left to those who *can* fight."

Sloane's eyes remained on the floor.

"'Tis late. You've been through an ordeal. In the morning, I shall return, and we'll discuss this matter further."

She remained silent.

"What say you?" The rough silk returned to his voice.

"Very well. But I mean to help."

"I'm certain you do. And I hope you will."

CHAPTER
23

Tolvar

He wanted to spit daggers. He wanted to bust stone walls. He wanted to slash his sword clean through a wooden pole.

On the walk back to the King's Pub, Tolvar wanted to pick a fight with every man he stormed past. Of all the empty-headed, stubborn, and feckless women he'd ever encountered. His hands shook. He'd saved her life! She'd be dead right now if he hadn't found them in time. And what thanks did she offer? Of all the idiotic women in all of Tasia, she had to be the one who knew the Edan Lore and had the crackbrained idea she should withhold that. And for what? What did this Sloane think Tolvar was going to do? Knight her?

Did she even know the Edan Lore? Tolvar wanted to think not, but for some foolish reason, he believed her. It was those eyes. Those onyx eyes where his own image was reflected. Where he could get lost. Those enormous eyes that looked at him with shock and naivety when he'd said she couldn't join the Order of Siria.

And stars bless him, she thought it was because of the way she walked. He'd read it on her. That *Sloane* thought he judged her disability. How about, "you're too small, too young, too innocent to join the ruthless Order?"

"Blast!" Tolvar shouted and four men in the street jumped away from him.

It should've been Ghlee. He should've been there. He'd have that woman eating out of his hand.

"Where in stars did you go?" Ghlee asked when Tolvar flumped back into his seat at the King's Pub. The place was sparsely occupied now, and Tolvar found it disconcerting after being surrounded by people all night.

"Don't ask. Not until I have a drink in my hand."

Ghlee gave him a once over. "That bad?"

"Mayhap worse."

Ghlee tsked. "I distinctively remember someone saying something about not drinking into a stupor."

"Save your talk of virtue until you hear my tale."

Ghlee opened and closed his mouth, waved to his barmaid, and ordered two fresh pints.

Tolvar exhaled and told Ghlee everything. When he finished, Ghlee's eyes gleamed in a manner that Tolvar did not care for in the least.

"Wolf, this is glad news. In the morning, we'll simply talk this feisty thing into telling us. Tremendous." He ignored the pointed look Tolvar gave him. "Especially considering the remainder of my night."

"What happened? Why did that scholar hop in and out of here like a hare?"

Ghlee scanned the pub to see who might be listening. "Someone was supposed to give us information tonight. About the Edan Lore."

"The Azure Moon?"

"Uncertain. I sat here all night, and no one ever came. Frightened off or a jest of some sort, mayhap?"

"It has to be the Chief Scholar," Tolvar said after a moment.

The way Ghlee tightened his jaw gave Tolvar the impression he'd had the same idea. And if it was the Chief Scholar, why had she withheld information only to try and tell them later in private but then be spooked off? Tolvar couldn't quite assess what Ghlee was concluding, but there was one thing Tolvar knew. He didn't like it.

☾

Tolvar and Ghlee had sat with Sloane and Alvie in their inn for an hour's time, Sloane picking at more than eating the porridge in front of her, Alvie helping himself to three bowls after Ghlee said he'd pay for their breakfast, and Ghlee was no closer to coaxing from Sloane her knowledge of the Edan Lore.

Apparently, her tactic was to offer silence on top of more silence. Meanwhile, this Alvie, his silver tooth catching the morning sunlight every so often, was remarkably skilled at chattering one's ear off. He'd told them about the year he'd spent traveling with troubadours as a juggler and had entertained the sovereign's own steward. The time he'd apprenticed for a nature scholar studying field eels. A tale about an encounter with a real hoshefer, rare creatures that supposedly had the softest fur on the continent. Now he was working his way through a story about their caravan being chased by Ravyns days ago.

Worst of all, Ghlee appeared wholly captivated.

"If any of this is true, that is astounding," Ghlee said. "Now, if you could get back to the—"

"Astounding nothin'! Wait 'til I tell you about Sloane surviving the Befallen three times."

"Three times!" Ghlee stammered.

"Alvie!" Sloane chastised, then faced Ghlee. "I didn't, Sir Ghlee. Alvie has it wrong. I didn't survive. I wasn't there."

"Don't matter." Alvie scooped up more porridge before talking with his mouth full. "You were supposed to be." Then started right into his next story, an outrageous tale that turned Sloane into a being close to a seer. When he finished, with more food leaking from his mouth, he said, "Lucky that, wouldn't you say?"

"I would say," Ghlee agreed. "And because of that, you of all people, Sloane, must know how important it is you share your knowledge of the Edan Lore with the Order of Siria so we can strategize on how to defeat the Befallen. All this talk of the Azure Moon makes matters more pressing. Especially as it *should* rise within this year."

"Indeed. What's more, the Edan Lore states the Unsung must be in a certain place when it does rise. I am happy to share it with you. Once we're at Dara Keep and you vow that you'll allow Alvie and me to stay."

Siria's skirt. Tolvar eyed a keg behind the bar.

"I'd like to make that promise, but we cannot take you to Dara Keep. Even if we did—" Ghlee said.

"This is a waste of time, Ghlee." Tolvar had had enough. He tossed three coins onto the table. "Let's go."

He didn't wait to see if Ghlee was following him. He wanted out of this inn and away from this stubborn woman. The dock wasn't far, and he soon found himself staring out into the turquoise waters of the sea toward Seabeckon. Home. He wanted to go home. It stung to think he wasn't welcome there. The Wolf. The war hero. Oh, aye. The failure.

Had that woman really been that close to the Befallen and skirted her fate three separate times? How was a woman that size not afraid of her own shadow after all she'd been through? Why did she want to have anything to do with the Edan Lore?

Realization bristled within him. He knew. It was the same reason why Tolvar stood here on a dock in Deogol. He wanted to earn back his honor. His life. This woman, this Sloane, wanted to earn back her life and ensure no others had theirs taken away.

"Damn."

He could not take these two to the Order of Siria. He'd been banished with strict instructions to not dare return until he'd found recruits of quality. Pharrell would kill him. Then banish him again.

There were too many pieces to this puzzle, and Tolvar recognized he was not putting everything together. And now added to everything else, the Unsung supposedly needed to be in a specific place, too?

He felt the presence of someone next to him and was surprised to see it was not Ghlee, but Sloane. Stars, she was small. Shorter than the princess. The top of her head barely reached his collarbone. She, too, peered at the sea.

"I'm not asking to be a hero, Sir Tolvar. I'm not the Unsung. I should be dead. I just know I need to be a part of this. Certainly, if you're a knight, you can understand that."

She had no idea who Tolvar was. Had no idea she stood beside the famed Wolf. It was both odd and refreshing.

"I think I can," Tolvar said.

"Then you'll let Alvie and me join the cause?"

"Him, too?"

"You never know when a tale-teller may come in handy."

"I must be daft. We better begin making arrangements," Tolvar said, his focus never drifting from the direction of the Capella Realm.

CHAPTER 24

Tolvar

Dara Keep, the headquarters of Deogol's Order of Siria, was no Thorin Court. Not even close.

Thorin Court, Tolvar's home, or what *was* his home until he lost it in Crevan's deceit, was a sprawling stronghold, consisting of several beautiful, white-washed stone buildings, including the inner keep itself.

Dara Keep was smaller in size, though its walls were thicker and taller. The larger training yard was a stark, gravelly quad, so unlike the fine grassy training yard his father had proudly kept at Thorin Court. The Great Hall of Dara Keep wasn't near so bright; Tolvar remembered the large windows with diamond panes of glass in the hall of Thorin Court.

Frankly, Tolvar cared little for the Order's headquarters. But Dara Keep was a far cry from his quarters at the inn or the oppressive air of the sovereign's castle.

It'd taken a half-day's ride to reach Dara Keep after finally receiving a reply they could return with their nine recruits—Tolvar still incredulous he'd allowed Sloane and Alvie to come. Pharrell made them wait a full week for his reply. A waste of time. He was simply reminding them who was in charge, making them sweat about whether he would allow Tolvar to reenter. Ghlee wrote of their newfound knowledge of the Edan Lore, which they didn't actually have yet, but they'd used as a means to return to Dara Keep. Their time of interviews, chasing messengers, and random brawls in Kestriel was over.

"Of course," Ghlee had laughed, "This could all backfire on us."

Aye, too much trust was being put on Sloane. Too much for Tolvar's tastes. If there *was* a missing piece, she'd better be out with it.

Pharrell's reply had been brisk. *Don't disappoint me again.*

Tolvar eyed Sloane, sitting next to Alvie in the wagon he drove, carrying the supplies Pharrell requested they bring.

She better not be lying.

Pharrell might see him drawn and quartered. Though the seven other recruits weren't of note, Tolvar was quite certain he and Ghlee were about to be the butt of many a joke. Even with training, Sloane and Alvie would be at a disadvantage. He didn't like it. He didn't like the way the other recruits gave sideways sneers, knowing he could best all seven of them at once with his eyes closed. Ghlee had mentioned it, too.

"We're going to have a fight on our hands, Wolf. And even if *any* of them make it into the Order of Siria, none of them is the Unsung."

The muscle in Tolvar's jaw twitched. He was always ready for a fight. He better be damned sure he knew what his move was if Sloane deceived them just to sneak a gander at the Order of Siria's new Deogolian headquarters.

He'd feel much better if Ghlee's messenger had come through. They still couldn't be certain it was the Chief Scholar who'd sent the two messengers. Both had turned into nothing. The second one had found Ghlee as he'd been leaving his inn three days ago. Ghlee maneuvered up and down Kestriel's city blocks, ducking into shoppes, even looking in on his gran, trying to lose anyone who might be following him before he made it to the spot on the docks where he'd been instructed to wait. But no one had ever shown, and there'd been no third messenger.

It had to be the Brones who were scaring off the messengers. Whoever it was, no chances were being taken. They'd considered lingering in Kestriel one more night to see if another messenger would approach them, but Pharrell's command for return outweighed the risk of finally connecting with whoever this skittish person was.

Tolvar was no novice to spending the day on his horse, but his backside still ached. Hopefully, Pharrell would allow him to join the Order's nightly feast. The last night Tolvar was here, he'd not been welcome.

"Who goes there?" a voice called from atop the battlements of Dara Keep.

He grimaced up at who he thought was Nevin. A thick man with a red beard. Stars almighty, was Tolvar ready to return?

Tolvar still clung to the fact he'd been correct in questioning what the Order was doing. Stars, they were no closer to defeating the Befallen than when he'd arrived.

He still wasn't sorry for punching Pharrell. Not at all regretful for stabbing Kek in the shoulder with his dinner knife. They'd clearly forgotten it was *they* who'd brought *him* to the Order of Siria. Tolvar was the Wolf, and he'd made no concessions about that. If that included a high temper or a short tolerance of fools, that was not something for which he was going to grovel for forgiveness from Pharrell.

However, Tolvar supposed he had been in the wrong to snap Kek's prized bow. That seemed a bit much now, thinking back on it.

Stars help him.

"Nevin, you blind fool, open the gate," Ghlee shouted up to the battlements astride his own mount. He turned to Tolvar. "Try not to get kicked out our first night back." Ghlee's eyes twinkled.

Tolvar growled. "Mayhap not the first night anyway."

Ghlee regarded Sloane and Alvie on the wagon. "Here goes everything."

TOLVAR WAS NOT INVITED to the Great Hall. In fact, upon entrance into the outer keep of the fortress, he'd barely seen anyone. Kek met them, his cold green eyes the epitome of unforgiveness.

"You're to house in the sixth barrack," Kek had said. The sixth. The last barrack. "There's a cookfire going. Cook will send out food so you can prepare supper for yourselves. Keep the recruits with you. Any stranger nosing around will be run through." He said this last part for the benefit of the nine frightened faces staring at him.

So Tolvar spent the night on a small cot in the corner, giving command that the recruits were to sleep on the other side of the small barrack.

Housed like a new squire, Tolvar thought, staring up at the thatched ceiling. Pharrell was certainly making his point.

In the morning he found the recruits already at the cookfire again, waiting for a lanky, pale trainee to finish their meal. Tolvar found the privy and when he came out, Sloane stood there, her large brown eyes searching his own.

"Why did you sleep in the barracks with us last night? Sir Ghlee was housed in the keep."

Insufferable woman.

He ignored her and walked toward the training yard. The *clang* of swords could be heard, and Tolvar was anxious to take his bad night of sleep out on someone.

"Sir Tolvar, when shall we meet with your commander to discuss the Edan Lore? Time is of the essence."

He spun around. "Now 'tis of the essence? Where was this while Ghlee and I have been trying to get it out of you?"

She held his gaze, quiet.

"I would assume Pharrell will inspect you and the others this morning before promptly throwing you all out." Tolvar continued toward the yard. He needed a good practice fray. That would settle what heat was roasting him within. The sixth barrack.

"Is he more like you or Sir Ghlee?" Sloane attempted to keep up.

"How do you mean?" He stopped abruptly.

"Is he affable like Ghlee or sour-faced like you?"

Tolvar glared at her with the intensity of the Wolf. She staggered back, her cheeks turning pink. Good. At least, that was how he *wanted* to feel. But making this insolent, small woman cower gave him no pleasure.

"You've quite the tongue."

"Alvie told me who you are. The Wolf, I mean. I can see how you've secured that reputation with that gaze, but I'm not your enemy, Sir Tolvar. I am here to help you. If I know what sort of man your commander is, then that might help me win him over." She ignored his pointed look. "I do not fool myself to think that once you have the piece of the Edan Lore, you won't throw me out on my ear. But I mean to stay. What sort of man is your commander?"

"Pharrell is not my commander."

"He's not? But I thought—"

"I am here as a courtesy to the Order. I am not part of it. Those who join must make a sacred vow. Ghlee recently took his, making him the first Deogol-born Order member in an age." Tolvar glanced at his sword. His father's sword. "But I am not the vowing sort."

Her brown eyes stared. Pharrell and Kek were going to toss her out the moment they had what they wanted from her. "Pharrell is... difficult." Tolvar sought the words. "He likes to be right. He suffers no fools—"

"Is that why you slept in the barracks with us? Did you act the fool?"

Stars, this woman had no idea how close he was to drawing his sword on her. "Pharrell and I did not see eye to eye on a matter, so he's reminding me he's right and commander here."

"But I thought—"

"You would do well to remember there is much pride in the Order. Act as though you already belong here."

Sloane nodded like she'd learned an important lesson. Tolvar hated how it softened his anger.

"Look Pharrell in the eye but do it in a way that lets him know he's in command."

"Aye. I will." Sloane smiled, and his fist unclenched. Bah. This was all ridiculous. He frowned and walked away from her.

"My thanks, Sir Tolvar," she called behind.

Tolvar unsheathed his sword. He was in desperate need of a fight.

CHAPTER
25

Sloane

S loane was glad the weather had turned to the pleasant coolness of autumn. Not yet chilled, no longer hot. It allowed her to not shake or sweat more so than she was. Dressed in a simple tunic and hose she'd been given, both of which drowned her, she stood at the end of a straight line with Alvie and seven others. They'd been pleasant enough to the two of them, though she still caught stares and had walked up to cut-off conversations. It didn't matter, though. She knew what she was doing here.

The Azure Moon comes.

And with it, the goddess of the Azure Moon would give the Unsung the secret to defeating the Befallen, a weapon only *she* could give. The Azure Moon's sole night was impossible to pinpoint, but Sloane hoped that to give them more time it would be after the Hoarfrost Moon, which was the moon that followed the Falling Leaves Moon, the next full moon.

There was someone who *did* know exactly when the Azure Moon would rise. However, that information Sloane was holding onto until after she'd met the reaction of the Order regarding her knowledge of the Edan Lore. Tolvar and Ghlee had promised her nothing, but she didn't doubt this Pharrell would force her out when he had what he wanted.

Someone needs to do something. Sloane straightened her back.

Ghlee stood in the small group of uniformed knights, fewer than she expected, who were standing in what must have been a military formation. She'd never seen backs so straight, faces so serious. Tolvar was not there, and she wondered if it was because he didn't want to witness Pharrell's inspection of them or because he'd not been allowed.

The doors to the keep opened, and out strode two men. They wore the same uniform that Ghlee and the other knights did, black trimmed with thread-of-gold. On the chest of the uniform was an emblem made up of five stars. Sloane knew stories of the Capella Realm; they worshipped the stars differently than Deogol.

When the two men stood in front of the line, Sloane guessed instantly who Pharrell was. The bold sneer, tight mouth, and vein popping out of his thick neck gave him away. He had pale blue eyes, a broad nose, and a neatly trimmed greying beard. Aye, this man was in charge. Sloane now understood Tolvar's words.

Next to him was the man who'd 'welcomed' them last night, Kek. His tanned skinned and sun-stroked beard gave him the air of someone with more time to train than Pharrell, and those harsh green eyes dared anyone to question him.

"Ghlee," Pharrell said, and Ghlee jogged toward them that instant, the gravel crunching under his feet.

"Aye, sir."

"You cannot be serious," Pharrell said. His shoulders were broad, accentuated by the stiff coat of his black-and-gold uniform. When he stood in front of Sloane, she forced her eyes to not study the ground.

"When have I ever not been serious, Pharrell?" Ghlee moved to stand next to Sloane and smirked at his captain.

The very presence of Pharrell threatened her loss of balance, but Sloane knew this would be her only moment.

Pharrell snorted, gesturing toward Sloane. "I instructed you to find me soldiers, not—"

"Not what?" Sloane said in a voice deeper than normal, which caused Ghlee to eye her.

"Not children." Pharrell bent so they were eye-level. "*Small* children, at that."

Sloane wondered if the thumping of her heart was audible to Pharrell.

"We need recruits. We need an Unsung. This is who I've found." Ghlee folded his arms over his chest.

"You idiot. No doubt you found her in a village orphanage. I've no time for your jests." Pharrell ran his fingers through his neat hair, ruffling it, and glanced toward the stone castle behind him. "Things have...changed."

Ghlee searched the face of the older man.

Sloane, too, shot a glance to the castle—was someone up there watching them? —before shifting solely onto her right foot, hoping she appeared at ease. In the background, the men who stood in their formation stared openly at them. When Sloane looked again at Pharrell, she found that he, too, was staring at her, jaw muscles clenched.

"Have you *any* training, girl?" Pharrell asked.

"Aye," Sloane said, straightening her shoulders. He'd not asked what *sort* of training she'd had.

He and Ghlee lifted their eyebrows in response.

"I'm a leatherworker. You must have a need for someone with that skill?"

Pharrell rolled his eyes at Ghlee. "This is our last chance. This was *your* and Tolvar's last chance. Can you not understand what is at stake for the Order being back in Deogol?" he said. While his voice was commanding, Sloane thought she caught a slight weakness in the tone.

Ghlee unfolded his arms, adjusted his footing, and kicked at the gravel. "I told you in my letter, this is the girl who knows—"

"Get rid of her." Pharrell nodded to Kek.

Sloane drew her brows together and shrugged off Kek's hand.

"Sir. Pharrell," Sloane said, forgetting to deepen her voice, "'Tis true, I do not have combat training, but I'm here. I am strong. And I see a training yard only half-filled."

Pharrell's jaw tightened. Her left leg began to buckle under her.

"I am ready to join you. Don't turn me away. I have naught to lose, and you have everything to gain."

His glare was almost as terrifying as Tolvar's.

"And what would one half the size of the rest of my soldiers have to offer me?"

"Precisely what Sir Ghlee was telling you. I know the Edan Lore. The *full* Edan Lore."

She caught a slight twitch of his mouth, and his eyes glanced up at the tower of the castle again. Who or what was he looking at?

"Can you use a bow?"

"A bow?" Sloane repeated. She began to sweat more.

"Aye." Kek's face twisted into an unfriendly smile. "'Tis used to shoot arrows."

"I'm certain I can." She disregarded Ghlee's wince. What was she doing? She'd never so much as touched a bow before.

"Very well. Run to that corner and fetch yourself one to try out."

"Pharrell—" Ghlee started, but Pharrell held up a hand to silence him.

Sloane frowned at the rack of bows at the farthest end of the yard. Jog?

"Run to those bows over there?" Sloane pointed.

"Those very ones," Pharrell said, clasping his hands behind his back while Kek frowned.

He knows, thought the shaking part of Sloane.

This is your only chance, retorted the other part, which wiped sweat from her brow.

"Aye, sir," Sloane said. Although she'd managed to cinch her leather belt around the tunic and hose to hold them up, she gave a tug on the garments, ensuring they were securely in place. She began her jog, ignoring how clumsy she must appear. She dared not look anywhere but at the rack of bows she trotted toward.

When she finally reached the rack of bows, the crunch of gravel followed behind her until Pharrell stood beside her.

He nodded at her leg. "Permanent?"

"So far."

"You said you were strong?"

"I am strong. There's more to strength than legs." Sloane half-yelled.

She kept her eyes fixed on his. It would not be she who turned away this time.

There was a pause before Pharrell spoke again. His gaze at the castle this time was not a glance but one of deliberation.

"I will see what you *really* know and make my decision then. For now, grab a bow, and let's see what you *can* do. All of you!" he yelled to the rest of the recruits.

Sloane kept her composure serious. The sight of Tolvar leaning against the wall in the far corner of the training yard caught her eye.

"Girl," Pharrell said. Sloane was the only one who didn't have a bow in her hands.

"Sloane, sir."

Pharrell nodded, stealing a glimpse at Tolvar in the background. "You better not be having a sport here. Tonight, we shall meet, and you will tell us what you know of the Edan Lore. *If* we like what you say..." He clearly didn't know what to do with her. "Well, we shall see."

Sloane dared nod toward Tolvar. "Only if Sir Tolvar may accompany me."

Pharrell's forehead furrowed. "Curb your tongue, saucy girl. I've killed men for speaking less out of turn."

Ghlee walked up to join them, worry knitted across his brow.

She blinked. The bow in her hand shook. "Sir Tolvar is fighting against the Befallen, too. He is the one who found me. He should be there. Punish him no longer. Please."

"I should throw you out now with the rubbish. Is she always like this?" Pharrell asked.

Ghlee quirked a smile. "Let us hope so. The Order could use entertainment. Wait 'til you meet Alvie."

CHAPTER
26

Sloane

S loane changed out of her tunic and hose into her worn brown
dress. She had no looking glass but still unplaited her hair and
gave it a good brushing, letting it fall to her waistline. Nothing she did
to her appearance would lessen her nervousness about meeting with
Pharrell and the others. She started to re-plait her hair but dropped
her hands to her side.

What am I doing here?

After you tell them, they're going to toss you out of here, sneered
the part of Sloane seeping with cynicism.

She rubbed her face. *Aye, probably.*

She still had the *other* piece of information, though. Mayhap that
would buy her some time. But would that be enough? She needed to
find a way to make herself useful.

When she entered the stables, the smell of straw and manure
greeted her. To her surprise, the stalls were half-empty. Just like the
number of knights this morning. Wasn't the Order of Siria supposed
to be this imposing army? Alvie had filled her head with stories about
the prestigious Order from the far-off Capella Realm who seemed
larger than life itself. But this rundown fortress with its dozen or so
knights, well-uniformed though they were, did not seem the stuff of
fairy stories.

"Hello?" Sloane said, hearing nothing but the occasional snort of
a horse. There had to be some stableboy here, at least. "Hello?"

Nothing.

Well, for what she'd come to the stable for, she didn't need anyone. She found the tack room filled with saddles, bridles, reins, and other gear. Happy that the saddles were held on racks closer to the ground, she managed to pull one down. The heavy thing unbalanced her for a moment, but after setting it on the ground, Sloane assessed the piece while taking oil and a cloth from a nearby shelf. She rubbed it along the leather, noting that it was in good condition. So was the second saddle. The third, however, had a broken stirrup. She'd need a new strip of leather. And some tools.

Blast those Ravyns!

She did have Father's stitching needle with her and, luckily, found most of the other tools she needed. She could make do without the awl. In a wooden crate were worn harnesses. She hoped no one would notice that she cut one. She cut the edges of the stirrup with the knife she'd found, covering the torn portion with the harness patch she'd made. Chewing the bottom of her lip, she inspected where she needed to stab the hole. An awl would make it much easier. The knife's tip would have to do. She created a hole, and, using a thin string of leather Sloane made, she sewed the patch to the stirrup. When she finished, the warmth of satisfaction filled her. Father would be proud.

"Where did you learn that?"

Sloane gasped and spun around. "You gave me a shock, Sir Tolvar!"

The corner of his mouth quirked as he entered the room and picked up the saddle, setting it back on its rack. Though Sloane was glad for the assistance, after using that bow this morning, her arms were weak, she still shot Tolvar a look.

"I could have done that," Sloane said.

"You're most welcome," Tolvar said, taking the repaired stirrup in his hands to examine. "Where did you learn how to do that?"

"I told you I was a leatherworker. Were you not listening?"

"I didn't think you were serious," Tolvar said, facing her.

"You do not appear to take much I say seriously."

"Tell me you aren't going to sentence us all to death in that meeting, which you are late for, I might add."

"Late?" Sloane stood, gathering the tools to put away. "Stars, we must go. Do I look all right?" She smoothed her skirts, not focusing on how ratty they were.

Tolvar coughed. "Aye, you do. I—didn't know you had so much hair."

Sloane felt heat under her cheeks. "I—I could put it back in a plait."

"Nay. I like it." She met his eyes. "But, Sloane, just tell me."

"I shan't disappoint you. The Azure Moon comes." Something crossed over Tolvar's face. Familiarity? Understanding? Dread? "Are you well?"

"Aye, just thinking about how all this will tie together." *What did that mean?* He grimaced toward the door, shaking his head. "By the way, Sir Ghlee will not be there. But do not mention it. 'Tis my hope his absence will not be noted."

"Where did he go?" Sloane asked, puzzled further by these words.

"Hopefully to gain something useful this time."

Sloane still didn't understand but was quickly learning Tolvar was not a man to press for information.

When they approached the large double doors of the Order's council room, they were stopped by two knights standing guard.

"Where you think you're going?" The taller one with a slender nose asked Tolvar.

"In there." Tolvar barely acknowledged the knight.

"We have orders that you two are to wait here."

"We're late. We're supposed to be in there," Sloane explained.

"And who are you to even be speaking?" the other guard, a freckled man with hazel eyes, asked.

"You would do well to watch your tongue." Tolvar stepped so close to the knight their noses practically touched. "Now, step aside before I throw you aside." His tone was quiet, but it was as if Tolvar's presence filled the whole corridor.

"One day, you're not going to be able to bully your way around here anymore," the knight said in a wavering voice.

"I don't plan on being here that long," Tolvar said, shoving the knight away with his shoulder and opening the doors.

Inside, as the light from the corridor flooded the room, Sloane almost gasped. The walls of the council room were covered from floor to ceiling in black silk. Embroidered gold swirls, circles, and diamonds were sewn in a scattered pattern. In the middle of the room, which was smaller than Sloane had imagined, stood a long table with two dozen chairs around it. Candles covered the table and surrounded the room. The door shut, and the room plunged into near darkness. The candlelight bounced off the intricate gold embroidery work, making it appear as if it glowed. Like the stars. She searched for a symbol of the moon, finding none. This room symbolized the sky of the Nay Moon. Moonless nights belonging only to the stars. So, it was true. The Order of Siria did not worship the goddesses of the moon. Could Sloane convince them how important the Azure Moon was?

At the table sat six men, all silently gaping at Tolvar and her.

"This is a closed meeting, Sir Tolvar," Pharrell said, his face difficult to make out in the darkness.

"You cannot take back your invitation now, Pharrell. I'm here."

"Where's Sir Ghlee?" Kek asked.

Next to Sloane, Tolvar tensed momentarily. "He had business to attend to. He'll be here shortly."

"Wait outside until he arrives." Pharrell stood.

"Don't you want to hear the Edan Lore?" Sloane spoke up. "Time is growing near. The time of the Azure Moon."

"I've sent a message by raven to the scholars of Kestriel," Pharrell said, striding to them. "I expect a return message tonight. We shall see about this Azure Moon that seems to make people jump as if they were a hen sensing a fox."

Again, Tolvar tensed. "What do you mean by that?" he asked. "Who else has come to you about the Azure Moon?"

Pharrell paused before speaking. "Tolvar, you of all people should know by now that I need not explain myself to anyone."

Sloane scanned the others at the table, her eyes growing accustomed to the darkness. Mouths set in hard lines, eyes never leaving Pharrell. In the far corner, someone sat there whom she hadn't noticed before. Whoever it was, his face was shadowed. He didn't appear to have a uniform on, but rather was cloaked in a long robe, or mayhap that was merely the effects of the shadow.

"Now, remove yourself from here until you're given command to enter, or I'll have you removed."

Tolvar stepped closer to Pharrell. In the candlelight, his massive form might have been Pharrell's own shadow, or mayhap Pharrell was his. The flickering light was playing tricks on Sloane's mind.

No one said anything, and Sloane could feel the eyes of the shadowed figure on her.

"We've no time to waste," Sloane said. "The Azure Moon—"

"Enough," Pharrell said. Before his guards could lay a hand on Sloane, Tolvar was between them.

"We'll be in the library," Tolvar said, pushing Sloane out the door.

Sloane hurried to keep up with Tolvar, whose pace doubled from what it usually was when he walked with her. The library was larger than the council room, furnished with several chairs, most of which were covered with worn, faded fabric, a few desks that needed dusting, and mayhap twenty books on a lonely shelf. Not quite what Sloane had imagined a library would look like.

Inside, Tolvar paced the room.

"What happened? Why wouldn't they meet with us?" Sloane asked, receiving no answer. She sat in one of the chairs. "Who was that man in the corner?"

"What man?"

"Didn't you see him? He sat shadowed in the far corner."

Tolvar's nostrils flared as he paused. "Your eyes must have deceived you. There was no one there. I would have seen him."

Sloane wanted to laugh. "You're saying there was no one there simply because I happened to see him, and you did not?"

His eyebrows rose, letting her know what he thought of that idea, and he resumed pacing, muttering to himself.

"What did you say?"

"Nothing for your ears," he snapped, making Sloane drop her shoulders. Some of the lines disappeared from his brow. "I said, something is going on around here. Pharrell may hold a grudge, but he's a man of his word. If he said we were to meet tonight, then he would keep that appointment. If he thought there was something that would help the Order in this quest against the Befallen, even through motives of his own glory, he would hear it. And what did he mean about sending a message to the scholars about the Azure Moon if he didn't even want to hear *your* words?" He placed his hands behind his back. "Ghlee told me this morning that Pharrell said something has changed. I don't like any of this."

"What if?"

"What if what?" Tolvar halted.

"Would Pharrell see us if there was more to tell than just the Edan Lore?"

"More to tell? You haven't even told us that!" Tolvar muttered again and the only words Sloane caught were "doubt" and "daft."

"I'm not daft. I need assurance you won't toss me out!"

Tolvar snickered, did an about face, and it was as if Sloane was invisible.

For hours they stayed, Sloane slumped in the chair, Tolvar pacing. Neither spoke, Tolvar seemingly lost in thought and Sloane not wanting to be snapped at again. The shadows outside grew longer until they disappeared altogether into night. Tonight, was the Nay Moon. She'd forgotten. The Falling Leaves Moon would rise in no time. The weather would change soon, harkening in winter and with it first the Hoarfrost Moon and then the Solstice Moon.

And the Azure Moon?

She wished Alvie sat here with her. He would put her at ease. Every now and again, Tolvar would stop and glare at the wall, the ceiling, even her.

He looked like a man at a chessboard determining his next move, desperate to not be cornered into checkmate. Nothing like the famed knight Alvie told her about.

I should just tell him the Edan Lore, and mayhap even the other piece of information, part of Sloane thought. She wanted to help, after all.

But with no next move of her own, she bit her tongue, hoping she wasn't jeopardizing all their fortunes with her own desperation. She wanted to stay, after all.

Instead, Sloane asked, "Why does the Wolf from the Capella Realm come to Deogol? This place of death."

Her words appeared to press down on Tolvar; gone were the harsh lines from his face. He regarded her, his face naked. He wasn't here by choice, was he?

The vulnerability evaporated. The harshness, a barricade once more.

"Death has already found me before."

CHAPTER
27

Tolvar

Tolvar trained his eyes everywhere except the girl. If he slipped up, it was easier now that she'd fallen asleep cuddled up in the chair in the library, where they still were close to dawn. Her hair was like a thick brown blanket covering her shoulders and torso. How did she keep all that hair in such a tight plait all the time? Sloane's steady, rhythmic breathing seemed to still something inside of Tolvar. His anger at being dismissed this evening was a terrible thing, but the sleeping form of Sloane calmed him.

Confounded woman. He had a desire to carry her out of this place before it hardened those smooth cheeks. He could sail her across the sea and hide her away from suffering any more misery. Damn it! What was he doing? Fantasizing about some woman when he should be focusing on what Pharrell, Kek, and the others were up to. Something was off. He loathed to think his guard had been off enough to not notice someone in the corner, but there was no reason not to believe Sloane.

Why wouldn't she tell him what she knew?

But if the roles were reversed, would he be so quick as to tip his hand? He chuckled. Nay, of course not. Mayhap she was smarter than he gave her credit for.

He'd simply have to piece together what he could right now.

Let's see. Right now, there was some part of the Edan Lore he was missing. That missing piece had to do with the Azure Moon. There was some company or other called the Brones waiting for the

Azure Moon, so they could gain something they thought could send the Befallen elsewhere. Tolvar huffed. Not to the Capella Realm. He could not let that happen. The leader in the street that night, he'd spoken of the Curse of Adrienne. A dark magic so foul, its name was not to be uttered for fear it could bring the curse directly upon the speaker.

Tolvar touched the spot behind his ear where his mess of hair covered the small dark scar that still appeared as fresh as the day he'd received it. If anyone knew how close the Wolf had been to succumbing to the Curse of Adrienne that winter night during the Battle of Reva... If Crevan hadn't been there, mayhap he would have.

Odd. He'd thought of his brother and not had the urge to tear something to shreds. Had Crevan suffered the effects of Adrienne that night he'd pulled the threads of the curse from Tolvar? It was said no man could touch it.

Had Crevan been brought to madness somehow? Is that why he'd killed their father? The Knight Captain? And after the siege, King Rian's cousins—for that's how Tolvar thought of them now, mere cousins. Crevan had been the leader of that band of scum who'd invaded Thorin Court, leaving Tolvar to bleed to death. The Leader!

A snarl knotted in Tolvar's throat. And the outcome? *Tolvar* had been hunted like a criminal by the royal guard of King Rian, grieved and outraged for the loss of his cousins. The famed Wolf, an outcast.

The decorative carving on the back of the chair that Tolvar gripped snapped off.

So much for thinking of Crevan without seething rage. He tossed the broken piece of wood onto the seat of the chair and dropped his hand from the scar. If the Curse of Adrienne was stirring in Deogol, what would anyone be able to do against it? They had no StarSeers to protect them. And these people could not hope to destroy the Befallen *and* fight off Adrienne at the same time. It would be the end of Deogol.

And here he was, right smack in the middle of everything.

He had to find the Unsung and stop this. Only then would he be welcomed back into the Capella Realm's good graces.

The door opened, and in peered Ghlee's blonde head. "Wolf, what's going on? The council doors are still closed, but the guards said you weren't there."

"We were uninvited," Tolvar nodded toward Sloane's sleeping form. "Have you met your messenger?"

"In a way." Ghlee didn't seem pleased. "We need to talk."

It'd been Tolvar's hope that Ghlee would be able to solve at least one piece of this puzzle. But the fret covering his face did not bode well.

Woe is that time when the lee of the island befalls
When havens are vanquished, and the threat of death
   calls
For none shall be spared when cursèd shadows arise
If not for the Unsung, 'twill be the whole of demise
Powers of both temperance and that of great strength
Yea, a hero Unsung, bearing the fortitude of faith
'Tis the Unsung's winding and shadowy path to
   the end
That will cease the Befallen, confronting death to
   transcend
And to conquest over this curse lest it strike land
   anew?
The secret is held with the goddess of the moon
   Azure blue
At Ayla, a weapon she'll give the Unsung on her sole,
   obscure night
Its power will bury the curse and restore the world
   aright
Beware, the night of the Azure Moon comes every
   years ten

The Unsung has one chance aflame, else all must begin again.

TOLVAR READ the Edan Lore again using the eyeglass Ghlee handed him. It was inscribed on the smallest piece of parchment he'd ever held, roughly a third the size of his palm. And there they were, six more lines after...*confronting death to transcend.*

Important lines.

"Sloane was telling the truth. There is a second part." Tolvar frowned, handing the tiny Edan Lore back to Ghlee, who hastily tucked it into his rolled-up sleeve. They stood in a study, a small room with no windows. A single lantern gave the only light. "A weapon. Stars, we cannot let anyone—especially the Brones—get whatever this weapon is first."

Ghlee poured them both a glass of wine. "Aye. But what concerns me most at present is how I came to have this."

"What do you mean?"

"Where I was supposed to meet the messenger, there was an animal carcass. Its tongue had been stretched out of its mouth. This parchment was on it."

"Who is behind this?" Tolvar asked. This didn't sound like the work of the Chief Scholar. The Brones again? But why would they offer up the missing part of the Edan Lore to them?

Ghlee took a drink. "I would say the Chief Scholar, as the other messengers have been hers, but the manner in which I found this, I cannot be sure."

Tolvar had ceased being amazed ages ago that Ghlee and he were so often in sync with their thoughts.

"I take it you wanted to show me this in private for a reason?" Tolvar eyed the door as he set down his goblet rather than taking a drink.

"I was going to bring this to the whole of the council, but when you weren't there..."

"What are you not telling me?"

"At last night's feast, Pharrell wasn't himself. He was jumpy. And kept talking of returning to the Capella Realm to seek the advice of the StarSeers." Ghlee gulped his wine.

"He's pledged to stay in Deogol until this is over," Tolvar leaned forward in his chair. "He said the StarSeers Saw his fortune."

"Aye, but since we've been in Kestriel, I discovered Pharrell allowed eleven Order members to go back to the Capella Realm."

"What? Cowards."

Ghlee nodded. "And I overheard Kek say to Danton that Pharrell has no intention of leaving Dara Keep for any reason until he leaves the island. Unsung or no."

Aye, Tolvar wasn't imagining it. Something was going on.

Someone walked by in the corridor, and they both tensed toward the door.

"Tolvar, I am bound by my oaths to the Order of Siria now. I must share what I've learned of the Edan Lore with Pharrell, but in the meantime, mayhap there is something you can do as you are bound to no such oaths. Before riding out this eve, I received a raven of another meeting our messenger wishes to arrange."

"Another? Why not give you everything tonight?"

"I know not, but I think you should go in my stead."

Tolvar did not miss the sweat on Ghlee's brow. He did not want to give this Edan Lore to Pharrell, but the stars held him to his vow.

Tolvar picked up his goblet and downed the entirety of its contents before eyeing the bottle on the table. "You know you need not ask. Of course, I'll go. I'm anxious to begin solving these mysteries."

"I better make my way to the council room." Ghlee stood, looking grey. "Be on your guard."

"You as well," Tolvar said, then, "Ghlee, what animal was the carcass?"

Ghlee's hand froze on the doorknob. He didn't turn around to face his friend, but Tolvar knew the answer before he spoke. "A wolf."

CHAPTER
28

Sloane

S he might tell herself otherwise, but Sloane felt like a sook many times. Enthralled though she'd been for the adventure of seeing the Order of Siria's headquarters, she found she did not like this place. It frightened her—the towering guards, the way knights slunk through corridors, the tightly shut doors.

But when she awoke and found Tolvar gone from the library, she abandoned her nervousness and made her way back to the council room alone.

She didn't think about the sight she must be—small, delicate, no doubt a red mark across her cheek from the arm of the chair—as she demanded the guards let her into the council room. One of the guards chuckled, the other opened his mouth to no doubt send her away, but the double doors opened, one of the black-and-gold uniformed knights, a beardless, squat man, whispered in the guard's ear, and Sloane was beckoned inside.

"Where is Sir Tolvar?" Sloane asked, scanning the room. The shadowed figure no longer sat in the corner. "I thought he'd be here."

"Why is that?" Pharrell barked. If Tolvar wasn't here, where was he?

"Um, no reason, sir," Sloane tilted her head in what she hoped was an amenable bow. It seemed to have the opposite effect; Pharrell bristled. Her legs shook.

"All right, you can forgo the courtesies; we heard you well enough in the corridor."

Sloane was glad for the darkened room that hid her blush.

"We have decided. And though we thank you for the honor you've displayed coming here, 'tis been decided the Order has no need of your information. You and your companion will leave on the morrow."

"You cannot send me away. You need this information about the Azure Moon!"

"Enough!" Pharrell slammed his fist on the table as the double doors opened and Ghlee strode in holding his fist outstretched.

"I have the Edan Lore, Sir Pharrell," Ghlee said before noticing her. "Ah, Sloane. I'm glad you're here."

"Thank you, Ghlee. But—" Pharrell regarded Ghlee with boredom.

Ghlee did not wait for Pharrell to continue but thrust a tiny bit of parchment at him.

"Read it."

The men at the table shifted uncomfortably.

"'Tis real." Ghlee nodded toward the parchment scrap. "And all there."

"Stars be good, I cannot read this." Pharrell called for an eyeglass and a torch to be brought in.

"No need," Sloane said, and, without waiting for permission, recited the Edan Lore in its entirety, ending with, *"The Unsung has one chance aflame, else all must begin again."*

When she finished, it was silent. She dared a side glance at Ghlee, who gave a subdued smile.

"How did you come by this?" Pharrell finally asked, inspecting the tiny parchment to match it the words Sloane had just spoken. "I thought it was forbidden to write this down."

"To that I cannot speak," Ghlee said. "A messenger gave this to me by curious means, but it *is* the full Edan Lore, and it gives us many details we must consider. Starting with that weapon."

No. Starting with the Azure Moon, Sloane thought.

Pharrell stood and nodded to two knights sitting near Sloane. "Very well, I'll consider it," he said.

Sloane couldn't believe his words. Her arms were gripped, and she was escorted from the room.

"Don't send me away," Sloane shouted. "The Azure Moon! We must consider the Azure Moon, and I have more information you need!"

The doors closed on her again, Ghlee offering her a pitying look before they clicked shut.

"And then they tossed me out," Sloane said to Alvie, whom she'd found entertaining the other recruits and a few of the Order knights around what was either a *very* late night or *very* early morning fire outside barrack six. The two had walked to the deserted training yard, Sloane spilling out much of the story before they arrived.

"Blimey. So, what happens now?" Alvie asked.

"I know not. Pharrell said we had to leave in the morning, but..." She drifted off, turning her attention to the dregs of the night sky effervescing into dawn's first light. If she'd been able to pray to the Nay Moon stars this night, would they have directed her to her fortune?

"Fact o'matter, Sloane, I'm not surprised." He shrugged, picking up a handful of gravel and sifting it between his palms. "Don't matter. We'll go back to Branwell."

"I'm not meant to go back there." Sloane was still searching for any last sign of stars.

"What you mean?"

"There's still help I can give. Information they don't have."

"Oh?" Alvie gazed at her with such earnestness, making it clear he'd listen and believe anything she said. Alvie, the heretic.

"We need to find a way to stay here for now."

"Then we'll think of somethin'."

"I mended one of the saddles. 'Tis doubtful anyone will even notice."

"You never know." Alvie stood, wincing as he did.

"What's wrong?" Sloane frowned up at him.

"Nothin'. My leg ain't the same since...that night. It's fine. Anyway, I gotta find the privy. I'll be back."

Sloane watched Alvie's gait. No doubt the rope contraption on the peg had gotten worse since their alley encounter in Kestriel.

Movement from a tower window caught her eye, but when she focused, nothing was there. Sloane had the sense she was being watched.

The sound of footfalls made her turn, but instead of Alvie, came Tolvar. His tread was swerving and sloppy. When he approached, she smelled the sourness of wine.

"Where did you go?" Tolvar mumbled.

"Me? Where did *you* go?"

She made to stand, and Tolvar reached out.

"Let me help you." In his inebriated state, rather than help Sloane up, he managed to half-push, half-drag her back to the ground. She yelped when her already-aching shoulder hit the ground. "See? You need help. 'Tis a wonder that you've gotten this far."

He belched and jerked at her arm again. His breath reeked to the sky.

"Get away from me. I need not your help or anyone else's." She stood, breath heaving not from effort but from anger.

"That's not true. You would have died without me!" Tolvar's voice rose into a slurred shout. "I saved you!"

"All right!" Sloane yelled back. "So what? You behave as though I owe you something. I don't doubt you've saved many people. Doesn't mean I'm incapable."

Tolvar's jaw slackened, his eyelids heavy.

"I haven't always saved them."

Sloane had no idea what those words meant, but he looked wounded.

"I shouldn't be here. I'm doing no good. Repenting for nothing. This quest is a fool's dream." He slumped to the ground, his eyes red. The scruff on his neck made him appear younger, vulnerable somehow.

"Sir Tolvar." Sloane placed a hand on his shoulder.

Their eyes met. Why was it she felt he could see everything inside her, and she read nothing?

His eyes hardened. "You shouldn't be here either. If you think you're to play a heroine, you ought to look in the mirror, foolish woman. You're weak, too."

Sloane's slap left a reddened imprint immediately on Tolvar's cheek.

"And you're naught more than a drunkard."

Before he saw the tears forming in her eyes, Sloane hobbled away. And she'd never been keener of her own gait.

CHAPTER 29

Sloane

The scratching scrub of the bristles was the only sound in the tack room. There was so much dirt and grime on this piece of leather; Sloane needed to see the true condition of this strap. There would be no replacing this piece later.

She went cross-eyed as she studied the thin piece. It was filthy but not worn. It would work. It felt good to be using her hands. Father would be proud. Mayhap on the Falling Leaves Moon, she could show him her work, for that was a night when the veil between the living and dead was blurred. She'd lift her work to the stars and show him.

In the days since she'd been thrown from the council room, she'd not seen Pharrell, Kek, Ghlee, or any of the council knights. Or Tolvar. She'd braced herself that first morning, waiting to be tossed out, but no one came.

But she'd noticed an edginess to the few dozen knights here. When Sloane passed one in a corridor or watched them training, they didn't seem like how she imagined knights behaved. Sloane couldn't quite discern what it was, but the air here was akin to smelling smoke before seeing flames of a fire.

Despite being ignored, more than once did Sloane feel she was being watched. But no one was ever there.

Since no one had bothered to remove them from Dara Keep, she and Alvie spent hours training with the seven other recruits, though she'd been last, slowest, or worst at every exercise or skill they'd trained in. If she knelt, she found that she was growing more accustomed to using the bow, but swordplay—even knife play--had been hopeless so far. She didn't have the balance nor the upper body strength—especially if wearing a breastplate—to lift a heavy sword. Wielding a knife was at least manageable, but Sloane often dropped her weapon or tripped backward when any practice partner charged her. Her cheeks grew hot, thinking of what a sook she was.

Alvie, at least, had performed well these last days. Even with his peg leg, he was near as nimble as some of the other recruits, although Sloane knew the rope around his stump still bothered him. Alvie picked up a sword like it was something he was meant to hold. Her smile stretched, remembering the light in his eyes the first time he'd gripped the hilt.

"This is way better than slingin' bags of barley." Alvie sliced the air. "Fact o'matter is, I could get used to this, I say."

Alvie disarmed one of the other recruits, a man taller than Alvie, but with a slighter torso, in only a few minutes. Sloane hadn't missed the rise of eyebrows of the three Order knights watching. Two even nodded in approval. Mayhap Alvie had found his place, and they wouldn't toss him out. And that was why Sloane needed to finish this work.

She drew back her hand from where she'd pricked her finger on her stitching needle. She put it to her pursed lips, annoyed at the careless wound.

"If you cannot suffer the sting of a needle, you won't handle a sword wound well."

Sloane kept her back to Tolvar, who appeared in the doorway.

Had he been the hidden one watching her? No, for some reason, she knew it wasn't him.

"You certainly seem to enjoy sneaking up on me, Sir Tolvar."

He remained quiet behind her. Sloane decided to ignore him and went back to work. His dark eyes pressed into her back.

"That is no mended stirrup. What are you making?" He

crouched beside her, inspecting the leather strap she held. Would he tell Pharrell she'd taken more leather from the crate?

"'Tis something for Alvie," Sloane said. He watched her, and, from the corner of her eye, Sloane could tell he was piecing together what she was making.

The part of Sloane, who was most certainly not ignoring Tolvar, wanted to give in to the unease of the last few days and ask what the Order was doing about the Edan Lore.

And mayhap you should tell him the other information. The Cibil of the Nay Moon is our only chance.

But Tolvar's words cut off both her contemplation and her desire to tell him.

"Why not make one for yourself? Surely you could fashion some brace to make things easier on you."

"I need no brace, nor anything else. I am quite accustomed to being me." She kept her voice brittle. He stiffened next to her before standing.

"Then I'll leave you to your work."

"Where are you going? You're dressed for travel." Sloane was angry at herself the moment the words came out. Where Tolvar went and what he did was not her concern.

"I'll be back."

She rolled her eyes. "I forgot. The Wolf only gives short, cryptic words when he speaks."

For some reason, this made Tolvar crack a half-smile. "Worry not, I'll be back."

"I'm not worried!" Sloane shouted.

He picked up a saddle and reins, nodded to her, and was back out the door.

Sloane wasn't certain how long she sat there, dumbfounded, picking at a hunk of some grime on the piece of leather, but she was about to clear and hide her work, ready to leave the tack room and find Alvie when two voices entered the stable.

She couldn't let anyone see her work. They would take it away from her. Grabbing her work and the lantern, she moved to the corner away from the tack room door. She blew out the light and stood crouched in the dark. With hope, they wouldn't enter the tack room.

"It won't matter one way or another," a deep voice said from outside the tack room. "Pharrell's given strict orders that as long as the baron is here, we're stuck sitting on our thumbs."

Baron?

"Should we send word back home to Commander Goodsell that we haven't left here in over a fortnight? He ought to know what's going on. This isn't what the Order signed up for," returned the second and more tenor voice.

"You mad? You fancy goin' out there? What can we do but wind up dead like the lot of them? We've no protection here. This was a ridiculous notion, and I'll be glad when this place is to our backs, and we're back in the Capella Realm where we belong."

"We did swear to—"

"Our oaths are to the stars, Marvone. Before we arrived, Dara Keep didn't even exist anymore. 'Twas foolish to reinstate the Order in a place that'll be wiped out soon."

"Ghlee means to be steward of this place when it's all over. He means for Dara Keep to remain an Order of Siria headquarters like the olden days. Mayhap that's why he *really* brought in those newbies? Sucking up," Marvone said.

Sloane strained her ears. They were moving away.

"You're dumber than you appear if you think any of *them* will be able to join, especially that cripple. What was Ghlee thinking? But don't matter, Pharrell's not making the orders around here anymore. The baron is here on the sovereign's orders, and he ain't going to let us do anything even if one of them *was* the Unsung."

A grimace formed on Sloane's face as her breath stopped.

The sovereign?

What did that mean? The sovereign was *seeking* the Unsung. Wasn't he?

The second man gave a response, but their voices were too faint now. As she sat in the quiet dark, pulse rushing, Sloane was both glad she heard no more and fearful that she hadn't heard enough.

CHAPTER 30

Tolvar

He'd chosen to arrive at the meeting place early specifically so he could survey the area in the light of day. The meeting was set for twilight, and the Wolf was not in the habit of allowing himself to be surprised when he could help it.

The meeting place was set on a sloping hill at the ruins of an ancient Delara, a temple for those who worshipped the stars. The ruins were merely one crumbling wall and a few piles of stones where the corners once stood. Tolvar rarely entered Delaras back home in the Capella Realm—he wasn't a praying man—but the temples were quite a sight to behold, white and gold, spacious and divine. He'd never seen the ruins of one before, but after being in Deogol for a year, it didn't surprise him to find one whittled down to rubble. This island had forsaken the stars, and that was saying something for him.

Still, a tingling sensation went up the back of his neck as he thought about this Azure Moon. Now that he had the full Edan Lore, was he beginning to put more clout in the beliefs surrounding the goddesses of the moons?

Bah.

From where Tolvar stood on this hill, leaning against the tumbling wall a tad shorter than he was, he had a nice vantage of the surrounding landscape. The fields were autumn's gold; he couldn't help but think of the fields that surrounded Thorin Court. There was a large pond in those fields where he and Crevan had played as youths.

Stars, had he let himself slip into thinking about his brother again? That bastard. Tolvar's mouth twitched, thinking about the skin of wine tucked in the saddlebag of his horse, Valko.

Drunkard. Sloane's words came back at him. As they'd been doing these past days. And in the stables she'd hissed at him again. He'd only been making a suggestion.

Stars, that woman could craze a lunatic.

He continued to scan and learn every detail of this surrounding area. A wide road to the east. A sole crofter's cottage a quarter-mile west of here. A few dew fruit trees a sprint from the hill to the south. A grove of trees swayed in the breeze north of the hill. That was the only problematic aspect for preparing for danger. It'd be easy for someone to hide amongst them. But that was why Tolvar was here early. This was a different meeting place than the one where Ghlee had discovered the wolf carcass, but if anyone thought to perform a similar stunt here, Tolvar would be ready.

He unsheathed his sword and took a few practice swings. After a time, he grew bored. What was the fun of swinging a sword if there was no enemy on the other side of it? Tolvar inspected the blade, knowing it was in perfect condition. He'd never see his father's sword in anything but. His father's sword. The late afternoon sun cast a beam off it.

So much blood.

When Tolvar helped to vanquish the Befallen, would he feel as though he'd done his father justice? The cousins of King Rian justice? Would he regain his honor? Would he ever feel redeemed?

He'd continue to carry his father's sword until he'd avenged his death somehow. And earned back his own sword, a beautifully crafted weapon currently held by King Rian.

Tolvar placed the sword to his forehead. "Someday, Father, your sword will rest, and I shall earn the right to call myself your son once again."

He was hard-pressed to think of anything he'd done in the past year that would earn the pride of his father. His stomach was heavy.

He wanted to apologize to Sloane for the drunken remarks he'd made, but...well, the Wolf didn't easily apologize.

After a few more swipes of his sword and another survey of the area, it was still at least an hour's time until twilight. Would the messenger be on time? Was there even a messenger at all, or was this a set up? Whatever the case, it would be a while before Tolvar found out.

If only I'd been this prepared that morning at Thorin Court. Father. The knight captain. King Rian's cousins.

So much blood.

The itch for the wineskin returned. He did have time. At least for one drink.

"SIR GHLEE, IS THAT YOU?" a light, frightened voice made Tolvar open his eyes. He was slumped against the crumbling wall, the skin of wine next to him.

Tolvar stumbled up, the grey-purple hues of dusk overhead. In front of him stood a scholar. A young man. Probably young enough he hadn't grown his first beard. That stupid hat sat upon his head, the reins of a chestnut mare in his hand, the scholar studied Tolvar as though he were a prowling shadow cat.

"I'm here in Sir Ghlee's stead. Sir Tolvar of Askella." The words came out thick. Tolvar balanced himself on the wall. "I'd hear your message."

"The Wolf?" The scholar's eyes widened. "I have copied many of your tales for the sovereign's records. Have you really met a witch of the Skyward Mountains?"

Of all the tales for this gawker to ask about. Tolvar hiccupped slightly. "Aye. I did. Stabbed her in the eye."

The scholar's expression changed to one of intellectual interest. "I would hear that tale from your own lips so I may add to my account."

Siria's skirt.

"Mayhap after we are finished here. What is your message?"

"'Tis meant for Sir Ghlee."

"Sir Ghlee is my brother in all ways but birth; your message is safe with me."

The scholar scrutinized the area as if waiting to be scolded if he shared his information with Tolvar. Nay, not that. He grimaced as if in fear.

"What are you looking for?" Tolvar's head swiveled, too, though not as deftly. His foot kicked the wineskin.

"First, tell me that Sir Ghlee found my message."

"The Edan Lore? Aye. He did. Though you had a strange way of leaving it."

The scholar let go of his horse's reins and fished around in his pocket. "That is part of my misgivings. That corpse of the wolf was already there when I arrived to meet Sir Ghlee."

Tolvar straightened. "Aye? And what of the parchment on the tongue?"

"I replaced the message there with the parchment. Someone knew of my meeting and left a message of their own in that horrific way before I arrived. I didn't know what to do with the carcass, and I was frightened I was being watched, so I left it there for Sir Ghlee to find. I beg your forgiveness."

"You say there was another message on that tongue?" Tolvar glanced in the direction of the grove. Were they being watched now? "What became of it?"

"I have it here." The scholar gave Tolvar the item from his pocket. A piece of parchment almost as small as the Edan Lore.

The Curse of Adrienne has been unburied. You know what that means. –The Brones

"Stars' shadow." Tolvar had to think fast. The darkening night seemed to make that more difficult. Tolvar kicked the wineskin again. "Why this second meeting? Does anyone know you're here now?"

"Only m'lady."

"The Chief Scholar?"

The scholar nodded.

"Why all this secrecy? What is the Chief Scholar trying to tell us?"

"The first you know already. The Edan Lore. You have in your possession the only copy. A copy kept in secret these hundred years by the Chief Scholars alone. The second, none but a few know. I was bid to come here in person because it is a message that dare not be written."

"What?" The back of Tolvar's neck sweated.

"You now know you must find the goddess of the Azure Moon at Ayla. But what you do not know is that no one may find nor speak to her who does not have the Edan Stone."

"What's the Edan Stone?"

"'Tis a small, flat kernel of stone. Seemingly smooth, yet rough. Pale, grey, and as black as midnight all at once. Broken off from the moon itself and cast down."

"Where can I find it?"

The scholar's nose twitched as he gave a small frown. "M'lady does not know where it is, but her forebearers made record that none but the Unsung shall know it."

Tolvar's mind raced as he took in the scholar's words. Then a mantle of unease hovered on his shoulders. It was clear from the scholar's leveled shoulders that he sensed nothing.

"Scholar, one last thing. Why has the Chief Scholar kept this hidden? We asked her about the Edan Lore, and she proclaimed to know nothing."

Beads of sweat appeared on the scholar's forehead. "M'lord—" he began.

An arrow pierced the ground, not feet from where they stood. The scholar's face drained of color. Tolvar felt heavy as he picked up his sword from where it stood next to the wineskin. Curses. Was he as prepared for his enemies now as he'd been earlier?

Another arrow grazed the scholar's shoulder and he fell to his knees, crying out. The whites of his eyes were enormous.

"M'lord!" the scholar yelled, holding his shoulder, his eyes fixed behind Tolvar.

Tolvar turned to two men wearing red tunics, standing on the crumbled wall, wielding swords in his direction. Before one of them brought down his sword, Tolvar sliced through the man's belly. His grunt was like the bleating of a goat as he dropped off the wall. Tolvar had no time to finish him. He was met by the other man's sword. Tolvar stepped back to give himself more room, knocking the scholar out of the way.

"Crouch against the wall," Tolvar shouted, another man advancing on him. He deflected the blade, trying to regain his stance. There wasn't enough room here on this hill. Why hadn't he moved the scholar to a wider area? Another man leaped from behind the wall, and Tolvar changed his stance to fight two at once. Already, sweat dripped down his temples. As Tolvar parried and hacked at the two, Tolvar saw two more, also in red, striding up the darkened hill on the other side.

"Get my knife!" he yelled to the scholar, who cowered against the wall covering his face. "It's in my saddlebag." The scholar didn't move. "Go!" Tolvar growled, the Wolf growing more alive within him.

Three now. Tolvar pivoted to create the room he needed to take on all of them. His training taking over, he sliced and slashed his sword against the others, narrowly missed by his opponents' blades.

Finally, the second man who'd joined his comrades made an error in his block, and Tolvar was able to strike him across the neck. Beneath the clangs of blades meeting, there was a small gurgling sound as the man held the gaping wound and fell to the ground. There was now enough blood that the air held a metallic twinge. Tolvar must defeat one of the others before the next two made it up the hill.

Another arrow hit the ground feet from Tolvar and he almost laughed at this imbecile archer's aim.

The first man found an opening and slashed Tolvar's shoulder. It sagged in pain, but the Wolf didn't cry out. Not for a mere wound such as that. He was able to return the wound to his opponent, openly laughing when the man howled as if Tolvar had whacked off his arm. The third man took the opportunity to strike at Tolvar's back. A coward's move. Tolvar lunged back at him, feinted to strike his right arm, and then caught the man in the chest. The man stumbled back, stunned, and Tolvar stepped forward, thrusting his sword into his chest.

"That is how a man attacks," Tolvar whispered to the man, removing his sword, then knocking him downhill. Tolvar gave only a brief sigh, regripped the sword, and parried against the first man. The man's eyes were wild now, and Tolvar chuckled again. His laughter caused his opponent to lose control. Tolvar advanced, glancing at the location of the two climbing the hill. More arrows flew into the area, but nothing close. Tolvar swept his sword first left, then right, the man retreating. Stars, this was beginning to feel easy. He blocked the man's slash with ease. He almost had him backed against the wall, when the additional two made it up the hill.

And then two others leaped over the wall behind Tolvar.

He was near the scholar, who was still crouching against the wall, the knife held loosely in his hand.

"You're going to need to use that now," Tolvar called to the scholar, taking stock of all the opponents.

"You're surrounded, Sir Tolvar," said one of the men who'd come up the hill. It was him. The leader with the club. He held it at his side. "Why don't you tell us what you two were having such a lively discussion about. Mayhap we'll make your death quick."

Tolvar said nothing. He sized up each man, their stance, whether they appeared frightened or ready for attack. How should he go about this? The scholar was of no help. Tolvar would have to protect him at the same time he fought.

"Been drinking again, I see." The leader with the club nodded at the wineskin. "This should be easy then."

Before the attackers took two strides, Tolvar drew his dagger from his boot and flung it into one of the men on the wall. Before the attackers took four strides, Tolvar dragged the scholar up to a standing position. And before they were upon him, Tolvar lunged to the side, his sword lacerating one of their arms. The man dropped his sword, the wound a bleeding, gaping thing.

But with two disarmed, there were still three. Sweat poured off Tolvar. He heard little but his own breath above the clash of swords. It seemed like hours; Tolvar's feet acted as fast as his sword arm. The man with the chest wound rejoined the fight. Stars. Tolvar shifted the fight closer to the edge of the hill before pivoting again and kicking the man with the chest wound. Through a loss of blood and strength, he tumbled down the hill. Now Tolvar could reposition himself back toward the scholar, who cried out every time a weapon neared him. The attackers ignored him.

Probably want him alive.

Tolvar's arms were heavier and heavier, the smell of blood more potent from several wounds he'd both given and received. He managed to whittle down his five attackers. One dead. One at the bottom of the hill. One groaning next to the wall, holding his side from the stab Tolvar had just delivered. Only two remained.

"You might as well run like you did last time," Tolvar said to the leader, dodging another swing. Every time that club swung into his sword, it was as though his whole being reverberated. What was it made of?

"I think not." The leader threw him a nasty smirk.

"Sir Tolvar, look out!" the scholar shouted.

Yet another new attacker brandishing a spear appeared behind Tolvar, and the scholar ran to block him. In the haste of his movement, the spear punctured the scholar. The cry that followed was that of a boy, and Tolvar's stomach sank. He whirled around to face the new attacker and was pummeled by the leader's club. It knocked Tolvar off balance and onto the ground next to the scholar, where, without hesitation, he dropped his sword, yanked the spear from the scholar's torso and pitched it into the man who stood next to the leader. The guttural noise gave the leader pause as he surveyed his comrade's damage. The man fell.

Tolvar reached for his sword and was kicked in the head. Blood spurted from his mouth. Before he could regain his bearings, another boot plowed against his skull. The world spun. Lying on his side, Tolvar pawed the ground for his sword.

"This what you're looking for?" The leader held Tolvar's sword in his free hand. The newcomer stood to the side, a dagger held at the ready.

The scholar coughed and moaned. The Wolf spit more blood onto the ground. His arms hurt. He had multiple gashes in his shoulders, one on his back, and his head pounded something fierce. Tolvar fought to focus on his heartbeat. Anything to block out the fuzziness he grappled against.

"What will others say when they hear stories of me beating the Wolf twice?" The leader chuckled.

Bile threatened to come up. Tolvar shifted to his back and closed his eyes.

The leader continued, "Though I do wonder if you might have put up more of a fight had you not been soused again. Soon, you'll be known as the Drunk, not the Wolf."

The newcomer laughed at this remark. Tolvar kept his eyes closed, his body motionless—save for his hand—and let them laugh.

Thoughts raced. *The Edan Stone. The Azure Moon. Sloane.*

Tolvar's voice was scarcely a whisper.

"I say. What was that?" the leader asked.

Tolvar, his eyes still closed, sensed the leader stoop down to him. And he sensed the newcomer move away.

"Sir?" The newcomer's voice was confused.

Tolvar muttered again.

"Spit it out, man." The leader was close now. Tolvar felt his breath on his throbbing face.

"Sir, this wineskin is completely full."

Tolvar drove the knife that the scholar had pushed at him into the leader, the club and sword making echoed *clangs* as they hit the ground.

"I said, 'I'm not drunk.'" The Wolf glared.

The leader shuddered, mayhap as much as from that glare as from the knife protruding from his chest. Crimson dripped from his mouth, the whites of his eyes growing bigger in the darkness.

The newcomer wasted no time. He leaped back over the wall and fled. Tolvar twisted the knife before jerking it from the leader's chest, picked up his club, and stood above him.

It had been said of the Wolf that he'd once killed a man with his gaze. Tolvar found that story the most ridiculous of all, but it did have an impressive ring about it. While he didn't plan to finish this man off with his glare, he didn't mind that it helped. He held his expression steady on the leader, who, at least, unlike his comrades, wasn't blubbering. Nay, this man was doing his best to keep his dignity. While Tolvar would soon see him dead, he did give him credit for that, at least.

"You're still too late," the man said, his voice weak and hoarse.

"Won't matter to you soon," Tolvar returned. "And now the Brones have lost their leader."

"You're a fool thrice over. I am not the leader." He gave a cough-laugh. "But you'll meet him eventually. And more of us are coming for you. For the weapon, too." His rasped laugh was maniacal. "Ah, I've made a believer of you. Good. It won't matter, though. We're well-prepared and have stirred the shadows of Adrienne's Curse again. We shall rid this island of the Befallen."

Tolvar did not flinch at the word Adrienne, nor allow himself to respond, but kept his glare resolute. He toyed with the club in his hands, getting a feel for its weight. What was this made of? He wanted to ask the leader, but renewed whimpers from the scholar changed his mind. Without another word, Tolvar bashed the head of the club into the leader's face. There was a crunch of his cracking skull.

He tossed the club aside and knelt beside the scholar. He inspected the wound, finding it to be deep. He tore the hem of the scholar's robes and pressed the cloth upon the wound.

"Stay with me," Tolvar said. The scholar's pale face was going lifeless. "Oi! Stay with me, scholar. What of the Chief Scholar? Why is she hiding? What is she hiding?"

The scholar convulsed and coughed. "The sovereign—" He managed to get out before turning still. His empty eyes stared at the night sky.

Tolvar closed the scholar's eyes. So young. Tearing more of the robes, Tolvar wrapped his shoulder as best he could. Then he opened the wineskin and took a swig that he'd abstained from all evening. The warmth of the liquid in his belly momentarily quieted the many questions and concerns. The sovereign. What was he to make of that? There was only one explanation. The sovereign had stopped the Chief Scholar from giving the Order of Siria the information she had. Which didn't make sense. Because it meant the sovereign was endeavoring to stop the Order from knowing about the Azure Moon. Which didn't make sense, either. Wasn't the sovereign desperate to find the Unsung? Desperate to find a way to defeat the Befallen?

His gaze fell upon the leader's corpse. *I am not the leader.*

Siria's skirt. More puzzle pieces.

He gingerly touched the gash on his forehead. These Brones seemed to believe that the Befallen could be defeated without the Unsung, that they could use the Curse of Adrienne instead. Something pricked up his spine.

And how did this group know this scholar was to meet here with Tolvar? If the only person who knew about it was the Chief Scholar? But mayhap she wasn't the only person who knew. Did the sovereign's raven keepers take her messages?

Nothing about the ideas that were flowing through Tolvar's mind made any sense at all. But he couldn't find a way to make the sovereign not be a part of all this. And now another thought penetrated his mind. This time about the Order.

CHAPTER
31

Sloane

Sloane drew back the string of the bow, took a deep breath, like Ghlee had shown her, checked her aim again, and let go of the arrow. It landed next to the target, but at least she'd managed to shoot it the distance she was aiming for this time. She adjusted her tunic and belt before shifting her balance from one foot to the other before trying again. She didn't want her legs to lock up.

She eyed the entrance again. Tolvar had still not come back, and it was well past midnight. The training yard was empty, but guards had left the torches lit for Sloane. Evidently, practicing well into the night wasn't an unusual activity at Dara Keep. At least she didn't feel as if she were being watched this time of night. Her lips tightened, Sloane redoubled her efforts to stop monitoring the entrance. She'd found Ghlee earlier, and he'd been completely unconcerned.

"The Wolf can take care of himself," Ghlee had said with a shrug. Did he know where Tolvar had gone?

She'd offered a prayer to the sliver of moon in the sky for Tolvar's safe return. Even if she didn't particularly like him right now, she still didn't want something to happen to him. Besides, she'd decided she must tell him about the Cibil of the Nay Moon. No more holding back, especially after what she'd overheard in the stable. She trusted no one else besides Tolvar, the only knight here not in the Order of Siria.

But, oh how she hated that she waited here.

What if the Befallen was close? Sloane's wide eyes fixed on the entrance again.

What's it to you when he returns? Thought the part of Sloane who still stung from Tolvar's remarks.

He's searching for a way to defeat the Befallen, same as me. I must tell him what I know, the other part returned.

That's not it, though, Sloane conceded to herself. She didn't want to lose one more person she knew. There were many broken parts to Sloane now, and she couldn't consider how she'd piece herself together again if she did.

Without giving thought to her form, she nocked the next arrow and shot it. It landed in the bottom right corner of the target.

"Better." Ghlee's voice startled her, and she dropped the next arrow she'd plucked from the quiver next to her. "Sorry."

He stood beside her, his focus on the target as if to prod her to shoot again. Sloane reformed her stance and missed the target.

"You're thinking too much," Ghlee said.

Another arrow shot; the target missed again. Sloane huffed out her frustration. This time, she didn't think. She grabbed the next arrow and shot it into the lower right side of the target again.

Ghlee chuckled. "You're consistent, I'll say that. What are you doing out here at this hour?"

Sloane hoped it was too dark for Ghlee to see her blush. "Training, of course."

Ghlee glanced at the entrance. Unlike earlier, his expression was pursed.

"You know where he went?"

Ghlee nodded, his jaw flexing as he kept his focus on the entrance.

"Is he in danger?"

"I hope not."

"Should we search for him?" Sloane asked, hoping her voice sounded steady. Ghlee's troubled face did not help.

"He'll be back." Ghlee's words were firm as he picked up a bow and arrow of his own. Without looking, he shot it into the center of the target. "I do wonder, though, why you keep vigil like this?" He was pointedly not looking at her.

"I'm not keeping vigil." Sloane raised her chin, fiddling with the fletching of an arrow.

"Suit yourself, but I wouldn't waste too many thoughts on Sir Tolvar." Ghlee shot another arrow into the center of the target.

Sloane's jaw slackened. "I don't. You may be sure of that. He's a drunkard and an oaf."

Ghlee chuckled. "Aye, he is. But he wasn't always this way."

Not wanting to ask, but certainly wanting to know, Sloane sharpened her gaze toward Ghlee. He glimpsed at her from the corner of his eye and continued. "Sir Tolvar, as you know, is from the Capella Realm. You and everyone else know him as the Wolf, a famed knight who's won more battles at age twenty-five than most men can boast in their lifetimes. But Tolvar is, *was,* also the eldest son of the Earl of Askella."

"Was?"

"Aye. Three years ago, the earl, along with King Rian's very dear cousins were killed by Tolvar's younger brother, who led a group of bandits Tolvar had spent moons tracking." Ghlee sighed. "He never imagined his brother could be their leader. Crevan was a sly one. Tolvar thought to set a trap for the bandits and instead left their castle, Thorin Court, open and vulnerable to attack. Crevan, himself, killed their father and one of the cousins, and left Tolvar for dead.

"King Rian was furious at his cousins' deaths and Tolvar's foolhardiness. Many died in retaking Thorin Court, and it caused upheaval in the Capella Realm that hadn't been seen for an age. He stripped Tolvar of his land and title and banished him from the Capella Realm until Tolvar redeemed himself."

"That's horrible," Sloane whispered.

"Aye, but the worst for Tolvar was the loss of people he suffered. He blames himself. For all of it."

"And that's why he's here in Deogol? He hopes if he finds the Unsung and defeats the Befallen that he may return home."

"Aye," Ghlee said. Through his story, he'd continued shooting arrows into the target. He hadn't missed once.

"What became of Crevan?" Sloane asked.

"For a time, he and his bandits held Thorin Court, the earl's stronghold, and King Rian was forced to call upon neighboring earls to seize it back. But Crevan still held hostage one of King Rian's cousins. Eventually, the castle was breached and taken back. But not before Crevan killed her. He was driven into hiding while his band was hunted down." Ghlee paused. "'Tis *believed* he's dead.

"Tolvar was not there for the siege; he was too wounded. I know he thinks he may have somehow changed the outcome. Though I cannot think how. 'Tis clear Crevan was mad."

"I cannot believe it. Why would someone do that to their own family?"

Don't think about Joah.

"Power. Tolvar's father was one of King Rian's most trusted advisors. And, of course, there was the matter of the cousin. Crevan thought he could leverage her into gaining status for himself, a second son."

"I don't understand," Sloane said.

Ghlee dropped the bow to his side. "The cousin, she was Tolvar's bride-to-be."

Sloane stared, stunned. "Bride?"

"'Twas an arranged marriage, but I do think Tolvar was fond of her. And he does blame himself that he couldn't protect her."

Her mind raced. No wonder Sir Tolvar sought ale and held on to his frown so tightly.

"So, I wouldn't spend thoughts on Tolvar, Sloane," Ghlee said quietly. "'Twill be a lost cause."

She didn't have a chance to respond. The rattle of the main gate opening, followed by the clopping of horses' hooves, took their attention.

In the shadowed light of torches, Tolvar sat slumped astride his horse, leading another horse behind him, a great lump slung over its backside. A body. Two of the night sentinels atop the battlements clambered down the stairs, spears ready. Their focus was on the body draped over the horse.

"You think I'd bring an enemy in here," Tolvar growled at them. He swung from his saddle, looking pained as he did so. "He's a scholar from Kestriel."

A scholar? Why would Tolvar meet with a scholar? And why did he seem as if he'd been through a war? He was covered with blood. Sloane couldn't help but think about a bloodied Tolvar witnessing his own father's death.

We have more in common than I thought.

"Captain Pharrell will want to be alerted," one of the guards said.

"You think to wake him at this hour? This can wait until morn. Bring me the raven keeper, though."

"And mayhap the healer," Ghlee said, moving forward.

When the guards just stood there, Tolvar growled again. "Have you gone deaf and dumb? Move!"

The two trotted away.

"What happened?" Ghlee said.

"Too much to talk here in the open." Tolvar's eyes scanned the training yard. "Let's wait for the raven keeper, then find someplace private."

Sloane eyed the wounds. His arms appeared lacerated, a cascade of blood soaking his shoulders and sleeves. Yet, here he stood as if his appearance was completely normal. He turned his back to her, and Sloane yelped. His back was soaked in blood. Tolvar looked at her as if noticing her for the first time. His furrowed forehead relaxed.

"I told you I'd be back."

"So you did," Sloane said. Could she see the pain there behind his eyes? Nay, Tolvar was a master of his emotions.

"You need not tremble your lip like that. It looks worse than it is."

There was the Tolvar Sloane knew. She wanted to strangle him.

"We'll see about that," Ghlee said as the raven keeper, an older man dressed in naught but a night shift and carrying a box, raced out into the yard.

"I'm here, m'lord," he panted. The raven keeper opened the box and took out some parchment, quill, and ink. "And prepared for your dictation." By the firm line of his mouth, this must not be too unusual.

"I'll write it myself. You have your seal?" Tolvar said, scratching a short message with his scarred hand. Aye, Sloane watched his movements carefully now. When he finished, he handed it to Ghlee, and Tolvar wrote a second message. He sealed both.

"This goes to the Chief Scholar in Kestriel." Tolvar handed the first message to the raven keeper. "And this goes to the sovereign."

"Aye, m'lord. 'Twill be done." The raven keeper hurried away, leaving puzzled faces on everyone who watched Tolvar.

"Well, back to your posts," Tolvar said, his shoulders a little too straight.

"What about the body, sir?" one of the guards asked.

Tolvar softened his gaze when he glanced at the body. "Wake Sessel. He'll take care of him. I've sent word to Kestriel. Someone will come to fetch it so he might have a proper send-off."

With that, Tolvar walked away toward the barracks, Ghlee keeping stride with him. Sloane doubled her strides to match their pace. Whatever had happened, it had something to do with the Edan Lore. She could feel it.

Good. We can all figure this out together.

"Where do you think you're going?" Tolvar threw over his shoulder.

"With you, of course," Sloane returned. "Sir Tolvar, I have something important to tell you."

"I think not."

"Oh, let her come, Wolf. She's been up all night waiting for you," Ghlee said.

"I have not," Sloane said, reddening again.

"Touched, though I am, the answer is nay," Tolvar said. "Whatever you need to say must wait. Good night, Sloane." Tolvar and Ghlee walked past the barracks and entered a side door of the keep, closing it behind them.

CHAPTER
32

Sloane

S loane had two choices. She could continue to sit outside the door Tolvar and Ghlee had gone through and wait, or she could go to the barrack and try to sleep.

Or you could leave this place altogether, thought the fuming part of her.

Or you could try something on your own to help. You cannot wait any longer. Sook. The other part of her shivered as she thought of the Befallen: dark, mysterious, and out there somewhere. But what was she supposed to do on her own?

Why wouldn't Tolvar let her join him and Ghlee? Was it her leg? He'd said she was weak when he'd been drunk. Weren't people more honest when drinking? Father always had been. Was it because Tolvar didn't like her? But if he'd brought her here, he couldn't find her that bad.

Sloane gave herself a sniff. Certainly better than Tolvar, who smelled of sweat and booze and sort of an earthy scent. Mayhap not all unpleasant.

Glory of the moon, what was she doing thinking about the way Tolvar smelled? She was glad no one was here to see her blush.

She couldn't sit here like an obedient hound—she needed to do something. Indecisiveness dragged at her. "You're a sook, Sloane," she whispered, shamed that she didn't move from her spot.

The dropping temperature in the air brought with it a thick fog. She yawned and stretched her arms overhead. Her eyes stung from being up all night, and she strained them to see even a few feet in front of her. The fog was so gradual, she hadn't noticed how murky the air was until now. Gone was the view of the stars in the sky. Everything was covered in mist.

How much longer would she wait? She didn't want to think about how foolish she would appear when Tolvar finally exited. It didn't matter. She already had the pangs of regret that she hadn't been forthcoming with Tolvar from the beginning. And now he needed to know what she'd overheard.

All these days here at Dara Keep wasted.

Sloane shivered, the wet air clinging to her sleeves. Was the Befallen like fog? Did those who succumbed to it feel damp and cold like this before choking to death? They couldn't wait around Dara Keep any longer. They needed to act before the Azure Moon rose. They needed to find the Cibil of the Nay Moon. She wished she had more information besides a fairy story about the diviner who granted anyone the answer to a single question on the night of a Nay Moon.

If one knew where to find him.

We must find him.

The next Nay Moon was mere weeks away. Instinctively, Sloane peered up for sight of the moon, but the fog blocked her view.

Or did it? What was that in the sky? A pale orb. But it wasn't the time of the full moon yet. The Falling Leaves Moon was still days away. Sloane's heart pounded. Was that orb turning red?

"*Addrriennne...*" whispered a voice like the one at the bog. It was a cursèd word. Never to be uttered.

Sloane winced and stood, wrapping her arms around herself, eyes fixed on the blurred moon through the fog that, aye, was turning crimson. What was happening? She wished for her moon cuff. She'd feel more protected.

She yelped as the door slammed open, and Tolvar entered the courtyard.

"What's happening?" he asked. Stars, did his eyes always have to penetrate her so?

"The moon. 'Tis turning crimson. Something is happening."

Tolvar kept his eyes steady on Sloane. "You need to stop pretending."

"What? Sir Tolvar, did you hear me? The moon. 'Tis red!" Sloane shouted.

Tolvar focused on his hands. They seemed to melt into the fog. "I need to find the Unsung. I need redemption."

She met his pleading eyes. She had to do something. "I know what to do. Listen! I need everyone to listen. The Cibil—"

"They will only listen to the Unsung."

The blood moon expanded. Growing bigger and bigger. Tears formed at the corners of Sloane's eyes. "You misunderstand. I simply want to help. I'm not the Unsung. Look at me. You said so yourself."

Tolvar studied his hands once more. With regret? Is that what she saw?

"Look at me! Why won't you share your thoughts with me? We're on the same side!" She went to touch his shoulders, but her hands passed *through* him. "Sir Tolvar! What's happening?"

"You cannot be the Unsung because no one even believes in the Edan Lore anymore." His words seemed labored as if every syllable pained him to utter.

She sobbed. "'Tis true. No one believes in the Edan Lore or even the goddess of the Moon. I know you don't. But I do. I believe. And I *know* what needs to be done."

"*Then do it.*" These words did not come from Tolvar but rippled through the fog.

What was happening? The fog enveloped Tolvar. He was disappearing.

"Wait! Where are you going? I need you! I cannot do this alone!"

"But you are alone, Sloane," Tolvar said, his voice sounding distant and echoing. He vanished, and the crimson moon filled the sky. Tears poured off her cheeks, her shoulders shook. She'd never felt more small.

"Someone needs to do something!" she screamed.

She startled awake. She panted, eyes searching everywhere. The night, waning into early dawn, was crisp, clear. No hint of fog. She rubbed her face.

The Cibil of the Nay Moon. That was her next step. No more holding back.

The echoes of her dream resounded in her ears, *No one believes in the Edan Lore.*

"Then I will find a way to make them," Sloane said, her tone sounding strange to her.

Sloane didn't read well. After all, she'd never been able to complete her studies with Mistress Semla, but she knew enough she could muddle through a few passages. Mayhap there was a book here containing information on the whereabouts of the Cibil.

The library was easy to find again, and she was surprised to see a few candles lighting the room. There was a faint scent of incense, which seemed to be no longer burning. Before, Sloane hadn't dared touch the books. But now, alone, she had purpose. Holding the first tome in her hand, Sloane's fingers roved over the leather spine and cover. Whoever had made this embossed cover had done an excellent job. She held the book to her nose, taking in the homey fragrance of the leather combined with the musty smell of parchment. This book seemed to be on war tactics. Nothing of help here. With the second book, Sloane again found herself spending more time admiring the leather binding rather than flipping through any pages. Not able to help herself, she put that book to her nostrils as well.

She had the third book pressed to her nose when she noticed the man sitting in the corner watching her. Sloane's grasp slipped on the book, but she caught it, her shoulders feeling as though they were next to her ears.

"That certainly is an unusual way to read a book," the man said in a pleasant voice. He had a greying mustache as his only facial hair, revealing a sharp, noble chin. He wore a lavish blue tunic with a plush, decorative doublet. It was how Sloane imagined the sovereign himself must dress. Through his amused brown eyes, Sloane recognized a kind face. Still, she flushed under his scrutiny. "Please. Do not cease on my account." He stood, walked across the room, and picked up one of the books to smell. "Leather has a good scent. Sweet, yet earthy. A most subtle scent of the strongest nature."

Sloane's expression softened, the man's words putting her at ease.

"I love it, too. My father was a leatherworker. I'm apprenticing—I mean— *I'm* a leatherworker, too."

"That so?" The man returned the book to the shelf. "I've an eye for fine leatherwork."

"Then you would have appreciated my father's work, m'lord. There was no greater leatherworker in all of Deogol."

"I don't doubt it, hearing that fervor in your voice." The man chuckled as he sat in a chair. "I find I have a difficult time sleeping here in this unfamiliar place. Mayhap you'll keep me company for a time."

"You want *my* company?" Sloane smoothed out her ill-fitting tunic.

"Certainly, if it suits you. I'm not so highborn that I can't engage a pretty girl with a bit of conversation." He observed her as she sat in a chair opposite. "Your leg. Does it pain you?"

"Nay, m'lord," Sloane said. Why was her leg always a topic of conversation?

"That is good. Tell me. What brings you here this time of night? Something more than a yearning to smell books?"

She fidgeted with the frayed hem of her tunic. "I hoped to find information."

"Books are usually the best place to start. What information do you seek?"

"I'm looking for information that I know will help defeat the Befallen."

The man leaned back in his chair. "A most grave topic. I lost my daughter to the Befallen."

"I'm most sorry to hear that, m'lord." Sloane hoped he sensed her sincerity.

"Aye, most tragic. Two years ago, this Gale Moon."

"I, too, lost my family. My parents and my younger brother."

"A rotten lot, indeed."

They sat in silence, both consumed by their own grief for a time. Sitting with this richly dressed man, eyes welled up, no doubt in memory of his daughter, made Sloane feel less isolated. Whoever this nobleman was, the Befallen had ravaged his life as it had her own. It heated something in Sloane's chest. She had to find information on the Cibil of the Nay Moon.

"I fear I promised you good conversation, and I failed before we even introduced ourselves," he said, brushing a hand across his cheek.

"I'm Sloane. Of Mohn," she said.

He nodded, "I am Henry."

"Henry? Are you not a noble?" Sloane said before she could stop herself. "My apologies, m'lord. I spoke out of turn."

"No need to apologize. I am a lord of something or other, and here at Dara Keep on the sovereign's business. But for tonight, Henry will do." He winked.

The sovereign's business? Sloane's heart quickened pace. But this Henry seemed so kind.

"And you're here in Dara Keep because of the Edan Lore."

Sloane tensed, suddenly on guard. "How do you know that?"

"As I said, I'm here on the sovereign's business. There isn't much happening here that I'm not informed of at present. For instance, you are *still* here."

"I am," Sloane said, struggling to see Henry as a force holding the Order of Siria hostage rather than the kind face regarding her. "The Befallen took everything from me. I should be dead, but instead, my path leads here. To help. I hope that is why you're here as well, Henry, being that you've suffered loss, also."

Henry was quiet for a moment. "You speak of your path as would a priestess."

"Certainly not. But my family is dead, same as your daughter. I have a means to help the Order with the Edan Lore. Mayhap the only means; I need them to listen. Someone needs to do something." Her voice cracked, and a flash of the crimson moon entered her mind.

"'Tis very noble, Sloane of Mohn," Henry said.

This statement emboldened her. "I fear the Order is doing naught to defeat the Befallen, Henry." He perked up an eyebrow. "Aye. Including learning what they can of the Azure Moon. They now know of the Azure Moon's part in the Edan Lore, but I've seen naught done regarding that. It'll rise *this* year and I have knowledge that can help." She decided to be brave. No more holding back. "Mayhap you've heard of the Cibil of the Nay Moon?"

To her surprise, Henry gave a nod.

"Well then, I tell you, the Azure Moon and the Cibil are key to everything. We don't have much time."

"My," Henry said, toying with his mustache, "you've much passion in your words. But I'm afraid you mistake my role here. I've little influence that will help you and your cause. But you've given me much to think upon. I'm glad I finally met you. My thanks."

With that, the finely dressed lord of something or other stood and left the library, leaving Sloane confused and mayhap a bit frightened about her outburst.

CHAPTER 33

Tolvar

He'd sat in this dungeon cell for two days, careful not to reopen his shoulder wound that he'd already split once being "escorted" down here. Pharrell's orders. A dripping sound coming from stars-knew-where was driving him mad.

Even still, he preferred it here in this dingy, mildewy space to the stale infirmary, where, thanks to Ghlee and his accursed meddling, he'd spent the day prior.

He didn't have time to be angry with Ghlee, however. He supposed getting his shoulder stitched *had* been the right course of action. He didn't even have time to be angry with Pharrell. He needed him to listen, for once.

The sovereign. It was the sovereign behind all this folly. Tolvar knew that now with every ounce of his soul—if he had one. The sovereign had hired the Brones to stop him. The sovereign had those men, those would-be Unsung recruits, murdered. The sovereign had stopped the Chief Scholar from sharing the Edan Lore with them. It all made sense now.

And yet, it didn't make sense at all.

Why, in stars' holy names, would the sovereign not want Tolvar to succeed? Not want to find the Unsung? Not want the Edan Lore shared?

Pharrell may be an idiot, but Tolvar had to make him see reason. And so, he sat, docile as a lamb until Pharrell assumed he'd taught Tolvar the valuable lesson of who the lion was.

Mayhap Tolvar should've told Pharrell everything three days ago upon his return as the commander had demanded so he wouldn't be sitting here. But he'd wanted to consider matters before letting anyone but Ghlee, to whom he'd recounted everything that first night, into his confidence. Apparently, Sloane had made several attempts to see him, shouting she needed to speak to him, but had been barred entrance.

Yesterday, Ghlee confirmed what Tolvar suspected would happen. Pharrell was sending all the "recruits" back to Kestriel, Sloane and Alvie included, along with the scholar's body. The Chief Scholar had written back saying a wagon would arrive today.

The sovereign had not written back.

What did that mean?

Tolvar's note to the sovereign informed him—as if he didn't know—a band calling themselves the Brones had attacked him. The last line said, *I defeated them all.*

Ghlee had paled when Tolvar related that part of the note. "Stars, you're going to get us executed."

But with no response from the sovereign, they could do little but continue to speculate. Tolvar had had naught but time for three days and felt no closer to understanding this mess. It must be this weapon of the Azure Moon. For some reason, the Brones, and thus the sovereign, must think the weapon was all that was needed. And what of the Curse of Adrienne? Did the sovereign know about that? He and Ghlee had talked themselves in circles yesterday.

"I've heard they leave within the hour," Ghlee said as he came out of the shadowed corridor, the light of the torch behind him making him visible. He stood on the opposite side of the bars, holding a flask in his hand. He outstretched it to Tolvar, who took it, nodding in appreciation. The fiery liquid was doing what nothing else had: calming him. Ghlee scanned the dank, stone corridor, seeing if a guard was in earshot. "And I've learned some news."

Tolvar took another swig of the flask. Was this news he wanted?

"The sovereign has commanded the Order to stand down."

Tolvar choked. It was like coughing on fire. "Stand down? What do you mean?" He leaned against the bars, apprehension burning on his tongue.

Ghlee leaned in as well, and his voice was barely a whisper. "The Order of Siria has been ordered not to leave Dara Keep. We're to remain here giving naught more than a pretense that we're making strides."

Well, this certainly confirmed everything about the sovereign. But why?

"Pharrell is contemplating leaving Deogol," Ghlee said, grabbing the flask and taking a healthy swig off it. "Going back to the Capella Realm. He said there's no point in staying. That will leave me and a half dozen others to man the keep. A waste. This isn't what I signed up for." He dragged a wooden bench close to the cell and slumped onto it.

This chance for redemption...if the Order of Siria *did* leave, what would become of Tolvar? He needed to find a way to make Pharrell stay here and make the Order keep the promise they'd made when they'd arrived in Deogol, not bow to the whims of a sovereign who Tolvar was becoming convinced was utterly mad. But he certainly couldn't do anything about it rotting in this dank cell.

"Has Pharrell mentioned when he plans on ending my incarceration?"

"Nay, but if he means to leave, he'll lose interest in punishing you."

"How came you by this information?"

Ghlee twisted the cap off the flask again and took a swallow before handing it over. "Sloane. But I confirmed it by cornering Kek."

"Sloane?" He held the flask frozen near his mouth.

"She found me this morning and said even though you sought to ignore her, she still had something important to tell you. She doesn't know where you are. Clearly."

"I'll be damned." Tolvar let the scorching liquid settle on his tongue a moment before swallowing. "And your research of the Azure Moon?"

"There isn't a soul in Deogol who can say when it will rise. Not a scholar, nor priestess, nor any book or scroll that the Chief Scholar has searched secretly for us. But 'tis funny you should ask."

Tolvar raised an eyebrow.

"Sloane ranted that she knew how to find the answer to that very question."

"And?"

Ghlee's lips pursed into a half-smile. "She wouldn't tell me. Because I was in the Order, she said. I think the conversation she overheard spooked her."

Stars. Although I can't say I blame her caution.

"You believe her?" Tolvar asked, passing back the flask. "This isn't another tactic so she doesn't have to leave?"

"Nay." Ghlee did not hesitate his answer. He set the flask on the bench at his side. "She wanted to tell me. I think she almost did. I could sneak her down here, but I'd need to find her now. The wagon leaves soon."

Tolvar's words had been so unkind that night he'd been drunk. He began pacing again, a nervous energy suddenly consuming him.

"Bah. We shouldn't involve her further. We'll solve this puzzle." Tolvar stopped pacing, picking at a chunk of worn stone on the wall. It crumbled and tumbled to the ground. "Besides, that girl is not built for this."

"Built for what?"

"This. All of this. She should be taken far from here where no more damage can be done to her."

Ghlee stood and leaned against the bars. "Wolf, I've never heard you so concerned for a mere girl before, not even—"

"Do *not* say her name," Tolvar interrupted, scowling. "And 'tis not concern, exactly. Do not think of putting words where there are none. Sloane's just too delicate."

Ghlee snickered. "Wolf, have you actually paid attention to that woman? She's far from delicate. She's passionate and willful."

"You forgot stubborn, hardworking, and good-hearted." Tolvar drew his mouth in a firm line. He would not look at Ghlee.

"Stars. You care for her."

"Don't be an imbecile."

Ghlee would not cease his gape on Tolvar. "Huh. I always imagined this day somewhat differently."

Tolvar moved to the bars so fast that anyone but Ghlee would've startled backward and tripped over the wooden bench. But Ghlee stood there, arms crossed, fighting Tolvar's glare with a pleasant one of his own.

"I do not *care* for the girl, Ghlee. Make no mistake. But she's trying to insert herself in this cause, and she will only hurt herself in the process. I do not wish for more deaths to be on my conscience."

"Suit yourself," Ghlee said, casually sitting back on the bench, picking up the flask. "Oh well. She's leaving anyway."

Ghlee was about to take another swig when a voice crashed down the stairs at the end of the dungeon's corridor. Ghlee stood, and Tolvar leaned against the bars to try and better his vantage.

"Sir Ghlee! The Befallen! Sloane!" Alvie's voice grew louder as he neared.

Close behind, a guard tailed him. "I told you, you cannot come down here!"

"What about Sloane?" Tolvar could barely contain the emotion in his voice.

"You gotta come, Ghlee," Alvie said.

"What about Sloane?" Tolvar shouted.

"Sir Tolvar!" Alvie said. "I didn't know you was down here. The Befallen struck Kestriel..."

"Kestriel?" both men said together.

"...they locked Sloane in the barracks. Awful scene. She was shouting at—"

"Unlock this door," Ghlee commanded the guard standing next to Alvie.

"I don't have orders to—"

"Unlock this stars-forsaken door," Tolvar bellowed.

Ghlee simply looked at the guard as if to say, 'are you going to disobey *that* command?'

"Right. Now." Tolvar growled.

"Aye, sir," the guard said, nervously fiddling with the ring of keys, purposely not meeting either man's eyes, before unlocking the door.

Tolvar stepped through the door, picking up Ghlee's flask. "Right. That's one way to be released. I hope Pharrell is in the mood for another fight."

CHAPTER
34

Sloane

They'd placed seven men around the barrack to guard her. Seven. What did they think she was capable of?

For the first hour, Sloane yelled in a constant barrage that she hoped would drive everyone mad. In the second hour, her voice grew hoarse, and when she asked for water through the door, silence responded in kind. Alvie spoke to the guards, but she couldn't hear much of anything that was said. So, in the third hour, Sloane, growing bored and restless, began singing. Her voice wasn't as good as Ma's had been, but it was better than Father's. She started with "The Knave and the Hoshefer," followed by "Shadow Cats Shan't Eat Me," light-hearted songs meant for children. They'd been Sherik's favorites. Eventually, she grew somber thinking of Sherik, and the songs changed as she recollected her little brother's curls, the laughter in his tone. Ma's sweet voice that would lull Sloane to sleep. Father's wink when he noticed Sloane wasn't asleep yet in the one-room hovel but didn't tell Ma. And Joah? Joah, who'd loved songs about hunting and heroes.

"Joah, how could you?" Sloane whispered, before starting into "The Lady in the Moonbeam," one of Sloane's favorites, about a woman transformed into anything she wanted when the light of the moon descended on her.

"*And the lady shall be whoever she'll be, and the lady in moonbeams will fly away free.*"

Sloane finished, humming the tune again, letting the last lyrics hang in the air.

She couldn't stop her thoughts. The Befallen had struck Kestriel. She couldn't believe it. According to the message tied to the raven, it had surrounded a few blocks of the northern end of the city. The note described it like a dark mist. Just like the witness of Slough Groth had said. Two incidents with witnesses now. Was the Befallen growing stronger?

She couldn't completely dismiss the pang of guilt. If she'd been forthcoming from the start, would she have been able to convince the Order to act? Mayhap have a plan in place?

But nay. The Order had shown their true colors.

And so coupled with her dream and the fact she was supposed to be dragged from Dara Keep today as soon as the wagon came, Sloane hadn't been able to contain herself any longer.

She'd spent the last three days—three days! —trying to do something, to make amends. But it was as if Dara Keep had become a deserted place. When she walked the corridors, knights spotted her and turned the other direction, disappearing. The library was perpetually empty, and she'd found nothing on the Cibil of the Nay Moon. She'd seen no one. Not Henry, whom she'd attempted to find to change his mind again. She'd even tried sending him notes via knights, who offered confused expressions in return. Not Tolvar, whom she was desperate to tell about the sovereign and the Cibil. Not Ghlee, until finally this morning, she'd found and told him what she'd overheard in the stable.

And meanwhile, waiting to be flung from this place, she'd watched knights do nothing. Nothing!

Nay, she hadn't been able to stop from throwing herself into a rage.

Someone needs to do something.

Did these knights think that their oaths to the stars protected them here? It couldn't be. When they heard the news from Kestriel, she'd scrutinized the faces of everyone in the courtyard, everyone except Tolvar, Ghlee—where were they anyway? —and Henry, who felt like a ghost now. Cowards. These were the faces of cowards. Including that tyrant Pharrell and that arrogant Kek. The Order of Siria had come here, sworn to find the Unsung. They'd sworn to help.

"What's wrong with you all?" Sloane shouted. "The Befallen claims more victims, and still, you stand here doing nothing! You're supposed to be brave knights! You're supposed to help! You have the Edan Lore now! You know we must act before the Azure Moon rises! Yet, you stand here like cowards!"

At first, everyone simply stood, dumbstruck.

"But nay! You let the sovereign and that puppet man control you!"

Out of the corner of her eye, she saw Henry coming to join them. She pointed a finger at him.

"You should be ashamed! You lost your own daughter! We could defeat the Befallen. All we need is to find the Cibil of the Nay Moon!"

"Cibil of the what?" someone asked.

"That's enough." Pharrell's grip on her arm hurt.

"Let go of me!" Sloane shouted, watching two knights hold Alvie back.

"Take her to the barracks and lock her in until that blasted wagon gets here!" Pharrell had shouted.

Coward.

Sloane stopped humming and balled up her hands. She wasn't at all sorry for her outburst.

Commotion sounded outside. Then the door to the barracks swung open, and Tolvar, Ghlee, and Alvie stepped inside.

"Let's find Pharrell," Tolvar said. "If your words can't sway him, my fists will."

In Pharrell's study, the door of which was now splintered and missing a doorknob courtesy of Tolvar, Sloane scanned the room. A tapestry, of what she assumed was a StarSeer, a radiant woman gazing to a sky speckled with stars, was the only decor. Apart from the desk Pharrell stood behind as though it were a barrier, the study didn't have much furniture. In the corner sat three grim men—two nursing new black eyes they'd received in their attempt to block Tolvar's entrance— and a shelf that held mostly weapons. Small wonder none had been used when they'd first barged in here.

The initial scuffle over, the room's air remained taut with tension. Next to Sloane, stood Tolvar, Ghlee, and Alvie. Kek stood near the door with five knights beside him. It was crowded. Missing though, was Henry.

"This is the last straw, Tolvar!" Pharrell said, pounding on the desk, "You're to leave immediately. You can take your chances with the sovereign or King Rian or the Befallen itself, but you go! And you," he pointed at Sloane, "should never have been allowed entry here."

"What is the sovereign paying you?" Tolvar said evenly.

"How dare you? I am a knight of honor."

"The stars must laugh at that phrase," Tolvar said.

Kek drew his sword, but Pharrell put up his hands. "Enough." He glanced at a side door. "We're following orders commanded by the sovereign, nothing more. We're outsiders, blast it all! But assuming we *did* have an Unsung, we're supposed to determine the night of the Azure Moon, and with it, a goddess who may or may not exist—"

"She does exist!" Sloane shouted over Pharrell's words.

"—who apparently has the only weapon to conquer the Befallen. Yet, again, we know not when the Azure Moon comes. No one does." The grey whiskers above his mouth twitched. "Believe it or not, I have actually made inquiries."

"The Cibil of the Nay Moon knows," Sloane said.

"Who is that?" someone asked.

The focus on Sloane was acute. But this is what she'd wanted. *Don't be a sook.*

Sloane took a deep breath and told the story of the ancient

diviner and his powers. She kept her fists at her sides, ignoring how childish it sounded—telling a fairy story to a band of knights.

"Your answer to this is a mysterious oracle who grants anyone who finds him on the Nay Moon the answer to one question?" Pharrell made a face that left naught to the imagination what he thought of that idea. "You're missing a detail. Even if he *ever* existed, if no one has a tale of him that is under one hundred years old, he must be long since dead."

"Girl, you are as daft as a spirit dancing in the Falling Leaves Moon," Kek said.

"Careful," Tolvar uttered.

"Have you not your own priestesses of fortune in the Capella Realm?" She put her hands behind her back so Pharrell couldn't detect them trembling.

"The StarSeers?" Pharrell sat and leaned back in his chair, his eyes glancing at the tapestry. "The Five's whereabouts and their guidance are well-known and not shadowed in unnecessary mystery."

Sloane didn't miss the pointed remark. She shivered, her dream and the crimson moon flickering through her thoughts. "Sir Pharrell, you say you're a knight of honor. You swore to help. If the StarSeers can exist, and the Befallen can exist, and the goddesses of the moon can exist—"

Kek snickered. This time it was Alvie who threw out a cuss to silence him.

"Where is Henry?" Sloane asked making Pharrell give an expression of surprise. 'Twas obvious he wasn't aware he and Sloane had met. "He knows about the Cibil. He's here on the sovereign's behalf. If we might convince him—"

Tolvar interrupted, clearly at his patience's end. "Aye. Where is this Henry who's manipulating your strings like a master of marionettes? I don't care if he is some baron. His eyes will blacken, same as any man."

His words brought new shoves, shouts, and swearing from everyone.

"Stop!" But Sloane's voice drowned in the racket. "We should all be on the same side!"

"That's quite enough." Henry stood in the open side doorway. In his arms, he held a large leatherbound book, the spine of which was barely holding itself together. The Order knights stood at attention.

"No need for more violence," Henry said, making his way next to Sloane and setting the book on Pharrell's desk. "Allow me to introduce myself properly. I am the Baron of Fenella. Lord Henry Gwynmyer."

Sloane's eyes widened. The baron. Henry was the baron for whom Father had made a saddle all those years ago. She was about to say so when Tolvar said, "I presume that's supposed to mean something to me."

Sloane expected more shouting, and mayhap a few more fists swung, but Henry held up a hand. "Peace, Sir Tolvar. Things are not as simple as you and Sloane would have them be. To go against the sovereign—"

"Defeating the Befallen is all that matters. No one should know that more than you," Sloane said. "Please, m'lord. I know you to be an honorable man. Years ago, my father made a saddle for you—"

"A saddle, you say?"

"Aye, and you wrote a letter of thanks to him, even though he was but a lowly leatherworker. A man who would send thanks in his own words must be a man of honor, m'lord."

"Enough of this!" Pharrell said, gesturing to the knights in the doorway before pointing to Sloane and Alvie. "They go!!"

The commotion started again. Tolvar, the loudest, proclaimed he would break the next man's arm who touched Sloane.

"Peace!" Henry held up his palm. He studied Sloane as though she were a freshly woven tapestry he was admiring. "So, I meet the daughter of an artist. Your father, too, was a man of honor. I've never had a finer saddle before or since. Honestly, any leatherwork." He paused. "I received your many, many notes. 'Tis difficult to ignore one such as you, Sloane of Mohn. You remind me of my daughter."

Henry cleared his throat to hide his eyes glassing over. "You truly believe that our hope lies in this Cibil?"

Sloane straightened her shoulders. "Aye, m'lord. I *know* it does. Like I know the moon shall rise in the sky."

Pharrell muttered something under his breath.

Henry quirked an eyebrow. "The moon that rises in the sky each night is a very contrast to itself the night before."

"While that may be true," Sloane said, "its constancy is reserved in that contrast. Our doubts may subside and then swell, but our faith is the light that shall persist, even when we cannot see."

No one responded until finally, Henry took Sloane's hand, his grip warm and tender. "Well said."

"This is a bloody mess," Pharrell said, scratching his chin and surveying the study.

"As I said, to go against the sovereign will most assuredly bring hefty consequences."

Sloane turned her eyes to the floor.

"But I've hung my honor in the balance long enough," Henry said. "My daughter would be...displeased." Then he addressed Pharrell. "'Tis time for light to persist, as this young lady points out. I've learned quite a bit of information as of late. First is this." Henry opened the book on Pharrell's desk to a map that covered both pages. It was a map of Deogol. The first place Sloane noted was a large green place. The artist had dotted it with tiny trees.

"Ayla!" Sloane exclaimed. There it was. The place reverently referred to in the Edan Lore.

"Aye." Henry bobbed his head. "But here," his index finger traced from there a few inches on the page to a grey spot, "is a swampland known as Kage Duna."

Multiple men shuddered. Sloane had never heard of the place.

"What's Kage Duna?"

"Only the worst place ever in Deogol," Alvie supplied.

"Aye," Henry said. "But look."

Next to his index finger there was a miniscule inscription. She couldn't make it out.

"Stars," Pharrell said, pulling an eyeglass from a drawer. He handed it to Sloane.

It read: *Home of the Cibil of the Nay Moon.*

Sloane gasped.

"After we met in the library. And after all those notes," Henry said. "I wondered if there might exist any clue about where the Cibil might reside. Tales, after all, begin in some sort of truth. After finding nothing here, I sent for this book—my own. Been in my family for generations. So, there it is. The Cibil, if he's still alive, resides in Kage Duna."

"You sent for this book. That must have been days ago when you made your decision about going against the sovereign." Sloane met eyes with Henry.

"Aye. That brings me to other information I've discovered. The sovereign isn't the only one with spies. Sir Tolvar, I feel certain you can confirm what I've learned about the Brones?"

Tolvar gave a brief nod.

"I'm afraid the sovereign has turned to new tactics, Captain Pharrell. One which I cannot condone. Right. 'Tis time we formed a new council. One without His Majesty's sanction. This has become bigger than all of us. Whether we sit on a throne or a sty. Isn't that right, Sloane?"

Sloane wasn't certain she'd taken in everything he'd said but nodded.

"Good. Then we'll begin preparations for travel to Kage Duna."

"You're certain about this?" Pharrell gruffed at Henry, eyeing the map. "This could be naught more than a fool's errand. And as you said, there will be hefty consequences. Surely the sovereign will desire to disband the Order of Siria all over again. Not to mention, it'll mean your title when he learns of this."

"'Tis no matter," Henry said. "We have something the sovereign does not." And his gaze on Sloane was as steady as it was kind. "The Unsung."

CHAPTER
35

Sloane

Was it possible to have so much occur in one day? In the time it took for the sun to rise and steadily plummet to the other side of the earth, could so much actually happen?

The air was changed, and not because it was the night of the Falling Leaves Moon; the veil between the living and dead blurred like ripples disturbing an otherwise still pond. Dara Keep was different. In one day, everything was different.

Sloane knelt alone in the courtyard, guards patrolling the ramparts of the castle with purpose in their step. The air of the Great Hall, which Sloane and Alvie had been allowed to enter for supper this evening, felt charged. Over the meal, plans were made and re-hashed and re-formed; so many throwing out ideas, and questions, and scenarios for problems that plans were remade again, tightened, and secured until every last obstacle was squeezed from them. Aye, it was as if the Order of Siria had been reborn. The drab and weedy lot of complacent men were replaced with the legendary knights of the Order of Siria. Brilliant strategists. Bold soldiers. Brave believers with a cause.

The only problem was Sloane felt utterly unchanged.

When Henry had proclaimed her as the Unsung, every part of Sloane wanted to duck into a crevice in the wall and burrow herself into oblivion. It'd not helped that the reactions in the study, except for Alvie, had been a mixture of laughter and lament. But Henry, like the night they'd met in the library, had put his tactics of ease to good use. And now, the whole of the Order of Siria was tiptoeing around Sloane as if she were a goddess of the moon. Even Alvie.

"I knew it!" he boasted. "You don't come out of the Befallen three times and not be the Unsung. It's been obvious to me all along."

The only one who wasn't treating Sloane as if she should be fallen over was Tolvar, who was his usual grumpy self.

I'm not the Unsung, the part of Sloane, who was so welled up with emotions she could burst, breathed out as she waited for the full moon to rise in the courtyard.

The other part of Sloane, who was paying more attention to the chilled breeze in the air, wanted to agree and disagree all at the same time. Someone had to do something, and although Sloane could not quite muster the courage to tell herself that, mayhap, just mayhap, there was something she could do. She could go along with Henry and the Order of Siria's theory if it meant *she* could do something.

And so, plans had been made and remade until Sloane's stomach felt it would jolt out of her being. They were going to Kage Duna. The Order of Siria was going to escort Sloane there to ask the Cibil the only question that mattered: When does the Azure Moon rise next?

But in all these plans, Sloane was having trouble keeping everything straight in her mind. Her head was still spinning about what Tolvar and Henry had revealed about the sovereign when they'd met in the council room last night.

Not only had the sovereign commanded the Order of Siria to stand down, but the sovereign apparently had a second company to rid Deogol of the Befallen, some band calling themselves the Brones.

"Naturally, I was keen on any idea that promised to save the country. The Edan Lore of the Unsung is ancient, clouded in mystery, and a foolhardy dream. That is, until I discovered exactly what the Brones were up to," Henry said. "We must rely on the Unsung now."

"Whether or not Sloane is to be the Unsung is not our most pressing topic," Tolvar said, his eyes scanning the room in a chiding manner as everyone else gaped at Sloane in a way that oscillated between reverence and being ready to send her into the den of a shadow cat. "We've no sign Sloane is the Unsung, and furthermore —" He did not finish. "The most pressing matter is the sovereign. He's lying to the people of Deogol, using these Brones to seek the weapon mentioned in the Edan Lore. The sovereign is going to try to send the Befallen elsewhere. To the Capella Realm."

Pharrell swore louder than the others at the table, some of whom pounded fists on its surface.

"I don't need to reiterate how disastrous that would be for not only the Realm but all of Tasia. There's no confining it once on the continent. At least here, on an island—" Tolvar cleared his throat.

"How do you know this?" Pharrell looked aged.

"I was told."

Sloane wondered if Pharrell would question him further, and from Tolvar's scowl, he seemed ready, but Pharrell merely exchanged glances with Kek and Henry and nodded for Tolvar to continue.

"What's worse is the supposed leader of the Brones spoke of the Curse of Adrienne."

Not everyone in the council room gasped at the forbidden word, but all flinched. The Curse of Adrienne, the unknown darkness buried thousands of years ago, wasn't it? Sloane didn't know what hushed stories about the Curse of Adrienne were true and what were told to frighten children into obedience, but it was never spoken of lightly. The word Adrienne was not spoken at all. And for Tolvar to speak of it in *this* room, one which appeared to be sacred to the Order of Siria, meant something graver than the Befallen.

"Could the two be connected?" Sloane wondered aloud, bringing silence with her question, not answers. There was true fear on many faces staring at her in the torchlight flickering throughout the room.

"What you're suggesting is more terrifying than one can ponder." Henry leaned forward, the torchlight making his fearful face garish.

"No one knows what the Befallen is," Sloane said carefully. "Could it be that this is a manifestation of...the Curse?"

"If that's so," said a knight to Sloane's left, "what do you believe it means that the leader spoke of the curse, Sir Tolvar?"

"Either the sovereign is not aware of the Brones' full intentions, or the sovereign is fool enough himself to think he may harness Adrienne's dark power. Mayhap with this weapon."

"Tolvar, you must cease saying that word," stammered Clive, the tan, clean-shaven knight next to Kek, the twinge on his face reflected on everyone's.

"I cannot believe the sovereign would try something so evil, no matter his desperation," Henry said firmly.

"He wouldn't be the first," Pharrell said.

"Then 'tis time we act," Kek said, standing. "Captain, the Order of Siria came to Deogol with a purpose and vow. We shall uphold that. Time to start planning."

"Hear, hear!" Four knights stood, too, Ghlee being one of them.

"We're all going to get ourselves killed," Pharrell said, but to Sloane's surprise, stood as well. Kek clapped him on the back.

"One last thing." Tolvar's expression was pained as he uttered his next words. "The night the scholar died, he told me one last piece of information that may help us yet will certainly end up being a curse."

"What is it?" Henry asked for everyone.

"This is all nonsense," Tolvar said, standing and moving to a side table where a bottle of wine sat. He poured himself a drink and did not speak until the contents were drained.

"Apparently—I cannot believe I'm going to say this—to speak to the goddess of the Azure Moon, one must have a small moonrock called the Edan Stone."

"I've never heard of such a thing," Henry said, turning to Sloane. "Have you?"

"Nay, m'lord." It was clear to her now why Tolvar looked pained. To him, this was all still rubbish. How could a knight sworn to find the Unsung be unwilling to believe in the goddesses of the moon? Could he not see that everything about the Edan Lore was connected?

The others started talking about what and where this stone could be, but Sloane didn't listen. Something was nipping at the back of her shoulders, as if she'd walked into the hovel to fetch something for Ma, only to forget what it was, yet standing there all the same waiting for the object to place itself again in her mind. Something strained to wedge itself into her mind. But her mind forced whatever it was aside when Tolvar spoke again.

"If we are to believe this, even finding the supposed Cibil of the Nay Moon will do us no good if we do, indeed, need this object."

"We are to believe this, Sir Tolvar," Sloane said. "And we shall find the Cibil, and we shall find the Edan Stone, whatever it is."

There was an uncomfortable pause until Pharrell broke it by speaking about the preparations they would need to make. Tolvar and Sloane did not make eye contact again.

She didn't want to think about that anymore.

Sloane exhaled, taking in the chill in the autumn air, the essence of the darkness covering the world, the din of knights busying themselves with preparations in the outer bailey beyond the wall, and brought herself back to the courtyard where she knelt. The Falling Leaves Moon would rise at any moment, and, if the goddess blessed her this night, she might glimpse a ghost of her family. For she was certain, contemplating everything that had happened the last day, Sloane needed the encircling comfort only her lost ones could provide. Aye, she had Alvie and the support of the Order now, but she needed more. Solace. Otherwise, part of her was going to easily convince the other part that she should simply run away.

The moon cuff twirled on her wrist, the fingers of her other hand stroking over the indentations of the moons. The Dew Moon, a flower; the Mead Moon, a goblet; the Rainless Moon, a droplet; and so on. When she grazed the Azure Moon, the cuff ceased to spin, and Sloane inhaled the significance of the symbol. Why had Father placed the Azure Moon on her moon cuff?

Something tingled at the back of her collarbone. Different than she'd felt yesterday. A realization? Panic? Or simply her deepest desire she could not utter aloud?

But 'tis on my moon cuff, reasoned the part of Sloane, who, in that moment, felt like her faith was wildfire.

You? A crippled daughter from Mohn, a village that is nothing now? Besides, deep down, do you even believe in the Unsung? The other part squirmed off the sensation.

Mayhap it is as I told Tolvar. Mayhap someone simply needs to decide to be the Unsung.

It's not you.

Sloane scratched the back of her neck, studying the moon cuff, and argued with herself no more. The moon was rising.

She held the strap she'd made for Alvie at her side. It was finished, and she couldn't be certain if she was more excited to show it to Father's spirit or to Alvie.

The glory of the Falling Leaves Moon was in its enormity. It hung against the ebony autumn night sky like an incandescent ivory sphere. Was it its size that blurred life and death? That chilled over the land? That ushered in the new season born bitter and biting?

Sloane shivered.

A prayer, then. For guidance. For assuredness. And, most of all, for the chance to peek through the boundaries of the heavens.

Just as she'd done near the bog on the Harvest Moon, Sloane formed herself into her prayer position. Hands. Heart. Head. All connected.

The prayer Sloane pleaded was in her heart. It swelled and filled her. She needed no words.

Gradually, the warmth that laced her being as she thought on her family spread through every patch of Sloane. In a moment all too short and all too peaceful, she was full of love and serenity and every goodness she'd ever had and ever been.

When at last Sloane dared, she opened her eyes, hoping to see something, anything that would be a sign of Father, Ma, and Sherik. But when she blinked into the ever-cooling darkness, the only sight in front of Sloane was the pale orb that she was convinced had created so much warmth not a moment ago.

Nothing.

Was that how it worked? True, Sloane did not know how the Falling Leaves Moon goddess parted the veil. She'd never prayed to see the dead before. There'd never been a need. Mayhap her family could see her, and even if she couldn't see them in return, she needed to trust, to believe that the smudges in the lines of heaven were there.

"Father," Sloane whispered. "Look." She held up the strap for Alvie, her lips forming a closed-lipped smile when she beheld her own embossment work on the leather. Holding it up, nothing felt different. She lowered it to her lap, her eyes fixed on the moon still.

"Tell Sherik I saw the sea. It smelled so salty. I never knew air could smell like that." For some reason, the stench of Branwell's bog entered her mind. "I guess I didn't know air could smell like a lot of things."

"Ma, I'm trying to live up to your goodness. I'm trying..." Great tears rolled down her cheeks. "I'm trying."

Nothing felt different, but Sloane hoped the goddess of the Falling Leaves Moon had granted her heart's greatest wish: to be with her family again.

As the warmth took leave and left naught but the night's chill, Sloane came back to the courtyard and to her surroundings, which all the while hadn't changed.

"Spying on me, Sir Tolvar?" Sloane turned her head to address him behind her.

"I've never seen anyone pray with such earnestness before." He crouched beside her, not looking at her but at the great circle of the moon above them. "What did you pray for?"

Sloane stiffened. For one so private, Tolvar certainly was impertinent about the privacy of others. "For you to cease your misjudgments of me."

Tolvar cocked an eyebrow. "Mayhap I am the only one who sees you for what you are."

"And what is that?"

How was it that Tolvar could so easily agitate Sloane? But she was ready for more of his disparagement. He would not slander her prayer or the closeness to her family she longed for.

There was that piercing stare again, as if Tolvar's eyes could dive into the very depths of her and pluck out her soul should he desire.

"A brave woman who is going to get herself killed."

Sloane snorted to escape his gaze. "If it would stop the Befallen, that wouldn't be so terrible. I'd see my family again."

Tolvar nodded, easing himself into a sitting position. Evidently, he planned to stay.

"In truth, I prayed to glimpse my family. The veil is blurred this eve of the Falling Leaves."

"That so?"

"Aye." She wasn't going to be baited. "The goddess parts the veil, and those who are among the stars may gaze upon those who miss them. And see."

"What do they see?" Sloane was quite aware Tolvar resumed his intense gaze of her, his eyes roving her face as if he sought to memorize it.

"They see that love can travel across the sky and the heavens, all the way to the stars."

Tolvar searched the specks of light. "In the Capella Realm, the stars are viewed differently. We pray not to the goddesses of the moon."

"I hope you're not starting an argument with me again, Sir Tolvar. I take comfort in my faith that my family is there above." She didn't mean to, but there was no missing the emotion in her voice.

"Nay, you mistake me. I find that I, too, take comfort in your faith. 'Tis a precious thing that not many are brave enough to carry— in either realm."

There was a lingering moment of naught but eyes meeting. It was broken when Tolvar procured a flask from his tunic and took a long pull from it. He wiped his mouth on his sleeve and turned back to her before noticing her grimace.

"What is it?"

"Don't you think that a knight such as yourself can learn to cope without that?"

"What am I to gather from *that* remark?" The flask disappeared back into his tunic, his face growing flush.

"Only what I've told you before, that you're a drunkard."

The scowl attacked her again, but she wouldn't cower.

"I do not answer to you, but if you insist on throwing out judgments of your own, you're welcome to your own company," Tolvar said.

"Stop," Sloane said, pulling Tolvar's sleeve to keep him from standing. Neither part of her could explain why she did. "I'm sorry. But you must realize what it's doing to you."

"You're starting to sound like Ghlee." Tolvar drew the flask back out, this time taking a longer drink.

Despite the many words simmering below the surface, Sloane chose not to make further remarks. She couldn't help but remember the story Ghlee had told her about Tolvar's father and the others. 'Twas a wonder, mayhap, he didn't drink more.

"Do you pray to the gods of the stars, Sir Tolvar?"

His laugh made liquor trickle down his beard. "Nay. I am not a praying man. The stars have nothing for me."

Sloane wasn't certain what that meant but was sure it had something to do with the incident at Thorin Court. What would Tolvar say if she told him she knew?

"And I am certain, given your constant cynicism, that you've never prayed to the goddesses of the moon."

He surprised her with his next words. "I have once. Ghlee talked me into it."

"What moon?" Sloane found herself asking.

"The Prodigal Moon, I believe."

"The moon of generosity."

"Oh aye, very generous."

"Why not pray now? To the Falling Leaves Moon. Mayhap you'll see someone you love."

Tolvar gave her a confused look, and she hoped she wasn't too obvious. "I'm not a praying man."

"'Tis never too late, Sir Tolvar. Come, I'll show you how."

CHAPTER
36

Tolvar

Tolvar allowed Sloane to arrange his hands into her prayer position. As she spoke of what she was doing, he gaped at the tiny woman, her words lost to him.

When she seemed satisfied with how she'd arranged his hands, her smile was as full as the moon.

"But I don't have one of those wristlets you wear," Tolvar pointed, unclasping his hands.

"You need not a moon cuff to pray. Prayer is for any soul with a genuine keenness."

"In that case, this is lost on me." Tolvar moved to stand, but Sloane tugged at him again.

"What are you afraid of, Sir Tolvar?" It was as if this absurd woman knew each and every nerve of Tolvar's to dance upon.

"I am afraid of nothing," he said, allowing her to again arrange his hands. Her smaller hands were not smooth like those of ladies at court. Sloane's were calloused and dry. The hands of someone who had purpose. Before Tolvar could stop himself, he ran his thumb over the veins that ran up to her arm.

She paused. She was so close. Tolvar could feel her sweet breath on his face. This close, even in the darkness, he saw three tiny freckles on the side of her small nose. Everything about her was delicate. Except mayhap her lips, full, slightly parted, and something he particularly wanted to kiss.

This time, Sloane broke the gaze between them. "Sir Tolvar, I—" She cleared her throat and wouldn't look at him again. Did she dislike him so much?

"Please, show me what to do." He could think of nothing else to say. The woman looked as skittish as a hoshefer. Sloane nodded, but this time, she didn't reach for Tolvar's hands; rather, she modeled for him what to do.

"Then you place your chin upon your fist. Aye, like that."

"And now?"

"And now you pray." She said no more but retreated into herself, her head bowed, eyes closed.

Tolvar could not force his eyes off her. That jutted chin, her dainty, yet determined, jawline.

Come now, Wolf. You've more discipline than this.

But he found moments passed before he finally dipped his chin to meet his fist as Sloane was doing.

With his eyes closed, Tolvar was even more aware of Sloane's soft breathing next to him. The bustling of some of the Order knights in the background made his legs ache to stand. How foolish he must appear sitting next to this girl, "praying."

But after a time, he sensed the beams of moonlight upon him. It wasn't warm like the sun or astounding like the glittering stars, but he felt something, nonetheless.

This may be the most witless thing I have ever done.

But no sooner had Tolvar thought that, then he remembered the time he'd been thrown from an unbroken horse as a boy because he'd boasted to his father that he could ride it despite its obvious wildness. He'd broken his arm that day.

"I should have listened to you," Tolvar found himself whispering. "I wish I'd had more time with you."

Through his closed eyelids, Tolvar sensed a bright light before him. He opened his eyes and found the transparent and fluttering form of his father before him. His neatly trimmed beard, straight nose, and creases at the corners of his eyes, all as he remembered him.

Tolvar dared not say a word but gaped, stunned, at what he was certain must be some sort of illusion.

Mayhap Sloane is right; I need to stop drinking.

His father had his familiar close-lipped smile, and it occurred to Tolvar that although he could see him, his father wasn't going to speak.

Then a voice above Tolvar, distant and echoed, spoke.

"To the one they call Wolf. Let go of your self-loathing. Let go of your regrets. Forbearance is in your future, and she shall need it."

Tolvar, sweat beading down his neck, scanned up and around. Sloane was completely still next to him, seemingly unaware of what was happening.

Had he truly heard something? Was the ghost of his father actually standing before him? Tolvar wanted to wipe his brow but worried if he broke his position, then his father would disappear.

I miss you, Father, Tolvar's mind yelled. *I miss you, and I'm sorry I failed you. I'm so sorry.* His eyes glassed over, making the sight of his father blurrier.

"To the one they call Wolf. We watch you. Do not forget. Forbearance. She shall need it."

He nodded slightly, wiping his eyes on his shoulder so as to keep his hands clasped together.

"Let go of your guilt."

Tolvar sobbed. How could he? How could he ever let go of that? His father stood before him as a ghost because of him.

"Look upon your father and see no sorrow."

Tolvar did. His father beamed at him, nodding approval.

"Have peace," the voice said, sounding more faraway than before. The image of his father faded, and Tolvar threw out his hands as if to stop him.

"Father, no! I'm sorry!"

"Sir Tolvar." Sloane's palm rested on his forearm. She was pale.

"You did this!" Tolvar yelled, not bothering to wipe his cheeks, giving her an expression reserved for enemies. "You did this!"

"Sir Tolvar! What—"

"Do not say a word." With shaking hands, Tolvar removed his flask from his tunic. It was almost to his lips before he gave it a long look and flung it onto the ground, walking away.

CHAPTER
37

Sloane

I t'd taken time to convince Alvie to remove his peg leg so Sloane could attach the new leather strap to it when they sat in the stable tack room later that night. On the underside of the strap, Sloane had sewn in wool that she'd asked Henry to find for her. This new strap would be stronger but wouldn't bite into Alvie's skin as the rope did.

She ignored Alvie's silence; for him to be without words meant something indeed.

"There," Sloane said, after she'd shown Alvie how to buckle the new strap across his leg. "How does that feel?"

Alvie shifted his leg, still quiet, admiring the strap. Sloane checked the tightness, ensuring the strap was snug against the leg, but not too tight.

"Fact o'matter is, Sloane, this is the bestest, most amazin' gift I ever received. I don't deserve a friend like you."

"'Twas nothing, Alvie. I'm sure I'd be dead on the side of the road somewhere if you and Lauge hadn't come along."

"My, my," Alvie continued to inspect the strap. "I might be able to run wearin' this thing. Maybe I could outrun Sir Clive. Blimey. They have to let me join the Order of Siria now, Sloane!"

His silver-toothed grin momentarily made Sloane forget about being cursed at by Tolvar. She didn't know what had happened, but she knew the face of fear when she saw it. Tolvar had seen something, or someone, when he'd prayed.

Part of Sloane was jealous. But the other part who remembered the whites of Tolvar's eyes shivered.

Alvie rolled his hose over his peg leg, then studied her in an alien manner. "You truly think the Cibil of the Nay Moon is out there?"

"Course. But I know you don't."

"I will if you say I should." It was a gaze of rare seriousness.

"Alvie, eventually, you're going to have to find faith of your own."

"Nah." He stretched out his leg, then stood, marching in place. "That's what you're here for."

"What if—"

"Don't start that. There is no 'what if.' Not no more. 'What ifs' are nothin' but the stench of fear tryin' to stink us out."

This made Sloane laugh. "You're never lost for—" She stopped.

"What is it?" Alvie scrunched his face in concern.

"The bog."

"What bog?"

"The bog at Branwell. Remember that night of the Harvest Moon? We saw something in the bog. You remember, don't you?" Her words spilled out, matching the beats of her heart. She had to blab them out before she forgot the clue all over again. "That night. I held something. Something in the bog."

"What're you talkin' about?"

"The bog. The stone. The—" The clue became a tangible object in her mind. "Oh my stars! I know where the Edan Stone is!"

Sloane had never stood so fast.

"What in stars' name are you talkin' about?"

"The Edan Stone!"

"I remember what the Edan Stone is, Sloane. What you talkin' about?"

"I had it." She paused. She could almost feel the weight of what she'd thought was an onyx pendant resting against her chest. "It was in Mohn. I found it in the elder's cottage." Stars. She bit her lip in remembrance. "Then it was stolen...by the Ravyns."

"The Ravyns?"

"Aye, that day they robbed me. They took it. If they don't still have it, they can tell us what happened to it. They can..." Joah. To find and face the Ravyns again, Sloane would have to face Joah. No one here even knew about Joah. Not even Alvie.

"Sloane, you need to slow—"

"We have to find Sir Ghlee!" And Sloane strode out of the stables, Alvie by her side.

For a group supposedly leaving for Kage Duna in the morning, there certainly were a lot of people still up. Sloane dashed around Dara Keep, asking everyone she encountered to find Sir Ghlee. The alarm in her voice caught everyone's attention, and soon, twelve or so knights raced in search of him.

They found him in a small room furnished with a desk and two chairs, Ghlee in one, Tolvar in the other. Surprisingly, Ghlee was the only one with a goblet in his hand.

Guess there was no hope of speaking to Ghlee on his own.

"What's happened?" Ghlee and Tolvar both stood, their stance ready for anything.

Sloane avoided Tolvar's eyes. "The Edan Stone. I know where it is!"

A knight standing behind Sloane said, "Wake Sir Pharrell immediately," and two knights sprinted down the corridor.

"How can you possibly know where the Edan Stone is?" Tolvar asked, his tone guarded.

"I unknowingly had it two moons ago until I was robbed by the Ravyns. They took it." This time, she did face Tolvar. "And you need not scoff. I'm absolutely certain."

CHAPTER
38

Sloane

"If death be my destination, may my journey live on." Sloane whispered the traditional traveling prayer from where she sat atop the chestnut mare Tolvar had helped her mount.

She shivered in the late autumn morning air, the droplets of frosty dew stifling the surrounding fields. Sloane wrapped the cloak tighter around her as she waited for the others to finish preparing the last supplies for the journey. Was she really going to face the Ravyns again? Joah again? Part of Sloane was still in awe she was here. No one had been in support of her coming, not even Alvie.

Henry had said she was too important. Some other words had been spoken by others about her abilities. But the part of Sloane who was exhausted from being questioned found just the right amount of rage and demanded to go.

"Besides, I'm the only one who knows what it looks like," Sloane said.

She again suppressed Henry's words about her. The Unsung.

She glanced at Tolvar, who was throwing out commands as if they were axes in a tournament. He'd been the most vocal about Sloane staying behind.

Alvie trotted over on his own horse and eyed the mare. "You sure you're going to be all right ridin' that?"

"I'll be fine," Sloane said. "You?"

"Nothin' to it," Alvie said. A strange club hung from his saddle.

"Though I imagine my backside will feel like ground meat by the time we get there."

"Where did you get that?" Sloane pointed to the club.

"Tolvar gave it to me. Neat, huh? It ain't wood neither. 'Tis some kind of metal. Tolvar didn't know what. But you know what I think it is?"

Sloane waited.

"Starstone."

"You can't be serious." Starstone was an incredibly strong—and outrageously rare—metal. There was even a legend that surrounded it. But this club appeared to be the texture of wood. "Why would Tolvar give that to you?"

Alvie shrugged, giving the club a pat. "Said he didn't want it. Mine now."

Sloane disregarded the club she was certain was *not* starstone, silently counting the knights. "Do you think we have enough?" Nineteen. And Alvie. With his new club. How many Ravyns were there? Two dozen? The day on the road to Asana seemed like years ago.

"Sloane, these are only the most famed knights in all of Tasia. And we got the Wolf, and me, of course."

"Of course," she said, counting the knights again.

They'd spent the last days planning—more planning—on how to find and overtake the Ravyns. The raven keeper had sent out a dozen of his black-feathered messengers asking for sightings of the bandits. Late last night, a raven came back with a reply—the Ravyns had been sighted on the Nerezza Plains, a mass of rolling fields that would resemble a sea of dried earth this time of year. Only one day's ride away. Which was good. The Nay Moon was eight days away, and if they didn't get to Kage Duna by then, they would need to wait an entire moon before they could find the Cibil again.

Was eight days enough? Depending on exactly where the Ravyns were, the Nerezza Plains was about a four-day ride from Kage Duna, but what if the Ravyns left? What if they didn't have the elder's wife's necklace any longer? To think that she'd mistaken a piece of the moon as rough onyx stone, Sloane could hardly fathom it. How had the elder's wife come by it?

"Are you certain you can't be talked into staying?" Henry asked, walking up to Sloane's mare. Sir Pharrell, a handful of Order knights, the last two recruits—the others had left days ago back for Kestriel—and he were staying behind.

"M'lord, I've made my case over and over. Surely you can understand how important it is that I go. We've only eight days until the Nay Moon."

Henry's brow wrinkled, but he nodded. "I'm counting on you. We'll send word if anything here changes. 'Tis my hope the sovereign won't hear of this quest until you're well on your way to Kage Duna. I'll continue my correspondence with him as if naught has happened."

When Sloane scanned the area again, she found Tolvar staring at her crossly. Well, he'd have to make peace with her going. She gathered the mare's reins and gave the animal a pat on the neck, hoping her nonchalant movements would fool him—and herself.

It was a backbreaking ride, and, at the end of the day, Sloane's body screamed that she should have stayed behind. She was helped off the mare, her legs buckling instantly, and she was only too glad it wasn't Tolvar who helped her. If Alvie only knew how right he'd been about her behind feeling like ground meat.

As camp was made, a half dozen scouts set out to spot the Ravyns' camp. Such was Sloane's exhaustion, she barely noticed the hunk of bread and cured boar placed in her lap by Kek as she sat by the small fire. The throbbing in her left leg was unbearable, but she buried the pain deep inside herself and didn't let either part of her acknowledge it.

She must have drifted asleep, because when she opened her eyes, the sky was dark and speckled with a sea of stars. It appeared half their group was asleep, the other half on guard duty, stationed in a circular manner around their camp. She couldn't make out Alvie's form anywhere, asleep or otherwise. She couldn't decipher anyone: Ghlee, Kek, Clive, anyone.

"How's your leg?" a voice next to her spoke softly. Tolvar.

"Fine," she said, shifting her position and wincing despite herself. Tolvar didn't acknowledge it, though she knew full well he'd heard it.

"The Ravyns have made camp three miles southeast. We ride before dawn and will take them by surprise. We'll surround them swiftly. You'll stay here."

"But—"

"Only until we've dealt with them. You need not be part of a battle."

"Do you mean to kill all of them?"

Joah.

"We'll capture those that we can, but our task isn't to bring them back to Kestriel so they can stand trial. You said so yourself, our days are numbered."

Could she tell him about Joah? Should she, the other part still debated. Would it matter to him that her brother had turned criminal?

"You'll come to the site once it's over, and you can identify the Edan Stone. And do not argue with me. If I must tie you to a tree and leave you here, I will."

"Don't kill anyone. If the Edan Stone is gone, we'll need to know where it is."

"I cannot promise that no one will die. But I'll keep your words in mind."

"Is Alvie staying here?"

"Alvie isn't my concern."

She couldn't even mutter two phrases together.

"Edd and Michell will stay and keep you safe until I can again. That is, until the Order can again."

There was something in the way Tolvar looked away, combined with what he'd just uttered, that made the words on Sloane's tongue drop back down her throat.

CHAPTER
39

Tolvar

From atop the hill, mounted on Valko, who snorted and flicked his ears back, sensing what was about to happen, Tolvar spied at the shadowed forms of the Ravyns, still bedded and unstirring. He waited for the signal that would come from the other side of their camp when Kek and his group reached their spot of attack. The place of their camp certainly was a foolish one—a small valley surrounded by slight hills with a nearby clump of trees where an enemy could easily hide.

Hmph. The Ravyns. All the stories Tolvar had been told about this infamous mob, and here they were, looking as unprepared as a squire lifting his first sword. Truth be told, Tolvar had been itching to encounter this band of robbers. It was unfathomable to him that the sovereign allowed them to run wild over the island. It was an island. How difficult could it be to capture and hang the lot of them?

This thought tugged at another one that Tolvar kept tied down. The "leader" of the Brones had said more of them were coming. Tolvar scanned behind him. Nothing. He was sure of it. The only thing he needed to concentrate on right now was how good it would feel to run these men through. He supposed he must keep a few alive for Sloane's sake, but they didn't need to *all* live. Alvie and his big mouth had given him more detail of Sloane's robbery, and Tolvar wouldn't have the least bit of conscience about eliminating these terrorizing bullies from the earth.

He didn't need to yet, but he unsheathed his sword from the

saddle, gripping it in anticipation. Aye, the Ravyns wouldn't have time to cry out, let alone grab their weapons.

When the signal appeared from the opposite hill, Tolvar silently counted to ten, kicked his mount's side, and raced down the hill, the knights who surrounded the perimeters following suit. He gave Valko his head and let the animal lope down the hill, the sound of all the steeds creating an echoed cacophony in the valley where the Ravyns were still abed.

Closer and closer, he raced, his blood keeping time with the thud of galloping hooves. He was ready, so ready to release the aggravation he'd had to stanch these past weeks. Closer and closer, Tolvar gripped his sword. The Ravyns had yet to move.

Yet to move?

With this thunderous noise, even the dead asleep should have awakened by now. Closer and closer. And the Ravyns, who were known for their cunning, should definitely be roused.

They were close to the encampment. Tolvar could smell the ashes of the putout campfires but saw no one.

Stars!

"Turn around, it's a trap!" Tolvar's voice bellowed, jerking Valko's reins so abruptly that, had it not been for its training, the horse might have lost its footing in the maneuver. He turned, his comrades doing likewise around him, and there at the top of the hill was a line of men on horseback, weapons drawn.

How had he missed that detail? Of course, the horses had been missing from the camp. So eager had he been to fight them, so preoccupied with keeping Sloane safe, so cocky in his position, he'd missed it.

"I say," called a man in the line's middle, "What're you doing all the way down there?"

The Order knights gathered next to Tolvar. "Well, this is unpleasant," Ghlee said beside him.

Tolvar scouted behind him. The Ravyns had not spaced themselves to surround them as Tolvar's men had done. There was that. And their numbers were about evenly matched. And despite Tolvar finding himself at the bottom of the hill while his enemy peered down at him from the top, he did not lose the calm force of the Wolf that flowed through him, ready to tear these men apart.

The Ravyns chuckled above.

"You've had your last laugh," Tolvar called. "With the sun rising, so too does the justice you answer to now."

"That so?" the same man said, lifting a hand to silence the laughter. If there was a doubt before who the leader was, that put it to rest. "Well, then, why don't you ride up here and give it to us?"

"I think we'll wait for you," Tolvar shouted. He was not going to be provoked into huffing it up the hill to attack, giving the Ravyns even more of an advantage. "In the meantime, mayhap we'll rob you."

Tolvar dismounted, casually walked to the closest pack, and rummaged through it.

"Be my guest," the leader called. "I suppose we have it coming to us." This gave his men leave to burst into laughter again.

There was nothing of note in the pack and certainly nothing that looked like a piece of moonstone. One of the campfires still had embers glowing. Tolvar took what appeared to be a rudimentary map and held it to the orange glow. Gently, he blew on it until the map ignited.

"Mayhap we'll just burn your camp. I've heard tales of you burning a village to the ground."

"You heard wrong."

Tolvar shrugged, though in dawn's faint blue light, he wasn't sure they caught the gesture. "Regardless, we'll send your ill-gotten possessions to the afterworld properly."

Tolvar walked around the camp with his makeshift torch, kicking packs, blankets, and crates of food. He threw a whole sack of potatoes onto the fire he'd revived.

"You have his attention," Ghlee said quietly, his eyes fixed on the Ravyns. Tolvar finally found what he searched for. A sack of six silver goblets. Something the Ravyns wouldn't want burned.

"Very beautiful." Tolvar flashed one of them above his head. "Pity." He threw the sack onto the flames.

No verbal command sounded; the Ravyns simply broke their mounts into a run, charging at them.

Finally. Tolvar remounted Valko.

"Let's show these bastards what real cunning looks like," he said, drawing his sword. "Let them come to us." His eyes were on the leader. That one was his.

As soon as the first Ravyn horse hit level ground, Tolvar charged Valko into him. The man fell as his startled horse kept running. Next, Tolvar sliced through a Ravyn's torso as another to his side whacked his spear into Tolvar's newly stitched shoulder. Tolvar tightened his thighs around Valko and managed to stay seated, swiftly swinging his sword in the opposite direction across his enemy's shoulder. The man screamed and dropped the spear. Tolvar maneuvered Valko into the side of his horse and hit him with the pommel of his sword. The man fell unconscious to the ground. So far, Tolvar had kept his promise to Sloane. He'd downed three men and killed no one. Well, mayhap. A sword through the middle was never good.

The thrill of battle wafted through the air around him. The clang of sword on sword, the cries and commotion of fighting, the screams of startled horses. Sweat drenched his sleeves and chest, the stench of blood mingled with the odor of other men combatting one another.

Tolvar had managed to disarm and down two more when he noticed Alvie fighting a man twice his size. Through Tolvar's well-trained eyes, he could see Alvie was moments away from being downed.

He clicked Valko into motion and was almost there when the big man swung his sword again, knocking Alvie from his horse.

"Alvie, get up!" Tolvar yelled over the din of the battle.

As Alvie seized his club, straining to stand as he did it, the man brought his sword above his head. Tolvar wasted no time. He launched his sword into the man, the weapon sinking into his chest.

Blood trickled from his mouth as he fell backward onto the ground, his horse bolting away.

Tolvar dismounted before Valko came to a stop.

Alvie, panting, grinned. "Now don't you go showin' off, Sir Wolf."

Tolvar handed Alvie the club and the peg-legged man swung back into the saddle as if it took no effort.

He wrenched his sword from the man's chest, never breaking eye contact as he did, the sound of labored breathing emanating from him. Tolvar's sword was crimson-stained. As he contemplated putting him out of his misery, the Ravyn took his last breath and stilled.

Scanning the field, Tolvar took a quick survey. Over a half dozen bodies lay on the ground, but none seemed to be Order knights. Where was that dark-haired leader? He'd be the key to finding the Edan Stone. At last, Tolvar saw him on the other side of the encampment, fighting Kek. Tolvar mounted Valko and sprinted to their position.

Up close, Tolvar was surprised to see the leader was a younger man. Younger than himself.

"Kek, this one's mine," Tolvar said. Kek took a few more swings then nodded and directed his horse away. The leader turned his horse in Tolvar's direction and lifted his brows in delight.

"Oh goody. I was hoping I'd have a chance to meet the great Wolf. Don't look so surprised. Your reputation precedes you, magnificent knight. Tell me, are the rumors true? Are you truly banished from your own kingdom?"

Tolvar flexed his jaw. This man was attempting to both buy himself a moment to breathe and bait him. The Wolf wasn't as green as this.

"If you've caught your breath, let's see what you have to offer up a Wolf for breakfast," Tolvar said.

"I think not; I think 'tis time we surrendered," the leader said, then brought his fingers to his mouth and gave a low whistle. Every

Ravyn stopped fighting immediately, dropped their weapons, and put their hands in the air.

"I believe you are honorable enough to accept a good surrender when you find it." The leader cocked his head. "As I said, your reputation does precede you."

CHAPTER
40

Sloane

Sloane couldn't stop shaking her leg as she sat next to the fire, watching in the direction where Alvie, Tolvar, and the others had gone.

"They'll be fine," Edd said yet again. Mayhap if Sloane counted how many times he'd said that to her, she would've been able to properly distract herself.

"It's after sunrise," she said, her eyes fixed on the horizon.

"That don't mean anything. They'll be back before you know it."

Sloane couldn't decide what she was most nervous about. The Ravyns capturing them? Killing them? And what of Joah? Had Joah killed someone? Had someone killed Joah?

Michell came riding up. "No sign of anything yet," he said, dismounting.

"That's not bad news, Miss Sloane," Edd said. The smile he gave was one of reassurance. The smile she returned was weak. She couldn't wipe away the layer of anxiousness coating her.

"I'll make something to break our fast. They'll be back in no time," Michell said.

Sloane offered to help, but he waved her away.

She was handed a cup of hot cider, the warmth of the sweet liquid's scent making her nostrils sing, when the arrow pierced Michell's back.

His eyes were a storm of confusion and pain and disappointment all at the same time. He fell to his knees and then thumped to the ground, face first.

Sloane screamed.

Edd grabbed his sword, examining the direction where the arrow had come, from the tall grasses of the meadow in the distance.

"Sloane, get down," he commanded before yelling, "Who goes there?"

Sloane pinned herself to the ground, blood throbbing through her temples. She dared peer to where the arrow had come from, saw a head bob up before another arrow whizzed through the air at them. Edd managed to sidestep it, but another followed and hit him in the shoulder. He groaned but kept his stance.

"Cowards, come out and fight." His face drained of color.

Another arrow split the air and punctured his other shoulder. The sound from Edd was a chopped moan. And Sloane lay on the ground like a sook.

"Enough," she yelled, kneeling. "Enough. Come out."

Edd sunk to his knees in pain and was eye-level with her. "What are you doing?"

"Saving you," Sloane said.

"They're going to kill us both." His voice was strained.

"I'm not afraid to die." Sloane inched her way in front of him. "Come out," she yelled to the tall grass. "If you're going to kill us, do it looking us in the eyes. Not hiding like field eels."

The new day's sun had shifted and made the horizon pale. Sloane lifted a hand to shield her squinting eyes. Three men stood in grass up to their waists.

When they began walking toward her, when she now remembered she was unarmed—as she seemed destined to be whenever trouble struck her—when she now worried about Alvie and others for a different reason, then did she summon fear for what would happen next.

The men came out of the glare, and Sloane gasped. "Joah." A single word she'd hated for moons, which bore the brother, who, in a way, had caused more grief than the deaths she'd suffered, who had made Sloane fling curses out in the middle of the night.

Joah stood in front of her, rigid, almost unrecognizable.

"Stay back," Edd said, unable to keep the strain from his voice, working to stand again.

The two men on either side of Joah passed Sloane and hauled up Edd by his arms. One pulled out a knife.

"Stop!" Sloane pleaded into her brother's eyes. "Don't let them kill him. Please!"

"Kerr?" one said, furrowing his brow, his knife too close.

Joah's face was a stone wall. Nothing. "Please," Sloane whimpered. "Don't."

"Wait!" the third man said, pointing his free hand at Sloane. "'Tis her! The girl we robbed a few moons ago. The one with them tools."

"Stump, you're right," the other said. Joah kept quiet. "What you doin' with the Order of Siria?"

"Best to answer," Joah said in a tone that told Sloane they had best stay strangers.

"What's it to you? Cowards now just as before," Sloane said, glancing down at Michell sprawled on the ground. Unbelievably, he moved and moaned.

Joah searched Sloane's face, then studied Edd, who was growing paler by the moment. "Hux was right. They did leave you guarded. You're important for some reason. Why?"

Sloane kept her jaw firm.

"Very well. Doesn't matter," Joah said, his tone so unfamiliar. Sloane bit her lip so she wouldn't cry.

"We have our orders," Stump said. The knife slicing across Edd's neck made Sloane gag.

CHAPTER
41

Tolvar

The leader smiled. Tied up, sitting on the ground, the rest of the remaining Ravyns—seventeen in all—bound as well, and here was the leader, smiling up at Tolvar as he cleaned off his blade. The Ravyns had suffered six losses, the Order two. Both had four wounded, Ghlee being one of them with a gash down his left arm. Surprisingly, Tolvar's shoulder stitches hadn't torn. Tolvar inspected the blade before giving it one last polish.

"Shall I cut off your lips to make that smirk disappear?" Tolvar didn't look at the leader, but the chuckle he gave conveyed he'd heard well enough.

"My apologies, great Wolf. I'm simply wondering why the Order of Siria has cause to hunt us down. 'Tis well known you've been here for almost a year. Surely, you have more important things to do. For why not track us sooner? Even the sovereign has not sent his great army after us. My guess is we have something you want."

Tolvar rewarded the leader with his scowl.

"Ah, aye, that is a look that would scare any man. But you must understand, we are already outlaws. Already hated and hunted. Why don't you simply tell me what it is you want? Then I shall be able to tell you the location of what *you* want."

Tolvar must have flashed an expression of confusion because the leader's grin deepened. Next to him, an older man with an incredibly unkempt red beard, chuckled.

"Sir," Clive said, approaching Tolvar. "We've searched every bag. There's naught that meets the description Sloane gave us."

Tolvar frowned. Had they sold it somewhere? Mayhap one of them was carrying it?

"Sloane? Is that the girl's name?" the leader asked.

A sensation like ice swept over Tolvar.

Joy rushed into the leader's face. "I only saw her from afar, but I sensed she was special."

Next to him, the disheveled man chuckled again.

Tolvar held the leader by his collar at eye level. "Speak your next words plain and true."

The leader remained unfazed. "Seems I was right." When Tolvar tightened his grip around his collar, tightening it around his neck, his voice was breathy. "Isn't it obvious? We've captured her. Only two men left to guard her? Tut-tut."

The sound of the Ravyns' leader hitting the ground after Tolvar threw him down made Clive wince. Tolvar strode to Valko.

"Wolf, where are you going?" Ghlee shouted behind him.

Tolvar mounted and kicked Valko into a gallop, charging up the hill back toward where they'd left Sloane with Michell and Edd.

Stars be good, Tolvar thought. *Let that man be a liar.*

VALKO WAS FOAMING at the mouth when Tolvar reached the encampment, the tiny fire's ashes still smoldering.

Edd lay on the ground in a pool of blood, eyes empty, Michell huddled next to him, shivering with an arrow sticking out of his back.

"Where is she?" Tolvar dismounted before Valko came to a halt and picked up Michell by the collar as he had the leader.

"Gone," Michell winced. "Three men took her. Rode south." Michell was white and covered in sweat. Tolvar inspected the wound in his back. He needed to breathe so he stopped seeing red. This would not be another Thorin Court. He was not going to lose Sloane.

"I need to remove the arrow," Tolvar said, going to the pack that held strips of cloth and healing herbs. Michell paled further but nodded.

Tolvar pulled the arrow and was wrapping Michell's torso when two riders approached. Ghlee and Alvie. Ghlee's arm was wrapped, and his face was firm, but he was almost as pale as Michell.

"Sloane!" Alvie yelled, his already bugged-out eyes wider. "Where's Sloane?"

"Taken." Tolvar focused on the bandage so he didn't have to acknowledge the emotion that had escaped his voice. "We're going to get her back."

"Wolf, the leader must know where she is," Ghlee said calmly. "Let's get Michell to the others, and then we can have a little chat."

"If I speak to that man again, it will be to say a prayer over his corpse," Tolvar said, helping Michell to stand.

"They'll want her alive," Ghlee said. "Come on."

IT HAD BEEN SAID of the Wolf that his strength was that of a pack of beasts. And Tolvar felt that could almost be true when he picked up the leader again from his collar and tossed him feet away. The dark-bearded man landed on his back with a *crack*. The leader uttered a closed-mouthed groan and twitched his neck as if to shake off the wind being knocked out of him.

Tolvar held his sword to the leader's neck, holding all his rage within the hilt. Everyone was quiet: Kek, the rest of the Order knights, all the Ravyns, even that smirking, red-bearded man, who blanched when the leader landed.

"I ask questions but once," Tolvar said, "Where is she?"

"And I answer to no one," the leader said. "I'm a wanted man. And I have no faith my life isn't forfeit as it is. What are the odds you don't kill me one way or another? Nay, I say, by the look on your face, I have provided myself the only escape plan possible. Again, why don't you tell me what it is you want so we may begin our negotiations?"

"You must know the Wolf doesn't negotiate with anyone."

"Then you may as well kill me now and be done with it."

Never had anyone stared back at him so emphatically, save for Ghlee, and mayhap Sloane. Curse the stars, anyway. Tolvar lifted his sword and ran his hand through his hair. The Ravyns couldn't know what they searched for. That decision, he'd already made. And there was a chance they might not even have the Edan Stone anymore.

"Tell me what you want and swear you'll spare our lives, and, in return, I'll swear to spare the life of the girl." The leader finally sat up, a task he made appear easy even with his hands bound behind him. "But I must warn you. If my men do not hear from me by sunset, they have strict instructions to kill her. And I'm never disobeyed."

Tolvar exchanged a look with Ghlee, who put up a hand to stop Alvie from speaking, then scanned over the captured Ravyns, each sitting straight and tall. For a group of bandits, there was no mistaking their discipline. Tolvar grit his teeth together. This man wasn't bluffing.

He walked away from the group, Ghlee, Alvie, Kek, and Clive following.

"What do you think?" Kek said softly when they were huddled together.

"We must get to Sloane by sundown," Tolvar said. "There was no lie behind his words."

"Tolvar, we can't—you can't—we must—" Alvie was a jumble of words. The small man appeared he might faint.

"Get a grip," Tolvar said, shaking Alvie's shoulder.

"We haven't tortured them enough," Kek said. "They'll break. We just need some more time."

Tolvar viewed the sun. It was nearing midday, so that gave them a few hours. Hopefully. Who knew where they'd taken Sloane? Mayhap they could simply split up and try to find her?

"I say we bargain," Ghlee said.

"I'm with Ghlee." Alvie's voice croaked. "Anything to save Sloane."

"We can't let the Ravyns go now that we have them," Clive said. "They must be taken to Kestriel."

The sovereign. Tolvar was not going anywhere near Kestriel. What *was* their plan for the Ravyns? There were too many of them to hold captive. They'd simply slow them down. They could leave them tied here to rot. That wasn't a bad option to Tolvar. Except the leader. Tolvar wanted to rip the man's eyeballs out with his bare hands.

Sloane. What were they doing to her? Blood pulsed through his veins. He imagined seeing her balled up in the alley that first time. So small. For all that woman's spirit, he saw a fragile creature who was his duty to protect. He'd saved her from death in that alley, and he wasn't going to fail her now.

"Everyone. Search again for the item. And search the Ravyns as well. It may be on one of them." He caught a gleam in the eye of the leader. "And Kek, let's give our fists someone to punch."

CHAPTER 42

Sloane

Stump, as he'd been referred to by Joah and the other Ravyn, had socked her only once in the nose, but it bled like liquid being poured from a pitcher. Sloane spit repeatedly to remove the metallic taste from her mouth, and the front of her dress was soaked in blood and saliva. The stench made her queasy, but she couldn't wipe off the blood—which was drying into a crisp layer on her face—as her hands were bound behind her back. The thick rope dug into her wrists. She'd only bothered with an attempt to escape the rope for a few moments before it rubbed her skin raw.

The four of them crouched in a small hut on the edge of a cluster of trees. It was cramped and uncomfortable—not that Sloane would be comfortable even on a plush chair right now. Stump and the other man passed the time by either glaring at her or sharpening their knives, which Sloane was certain was an activity meant to scare her. Joah—or Kerr—ignored her completely, leaving every so often to scout the area. They'd left the horses a quarter-mile away near another hut of sorts and, with the use of a spyglass, they could detect anyone approaching the decoy hut from the direction of Sloane's encampment.

No one spoke to Sloane, and she hadn't bothered to speak either. After midday, Stump said to Joah and the other that only four hours remained. They were obviously waiting for someone.

Was it the young dark-bearded leader, Hux, mayhap? Sloane remembered the other one in command with the wild red-blonde beard. His name started with a "B," she recollected. She was, at least, glad it couldn't be Rhiner. The whole first incident with the Ravyns came rushing back, and Sloane found herself biting her blood-crusted lip to keep from tearing up.

Nay, you are stronger than you were, one part of Sloane consoled her.

Yet the other part of Sloane hurt acknowledging Joah's presence. Doing naught to help his sister. His last family member.

She must have dozed off because the next thing Sloane knew, she was being hoisted up and slung out of the hut like a sack of barley. She was dropped onto the ground. The sun set low in the sky, and it'd grown cool outside in the autumn air. Sloane shivered, gazing through the orange-and-yellow tree branches at the vibrant red-and-orange sky, like it was on fire in the distance. Joah and the other two Ravyns each held a weapon: a sword, a dagger, and what looked like a mallet. No one said anything, yet the atmosphere chilled. And part of Sloane wondered if this would be the last sunset she'd ever see.

The Ravyn holding the mallet smacked it against his palm twice; the only sound.

Sloane dared meet Joah's eyes. She'd been so careful to avoid them. Careful to give no indication to the others that their comrade's sister knelt before them. She searched his face. In some ways, Joah now resembled Father more. He'd grown into his forehead and had the same petite nose. Joah's beard was mere scruff and Sloane recognized her own chin, Ma's chin. The mask of hardness fell from Joah's eyes, and Sloane saw her fate there. They were going kill her.

I almost thought I could be the Unsung.

Almost, agreed the other part of Sloane.

"Well, what we waiting for?" said Stump, holding the dagger. "'Tis sunset. Hux gave the orders, and I'm not going to end up like Leonard did. We don't do it, you know what'll happen."

"When I'm among the stars, I'll try to forgive you," Sloane said, her eyes fixed on the sunset sinking into the horizon. She met Joah's eyes again. "But I know you won't be able to forgive yourself."

"Right then." The Ravyn with the mallet ignored Sloane's words. "Let's get this over with."

"I know how to stop it. The Befallen." Sloane held Joah's gaze. "That took our parents. I know you saw them."

Sloane was kicked and dropped onto her stomach. She spat out dust.

"That's enough." Stump brought his dagger close to her cheek. "The dead don't talk." From the corner of her eye, Joah raised his sword, his focus intent on her back.

She closed her eyes. Let it be quick, she prayed, wishing the moon had risen.

Let Alvie and Tolvar and Ghlee and the others keep going. Let them find the Edan Stone and the Cibil and the goddess of the Azure Moon. Let them stop the Befallen.

And while Sloane prayed and waited, the sound of a sword swished through the air and embedded itself into flesh. There were shouts and groans and steel hitting wood and the *thunk* of something hitting the ground. Men scuffled and swore at one another until finally, the second sound of impaled flesh came. When Sloane dared open her eyes and turn over, Joah sat near her, arms resting on his knees, panting, and bleeding from his temple. The two Ravyns lay motionless.

Despite Sloane witnessing more deaths than she could count, the sight threatened bile to come up, and she turned away to stop herself from vomiting. From behind her, Joah rose.

He crouched before her, tears streaming down his dirty face, as he untied Sloane's bindings, the relief across her wrists instantaneous.

"Sloane," he croaked out. "I'm sorry."

She let herself weep then and flung her arms around her brother, his scent familiar as she pressed her cheek into his shoulder.

"I'm so sorry," he sobbed the words over and over.

Finally, she broke their embrace. "Joah, we have to bandage your wound." It looked bad.

Joah placed his palm to his temple. "I think we have something in the hut," he said, standing.

The chain hanging around his neck under his tunic caught her eye.

"Joah! What's that you're wearing?"

He froze, then glanced down. He pulled the chain from under his collar, and there it was. The Edan Stone. The pendant Sloane had mistaken for a rough piece of onyx, here around her brother's neck.

He gripped the Edan Stone in his hand. "I stole it from Hux after we—you know. I wanted something to remember you. And your bravery."

"You've saved my life twice." Her eyes clung to it. "That pendant. I need it back. 'Tis going to help me stop the Befallen."

"You were serious about that?"

"Aye. You remember the old Edan Lore?"

"Course. Everyone knows it."

"But not everyone does, apparently. This pendant is a piece of moonstone, you see. 'Twill allow me to speak to the Azure Moon's goddess."

Joah sniggered. "I know Ma and Father taught you to believe, but you don't really—"

"Of course, I do. And you should, too, Joah. For their sake as for any reason."

Joah's face grew rigid, then contrite. He loosed his grip on the Edan Stone. "I will admit, wearing this, it made me feel...safe, I suppose is the word?"

"Safe?"

"Aye." He looked around as if about to tell a secret. "Before this, we were always worried about the Befallen, you know, like everyone is. But wearing this, 'tis like I've simply known the Befallen isn't around. That sounds stupid."

"Nay," Sloane said. "It sounds like...magic."

They grinned in unison. *It sounds like magic* had been a phrase Ma had used to describe good things. Happy things.

"Here," Joah said, handing Sloane the chain. "'Tis the least I could do after—everything. Sloane, I'm so sorry."

"I know." She studied the small piece of the moon, then placed the chain around her neck. "Now, get your supplies so I can help you bandage that wound."

Joah wobbled to the hut.

Then, the sound she'd waited for all day finally came. Galloping hooves. In the distance, Sloane could faintly see—for the sun had gone down—a dozen riders racing in her direction. It was only because she so clearly recognized Tolvar's movements that she was certain they weren't the Ravyns.

"Joah," she whispered. What was Tolvar going to do? "Joah! Stay in the hut. Don't come out." She wasn't going to chance Tolvar simply killing Joah on sight.

"Sloane, no," Joah said, standing in the doorway.

She turned on him. "Go back in. I'll not lose you a third time." She burned her gaze into him.

"I'm not going to hide."

"Do as I say!"

Joah slunk back into the hut. Sloane turned back to the riders, confident it was too dark for them to have seen Joah standing in the hut's doorway.

She needed to stand, to show she was strong. She brought herself up onto her good leg, then waited, heart pounding. How was she going to keep them out of the hut? How to protect Joah? And at the same time, the other part of Sloane was absorbed in watching Tolvar grow closer and closer to her, his mount a good lead ahead of the others. In the dark, she couldn't see his expression, but she felt his eyes on her as clearly as if she were being bathed in moonlight.

When Tolvar dismounted, a breath away from Sloane, he wasted no time in lifting and embracing her into his arms. She breathed into him, loving the sensation of his hand cradling the back of her head.

"Are you hurt?" he whispered.

"Nay," she replied, and she felt him relax. He pulled her away, but only slightly, and their eyes met. Stars, his face showed...what? Tenderness, she decided.

"Sloane!" Alvie shouted, dismounting his horse, and joining them. Tolvar set Sloane onto her feet so she could hug her friend. "Sloane! Don't you ever go doing that again!"

"Doing what?"

"That! Being captured! From now on, you stay with me so I can protect you!" His voice was merry, but his face revealed his worry.

Ghlee and the others grouped around them, each of them exclaiming their joy at finding Sloane alive and well.

"What happened here?" Ghlee asked, kicking one of the bodies. "You?" He pointed to Sloane.

"Nay. Listen. There's something I haven't told you all. My brother—my brother is—"

At that moment, Tolvar's eyes darted to the hut behind Sloane. She turned. Joah stood in the doorway.

"It's one of them. Kill him!" Tolvar's voice boomed as he drew his sword and strode toward Joah.

"Nay, Tolvar, stop!" Sloane yelled, racing behind him. She wedged herself between Tolvar and Joah. Tolvar lowered his sword.

"What is this?"

"This is my brother," Sloane said, reaching her hand behind her and placing it on Joah's forearm.

"A Ravyn?" Ghlee stuttered.

"He just saved me. You cannot harm him," Sloane said. "He's my only family left."

Alvie huffed.

Sloane had never fallen victim to Tolvar's glare, but the scowl he assaulted Joah with frightened her. Joah stiffened behind her. She dared not leave her place between them.

"What kind of brother betrays his sibling?" Tolvar's voice was so low, so taut with hatred, Sloane made ready to be thrown aside and watch Joah be run through. There was no doubt Tolvar was thinking about Crevan.

"Tolvar." Sloane's voice was equally quiet. "He saved me."

Ghlee came and stood beside Tolvar. "Wolf. Let this be her decision. Not yours."

Tolvar's eyes did not budge from Joah. "Look at her, Ghlee. Look at her face. He either did this or did naught to stop it."

Sloane gently touched Tolvar's forearm. "Please, sir knight. Take me back to camp. I'm famished and unnerved. We can speak of Joah later."

Tolvar finally dragged his dark expression from Joah, sheathed his sword, and gave the briefest of nods. He swept her into his arms and carried her to the waiting horses.

"I can walk," she said.

He did not respond; instead, he lifted Sloane onto Valko, mounted the horse behind her, and wrapped an arm protectively around her.

"If the brother can make it back to where we hold his comrades before we leave, we can speak of what's to become of him. If not, he's considered an enemy and will be killed on sight," Tolvar commanded and kicked Valko into a gallop.

"What?" Sloane said, turning in the saddle to look back at Joah, but it was too late. "You can't command that!"

"I just did," Tolvar said. "'Tis up to him now. We'll see what he's made of."

It was no use arguing further. Hopefully, Joah would hurry after them.

Unless he uses this moment to escape, part of Sloane worried.

As they sped along, the war of emotions made Sloane realize how exhausted and unnerved she was. She wasn't sure what she felt, but as her back melted into Tolvar's chest, Sloane felt completely safe for the first time in moons.

CHAPTER
43

Sloane

The camp at the bottom of the hill resembled a mini village with six different campfires dispersed throughout. In one corner, the Ravyns were clumped together, hands tied behind their backs. Sloane massaged her sore wrists.

"What will you do with them?" Sloane asked Tolvar, half surprised to see them still alive.

"A message has been sent to Pharrell. He will decide. But we cannot waste time."

"At least we have this now," Sloane said, turning around in the saddle and showing Tolvar the Edan Stone hanging from her neck. "Joah had it. And gave it to me. See? He's not bad."

She'd hoped he'd look pleased, but at the mention of Joah, Tolvar was unreadable again.

They'd just dismounted when Kek said they needed to make new plans. They had seven days until the Nay Moon to make the four-day ride to Kage Duna.

Sloane kept clutching the Edan Stone. The moon was half of itself this night, a time when men could most easily be led to division, some stories said. But Sloane had witnessed enough division these past moons to know the moon had naught to do with it. And this night was one of thankfulness. Moon cuffs may be for the full moon only, but Sloane found herself sliding on the wristlet and bowing her head in gratitude for a time.

When hunger drove her out of her prayer, Sloane sought food, and attempted to ignore the fact that Joah had not appeared. He did have a horse. She skirted the area where the bound Ravyns were seated on the grass with half the Order surrounding them.

"So, it *is* you," a voice called to her.

She turned and faced Hux, the dark-bearded leader of the Ravyns, who'd taken everything she owned. His faced was bruised and his head was bandaged, but he carried that same casual countenance. Next to him was the red-bearded leader, Brinley, Sloane remembered his name. His left eye was so swollen, Sloane wondered if he could see.

"One of my men thought he recognized you when we were scouting. Seems you've made important friends."

Sloane didn't want to speak to him but found herself edging closer. The guard closest to Hux puffed his chest.

"Seems I have."

"How did you escape my men? You should be dead. I know they didn't arrive in time, but no one will tell me anything. One of the nuances of being a captive, I s'pose."

Now, Sloane worried what Hux would do if Joah entered the camp. If he were to escape, what would he do to Joah?

"I overpowered them." Sloane raised an eyebrow, letting him know that was all the answer he'd get.

He laughed, then said, "Are they going to kill us?"

"I don't know," Sloane said truthfully.

"Can you stop it? Overpower *them*?"

"I doubt it. Besides, why would I help you? You took everything from me. My tools, my supplies, my horse."

"Aye. Strange horse, that. You're welcome to have him back. He's over there." He nodded to the group of horses corralled together.

They still had Kenn?

"What do you mean, strange?"

"Something tells me that you know." Hux's eyes twinkled. "I hear your name is Sloane, mighty one."

"Mighty? Having a jest at my expense?" She crossed her arms.

"Nay. You mistake me. I saw you praying. Seen the way everyone is looking at you. You're the true leader here."

Sloane's half-suppressed laugh was meant to show his statement's falseness.

"And I swear to follow you if you'll have me and my men." Hux's bruised face expressed earnestness.

She couldn't help but chuckle. "And what's the word of a Ravyn?"

"Nothing. After all, I did give the order to kill you at sunset. But I swear here and now if you find a way to let me and my men go, we'll be sworn to aid you in whatever cause you ask."

The Edan Stone became a weight around Sloane's neck. Hux noted it for the first time.

"Is that what they were searching for? I was certain that'd become lost."

Hux's calmness did nothing to stop Sloane from thinking he was puzzling some things together in his mind. She very much did not want Joah to find his way here.

"Lost? You *stole* it from me moons ago."

"I remember." Hux focused on it in the moonlight. "Why is it so important?"

Sloane shrugged. "I like the way it hangs on my neck."

Hux laughed again. "I do remember you had a bit of bite to you that day." Then more seriously, he said, "Do think on my words. My men and I are at your service if you'll convince them to release us."

Sloane surveyed the beaten, wounded Ravyns. She should be happy at the sight. She should not trust Hux nor help him. But counting their number, seventeen in all, she wondered how many more deaths she'd need to witness. Wasn't the Befallen enough? Wasn't the whole point to *stop* deaths, not add to them? Besides, if she helped them, then she could do something about Hux's anger when he found out that Joah had betrayed them.

"I'll consider it. But do not trust I have influence. And do not think to play me false. The Wolf, himself, will see to your deaths."

Hux's bruised face did naught to curb his smile. "I knew you were the leader. In more ways than one."

AT MIDDAY, when the Order finally—*finally*—decided to humor Sloane's request to discuss the fate of the Ravyns, Alvie was the only one to side with Sloane, and she wasn't entirely sure he hadn't done that simply so she wouldn't be alone.

"Besides," Ghlee said, "Pharrell already sent word to Kestriel that the Ravyns were being held on the Nerezza Plains, and the sovereign should send his army. This message can't be undone. It'll look suspicious."

As she'd known he would, Tolvar did not mince words about taking the option to simply kill the Ravyns, or at least Hux for giving the command to kill Sloane. No doubt he'd still like to add Joah to the list, especially as he still hadn't shown up.

"How can we say our quest is to stop this killing curse when we choose the death of others?" she asked.

"We're talking about thieves, low-lives, people who don't deserve to live." Tolvar gritted his teeth.

"They're still people," Sloane shot back. "Besides, what if we need more men?"

"For what?" Clive scoffed. "We're the Order of Siria."

"The Brones may come back. I've heard you all discussing it."

No one said anything.

Ghlee pulled Tolvar into a two-man huddle and spoke in hushed tones before saying he would consider it. At these words, Tolvar cursed and launched the knife he'd been toying with into the ground.

"At any rate," Alvie said, "we ought to think about goin' soon, or at least makin' shelter. Fact o'matter is, those clouds look awful big."

In the argument, which had dragged on all afternoon, no one had paid attention to the weather, but now Sloane's breath caught as the enormous black cloud unnaturally stirred toward them. The Edan

Stone's weight tugged at her. The rough stone, black as tar, was...
glowing? Not glowing—radiating. It had turned grey like the smoke of
a billowing pyre. She gaped from the moonstone to Tolvar. He saw
it, too.

"That's no storm cloud," Sloane whispered.

Everyone paled.

"'Tis the Befallen." Tolvar finished her thought.

"Run, everyone!" Ghlee yelled.

The blackened mass, seeming less and less like a cloud, sliding
closer and closer to the camp, rippled and ruptured like gurgling,
boiling pitch. A constant spume of darkness. Like it could swallow
everything good and bright in its path. And Sloane couldn't make her
legs move.

"Sloane! Let's go," Alvie called, mounted on his horse. How had
he already reached his horse?

Coming to, Sloane realized she was the only one who hadn't
sprinted into action. Chaos infused the undercurrent of fear in the
air. The squeals from the men—knights, brave knights—could have
been those of frightened children. The whites of their eyes revealed
sheer terror as they rushed for their lives, jumped onto horses,
galloped away, all while the Befallen—the cold, dark death—creeped
upon them like a tempest's grim hand.

"*Adrienne.*" The word quavered through her, pinching her
nerves, petrifying her limbs. But the voice. The voice drove cold
sweat down the back of her neck. Saying the distant, frosty tone was
unnatural would have been an understatement. "*Adrienne, I come.
Soon.*"

The hairs raised on her forearms. She couldn't raise her hands to
her ears.

Move, every part of Sloane shouted in her mind. A stumbling
mess, her legs shaking, Sloane raced to the waiting horses as she was
shoved and pushed by panicked men blinded to anything but their
own escape. When she reached the horses, she noticed the Ravyns—
hands still tied behind their backs—tugging in vain against the ropes

that tied them to posts in the ground. There'd be no escaping. No fleeing the monster of death.

"No." Something else besides fear gripped Sloane.

Alvie appeared on horseback, his arm extended to her. "Come on! Grab my hand."

"We have to help the Ravyns!" she screamed over the din.

"You mad?" He hauled Sloane up behind him astride the horse and kicked it in the opposite direction of the Ravyns.

"Nay, Alvie, I'm not jesting! Go back!"

"I have to get you outta here!"

"Alvie." Her voice was low. "We have to."

No one but Alvie would have listened to her. No one. But Alvie and Sloane had shared too much, were too close to the same person in so many ways.

He turned the horse, galloping to the Ravyns wrestling to free themselves from the posts.

"Sloane, no!" Tolvar's voice hollered from behind them, but they ignored him.

"Here," Alvie said, handing her a knife. He halted the horse, jumped down, his peg leg not the least bit wobbly, helped Sloane dismount, and ran for the nearest Ravyn, immediately sawing at the bindings. Sloane rushed to Hux and did likewise.

When he was free, she handed him the knife that hung from her belt.

Hux wasted no time in helping to free the others.

"It's getting closer!" Brinley yelled, his voice cracking.

"Sloane, we have to go!" Alvie pulled at her.

The Befallen now *was* the southern sky, and Sloane tasted something foul. "We have to help!"

"No, you don't!" Tolvar joined them, picked up Sloane as if she weighed nothing, and threw her onto his steed. The jarring sensation forced her jaw together. He mounted Valko behind her, ignoring her shouts and punches. "We cannot stop the Befallen if we die!" He yelled in her ear.

"Alvie! Is Alvie coming?" She changed the subject of her shouts. "Alvie!"

Tolvar didn't answer, instead yelled, "Valko, go!" Tolvar whipped the stallion's behind with the reins and the horse dashed up the hill and bolted into the vast plains toward where the sky was still unbelievably blue.

"Alvie!" Sloane yelled again. "I won't leave Alvie!" She turned in the saddle to see if Alvie followed them but could see naught except Tolvar's massive form.

It grew darker.

She would not leave Alvie. She grabbed at Valko's rein in attempt to steer the horse around.

"What in stars' names are you doing?" Tolvar yelled, resetting Valko's direction.

Sloane continued to call for Alvie, hearing nothing in return.

It was as if all color faded from the world, and the entire sky was clogged with smoke.

"Stop fighting me," Tolvar yelled again, "I'm saving you!"

But Sloane kept struggling. She had to help Alvie.

The tussle between them made Tolvar lose his grip on Sloane as he righted Valko once more. She slipped, tumbled, and banged to the ground.

Valko whinnied in terror. She lay in the dirt with her eyes closed. Tolvar cursed and yelled, but rather than his voice growing closer, it became more distant.

Open your eyes, ordered the part of Sloane, who had a notion the journey was over.

Open or closed, you're still dead, the other part soothed. *Best not to watch.*

Sloane tightened her eyelids closed and waited until some biting, bitter something slammed into her. Her breath cut from her lungs.

Then it was over and, opened or closed, her eyes would have seen naught but blackness.

CHAPTER 44

Tolvar

Tolvar had lost his father. His betrothed. Good men he'd followed and led and fought alongside. He'd even lost Crevan. But the thought of losing Sloane drove Tolvar into a state unlike he'd ever experienced.

When he finally gained control over Valko's neck-breaking gallop, Tolvar turned him around, but it was too late. The cloud of death covered everything behind him. He saw nothing. Nothing but a darkness that made him question his bravery. And the scar on the back of his neck, the would-be of Adrienne's Curse, itched.

It had been said of the Wolf that he was one of the most cunning and brave knights who'd ever lived. Tolvar felt like a fool—and a coward—as he dismounted Valko and simply stared at the darkness, the long-last revealed form of the Befallen in the distance. It was the most hideous sight he'd ever witnessed. But like a cloud they'd first mistaken it for, it silently hovered across the plains, a voluminous shadow, the very meaning of menace drifting over the valley until, without warning, it vanished. Disappeared as though it had never been.

It took time for Tolvar to regain his senses, to understand that the Befallen *had* withdrawn into nothing, leaving the impression it had never appeared.

But the bodies. The bodies strewn across the field is what made Tolvar fully recover from any doubt it had simply been a nightmare.

Sloane.

Tolvar trembled.

He had to check. He had to see for himself.

And he'd never even told her...

Even so, he stood planted, eyes darting from one body to next. Not Sloane. One of those poor contorted beings could not be Sloane. The dream—or haunting—of his father's ghost slipped into his mind. *I've failed again. I've failed.* Something stung the back of his throat. The Wolf never shed tears.

"Wolf!" Ghlee's voice came. On horseback, Ghlee trotted toward him, his hair tousled, his face blanched. The wound on his arm had clearly reopened as the bandage was stained red. "How bad is it? Who's left?"

Whatever was caught in Tolvar's throat thrust a hitching noise from Tolvar. "I don't know."

Ghlee followed Tolvar's eyes to the scatter of bodies, unnaturally sewn across the fields, rooted motionless there forever.

"Stars," Ghlee whispered. Then, "We'll find her."

Ghlee's presence gave Tolvar the strength to continue and, one by one, Tolvar forced himself to meet the dead eyes of his companions, friends, and even Ravyns. He did not want to count, but being a soldier created practices within him that Tolvar couldn't escape. Eleven so far.

But no sign of Sloane.

At one point, Tolvar considered calling her name, but he didn't think his ears could bear the sound without hearing her reply. So, he trudged along, scanning the fields like a dying man seeking water.

Finally, Tolvar stopped. There, not a stone's throw from him, was a body of a small woman laying on her side facing away from him, her crumpled skirts covering her legs, her body curled into an inconsequential heap, unmoving.

He did not call to Ghlee at the other end of the field to tell him he'd found Sloane. He wanted to say the words to her she would now never hear but that he must speak.

Gently, so gently, Tolvar scooped his arms under her frame and rolled her over onto her back, the chain holding the Edan Stone sliding around her neck.

"Mmmm," Sloane moaned. Her eyes remained closed, and her face was as pale as the moon, but Sloane, cradled in his arms, was alive.

"You're alive," Tolvar choked out, sniffling, but holding back firm the dam of tears threatening to cascade over him.

Sloane opened her giant brown eyes. "So I am. Help me sit up?"

Tolvar rocked her up but kept her cradled to his chest. Sloane squinted and squirmed but otherwise didn't seem to notice that she sat enveloped in his arms.

She turned to him with surprise. "What is it?"

"How?" was the only word Tolvar could muster.

"How what?"

"You're alive. You've escaped the Befallen. Again."

They both regarded the Edan Stone resting against Sloane's chest. "It seems I really have this time." She held the moonstone. "This must have protected me."

The words he wanted to say lodged in his throat. And there was even more he wanted to say. He wanted to shout that she must be the Unsung. He wanted to yell that she must be a damned fool for worrying about anything else but saving her own hide when the Befallen had come. He wanted to threaten to lock her away and keep her safe for the rest of time.

Instead, Tolvar simply squeezed her into an embrace and held her.

FIVE. Five people had escaped the fate of the Befallen. At least five who Tolvar and Ghlee could find. What Ravyns had survived had evidently fled, Hux and Brinley being two of them, for their bodies could not be accounted for. Neither could Alvie's.

Sloane's sobs were a storm of rage and despair.

"We don't know Alvie is dead," Tolvar repeated, "We haven't found him." But she was not consoled.

So, there were five. Tolvar, Ghlee, Sloane, Kek, and Clive. Everyone else dead or run off, in the case of the Ravyns. If Tolvar had counted the bodies correctly, only eleven of the Ravyns had survived.

And now, as Tolvar studied Sloane, curled next to a pitiful fire, the light bouncing across her blotched face, looking as though she'd like to throw herself into it, he knew he had to be the one to keep them going. There was a plan. There was a deadline. The Nay Moon grew closer, and, with Sloane's survival courtesy of the Edan Stone, Tolvar found he was a fledgling believer, though he wouldn't say this aloud.

He found Ghlee kneeling in the dark, praying over the body of Ridden.

"We need to leave first thing in the morning," Tolvar said.

"Aye," Ghlee agreed. "What about the sovereign's men who are coming?"

"Damn the sovereign. Anyway, 'tis probably better we're not here. We don't want to be questioned about what we're doing." Tolvar glanced east. "I think we're being followed anyway."

Ghlee nodded. "I've felt it, too. The Brones, you think?"

Tolvar nodded.

"They're being awfully clever about it."

"With only five, we should be able to make the journey to Kage Duna with more haste." Tolvar's focus drew to where Sloane sat by the fire. "She's really the Unsung, isn't she?"

Ghlee's eyes followed Tolvar's. "Aye. And you're going to have to *let* her be the Unsung, Wolf."

"Meaning?"

"You won't be able to protect her from everything. You're going to have to let her be the Unsung."

The firelight danced through Sloane's hair. "That's what I'm afraid of."

CHAPTER
45

Sloane

Sloane had uttered many prayers in her life. But the prayers to the Falling Leaves goddess and to the gods of the stars and to the forthcoming Hoarfrost Moon goddess for Alvie's life were of a fervor Sloane hadn't known was inside her.

But in the morning, Alvie still hadn't returned. Ghlee wondered aloud if mayhap Alvie had simply ridden off in the opposite direction and then become lost, but here on the sparse plains of Nerezza, it didn't seem likely that Alvie couldn't have found his way back.

Still, Sloane knew—even with her stinging, red eyes reminding her of yet another loss—the Nay Moon couldn't wait. And anyway, Tolvar had uttered something about wanting to be gone before the sovereign's soldiers arrived. They packed up. It felt wrong searching the packs of the dead for supplies. Like she was robbing Mohn and Asana all over again.

One oddity they'd discovered—the second time for Sloane—was a single grey stallion alive amongst the cluster of poor felled horses. Kenn, the elder's horse, fretfully whinnying and stomping the ground. The sight gave the men pause; no one moved toward the stallion. But Sloane met Kenn as an old friend and threw her arms around the beast's neck, despite both the woman's and horse's initial skittishness. The two last survivors of Mohn together once more.

Sloane might never be a horsewoman, but she was quick to take responsibility for Kenn and informed Tolvar she'd ride the stallion to Kage Duna. Still stunned at finding the horse alive and well, Tolvar and the others simply nodded, Ghlee mumbling he'd find a saddle for Sloane.

Now, kneeling in the dry grasses since before sunrise, Sloane prayed to the morning star that if she couldn't have her friend back, that the stars would embrace him into the heavens, even if he was a heretic.

Her legs ached, especially her left one. She stood, rubbing her hip and feeling less confident about riding Kenn all day. The Edan Stone was a ponderous thing around her neck today. So much loss. And yet, she must keep putting one sore leg in front of the other.

She found the men, horses saddled and laden with bulky sacks standing nearby, studying a rudimentary map together. The map didn't seem to be parchment, but rather made of cloth. The drawings were faded, and some of the names appeared as though they'd bled from being hit by liquid, so blotchy and unreadable they were.

Ghlee ran his finger along the map. "After we've left the Nerezza Plains, we'll cut here, across the Mort County."

"There'll be dust storms building up this time of year." Kek frowned. "That place is unbearable."

"Better than the early winter storms that might find us if we take the road through Fannar." Ghlee said. "Besides, we still have six days. We can stop on the border of the Mort if we need to."

Tolvar stared at the map as though his life depended on it. "Kage Duna isn't huge but does cover six leagues. How are we supposed to know where the heart is and how to find this Cibil?"

No one said a word. Six leagues? It could take them six days to comb that area. Sloane looked behind her. It was as if someone had brushed the back of her neck. But nothing. Only the chain draped around her. She studied the stone. It could be naught more than a rock. It appeared insignificant. But...

"This is how we'll find the Cibil." She held up the Edan Stone.

"How?" Tolvar said, not with disbelief but with surprise. This gaze was new to her.

"I don't know, but it will," Sloane said, fully expecting more questions. But no one said anything.

Ghlee returned his attention to the map and charted their route across the Nerezza Plains one last time.

DEOGOL's diverse terrain had existed in stories only. Life in Mohn had been vast fields of wild vegetation alternating between the vibrant green of the time of the Gale Moon, transforming through a variety of golds and browns before turning pale in the Hoarfrost Moon.

But the many settings of Deogol were anything but tales. The landscapes she'd traveled through were like her journey itself, pieces of diverse scenes and experiences—creating their own colors, feel in the air, even their own unique scent of the dirt—patched together like a quilt.

The Mort smelled like rotting bark and a staleness that told Sloane it didn't rain here. She hadn't noticed it all at once. Nerezza's dry plains gradually became a ground solid and hard, the grasses turning shorter and shorter until all that was left was the occasional thorny patch of brush. The Mort stretched into an eternity of dirt. Yet though it appeared hot, gusts of wind whipped at the party, and even wrapping her cloak tight around her did nothing to keep the wind feeling as though it blew through her.

"Should only take us one day to cross!" Ghlee yelled against the wind.

"And then we reach Kage Duna?" Sloane yelled back.

Ghlee and the others nodded. The wind picked up, and dust blew into Sloane's face. She squinted and tucked her cloak closer. Kenn pranced underneath her.

"Should we wait until the wind dies down?" Sloane said, hoping she was imparting some brilliant idea no one had considered.

"The wind is only going to worsen," Kek said, giving her what he surely hoped was an expression of encouragement. "Better to keep going while it's not bad."

Not bad? You're never going to make it, thought the part of Sloane watching dust build up. She couldn't see twenty feet in front of her.

Another gust of wind smacked at Sloane and blew her cloak off her face. She fought to get it back over her head.

Enough, the other part of Sloane quelled. *There can be no more doubt.*

The sound of the wind was a low whistle, and Sloane pictured banshees menacing out here. She tightened her grip on Kenn's reins. She knew the men were waiting for her.

Such a long way from home. A place that didn't even exist anymore. The only direction was forward. Sloane snapped Kenn's reins.

She wanted to stop. Oh, she wanted to stop. Her rear throbbed to an extent it'd simply gone numb. And her temples ached from the constant wind bellowing in her ears, her eyes stung, and her nostrils were caked and clogged with dust. And her fingertips, too, were numb from the biting cold. But most of all, her legs screamed. A single tear ran down her cheek when Kenn took a misstep and she'd been jarred in the saddle. Oh, she wanted to stop. But she didn't want to stop in the Mort. Not here. Not in this place saturated with sound, like the world would never be silent again, the incessant wind pounding on Sloane as if she were scarcely a speck of dust herself.

"We should be crossed just after sunset," Tolvar yelled next to her from atop Valko, his beard coated with dust and dirt.

Sloane could only nod, not wanting to open her cloak, let alone her mouth.

Ghlee, in the lead, halted. The others did as well, so Sloane tugged Kenn's reins to stop. The dust in the air made it impossible to see what Ghlee was doing. Tolvar trotted to Ghlee. Were they talking? It didn't look like it, and no sound reached her.

A moment later, both men turned their horses around. The five made a huddle of sorts.

"We have to find another trail," Tolvar said.

"What?" Sloane cried.

"What is it?" Kek said, turning toward what might as well have been a blind view.

"Trust us," Sloane thought Ghlee said. "We need to find a different path."

"We can't go back," Sloane yelled, forcing away other tears.

"We won't," Tolvar yelled. "We'll just sidetrack a bit."

The Unsung would never give up, sit on the cold, harsh ground, and wish she could command the blowing dust to bury her alive. But Sloane wasn't sure she could continue.

Don't be a sook!

"Sloane," Tolvar yelled, Valko so close he was touching Kenn. "You can do this."

More dust blew into Sloane's eyes, and she cried out, the tiny particles feeling like daggers.

"Hold on to your saddle." Tolvar grabbed Kenn's reins and led the stallion behind him. "You can do this!"

Sloane nodded, inched her cloak's hood further over her head, and hugged around Kenn's neck, trusting Tolvar to find a new path.

CHAPTER
46

Sloane

"The Befallen comes for you. For every soul. For it belongs to a darkness that shall bury light.

"And it comes for you soon."

Sloane hadn't bothered to shake the dirt out of her plait, though she could feel how the dust that had embedded itself there weighed it down. But even without the dust of Mort covering Sloane's entire being, she'd still feel heavy. Still feel wrecked. The nightmare she'd awakened from revealed to her the end of a world. The end, not only of Deogol, but all of Tasia. And the last words, spoken by a voice so chilling, made Sloane shiver as she stirred awake and sat up.

The voice she'd heard in the Befallen that day she'd lost Alvie. She'd forgotten. But her dreams dug underneath the depths where Sloane's mind had concealed it and brought it back. The voice in the nightmare was the same as the one she'd heard in the Befallen.

"Adrienne, I come. Soon."

Sloane scratched behind her ear and felt dirt underneath her fingernails.

The Befallen and the Curse of Adrienne were connected, and the only thing Sloane was certain about regarding that information was that she was not brave enough. Not brave enough by half.

For the thousandth time, she wished she knew the whereabouts of Alvie. She surveyed the sleeping men, Tolvar standing guard a few yards away. Could she tell him what he'd suspected about the Curse was something she *knew*?

Though she hadn't made a sound, Tolvar noticed her and came to crouch next to her, the intensity in his eyes never leaving as he continued to scan the area, still on guard.

"You should be sleeping."

"The ground woke me," Sloane said.

"I don't doubt that," Tolvar said, still swiveling his head. It was as if she could see his ears perked in the feeble light of what soon would be dawn. "Did you sleep at all?"

"Aye," Sloane said. "Though I feel as though I'll carry the sound of the wind with me for all time and eternity."

Tolvar smirked and then stuck a finger in his ear, drawing out dirt. "But you made it."

"Barely. Not without help. Your help."

"You did fine. Better than some knights I've been in company with," Tolvar said, standing and keeping his attention westward.

Sloane wanted to say something about her nightmare, about Adrienne. But Tolvar particularly resembled the Wolf right now, and she wondered what he might scoff at. Still.

"The Befallen seeks the Curse of Ad—Adrienne." She cringed like she'd bitten her tongue.

The only sign Tolvar gave that he'd heard was his nostrils flaring.

"When the Befallen came over me, I heard a voice. A voice like the meaning of horror itself. It said, '*Adri*—'" She paused and gritted her teeth. "*Adrienne, I come. Soon.*'"

"So, we guessed right at Dara Keep," Tolvar said, crouching again but still directing his attention to the west. "And we can have no doubt the Brones are trying to—or worse, already have—unearthed the Curse. They'll try to wield its power."

"Won't that make everything worse?"

Tolvar finally gazed at Sloane and offered her a half-smile that made her shoulders surrender in what might have been rapture had the topic and setting been different.

"If only everyone was as pure as you," Tolvar said. "Sadly, men have tried to wield Adrienne's power before."

"How?" Sloane asked, shifting her sore legs. "I thought the Curse was buried ages ago. Hundreds of years ago."

"Things buried may always be dug up," Tolvar said, pacing, his eyes searching, never stopping.

"Dug up?"

"I have seen it for myself. Men overcome with greed and arrogance, thinking they are stronger than the dark magic they hope to control. The Curse may have been buried long ago, but unless left undisturbed, the Capella Realm, Deogol, the whole of Tasia will never be completely safe. In the end, Adrienne needs to be destroyed, not simply buried."

Sloane's ears stung, but she let the words sink in.

Would destroying the Befallen destroy Adrienne as well? She could still hear the voice pummeling through her. *"Adrienne, I come."*

"What happened to your brother?"

For the first time, Tolvar seemed caught off guard. He quickly regained his composure. "I assumed you'd speak to Ghlee at some point." He paused. "Dead, I imagine. Like his allies who were hunted down and brought to justice for what they did." His focus had drifted far away, but each word emitted clenched emotions.

Sloane yearned to grip his hand.

The man standing guard before her, who was famed to have ripped out the bowels of a shadow cat with his bare hands, looked naught like a knight, but a tortured son lost in grief. She half-expected Tolvar to pull a flask from his pocket, but mayhap he had none.

"But before Crevan—before everything, he once saved my life. During the War of a Hundred Nights, in a battle, we discovered the Orlans had somehow infused their weapons with some sort of elixir that carried tiny droplets leftover from the Curse of—"

"Do not say it again."

"The Curse. Given to them by the Skyward witches of Grenden. I was struck."

Tolvar bent and lifted his hair off his neck, showing Sloane a small black line running behind his ear. Sloane's breath caught, though she instantly regretted her reaction. Tolvar covered the scar.

"Crevan *pulled* the Curse from the wound. Like a thread."

"How?"

"It was a strange night. So dark, a moonless night, and even the stars seemed to be veiled. And so cold. I remember stories as a boy..."

He had not answered her question, and he did not go on. They sat in silence, his face unreadable. He'd never unmasked himself to her like this. So she dared one more question.

"I know you saw something in the Mort. I know we went a different way because of it. What did you see? Why won't you tell me? I know you told the others."

"I didn't think it necessary."

"I made the trek, same as everyone else. I deserve to know."

Tolvar paced. "It was a body. With five stabbings through the chest. The dagger still embedded in one and a note that read, *Turn back while you still can.*"

He stopped and lifted an eyebrow as if to ask, *happy?*

Forget the Befallen; the Brones were obviously tracking them.

Sloane wanted her reaction to be outrage. She really did. She wanted to find some foundation of bravery that held her firmly to her faith that she was here for a reason. That the Edan Stone hung around her neck because she *was* the Unsung. She still hadn't dared utter it aloud, but stars, she *wanted* to be the Unsung. But her first reaction was a weight in her stomach that sank any kernel of courage she might have, and a squeal silently held in her throat.

Sloane noticed the three sleeping men had their weapons clutched tightly to them. Their legs facing outward, their bodies taut as if about to spring up any moment. Why, they weren't asleep at all. And Tolvar's constant vigilance and pacing didn't seem so precautionary now, but a thin shield between life and death.

Her palms shook. "I don't think I'm made for this."

Tolvar crouched beside her once more. His eyes penetrated—captured—hers. His hand took hers.

"You were born for this, Sloane."

CHAPTER
47

Tolvar

S he gaped back at him, those huge eyes wide and panicked.
His purpose for being in Deogol—this exquisite woman—
was inches from him, staring at him terrified. He did not want this
lovely creature to make this face. He loathed his feelings for her. He
hated what he knew in his bones. He did not want Sloane to be the
Unsung, yet there were some things the Wolf was never wrong about.
Instincts he could not ignore. Tolvar wanted to sweep her up and
carry her far from here, but instead, he'd ensure they continued their
two-day ride to Kage Duna.

He'd traveled to Deogol with an unyielding objective, and the
Wolf never turned back from his duties. Never.

Ghlee and the others stirred, and he appreciated Ghlee not
making eye contact with him, for he was certain they'd overheard his
conversation with Sloane about Crevan. Tolvar took the opportunity
to seek the privy and a moment of solitude.

Tolvar did not want to think about Crevan. Or his father. Or his
father's ghost on the night of the Falling Leaves Moon. Or most of all,
his failures. Nay, he wouldn't fail this time. His feelings for Sloane be
damned, he would *not* fail this time.

Despite rationing their water, Tolvar took a palm full and
splashed it on his face.

"Turn back while you still can"?

Tolvar would show these cowards the very meaning of "while
you still can." The battle with the Ravyns had merely been practice.

A warmup for the Wolf. He drew his sword. The voice of the Falling Leaves Moon had told Tolvar to have peace. And he would. As soon as he'd fulfilled his quest here. The Befallen, Adrienne's Curse, the Brones, all of them be damned. Tolvar was the Wolf.

And he was ready.

TOLVAR HAD JOURNEYED to the Skyward Mountains in Grenden, the deserts of Orla, and the lush moors of Ashwin, but the diverse landscapes of the eastern provinces of Deogol were quite something. He mentioned it in passing to the others, Sloane excitedly saying how amazed she was as well. Her expression was endearing and, again, Tolvar drove away how her enchanted countenance stirred something in his chest.

Kage Duna was a grey place. Hardly more than an enormous swampland. Here, the sky seemed blank and matched the dreary patches of bogs and saggy quag trees, a variety of tree that touched Valko's shoulders and were the color of nothing.

"A diviner lives here?" Tolvar said. "I wager he finds only destinies riddled in depression."

Kek and Clive snickered, but Sloane threw him a sour look. "He's here, and we're going to find him."

But after a day's search, they discovered nothing but more soggy marshes. Little of the land was dry, and they found themselves spending a wet night, practically everything covered in muck. While taking his turn standing watch, Tolvar marveled again at the quietness of this place. Nary a bird nor a night creature scurried about.

They'd also scouted the area and could find no evidence of anyone following them, though Tolvar didn't need to find the Cibil to know they *were* being tracked. His shoulders ached from the strain of being primed for attack. He would love a draught of some moon mead right about now. If he couldn't be physically warm, at least his insides could have the sensation of warmth.

The second night, Tolvar questioned everything. This was a fool's errand. *If* the Cibil ever existed, he was surely dead by now. Certainly not living in these frigid marshes. There was still no sign of the Brones' whereabouts, not so much as a muddy foot or hoof print, and Tolvar could plainly see the exhaustion on Ghlee's and the others' faces. Being prepared for an attack was a battle in and of itself.

And Sloane. She was withering out here, like petals succumbing to the chill. He didn't ask—he knew how she'd react—but after riding Kenn, her limped gait had grown much worse these two days. Every stride was a pain she stubbornly refused to show on her face, though Tolvar sensed it all the same.

And then it rained on the third night. It did not stop even as morning dawned. No one slept.

"There're only t-t-t-two m-m-m-more nights 'til the Nay M-m-moon." Sloane's teeth chattered so badly, she could barely be understood. She sat looking pitiful under one of the quag trees, it doing naught to help keep her dry.

Tolvar glanced up, great drops of freezing rain hitting his face. The clouds blocked everything. The sun, the stars, the moon, and their hope as well.

"The Edan Stone reveal anything yet?" Ghlee asked again. They'd asked that question dozens of times in the last few days. It seemed Sloane's notion that the Edan Stone would help to find the Cibil of the Nay Moon was wrong.

There was nothing to do but sit and wait for the rain to subside. Its patter against the cold ground and the scatter of bogs surrounding them shut out almost every other sound.

Almost.

Tolvar tilted his head. Had he heard something? He strained his ears.

If it was true that the Wolf's hearing was better than most men's, at this moment, he'd never been more glad for that trait. And had never been so discouraged.

For he *had* heard something. The Brones had waited until their party was as beaten down and as unsuspecting as possible.

His sword was unsheathed, resting against his chest. The three other men were sitting likewise. All three appeared poised to defend. Good. If it wasn't so blasted wet and cold, Tolvar might have smirked. Another huge droplet plopped from a quag tree branch onto his nose. He took in a sigh, no longer hearing their attackers exactly, more sensing them through years of combative instincts.

Sloane was in the middle of their semi-circle, her eyelids fluttering, obviously fighting to stay awake. There was only a moment, mayhap less. Tolvar frowned briefly, wishing he could throw her onto Kenn before this started. He'd given her command to ride away if there was an attack, and he was about to find out just how stubborn she was.

Tolvar heard movement again, impossibly, through the pounding rain, and this time he caught an accurate direction of where it came from. 'Twas time.

"Ghlee," Tolvar said. He only needed to say it once; his friend was as alert as he.

The blonde man, his wet hair deceivingly dark, immediately turned toward Tolvar, not a question of 'what?' in his eyes, but the question of 'where?'. He had the attention of Kek and Clive as well.

Tolvar inclined his head to the left, and the men nodded their acknowledgment.

He silently cursed that there wasn't time to alert Sloane, but as predicted, he'd been right. Less than a moment. Tolvar was on his feet, the others close behind, just as the first Brones attackers came out of the gloom and charged at them. Tolvar's sword blocked the one aimed at him with the first *clink*. The only sounds that followed, other than the rain and the clash of steel, were Sloane's scream and the startled whinny of the horses hobbled nearby.

Tolvar swung his sword, working to find his balance on the

uneven, drenched ground. Luckily, the Brones attackers were no better at finding their footing. The attacker who'd raced to assist his comrade fighting Tolvar slipped and fell into the shallow bog nearest them. It took a moment for him to struggle back to his feet, but by the time he had, Tolvar had disposed of his comrade. The man fell face-first into the muck with a sickening sound, his blood mixing with the bog and rainwater.

Tolvar brushed the rain off his face while also snorting water out his nostrils. As he parried and blocked the new attacker, Tolvar glanced to see what they were up against. It'd been a while since Tolvar had battled in the rain, the impenetrable sheets concealing those who might still be hiding. But he detected through the gushing torrent Ghlee and the others had also downed their first attackers and were combatting new ones. The red spreading on the ground was garish against the grey.

Meanwhile, Sloane, her back pinned against the tree no bigger than Tolvar, had drawn out her knife and held it out in front of her, white-knuckled, in both hands. She'd stopped screaming at least, drawing less attention to herself, but it would only be a matter of moments before one of the Brones spotted her as an easy target.

"Sloane, get on that horse and get out of here!" Tolvar bellowed.

Sloane gave a brief nod but didn't budge, her eyes wild and blank at the same time, her face as colorless as their surroundings. Stars, he *would* have to throw her on that horse, wouldn't he?

Tolvar pivoted, leading his opponent toward Sloane's direction.

Even with his ever-growing concern for her being smack in the middle of their battle, stars, did it feel good to be wielding a sword.

He was almost to Sloane, who still held her knife in a death-like grip.

"Sloane, move!" he shouted over his shoulder, dodging out of the way of his opponent's blade at the same time.

When he was close enough to stretch out his hand to her, Tolvar adjusted his fighting stance and modified his grip on his sword. He was finished fooling around with the man on the wrong side of his weapon.

Two expert swipes and the man sunk to his knees, falling like his comrades.

Tolvar took Sloane's forearm. "Let's go!"

He had her next to Kenn, the horse pawing and neighing like the other beasts, when Sloane screamed, "Look out!"

Tolvar turned in time to see the man he'd just downed, blood pouring from the wound at his neck, raising his sword at Tolvar's back. Before Tolvar could pivot around to defend himself, Sloane had lunged herself between the two and drove her knife into the man's chest. The Wolf wasted nary a second and followed her strike with his own, opening the neck wound wide to reveal the innards of his throat. The man gurgled and dropped in finality into the mud.

The pounding rain continued its merciless assault as Tolvar stared shocked into Sloane's eyes. Her knife had barely been fast enough—he'd been in enough battles to know— a breath faster than his own strike and had made the difference between Tolvar being wounded and standing here before her.

He expected to see trepidation tearing at her, but her expression was one of calm.

"My knife," she said, turning away from the body, the only sign she was affected by what had just transpired.

Tolvar retrieved her knife from the corpse, and handed it to her, not bothering to wipe the blade. The rainwater would cleanse it soon enough.

Sloane took it as though seeing the knife's point for the first time.

The underscore of steel against steel in the patter of rain brought them both back, and Tolvar now had one eye on the scene, one eye on Sloane, who, for some confounded reason, was not mounting Kenn.

"I can help," Sloane said before giving another yelp. Two more Brones appeared and attacked Tolvar together. His training and instincts drove him fully back into the battle.

"You can help by fleeing!" he yelled, moving the two he fought away from her and the horses, still whinnying to wake the banshees. One opponent was an inch taller than he, while the other was close to the size of Sloane. Together they fought as one, which Tolvar found to be in his benefit; there was no surprise in their attack. "Go! Are you here to find the Cibil or not?"

Those words seemed to finally drive some sense into the woman, and, from the corner of his eye, he glimpsed Sloane and Kenn trot off, the bog making it impossible to gallop away. When he no longer sensed her in his peripheral vision, Tolvar exhaled, gave his neck and shoulders a shake, and readied himself to give these two a real fight.

At one point, and mayhap it was the rain—Tolvar was uncertain how long they'd been fighting— but he'd downed six men so far, checking each time someone fell that Ghlee and the others were still upright. Ghlee's arm was bleeding, and Tolvar didn't know if it was his wound that'd reopened.

Fewer and fewer attackers were breaking into the fight, and Tolvar had a moment's fear that mayhap they'd focused their hunt on Sloane. But he reminded himself the Brones were after him, had no idea who Sloane was, and had probably not paid her any heed. She appeared too slight. As another opponent was downed, and the rain at last seemed to be subsiding, Tolvar had to smile at this thought. Too slight. Sloane was anything but that, wasn't she? Fools.

Wait? Was that it? Tolvar, Ghlee, Kek, and Clive found themselves standing together with no one else to fight.

"I would like to say that was easy, Wolf," Ghlee said, catching his breath, "but lying is for the weak."

Tolvar circled around, the light drizzle making it easier to scan the area.

He'd satisfied himself that the Brones had truly retreated when a group of half dozen men emerged from behind the mist into the clearing. It was evident by their swagging posture—soaking wet though they were—and their grim expressions, cutting and severe, that these men were more consequential members of the Brones.

Tolvar strode forward. Better to not waste time. They needed to find and catch up to Sloane.

"When are you going to send me a worthy opponent?" Tolvar said to a man, older, shorn, and with a disturbingly thin nose, who stood front and center. "You look no better for battle than these poor fools who've just suffered death."

The man's thin eyebrows raised above his angular eyes. "That so, Wolf, is it? I've heard much of you and have been anxious to finally meet you. Although finding you here speaks poorly of your intelligence as we've sent multiple messages to stop seeking the Unsung."

Tolvar's heart quickened, thinking of Sloane riding stars knew where in the wilds of Kage Duna. His only hope was that he hadn't misjudged the Brones. That they hadn't realized he had found the Unsung.

"I haven't received those messages, I'm afraid," Tolvar said, Ghlee snickering next to him.

"Aye, that's clear to me now. Which is why I was ordered to give you this final message," the man said. He nodded to the man next to him, who, as deftly as any of the best knights Tolvar had ever encountered, nocked an arrow into a bow, and fired it straight into Kek's chest.

Kek squeezed out a *humph*, and the stout man fell. As soon as he was on the ground, he writhed and contorted in morbid motions. Where the arrow had struck, an oozing, inky black something bled from the arrow's puncture.

"Stars," Ghlee whispered, crouching next to Kek. "Kek! Kek, can you hear me? Tolvar, 'tis—"

But Tolvar didn't need Ghlee to finish. For he'd seen the Curse of Adrienne for himself. Tolvar faced the men again, as two more arrows soared in their direction. He ducked and managed to dart out of the way, but Clive wasn't so quick. The younger man fell as well, succumbing to the arrow's poison in the same way as Kek, twisting and convulsing. What looked like ink dribbled from both men's paled lips.

Tolvar leaped up, his sword firm in his fist. "Cowards. Fiends." His eyes never stopped darting to and fro, waiting for the next arrow. But the men before them seemed content to fire no more. They were clearly enjoying themselves. Ghlee stood next to him. His brother.

Tolvar tightened his grip on the sword's hilt as if he could wield the force of an army behind it, as if the power of the stars' light could strengthen a common man such as he. He drove the glare of the Wolf into the men before him, knowing full well it would be the last of its kind.

He wished for faith. He wished for many things: self-forgiveness, redemption, and even forbearance—things he'd never find—as he took one last breath to call up all his strength. Most of all, Tolvar wished he could've seen his quest to the end. To see the Unsung, Sloane, fulfill her destiny.

But Tolvar had already encountered the Curse of Adrienne, and he'd, aye, finally, received the message. The will of darkness was stronger than the light of hope.

Tolvar noted the minuscule movement of the leader's hands. Saw some sort of signal between the men. Knew whatever was about to happen was going to be unstoppable.

"Ghlee," Tolvar said.

"Aye?"

"'Tis been an honor."

CHAPTER
48

Sloane

Sloane kept looking back as Kenn zigzagged through the swamplands. She couldn't help it. Tolvar. Ghlee. She had to go back.

What are you going to do to help? thought the part of Sloane, who kept jumping at branches and bubbles forming in the bogs.

Nothing. Nothing. But I left them. "I left them," she whispered.

She wanted to cry. She wanted to scream. She wanted to fall down and die like she had moons ago when she discovered the village of Mohn. She'd killed a man. She'd saved Tolvar, hadn't she? And then she'd abandoned them to their fate. Her emotions vomited from her. There was no controlling the jumbling mess of feelings retching from one extreme to the next. She felt everything.

The rain lessened, and as if that were a signal, it nudged away Sloane's feelings and brought thoughts to the forefront of her mind.

There was still the Cibil of the Nay Moon to find.

Teeth chattering, the adrenaline wearing away, Sloane wiped her face—the tears and raindrops indistinguishable—and began looking around.

Tolvar was right. Who'd want to live here? Did she really have enough faith to believe this was where a great diviner hailed from? The grey branches of the trees splintered the colorless sky, giving Kage Duna the appearance of cracked clay. She shivered, pulling her cloak tighter around her shoulders—though soaking wet, it did little in the way of warmth. Stopping wasn't an option.

The next day, Sloane couldn't remember what it was like to be dry. She was no longer sopping wet, but her gown, shoes, and cloak still clung to her in sticky dampness. She and Kenn's pace eased, and the horse meandered where he wanted.

She didn't want to admit she was lost. Not that she'd known where they were going before the attack. She'd trusted the others to know.

Aimlessly wandering, Sloane swallowed the pain of leaving Tolvar and the others. The sting of not knowing what'd become of Alvie. The ache of wondering where Joah had gone. She was alone, just as she'd been when the Befallen had taken everything from her. These past moons that she'd been surrounded by people who'd befriended her, challenged her, coaxed her on, seemed like naught more than a distant dream—mayhap from her time on the lonely road to Vithal, though she hadn't known where she'd been going then either.

The difference is, you're not a sook anymore, thought the part of Sloane who willed her to open her eyes more clearly to notice how the trees were beginning to change.

Aren't I? For the outlines of trees in her periphery still felt ominous.

But you're still moving. You're still trying. You still believe.

Sloane's hand found the Edan Stone and clutched it like it would give her direction, though all she felt was the cold smoothness of rock against her chilled skin.

The Nay Moon was tonight.

Not paying heed to where the horse headed, Sloane wasn't prepared for when Kenn stumbled into a puddle, deeper than it appeared. Dirty bog water splashed up, dousing Sloane. She was already wet, but the startled horse sidestepped, and Sloane, stunned by the new drench of water, almost fell.

As she tugged the reins to right herself, Kenn backed up, whinnying in alarm at the sudden shift in his mistress's direction. He reared his forelegs and Sloane cried out as she clung to his neck.

When Kenn regained his footing—snorting and stamping—Sloane's heartbeat was in her throat, her breaths thumping whimpers.

She slid off his back, hands shaking. *Not a sook, eh?*

A branch snapped behind her, and she spun, pulling her knife from her belt, only to find some sort of lizard plunge into one of the shallow bogs. "Sook."

She was cold, frightened, and lost. Sloane rubbed her sore rear as she also pried a chunk of mud from her hair. She'd never be a horsewoman. She could add that to the list. She'd never be a lot of things.

Sunlight streamed through the clouds and brightened a spot on the ground. The tiny beam bounced in front of her as the rain began to sprinkle again. New gleams of light jutted through the clouds, making the pattering rain sparkle. Aye, she would never be a lot of things.

But she wanted to be the Unsung.

Mayhap she had been right when she told Tolvar at their first meeting that the Unsung was simply the person who decided to be so.

"I want to be the Unsung," she whispered, still holding the Edan Stone. The words she'd at last dared to let slip off her tongue, the words that had been hanging there for fortnights as if dangling off a cliff had finally tumbled out. That made Sloane warmer, even as the scatter of gentle raindrops continued to kiss her face.

The first thing you need to do is gain your bearings.

Note the differences in your surroundings, Tolvar said in her mind. *Scan the vicinity and observe the distinctions in the landscape.*

Sloane wiped her cheek, letting the Edan Stone fall back to where it hung at her chest.

Bogs. Quag trees. More bogs. Nothing seemed distinct. It was all grey.

But. The trees to the right—for she couldn't say if it was the northeast or south or any direction—were different, weren't they? They clumped together and, like a stagger of stairs, grew taller in the distance. Sloane, careful not to wobble into a puddle, led Kenn that way. The trees in front of her were quag trees, but the ones a few yards away were taller, their branches fuller. The bark a light brown, not grey.

It couldn't be the Edan Stone that gave the sensation of being warmer—she'd let go of it moments before—but as she surveyed through the trees, growing denser as they stretched farther away, she did feel warm.

"This way," she said to Kenn, who merely huffed a snort and blinked at her.

The trees were so close together, she wasn't certain she could ride Kenn through them. Did she dare leave Kenn? How far did the trees lead? How far must she walk? Would someone stumble upon him, giving away her whereabouts? Did she want that to happen?

Enough. I have no choice.

She tied Kenn to a low branch of a quag tree. "You'll be okay. I'll be back."

But how to not lose her way? How to find her way back?

Rummaging through Kenn's saddlebags, she searched for something to aid her. Her hands touched something soft, and she drew from the bag the blue shawl she'd found in Mohn's elder's cottage. She'd rediscovered it scavenging through the Ravyns' supplies and had felt no reservations about plucking it back as her possession. Sloane inspected its beauty once more and held it to her nose, wishing the scent of home still clung to it. But it smelled like horses and some kind of herb, probably the sort that was smoked in a pipe. Even still, she hated to rip it. Save for the Edan Stone and Father's stitching needle, it was the last thing she had from Mohn, the rest of Father's tools never having been found among the Ravyn's things.

"Mayhap it was always meant to be this way," she whispered, finished with her hesitancy to rip it.

The next thing Sloane retrieved from Kenn's saddlebag was her moon cuff. She slipped it around her wrist. Certainly, it was not traditional, and she may be inviting misfortunate by wearing it on the moonless night of the Nay Moon, but Sloane needed to feel its strength encircling her. She then quickly packed her water pouch, a blanket, and some dried meat into her rucksack—not bothering to empty it of the stitching needle and the few tools she'd taken from Dara Keep—huffed it onto her shoulders and took her first tentative step into the trees. There was something familiar about this moment, but Sloane reassured herself.

She *wanted* to be the Unsung, and certainly, that person was no sook.

CHAPTER
49

Sloane

This was it. The pangs in her leg were forgotten. Whatever she'd felt the last week, doubt was no longer one of her emotions. This was the place. The heart of Kage Duna. Hidden in the plainness of the snarled trees, Sloane stood astonished at suddenly being under a clear, open night sky. She'd spent all day and evening trekking, surrounded by grey and gloom on the outside of the grove, tying fragments of blue to trees as she went. Her eyes took in the lake before her. So still, it might have been a looking glass, and it reflected within its waters the glory of glittering stars above, making her feel as if the night of the Nay Moon surrounded her entirely. Velvety darkness concealed the ashen groves encircling this place, and Sloane had the urge to place her fingertips on the cool ground to discover if where she stood was real.

"Hello?" Sloane worried if she took her eyes off the lake, the dark scene might disappear.

It had been an age since her eyes had feasted on beauty and devoured anything resembling peace. Yet, she had to skim them away from the lake if she were to find the Cibil, who could be viewing her from the other side of the lake or standing mere feet from her.

No sound returned Sloane's greeting. Not a creature fluttering in the trees, nor even a light breeze. Though it was well into autumn, the air seemed untouched by any season. Sloane, finally dry, felt as if she could be indoors. The air, like the lake's surface, was so still.

"Hello?" she repeated, not as bold as the first time. It felt wrong to disturb this place. She set the rucksack onto the ground, but her focus could not be withdrawn from the pinpricks of stars reflected in the lake, as if the sky had dipped into the earth before her feet.

"I see you, too, are drawn to the dark beauty the Nay Moon possesses." The raspy, deep voice next to Sloane caught her off-guard, but she simply replied, "Aye."

She sensed she was being studied, but whether it was the intoxicating draw of the lake or her apprehension that she would scare away the person next to her, Sloane did not turn toward him.

"You have traveled a far distance, Sloane of Mohn, daughter and apprentice of Corwin, master leatherworker of the Ordell Province." His voice creaked as though never used, which it probably wasn't.

The back of her neck tingled from being addressed so specifically by a stranger, but still, she didn't face him.

"I have. I've come to ask you a question," Sloane said. She itched to turn toward him.

"Hmph. From the look of you, you have many questions. You yearn to know many secrets." A rasped laugh met her ears. "And the longer you stand there, the more questions come to your mind: Is it true? Are you the Unsung? What *is* the Befallen? Does Adrienne stir once more in these parts?" At the word Adrienne, a ripple undulated across the lake. The Cibil ignored it and continued. "Who unearthed such a curse? Can the weapon destroy the Curse, too? What is this weapon, exactly? Where in Ayla are you supposed to go—for it covers many leagues, much more than Kage Duna? And how can you find the Befallen to defeat it? And, of course, the question that lingers there on your tongue. The only question that can possibly save you and this land, for Deogol cannot withstand ten more years of succumbing to the Befallen."

Sloane's heart drummed in her chest. He was right. She *did* have all those questions. And stars, she hadn't even thought of some of them. Repeating the questions in her mind, her shoulders sank.

One thing was certain: she needed to choose her words carefully.

He was obviously warning her that asking one question to the Cibil of the Nay Moon meant one question only.

It was then that Sloane could tear her eyes from the lake to fix them upon him.

The ancient man who stood next to her was short. Shorter than she was, surprisingly enough. His white beard trailed down his chest, ending at his belt, a worn piece of cracked leather. It was probably the leatherworker apprentice in her, but she couldn't help but trail her eyes down momentarily to notice his tattered leather shoes, too. The poor man's feet must freeze every winter if those were his only shoes. She could make out a few toes sticking out.

Peering into his shadowed countenance, she couldn't begin to count the lines drawn on his wrinkled face, threaded together as if it —like his belt—was crackled into unnumerable tiny folds. His eyes were as black as the moonless night. Like the lake, Sloane found herself pulled into them, though in contrast to the serenity of the lake's surface, the Cibil's irises dragged at her like a weight. The longer she stared into them, the more it seemed she would never be able to look away. It was as if Sloane detected the heavy shadows of information held within them and would drown at any moment under their force.

It felt somewhat like an impossible feat when Sloane ripped her eyes from his.

Her eyes landed on his shoes again. Then to the rucksack next to her. Her fingers itched.

"In truth, I thought I did know my question, but now that I see the beauty of Kage Duna, I long to linger here for a time. While I consider my question, I could mend your shoes, Master Cibil." She bowed her head low, as if he were noble, for mayhap he was—ages ago. When she straightened, the Cibil was regarding her with a high chin and a twinkle in those dark eyes.

"That so?"

"We have until dawn." Sloane had almost posed the words as a question but corrected herself in time. Carefully, she sat and rummaged through the rucksack. Blessed goddesses of the moon, at the bottom of the sack along with Father's stitching needle, was a leather string she'd not been certain was still there. She smiled into the bottom of the sack, keeping her eyes on the tools she set next to her.

"If your grace will kindly remove your shoes, I would be happy to patch them. You know I can."

The Cibil uttered a low sound like a cross between something contrary and approving. He sat, hitting the ground hard and giving an *oof*.

"You are either mad or wise, for naught much surprises me. But I warn you, one question only is all you are allowed."

Sloane nodded, taking the sweaty shoe in her hands and studying it in the darkness. The light of the moon would've come in handy. If ever there was a time for her to have her wits, it was now.

"Earlier today, I decided I wanted to be the Unsung, so there's that question answered," she said. Sloane withdrew a scrap of leather from the rucksack. She couldn't believe her luck at it being there. She waited for a response from the Cibil, but none came. No matter. She would stretch the time with her task.

But am I the Unsung? She could taste the question on her lips. Wanting to be the Unsung and knowing wasn't the same. She could ask, and he would answer. Then every part of Sloane would be satisfied. Her hands trembled.

"As for the Befallen," Sloane continued, using her knife to cut enough of the thick leather string to sew the first patch, "'tis connected with Ad—Adrienne and the curse that flows through its darkness. I heard the voice of the Befallen calling to it."

The glass-smooth lake wrinkled again upon her uttering the cursèd word.

Sloane waited for more silence from the Cibil. But the man stroked his beard and mumbled, "Interesting."

Sloane continued her stitch. "The Befallen is a form of darkness seeking Adri—the Curse, much like a kit seeking its mother shadow cat, or a flame seeking embers for more kindling..."

Did the Cibil just gasp?

"...Or a shadow seeking the solid to which it belongs." Her words hung in the air, her fingers hovering over the shoe she held.

She dared look into those dark pools, bracing to be dragged in, the answers lurking beneath the surface of his gaze. She blinked to keep from submerging in them totally.

"Was the voice male or female?" the Cibil asked.

"Male."

"Male. Hmph. Do you know what keeps the Curse of Adrienne at bay in this land?"

A chilled breeze stirred.

"Nay, Master Cibil." She wasn't going to ask a question. She was not going to be tricked and was glad she had her task to focus on. It was an empty silence before the Cibil continued, no doubt waiting to see if she'd slip up and ask.

"Faith. The Curse of Adrienne is naught more than corruption. Corruption, which, for humankind, is as ancient as our very existence. Tasia is too close to celestial light, you see. The continent cannot handle the dark forces that lurk and fester within humans..." From the corner of her eye, Sloane saw the Cibil shake his head. "...and so, it exudes anguish *incarnate.*"

Sloane took in the words but said nothing. It worked, and the Cibil kept speaking.

"The Befallen—that anguish: tangible and torturous—is a piece of that corruption that so many on the continent ignorantly assume, take for granted, was buried forever. Its desolation comes from the depths of Adrienne's corruption. Escaped from the cracks, of which there are many, in Deogol's beliefs."

Heart pounding, Sloane cut more leather with her knife, wishing for shears and the ability to ask questions. He would not be telling her all this if she wasn't the Unsung, would he?

"You know what beliefs I speak of. How many of *those* have you seen in your travels?" The Cibil pointed to her moon cuff. "I'd be surprised if you couldn't count on your hands. Nay, the light is dying. Replaced by arrogance and greed. The only way to truly destroy the Befallen and Adrienne is through belief."

The bluster from the word Adrienne stopped her from blurting out, "What about the weapon?"

With an inhale, her fingers steadied across her stitch and reground her. Nevertheless, her palms grew sweaty.

"I read you like a scholar chasing words across a parchment. The weapon." He snorted. "I hope you're ready for it."

"I hope so, too," Sloane said.

Aye, he was letting her know she *was* the Unsung. He would not speak of the weapon if she weren't. Would he? She gave one shoe back to the Cibil, and with satisfaction, watched him study her work, a slight upturn of his lips visible.

"And 'tis true that I don't know exactly where to go once I get to Ayla, but I found *this* place, so surely I'll find that place as well."

"You think so? What if you have no time to find it? What if the Azure Moon rises tomorrow?"

"Ca—" Sloane slapped a hand across her mouth. The question, "Can it do that?" had nearly leaped off her tongue. The Cibil gave her a smug smirk, and her attention quickly went back to her work. The sole of this shoe had worn away under where the big toe sat, but there was nothing she could do about it. She wasn't a cobbler. The most she could do was double up the patch. The needle stabbed into her finger, and she brought it to her lips.

Nay, the Azure Moon could not rise tomorrow. Could it? Could the sky go from the Nay Moon to a full moon in one night?

She decided *nay* at the same time the other part of her decided *aye*. It was called the Azure Moon for a reason. It must not follow the patterns of the other moons. It did not help that she'd never seen an Azure Moon; she had no experience to guide her. Her eyes drew to the lake, captured by the reflections of stars. Again, she fought for the answer within herself.

And this was why she *had* to ask the question she'd journeyed here to ask.

During this long pause, the Cibil had remained content to sit in silence, his eyes also on the lake.

The Cibil broke the silence but did not turn toward her. "That thing around your neck. Wield it with care."

The Edan Stone. In the darkness, it resembled a black half-moon.

"This saved me in the Befallen. It rolled right over me, and I was spared."

Questions burned within her. Sloane paused, praying the Cibil would explain. He said nothing but eyed the Edan Stone with familiarity. Sloane went back to her work, part of her wondering if she was going to have the strength to pull her needle through the patch and at the same time not rip the worn leather of the Cibil's shoe. How old were these? How old was he? What did he mean about the Edan Stone? If she was the Unsung, should she already know?

Just keep working.

She had almost finished with the patch on the big toe before the Cibil spoke again. "The Edan Stone will protect any who wears it from the Befallen. As well as give warning of its approach."

Wield it with care.

"It turned grey just before the Befallen overcame us," Sloane said, suddenly remembering.

"Aye, like a chunk of smoke. Like ashes of all the dead clumped together. It senses the darkness therein."

"I can track the Befallen with this," Sloane said, lifting the stone to eye level. Stars, this knowledge was both ponderous and freeing.

"Beware. That moonstone is not the weapon. You can't hold both at the same time." He exhaled and did not go on.

"I see," Sloane said. Well, at least the Edan Stone would help her track the Befallen. When the time came, with hope, she'd have the weapon. She wouldn't need the moonstone.

Through the hours they'd sat together, Sloane finished her repairs on the Cibil's shoes. It wasn't her best work, given that she didn't have everything she needed, but she still thought Father would be proud. The seam she'd resewn at the sole was barely noticeable.

She handed the Cibil his other shoe. Again, he did not thank her, but could not stop the pleased expression when he put his hand in the shoe and felt for himself that the holes were gone.

"'Twill be dawn soon," he said.

It was time to ask her question.

CHAPTER
50

Sloane

"**A**m I the Unsung?" Sloane blurted out, the words scattering in the air like dust in the wind.

"Fool!" The Cibil jumped up with the energy of a much younger man and headed toward the grove of trees.

"Wait! I didn't mean that!" Sloane yelled, staggering up. "Master Cibil, please! I didn't mean that. 'Tis your world, too! You must help me!"

She'd taken her first step, her leg stiff and tingling from sitting, when the Cibil abruptly turned.

She met his dark eyes—so dark she longed to escape them as soon as they captured hers. Even in the darkness, Sloane could see her own wide-eyed expression in them.

The question was a tangible thing, fettering her to the words she could still hear fleeing her. Sloane's intake of breath was the only sound for what seemed an eternity.

The Cibil would not release her from his gaze. "If you must ask that question, then you know the answer is nay."

Sloane's eyes glossed over, her small whimper like a scream. *Stupid, foolish sook!*

She nodded, and it was with a glimmer of conviction's inception that she dared utter the phrase, "Of course I am the Unsung."

His voice was low. "But a fool, nonetheless."

"Please help me," Sloane managed to whisper. "You know what I wanted to ask before I arrived."

Even through the blurriness of tears, Sloane was unable to draw her eyes away from the Cibil's. She leaned into him, like she could dive into the blackness of his irises and fall forever through the knowledge they carried. So much knowledge. Sloane leaned further, their faces almost touching. The smell of the Cibil's breath caught in her nose.

Sloane wiped her sleeve across her cheeks, but still, she looked. Further and further into the eyes of the Cibil of the Nay Moon. For hours. For eternity. Her legs ached. Her throat was parched and dry, but still, she looked. Her fingers found her moon cuff and outlined the symbols of the thirteen moons, and as she did so, she saw darkness. A true darkness not of the eyes of the Cibil but of something else.

She watched time pass in the Cibil's eyes, saw what seemed like a living smoke dash across a plain. People running, screaming.

"This has happened before," Sloane whispered, never even blinking. Scenes raced before her. "But not here and not like this. And it's going to happen again if I don't succeed."

Further and further, Sloane now longed to see into the bottom of the Cibil's eyes. She saw a child grow up to be a young man, watched him try and be denied joining the sovereign's scholars in a time when Kestriel was naught more than one main road and a single dock. Watched him pray and study the moons—and the stars! Observed him talk to the stars on nights void of the moon. Watched him attempt to warn the sovereign's steward, to plead to join the Capella Realm only to be rejected again. Watched him speaking with two women, so beautiful and illuminated that Sloane could scarcely not turn away, who gave him the words of the Edan Lore.

Were they the StarSeers of legends?

She watched him be driven from village after village until, astride a dark stallion, he found sanctuary in a swampland covered in sand and bogs, the stench making her nose crinkle. Beheld the Cibil dive to the bottom of a crystal lake on the night of a Nay Moon and rise to the surface, clutching something smooth and black in his hand. The

Edan Stone. Watched him and the stallion live in companionable peace—the horse's coat turning a lighter shade of grey by virtue of the Edan Stone's power—as the years passed. Saw the Cibil, an ancient man now, chance leaving his marshy home only once, it turning into disaster as he was robbed of his grey stallion and all his possessions—including the Edan Stone.

Sloane sucked in her breath. "Kenn. Kenn was your horse and that's why he survived—"

She couldn't go on. The robber, although hidden in the shadow of night, resembled a certain elder of a small, nowhere village called Mohn. Sloane's insides sunk under the weight of knowledge. But she couldn't linger there. She had to continue. Watched him, on a lonely night not long before the Harvest Moon, take something small that looked like what Sloane could only describe as a *shadow* from his pocket and dip it into a deep pool of murky water, whispering a name as he did. It submerged and traveled below the earth on a nonexistent path that was once a clear stream.

"You!" Sloane cried. "You called my name from here in Kage Duna and reached me on the banks of the bog outside Branwell. You gave me the sign of the Edan Stone in the waters."

Lauge's words of the Tale of Adria were true.

But even through realization and knowledge, Sloane didn't stop searching his eyes deeper and deeper.

She saw the Cibil transform his thoughts into a notion that transformed into an image that metamorphosized itself into the dreams of a small woman who, terrified, perceived a voice in the night as she stared at a moon blood red in Dara Keep.

"How did you do that?"

But there no answer. She must continue.

She saw a path in a land known as Ayla. On it, the same small woman, who walked slower than most, traveled.

And in her mind, the hoarse voice of a man ancient with knowledge: "Along the path of shadows, turn to the west when they stop. Across the plains you'll trek to find the realm of the shadow cat leading to the pool of crystal blue. In its reflection, the Azure Moon waits for you."

"The Azure Moon waits for you," Sloane repeated. Part of her didn't want to stop. Part of her wanted to sink into the shadow of the eyes for the rest of forever to learn everything the Cibil knew.

But the other part knew it would be her undoing, and besides, the Cibil had given her another gift, and she didn't want to tempt her fate further.

She peeled her eyes away from the Cibil with every fiber of her being, for that is what it took, and slumped onto the ground.

Sloane's voice was barely audible. "The Azure Moon rises in twenty-seven days. There will be no Nay Moon between the Hoarfrost and Solstice Moons."

Which meant that had she not arrived in Kage Duna on *this* Nay Moon, she would've been too late. She shivered with this knowledge. Stars, she was exhausted.

The Cibil of the Nay Moon's attention was back on the lake. "You'll find it difficult to stand for a few hours."

"Why did you show me that kindness?" Sloane asked. "I showed weakness, and still, you helped me."

The Cibil kept his back to her. "I suppose I *returned* a kindness, Sloane the Unsung. Besides," he turned, and when he gazed into her eyes, they didn't seem as foreboding, "you are the one who pried those answers from me. You are stronger than you know. And your journey from here will show you that. Now, dawn approaches. I must go."

And with that, the Cibil of the Nay Moon lurked back into the grove of trees and left Sloane to watch the first light of the new day touch her tired shoulders.

CHAPTER 51

Sloane

O n the first day backtracking out of Kage Duna, Sloane tried
not to consider the fact she saw no one. On the fourth day,
she let herself begin to worry.

The fragments of blue decorating the branches like a Solstice
Moon Tree led her back to Kenn at high sun the day after the Nay
Moon without error, the only thing that seemed to have gone right
since leaving the lake. Her stomach growled and her legs were weary.
She'd hugged the stallion, remembering the Cibil's memories and
wondering if it was the Edan Stone that'd truly led her to Kenn. The
Edan Stone that'd bonded itself to the stallion.

Since then, she'd become lost multiple times. She'd run out of
food, was close to running out of water, and it was becoming
increasingly cold. The blanket she'd taken with her was thin and
covered only half of her, small as she was.

It was useless to try and find the spot where the Brones had
attacked. There was no telling what direction it was, and it had been
days now. All she could hope was that Tolvar, Ghlee, and the others
would find her. If they were still alive.

Even if she knew what direction she traveled, she had to concede
that without a map, making the journey to Ayla was impossible.

Four days lost, the crescent moon's sliver-shape stretched bit by
bit. In no time, it would be the half-moon. Traditions be damned,
Sloane prayed night after night to the goddesses, gripping her moon

cuff like a tether of hope. Enough was enough. This felt too familiar. She wasn't that same lone girl on the road to nowhere anymore.

The worst part was she was alone.

No, the worst part was Ayla was too far away and she didn't know where it was. The worst part was even with the mantle of the Unsung placed upon her shoulders, she felt no better about the tasks at hand, about receiving a weapon—she could barely use her knife—about being the person who could, who *would* defeat the Befallen.

"How can I do it all?" Sloane whispered to herself in the cold, huddled near Kenn in the darkness. Being the Unsung did not mean being unafraid.

Aye, the worst part was she didn't know what had happened to any of her companions, and that was the true awfulness of being alone.

Four nights turned into seven nights, the half-moon looming. Sloane's stomach poked and pulled at her. She considered what the bark of quag tree tasted like. Her head rang with dizziness. Her water was gone. Whereas she had done her best at first to creep through the swamps of Kage Duna, lest she should run into the Brones, she now tromped aimlessly, yelling Tolvar and Ghlee's names. She did this every so often until, so tired, she dismounted Kenn, slumped to the ground, wrapped herself in the muddied blanket and closed her eyes.

"Sloane!"

Had it been a dream? Through the grey haze of Kage Duna, Sloane could tell it was morning. She was so tired. Best to close her eyes once more.

"Sloane!"

This time, Sloane sat up. Aye, she'd heard that. Kenn had wandered a few yards away, the stallion nibbling on something he'd discovered near a cluster of trees. Everything else was still.

"Sloane!"

"I'm here," Sloane called, her throat dry and scratchy. She didn't stand, though. She didn't have it in her.

The clomping through the brush and bogs grew closer. She held her breath. Her eyes squinted through the thicket. And through a parting in the brush was a man.

"Sloane!" he shouted when he saw her.

"Alvie!" Her voice was a teary laugh of disbelief.

She was lifted off the ground and embraced by her friend as she noted he was closely followed by Hux, more Ravyns, Ghlee and Tolvar, *and* Joah.

"Joah!" She hadn't the energy to cry, but her weary smile waffled somewhere between relief and desperation. She was saved!

Tolvar was next to her in three swift strides and pulled her into his arms immediately after Alvie released her.

"You must stop doing this," Tolvar whispered in her ear, lightly setting his scruffy cheek to hers.

She wanted to reply, but her thirst and hunger were too much, and, had Tolvar not steadied her, she would have fallen to the ground.

"Someone get my sister water," Joah said.

"She's so pale," Hux said. "When was the last time you ate?"

"I don't remember," Sloane admitted, feeling the world spin. "I need to sit."

Joah. He was here. And neither Hux nor Tolvar was killing him.

A water pouch was placed to her lips, and the cool liquid slid all the way down.

"Did you see the Cibil?" Alvie asked, the fear of the answer in everyone's eyes.

"Aye, I did. We have twenty days to find a crystal lake in Ayla," Sloane said, finding each word a tiresome burden to lift.

"All right, that's enough, Alvie," Tolvar said. "We can talk later. Right now, let's get a fire going and..." But the rest of Tolvar's words were lost, for Sloane closed her eyes and let herself surrender to his protective hold.

CHAPTER 52

Tolvar

The sensation growing in Tolvar's chest was entirely new to him. Aye, he had to admit it *had* been there for some time, and he'd done an adequate job ignoring it.

But now, it billowed throughout his chest and filled him with a warmth that gave him too much discomfort to ignore. He ached to let it out, knowing full well the sensation would expand even further if he did. But the Wolf had never been conquered like this before, and when he'd finally admitted to himself this sensation was made of permanence, he'd never felt so euphoric at the thought of being overpowered.

It wasn't the days they desperately searched for Sloane—his mind sick with gruesome possibilities—that'd made him realize this. It wasn't the fortnight they'd spent traveling toward Ayla, the sight of Sloane recovering like the bud of a flower in bloom.

Siria's skirt. He could not pinpoint the moment he had fallen in love with this delicate, determined woman. To his mind, it was as if the swell of love had always been there.

And it was for this reason Tolvar could *not* let anything happen to her again. Rescuing her from Rhiner and then the ordeal with the Ravyns had been one thing, but the dark places his mind had ventured while searching for her in Kage Duna had cut at him. Nay, naught else would happen to her whilst he was by her side.

Ghlee, of course, had offered him several looks, but ever proving his closeness like a brother, said nothing. Alvie obviously sensed his feelings as well but had also been smart enough to not verbalize anything either—a great feat for him, no doubt. And then there was Sloane's appalling brother. He'd been wise to stay clear of Tolvar on all matters. Bah. Blast it all, Tolvar knew his feelings must be perfectly plain to the eleven Ravyns who traveled with them, too— especially that stupid Hux shooting him pointed looks whenever he was near Sloane.

Was it plain to Sloane? He eyed her, her focus on the road they'd been trotting along all morning. Thank the stars she had her color back. Those first days, she'd been so weak, so pale. And like a blossom withered by chill, no one had been sure she'd fully come back to life. But as she'd proven several times already, her stature was not to define her. He shook his head, amazed again.

Sloane must have sensed him watching her. They locked eyes. Her nose crinkled ever so slightly the way it did when she smiled. The warmth in his chest swelled, and Tolvar could not deny that things needed to be said. And soon.

Of course, there was never a moment alone to tell her. Her brother lurked about her all the time. And if it wasn't him, even now, Hux reminded Tolvar they were surrounded. Astride his own mount, a great black stallion, the accursed leader of the Ravyns was singing again. He had a pleasant tenor voice mayhap if that sort of thing pleased you, but to Tolvar, it was merely a sharp reminder they traveled with the Ravyns. Criminals! Even if they *had* saved his and Ghlee's necks back in Kage Duna, even if they had fallen under his command—including Hux—as if he'd always led them, even if he found that most of them were far more interesting and colorful than most of the Order of Siria knights he'd spent time with, they were still Ravyns. Lowlifes. Including Joah. Sloane may want to forgive her brother, but Tolvar could hold a grudge in her place.

The Ravyns seemed to hold similar regards toward the brother they kept calling 'Kerr.' Alvie had informed him it had taken every bit of sweet-talking he had to stop Hux and Brinley from killing Sloane's brother when they'd made it away from the Befallen and run into

Joah. If Alvie hadn't reminded Hux that he'd pledged himself to Sloane, he probably would be dead. That was for the best, Tolvar supposed. It couldn't be a good idea to kill the brother of the person you loved. But he could enjoy the way that Joah was an obvious outsider among his comrades.

He shook his head once more. Brinley had joined and harmonized along with Hux's singing. Ravyns! Of all the company!

He had to keep reminding himself that these men—Hux, Brinley, and the rest—were all he had now. Save for Ghlee and those dozen left back at Dara Keep, the Order of Siria was no more in Deogol. And after they'd worked so tirelessly this past year to reestablish it here.

Tolvar shivered at the memory of Clive and Kek convulsing, blackness oozing from their lips. Had it not been for these lowlifes, Tolvar was certain his and Ghlee's fate would have followed theirs. Hux himself, had slashed the head off the archer barely in time. His command was to hack away at the Brones and ask questions later. Tolvar wanted to claim Alvie as the force behind the heroism of Joah and the Ravyns coming to their rescue, but it was because of Sloane that Hux had come. And in that, Tolvar had to admit these criminals demonstrated real quality. She seemed to bring that out in people, didn't she?

Realizing he still stared at Sloane, Tolvar broke off his gaze, averting his eyes from the others. Ravyns. Bah. 'Twas a constant war within himself to be on guard with them despite feeling that he owed them. But they were all he had. Two of the ambushed Brones, including the ugly thin-faced man, had fled. They'd be back.

His teeth clenched. The singing had ceased but Alvie had filled the air with mindless jokes and obnoxious tittering, including Ghlee's. Stars. Alvie could make friends with a floor mop and have it shaking with laughter.

Between Hux's singing and Alvie's jokes, they resembled traveling jongleurs. Sloane was the only other serious person on this journey. Something had happened in Kage Duna. And it was more than gaining information. More than what she'd recounted about the Cibil, his warning about the Befallen, and when the Azure Moon would rise. Her shoulders sat back, her chin leveled, and her focus fixed intently on the road. She'd entered Kage Duna as Sloane and left as the Unsung.

"Lord Wolf," Hux said and Tolvar turned dark eyes at the phrase. "I know these parts. We've reached Ayla."

Tolvar nodded, glad that he and Ghlee had made their calculations of the map correctly. Only one more week before the Azure Moon rose.

"Plenty of time now. Just need to find this path of shadows," Brinley added. "Whatever that means."

Tolvar still wasn't happy the Ravyns had been told of their purpose for coming to Ayla, but that blather-mouthed Alvie told them everything he knew before they'd met up with them, and Sloane and Joah had filled in the rest.

Hux continued. "I've been thinking, if we are supposed to turn west when this path ends, that must mean we are meant to travel south, for going the other direction will mean turning away from Ayla."

Tolvar scowled. He'd been pondering their direction and didn't like to admit Hux's words made perfect sense. Damn Ravyn.

"Aye. Let's head that way. Hopefully, our path of shadows will reveal itself," Tolvar forced out.

"By your lead." Hux beamed, bringing a snicker from Brinley, and Tolvar again had the thought the man toyed with him.

TOLVAR HAD AN APPRECIATION FOR TIME. He appreciated the timeliness of executing a perfectly strategized attack. He appreciated the time it took to master a new sword technique. He even appreciated how a journey must be timed exactly when rendezvousing with an ally. What Tolvar did not appreciate was the contradiction of the moon. The ever-changing dramatics the time of the moon caused.

Mayhap that was why the Capella Realm had abandoned their tributes to the moon centuries ago. The stars were constant. For all time.

Lying on his back, far enough away from the commotion around the campfire's light so Tolvar could take in the stars, like a marvel of diamonds, he decided he was right. The StarSeers, and those seeking their guidance in the Capella Realm, needed no special night to race to or wait on. But the supposed rising of the Azure Moon was only three days away.

He yearned for a drink.

They'd followed the main path to Ayla's southern border, finding naught resembling a shadow. They'd cut to four or five—he'd lost count in his frustration—lesser footpaths. Even in this late autumn air, Ayla was a place made up entirely of tall grasses and even taller trees. The autumn leaves had not yet all fallen. Strange for this late in the season. The Hoarfrost Full Moon had even come and gone. And even though it had grown more chilled by the day, kissing the ground in the morning with frost, the sunshine warmed their backs every day while they trotted along searching for a shadowed path. Nay, Tolvar did not appreciate the moon's tricks with time in the least.

In the morning, they would backtrack—again—along the main road in the hopes they'd missed something. But he doubted they had.

"May I join you?" Sloane said, standing over him and taking him by rare surprise.

"Aye," Tolvar said, rising. Blessedly, Joah hadn't followed her as he'd been doing since Kage Duna.

She sat next to him, her eyes fixed on the others enjoying themselves as they stuffed themselves—it'd been the first time in a week they'd found a deer. She wrapped her blanket tighter around herself.

"Joah keeps telling me that I've become much too serious."

Tolvar wanted to rip that idiot's head off, but he forced out a chuckle. "Well then, you've chosen wisely in your company."

"True." Sloane's eyes twinkled, the campfire light stroking her dark hair with reddish tones. "You're serious to a fault, so you are perfect company."

"You wound me," Tolvar said, feigning a knife being thrust into his chest. Sloane gave a small laugh before turning silent. Her hands fidgeted with the Edan Stone, something Tolvar had noticed she'd been doing more and more.

She'd told him details about the Edan Stone, about its ability to track and protect one from the Befallen and the Cibil's word about it not being the weapon. Sloane clung to it with a tenacious stare.

"The truth is, I find it difficult to be merry company when we're mere nights away from the Azure Moon rising. My faith is a flame," she uttered the old expression, "But this is our only chance. I cannot fail."

He offered no reply, not certain Sloane was talking to him anyway. Instead, he took in her exquisite features, his gaze lingering on her enormous eyes shaded by long eyelashes. How had he ever considered her not beautiful?

He eyed the group at the campfire. They were as alone as they might ever be.

Tell her, you fool.

But now, it was as if the swelling sensation he'd been battling with for weeks sealed off words from him. Tolvar could only continue his gaze.

Tell her, you fool.

"Why do you frown at me?" Sloane asked when she faced him.

"I'm not frowning at you." His voice leaked with defense. "I'm—just looking at you."

Sloane raised an eyebrow. "You think I will fail."

Blasted woman. At least this wasn't again about his dislike for Joah. Now Tolvar *was* frowning. "Nay. Why would you say that?"

"You gave no response to my words just now. And you always—"

"Always what?"

"From the looks you offer me, 'twould seem you still think me incapable at times."

Stars almighty, that woman knew how to pick a fight with him. But he bit back words. The nightmarish encounter he'd experienced on the Falling Leaves Moon darted into his mind. The thought quickly changed to the words of Lady Tara: *You shall require forbearance in your fortune.*

"I do not think that," Tolvar said in what he hoped was a calm voice.

"Oh?" Her nose scrunched, fist around the Edan Stone.

Tolvar peered into her. Aye, she may be the Unsung, but what mattered was that she was simply Sloane. She didn't need a title from a legend, Sloane had been readying herself for this her whole life. And she wanted—needed—others to know. To see her.

"You will not fail, Sloane. You are capable and will succeed. And I..." *Forbearance.* "I will make certain you do. You have my word."

CHAPTER
53

Sloane

A lvie had run out of stories. Hux had stopped singing. Joah had ceased asking questions. And Tolvar's scowl mirrored Sloane's mood.

The Azure Moon rose tomorrow. Everyone, including Joah—who'd been raised with the same belief in the Edan Lore as she—said, "was *supposed* to rise tomorrow," but Sloane was the keeper of the faith. There was no "*supposed;*" it *was* going to rise tomorrow. And they were still on the path in the open, the trees the only cover from the bright late autumn sun, with no clue to the shadowed path in sight.

It was difficult not to focus on Tolvar's back as he rode directly in front of her. Why had she picked a fight with him two nights ago? Their exchange had ended well enough, but they'd spoken little since. Their group—especially the last two days—had become increasingly alert, no one even relieved themselves alone, an embarrassing ordeal for Sloane, the only woman.

Tolvar cleared his throat, and Ghlee, Hux, and the others reached for their swords. Aye, increasingly wary and increasingly exhausted. Still, she wished she could say a few words to Tolvar. But what would she even say?

That you love him, thought the part of Sloane, who couldn't help but admire the girth of his shoulders.

Sloane, the no one, and the Wolf, the renowned knight? Not likely, retorted the other part of Sloane, ignoring the memory of Joah making a comment close to that last night. *Besides, the Unsung has more important worries.*

With that thought, she clutched the Edan Stone tighter and forced her eyes elsewhere.

Sloane felt different, and not in a brave Unsung sort of way. Something drove her toward something she didn't understand. And that made her awfully frightened. Her eyes darted to the Edan Stone, waiting for it to turn grey. Waiting for the Befallen to come and claim her before she could acquire the Azure Moon's weapon. But, like everyone else, the stiffness of her shoulders was from waiting for the Brones' attack. If the Brones suspected how close they were to receiving the weapon from the Azure Moon goddess, it could be at any moment, and that was why Tolvar had sent out pairs of Hux's men as scouts throughout the day *and* night. Nothing. But they would come. She didn't need to be a knight or a highwayman to know that.

Meanwhile, they were lost. Or felt lost, anyway.

Joah kept shooting glances at her. He'd begun to question everything. When Sloane had awakened in Kage Duna to see her brother alive and well, she'd felt new hope. She had a piece of her family back. And what's more, she'd learned that he'd run into the chaos in Nerezza during the Befallen's attack and had helped Alvie and the Ravyns escape death. At first, Joah had filled her with comfort in the face of thinking about weapons and attacks. They'd rambled through childhood and home memories in the way that only siblings can do. And Joah continually apologized for his part in her encounters with the Ravyns. She had her brother back, though she couldn't help but wonder if he'd ever explain *why* he'd joined the Ravyns. But she didn't want to ask. She wanted to forgive. Joah was the last she had of her family.

But for the past week, Joah's mood had turned dark, and, when they had moments alone, he needled remarks into Sloane: Are you certain *you* can be the Unsung? If the Cibil has given you so much information, why didn't he tell you exactly where the path to the

Azure Moon was? And are you certain that *you'll* be able to wield this weapon?

Every question stabbed her confidence. Sloane needed her brother on her side. But as the Azure Moon grew closer, Joah's questions grew bleaker. At least they'd stopped for the time being.

Everyone's silence brought out the sounds of their surroundings. Two crows flew overhead, their cawing splitting the air like a warning over the horses' hooves clopping. They'd passed this area before, even if it'd been a different time of day when they had. This familiar section of road had great trees—their hanging branches boasting golden leaves the size of her head—lining one side of the dirt road like a fence. An extensive field stared at them from the west, a grove of these same giant trees in the distance. There was nothing of note here. Sloane found herself focusing on Valko's hind legs in front of her, the bits of sunlight piercing the ground through the shadows the tall branches created, making shapes of light on the dirt road.

To distract herself from staring at Tolvar, thinking about the Brones, the Befallen, or the impending Azure Moon, Sloane searched for objects in the light on the ground as they rode. A snake. An egg. Mayhap what could be a hoshefer or some other furry animal? A crescent moon. A...

They'd passed the line of trees along the road. The shadows were gone. Sloane halted Kenn.

Along the path of shadows, turn to the west when they stop.

"Sloane, why'd you stop?" Alvie said, pulling his mare up beside her.

"A path of shadows," Sloane whispered. "This is it. The path of shadows." She peered behind her. The tall trees had created a shadowy path this time of day, and, ahead of them, nary a tree in sight. "We turn to the west," Sloane commanded, guiding Kenn to trot through the field leading to the grove of trees in the distance.

In front of her, Tolvar and Ghlee were putting together what she had. The grin on Ghlee's face proved it. "To the realm of the shadow cat!" Ghlee yelled.

"You sure?" Joah asked. "This might be a stretch, Sloane."

"Absolutely," Sloane said, turning away from him with her chin pointed up.

His doubts are not your doubts, the part of Sloane, who reveled in the cheers of Hux's men, reminded her.

Everyone pivoted their mounts west. Immediately, the mood in the air lightened. The Ravyns, Brinley in the lead, raced each other to the trees, Alvie and Joah kicking their horses into action to join them.

Sloane couldn't help but laugh in relief. "You coming, Sir Tolvar?" She flicked Kenn's reins.

Tolvar's eyes twinkled. "Aye, let's see if I might skin another of these beasts."

"Let's hope you don't add to your scars before you do, Wolf." Ghlee laughed and sprinted his stallion in front of them.

"Well done, Unsung." Tolvar winked, never letting Valko leave her and Kenn behind.

CHAPTER 54

Sloane

Tonight, settled by the campfire, everyone was in high spirits, even Joah. The forest—a never-ending army of the tallest trees Sloane had ever laid eyes on—had supplied them another deer. Though the setting sun had left the air chilled, the canopy of trees provided more warmth than they'd had in the countryside surrounding Ayla's open roads. What's more, scouts could keep watch above in the sturdy branches, making everyone relax a fraction.

The shadow cats, if they were near, kept their distance. Tolvar, usually a critic of Hux's pleasant songs, had told him and the others to sing as they'd traveled along the forest floor, the horses' hooves through the underbrush also creating noise. This would keep the shadow cats at bay, he explained. These creatures did not want to run into them any more than they wanted to meet these giant beasts.

And now, Sloane hung on every word uttered by Tolvar, who was proving to be a marvelous storyteller. Mayhap it was the last of the ale Ghlee had taken from his saddlebag and promised to Tolvar if he'd tell the tale of the Wolf versus the shadow cat that had convinced him. Possibly, Tolvar was showing off, but whatever had convinced Tolvar to share his impossible story, Sloane found herself melting at the sight of this rare side of Tolvar.

"And then what happened?" Alvie asked for everyone, taken in by the great pause Tolvar had constructed within the tale.

"Well, then, with a roll to the right, I managed to clutch my fallen knife, and I drove it into that cat's throat before he could get another slice at me."

"All while holding back his paw with your bleeding arm?" Brinley asked. The older man's usually gruff face was likened to an awed child.

"Aye, but that's not all. At that moment, the beast managed to break free of my grip. Its claws, long as a dinner dagger, swiped at my eyes. I only just dodged in time. There was only one thing left to do."

Another pause, and Ghlee smirked at Tolvar's dramatics.

"What?" asked Gaff, one of Hux's men.

"I jumped up, pinned its forelegs to the ground by my own weight, and ripped it open."

"With your bare hands?" Sloane said.

Tolvar only shrugged and sat.

Across the fire from her, Ghlee's smirk widened. "Naturally," he supplied.

"That is some tale," Hux said. "Almost believable."

Sloane expected to see Tolvar's familiar scowl, but instead, the Wolf gave only a sly grin. He rolled up his sleeve to reveal a long, jagged scar. Many in the circle gasped, and separate conversations sprouted, everyone wondering aloud the truth behind Tolvar's tale.

As if on cue, the guttural banshee scream of a shadow cat rang out in the distance. Many of the men rose to their feet, reaching for their weapons.

"Mayhap they're coming for their revenge, Lord Wolf," Hux chuckled, though it was a forced sound, indeed.

"Do you see anything?" Tolvar called up to the four scouts high in the trees.

"Nay," one shouted down.

"Be on your guard!" Tolvar's eyes moved so fast Sloane wondered if they saw anything at all.

A shadow cat's attack wouldn't likely come from the ground. Another reason Tolvar had posted the men in the trees.

Another roar sounded through the forest, and this time, it was answered by the eerie sound of others.

Sloane, one hand gripping the Edan Stone, even though it'd do naught to protect her, the other wrapped around her knife, scanned their surroundings, a trick of shadows mocking her. These monsters could be anywhere. A snap of a branch caught everyone's attention. And then another. This time closer.

"Milv, what's happening up there?" Hux shouted in the direction of the sound.

"I can't—" Milv's reply was cut off by a low growl, followed by a *swoosh*. Milv's cry was little more than a repulsive croak. Something thudded to the ground.

"Be ready," Tolvar commanded. "Hux, you and Joah protect Sloane."

Sloane didn't have time to process these words. A scream leaped from her as something black and as big as a horse sprung from above and landed on Frisk. His screams joined her own as the beast thrashed into his chest. One of the Ravyns, Sloane couldn't focus on who, shot an arrow into the cat, and it shrieked. Every hair on Sloane's arms rose as she covered her ears.

"Here comes another," Brinley yelled.

At that moment, the forest quaked with sound. Sloane wanted to be brave, but her eyes shut, and her scream was never-ending, bouncing off the trunks of the giant trees. At one point, she couldn't tell the difference between the shrieks of men and of the shadow cats.

Open your eyes, you sook!

It was chaos. Great monstrous shadows tore into some men while other men sliced at them like they were battling the very essence of Adrienne's demons. Sloane stood petrified, not an inkling of who would walk away from this.

And Tolvar, where was Tolvar? She spotted him, the great Wolf battling a beast, Alvie at his side, swinging his club. He got a whack at one, making it possible for Tolvar to drive his sword through the mouth of the beast. Sloane couldn't hear the sound through the mess of screams and was glad.

Two of the other cats dropped, but gaining her wits enough to count them, there were still three attacking. Tolvar and Alvie wasted no time in helping Gaff and Joah fight one, but not before she watched it shred into Gaff.

"Joah!" she screamed. She glimpsed her knife. She was a coward stuck standing there.

Someone needs to do something. These shadow cats were no different than any other trial she'd faced.

Joah scrambled up, the darkness swallowing him where Sloane's eyes couldn't follow.

Alvie's cry punched at her. He was on the ground, his huge club the only thing between him and a shadowed beast swiping at him. Tolvar was alone, holding off a beast three times his size.

Without thinking, Sloane dropped her knife, picked up a nearby stick from the pile they'd collected for firewood, tore a strip from her skirt, wrapped it around the stick, and plunged it into the fire. The cloth caught flame, and Sloane strode with her torch to save her friends.

As if the torch were an extension of her arm, Sloane stabbed the shadow cat with the mastery she used with an awl. She took two controlled steps back, adjusting her weight on her good leg. The shadow leaped back, then turned on its new prey. But Sloane was ready. She thrust her torch at the animal's eyes, knowing instinctively the Wolf—her Tolvar—would be ready, too.

His sword gored into its torso, and the animal dropped to the ground like a rock.

Sloane pivoted, ready to catch more beasts with fire but found the encampment deadly still. The echoes of screams still rang in her ears, making the moans of those injured not real yet.

Alvie stood, filling Sloane with relief. He seemed okay. Ghlee had a gash across his cheek, but otherwise seemed uninjured. She didn't see Joah. She was assessing Sy's injuries when Hux shouted, "Brinley!"

There lay Brinley on the ground covered in blood. His tunic was torn, revealing a long gash opening his middle. Sloane did her best not to glimpse his insides spilling from him.

She crouched next to Hux at his side, taking his hand. There was nothing to say.

"Brinley," Hux whimpered as he pressed a cloak into Brinley's chest. "Brother. You're going to be fine. I'll fix you."

"Nay, brother." Brinley coughed. "You've already done that these past years. 'Tis finally time I go." Brinley turned glassy eyes to Sloane. "I see within you now what Hux does, and glad am I that I've been part of your adventure." He coughed more blood.

"Brinley," Hux said, tears pouring from his face. "Stay with me."

"We shall meet again when the stars call you home." Brinley stretched an arm out to Hux but dropped it. His strength was gone.

In the background, the Ravyns held back sobs.

"And Kerr," Brinley said, focusing on Joah. "I forgive you. I hope you know what family means now."

Joah choked out a groan.

"Sloane," Brinley said, his voice weaker. "My thanks for your forgiveness. You have been my redemption."

Brinley's eyes went cold and blank.

Sloane had come to know the Ravyns. And she'd long since forgiven them for what they'd done to her when they'd robbed her. But it was still difficult to recognize any softness under their scarred, gruff, unshaven faces. But as the faces of Joah and the other Ravyns melted into agony, Sloane's own grief smoldered. She hadn't really known Brinley, not like others she'd lost, but his last words had been kind, not the words of an outlaw.

Each wail of grief was like a scorch to Sloane's heart.

But it was when Hux began bawling that Sloane rekindled herself with the gravity of loss.

"Was Brinley really your brother?"

Sloane sat with Hux against an enormous tree trunk. It was late morning and the ashes of the funeral pyre they'd built for Brinley and the others were dying out. Hux had asked Sloane to keep him company as the flames died. Tolvar wasn't far away, standing guard, no doubt. Sloane sensed his presence nearby. The others were either muddling their way through packing, shutting their eyes for a few moments—no one had slept—or mustering the stomach to eat before they continued on their way.

The Azure Moon was tonight.

"Aye," Hux said after a time. "I know what you will say. Ravyns are to have ties to no one. 'Twas why it was kept between us."

Sloane scanned the shrouded sky above. How many hours were there before nightfall?

"Don't worry, mighty one, I shall rise in a few moments. My grief shall not interfere with your quest. I promised you me and my men, and you'll have us until the end." Hux's face was a blankness that compelled only more sorrow from Sloane.

"May I ask you something?"

"Aye," Hux returned.

"Why did you form the Ravyns? You and Brinley and Sy and the others, you seem honorable men deep down. I would almost mark you as a gentleman. Why?"

"Ah." There was a hint of the familiar mischievousness in Hux's face. "That is a story."

He couldn't say more before Tolvar entered the clearing. His arms crossed; he seemed as if he struggled to not order them to their feet.

"Lord Wolf, I know that look." Hux gave a sad smile and stood. "Come, Unsung. You've glory to meet this eve. Farewell, my brother. Until the stars bring us together again."

Sloane started into the trees then stopped. The men weren't following her. They were talking.

"...you needn't have stood sentimental like a mother bear. As you can see, she's fine. I did not tackle her to ground, nor make off with her as my captive." Hux snorted a laugh. "What must I do, a lowly Ravyn, to earn the trust of a Wolf?"

Sloane could not hear Tolvar's answer, but Hux laughed again.

"I may not have chosen a knight's path, but you are not the only one with a sad tale in your past, Sir Tolvar. You carry grievance with you like a shield. Mayhap you and I could both take a lesson from Sloane."

Tolvar's response was again too low to make out.

"Agreed. But I'm not the one you should be watching," Hux replied, before their footsteps made Sloane rush away so they wouldn't know she'd spied.

CHAPTER
55

Sloane

"I must go on alone," Sloane repeated, nodding to the narrow path that poked through the trees.

"I forbid it," Tolvar snapped at the same time Joah and Alvie said in unison, "I'm coming with you!"

"You cannot forbid it. And you can't come with me. I am the Unsung. Didn't we just have this talk? The Azure Moon will rise in a matter of hours. You must trust the words of the Edan Lore." Her last remark was for Joah. "Trust *me*, at least."

Tolvar ran a hand through his disheveled hair, turning his attention away from her. The exhausting effects of the last day overloaded them. There wasn't a man standing here in this forest, the late afternoon light streaming through the trees to extenuate their wounds, who wasn't cut, scarred, bashed, or bone-tired.

Too much had befallen them. But now the moon was going to rise.

"Wolf, you must—" Ghlee started, but Tolvar cut him off.

"We're not sending her alone. That's final."

"You must," Sloane said, and held the Edan Stone up. "This will protect me. Besides, you said you thought we were out of the shadow cats' realm."

At that moment, no one appeared more tired than Tolvar.

"We're at least accompanying you to the lake. Don't argue anymore. We'll wait for you at the edge of the forest, but I'm not letting you trek for hours by yourself. Not with the Brones still hunting us, not for any reason."

'Twas the end of the argument for Tolvar. He wasn't going to let her do this alone. At least he hadn't said they were going all the way to the lake with her. It would have to do.

WHEREAS THE LAKE in the heart of Kage Duna had unexpectedly come into view, a contrast to the grey bogs encircling it, this unknown lake in Ayla was visible for at least a quarter of a mile. The trees gradually thinned out, the terrain sloped gradually, the orange light of sunset shimmered on its surface like the water was on fire, guiding her toward it like a beacon.

When Sloane arrived on its banks, the others hanging back in the forest as promised—even Tolvar—she took in the true vastness of the lake, more like a sea. It was enormous. How was this lake not on any map of Deogol?

The similarities between this place and where the Cibil dwelled connected for Sloane like ripples in the water, and she understood how this lake, surrounded by trees, served as a sacred place for those seeking the Azure Moon. Briefly, she wondered if the Cibil himself had once stood here and spoken to the goddess of the Azure Moon using the Edan Stone. It seemed certain.

Sloane glanced back, and as it was dusk, the lights in the sky transforming from grey to steel blue, she could no longer detect the others waiting in the darkened forest.

The Edan Stone was clasped in her hand. There was naught else to do but wait.

If the Nay Moon was tonight, no moon would rise, and the veil between the Hoarfrost Moon and the Solstice Moon would fall into place. Sloane would wait here all night, the stars as her only company. If it turned out to be a usual night, then her faith, invisible and as seemingly delicate as Sloane herself, might be shaken. But she was the Unsung.

Sloane, her moon cuff fastened around her wrist, her legs tucked under her, her eyes fixed on the stars who would not reign this night alone, merely waited. Her faith was no fickle thing. The Cibil, through eyes only an oracle could possess, had informed her the Azure Moon would rise this night.

And so, it did.

Sloane had presupposed she'd already witnessed the most breathtaking full moons in her life. The Gale Moon, even though it was the smallest of the full moons, had always been particularly pleasing to Sloane's eye, mayhap because it reminded her of her own small frame. She was enamored, too, by the Prelude Moon, for it was said that within its purity was a new beginning for all who feasted upon her. And of course, the Rapture Moon was always alluring with its tint of muted pink beckoning in the first signs of spring.

But the Azure Moon was something else to behold entirely.

When, over the silhouette of the tallest trees, the perfect circle of pastel blue touched the blackness of the sky as it rose, she openly gasped at its beauty.

When it had fully risen, the light of the Azure Moon's glow glittered across the water like a sea of blue diamonds.

Sloane wasn't certain what to do. So, she did the only thing she could think of. She let go of the Edan Stone, clasped her moon cuff in prayer formation, closed her eyes, and prayed. She said no words aloud but hoped the goddess would hear what was in her heart. That she would know why she'd made this winding journey, full of loss and fear and grief. That she would bless her—frightened though she was—with the weapon of the Unsung to destroy the darkness of the Befallen.

When she could bear it no longer, after what felt like hours, Sloane gazed once more at the Azure Moon, for the entire time she'd prayed, its beauty had never strayed from her mind.

The blue sphere, at this midnight hour, was even more radiant.

For the briefest of seconds, Sloane thought she saw the shape of a woman outlined in the center of the moon. Her eyes darted downward; surely they were playing tricks on her. She noticed the Edan Stone around her neck. It glowed the same blue as the Azure Moon.

"Look upon the mirror image of me. For no mortal may regard me as I truly am."

The voice was like honey and the velvet petals of Moonbeam flowers. Sloane warmed as she gazed into the reflection of the moon upon the lake. The blurred blue light illuminating the water where the moon shone upon it danced and rippled until there, in the center of the moon's reflection, standing *on* the water, was the form of a woman. The goddess.

She was pale white—iridescent—and her long, flowing hair, moving as if caught in a breeze, was the same hue as the Azure Moon. Even from the distance between her and where the goddess stood, Sloane noted her heavenly features. Her face, divine in all its perfection. And she glowed. Stars, how she glowed.

Sloane froze in amazement. Her eyes burned from the goddess's stunning form and were comforted by the grace bestowed upon her. She didn't know what to say.

"You have made it at last, Unsung hero." The goddess's rich voice made Sloane want to fall into a dream.

She could only nod in return.

"You seek from me a weapon."

"Aye," Sloane whispered, still in awe.

"By making it here, you have brought it with you."

"Nay, I've brought no weapon," Sloane said, almost scanning for it. It wasn't the Edan Stone.

The goddess's regal smile carried melancholy. "Indeed, you have, Unsung. But to wield the weapon to defeat the Befallen, Adrienne's own sycophant, there must be a sacrifice."

"I will give anything I must, but," Sloane bowed her head, "I've nothing to give."

"There is something."

Did Sloane detect a single tear streaming down the face of the goddess? The light from her being made it sparkle.

Sloane did not understand her words.

Until she did.

And now that she understood them, now that she realized what they meant, now that she recognized the meaning behind being the Unsung, she trembled in comprehension.

"You know what to do, Unsung hero. You must find the Befallen and walk into it without any hesitation. To hesitate means to show weakness. And weakness will only make the Befallen grow stronger. The Befallen will not be defeated until it has devoured bravery."

"But—"

"I'm most sorry. 'Tis the only way."

"What if I find another weapon?"

"Unsung hero, do you not understand? You *are* the weapon."

Tears dripped from Sloane's cheek. "I don't know if I can be that brave."

"Then all will succumb to the Befallen. And eventually, it will find a way off this land to other realms where it will only grow stronger. There are those who already seek that end as they believe it will save Deogol. But they are wrong."

She meant the Brones.

Not Tolvar's land, too. Sloane couldn't let that happen.

"I know you have shown great bravery. The faith you carry with you is evidence of that. It is why *you* are here. But it is the only way."

There must be a sacrifice. Sloane had not considered the Unsung would be a sacrifice. But now it began to make sense. Surely someone who *lived* through defeating the Befallen would be able to take part in the joy of a world free of this destruction that'd ravaged the land for too long.

But the Unsung would not know because she would not be here any longer.

"I understand," Sloane whispered.

CHAPTER
56

Tolvar

What remained of their party still hadn't regained any liveliness to speak of since losing Brinley and the other Ravyns, even though they'd left Ayla after the night of the Azure Moon. Not even Alvie.

Tolvar wasn't one for coaxing senseless racket from anyone, but stars' shadow, it certainly was quiet as they traveled. Mayhap it was the first snowfall. They'd awoken one morning, cold and wet, beside the road somewhere in the Gran Province to find the world blanketed in white. Despite the momentary delight with which Sloane had exclaimed at seeing the fresh coat of snow painted over this rugged ground, no one was glad to see winter had finally made its arrival. It only meant more difficult travel.

And where exactly *were* they traveling? No one could answer that as there was no way to know where the Befallen would next be. But Tolvar was no wanderer. They needed a real plan now that they —Sloane—had the weapon.

When Sloane had dragged herself back from the lake to them, she'd barely been able to put one leg in front of the other. And her face was as pale as the moon itself, yet she'd been radiant, as though she carried some light *inside* her.

Tolvar frowned at the memory as they trudged through the snowy road. It'd been a ridiculous thought then and was one now. Still, she did appear illuminated somehow: she simply did.

"Did you get it?" Ghlee asked as they'd helped her onto a pile of blankets to rest—they'd not seen anything but a reflection of moonlight on the lake in the distance. "Did you receive the weapon?"

"Aye," Sloane said. "I have it."

"Well, cough it up, Sloane," Alvie said. "Let's see it."

"Aye," Joah followed.

"You cannot," Sloane said, her voice like a flickering candle. "'Tis a weapon for me only."

He wasn't proud of it, but Tolvar had thrown up his hands and paced away from the group. It'd still been in the back of his mind that he might take the weapon—that burden—from Sloane and use it himself, but apparently, it was small enough for Sloane to hide, or mayhap invisible.

You are going to have to let her be the Unsung. Ghlee's words rushed at him, and Tolvar had walked back to them, but not before he saw the expression on Sloane's face. He'd wounded her. He told her she could do this, and yet, Tolvar couldn't help but want to stop her.

Tolvar cleared his throat and met her eyes. "Then we shall protect you and this weapon." Sloane nodded, but they both knew what he'd been thinking.

To make matters worse, he'd caught Sloane staring off many times over the last span of days. Riding Kenn—it was a damn good thing that horse was so tame—sitting by the campfire, even in conversation, she would simply break off. Something was off. He'd brought it up with Joah, much to his dismay, but her brother had simply made the excuse for her that she was tired and cold, unaccustomed to this much of a journey. But it was more than that. Tolvar saw through the barrier she sought to conceal her emotions behind. There was something she wasn't telling them.

"We may as well stop here for the night," Ghlee said, bringing his mount to a halt. "We can take cover under those trees over there. It looks as though it may snow again tonight."

Heavy grey clouds hung low in the sky. Tolvar nodded, pleased to hear Alvie and the skinny Ravyn, Sy, say they'd gather firewood. Sloane batted away Joah from helping her dismount, slid off Kenn, tightened her grip on the blanket cloaking her, and found a dry spot under the trees to sit. Everything seemed to be outside her grasp of notice.

"What do you think is wrong with her?" Ghlee said, walking up and taking Valko's reins to tether him with the others that Hux had started grooming. "She behaves as if she goes to her grave instead of to her glory."

"It must be that weapon she carries. It must be invisible, but heavy, is my only guess. Too heavy for her."

"Wolf, we're close. I can feel it. You are fulfilling your part in this. Let her do the same."

Tolvar wanted to throw one arm around his friend and smash his face in with the other. Ghlee knew him all too well.

He didn't say anything, for at that moment, both turned to scan the horizon behind them. All Tolvar saw was the snowy fields, looking grey themselves under this sky.

"You did sense that?" Ghlee asked.

"Aye. The Brones must be close."

Ghlee focused on Sloane, her back against a wide trunk, her eyes closed as if she'd drifted off. "Should we keep moving? We're only eleven fighters."

Tolvar didn't need the reminder. "Nay, we'll just have to be on the lookout."

"Being on the lookout and being able to defend ourselves will be different things, Wolf."

"And yet, we have no choice but to be ready for both."

CHAPTER
57

Sloane

"Ye know you can talk to me," Alvie said, settling next to Sloane. He handed her a piece of cured meat. She couldn't tell what it was from the taste, not that she had much of an appetite.

The most important thing, she'd decided, was to not cry. Crying would show these men she had weakness. She could not harbor weakness any longer. Although since hearing that she was to sacrifice herself to the Befallen, Sloane had felt nothing but.

She'd been given an impossible task. Weakness was the very essence of her makeup, wasn't it? Many she'd encountered in her life had certainly thought so.

But you're not a sook. Not anymore. You're the Unsung.

But how can I possibly be brave enough to walk into the Befallen, she argued with herself.

She'd had this argument repeatedly for the last week, and every time she concluded that she *was* brave enough, that her sacrifice would save Deogol, Joah, Alvie, Hux, Tolvar, and his realm, the fear wormed its way into her heart again. What if she couldn't do it? What if her faith wasn't enough? What if she wanted to live—

"Sloane?"

She'd completely forgotten Alvie sat next to her. Stars, she was having trouble concentrating.

"There's nothing to talk about," Sloane said, straining to remember what a smile felt like. "We just need to find the Befallen as soon as possible." *So I can die.* Her eyes shut.

"Something's wrong with you," Alvie said.

"I just want..." She could not tell him. "I have faith. But what if I'm not brave enough?"

"You are brave enough, Sloane. Think of all you've done since we met. Plus, you got luck on your side. You already beat the Befallen three times."

Sloane didn't have a response, but in sorting all this out over the last week, she certainly hadn't missed the irony. How many times had she cursed her luck for not dying with her family in Mohn? And now —she found Tolvar on the other side of camp—she longed to live.

She bit her lip to keep the tears swallowed up inside and nodded at Alvie. Her friend smiled his silver-toothed grin at her, obviously pleased he'd helped her.

But no one could help because no one was going to force her toward the Befallen if he knew what that meant, although she almost wished for that. But if that didn't make her more of a sook, she didn't know what did.

She caught Joah coming out of the shadow of trees. He rested his gaze on her like she was supposed to understand something. What'd he been doing?

"SLOANE, PSST, SLOANE, WAKE UP," Joah whispered.

She'd barely fallen asleep. There was a tinge of tension somewhere in the air. She sat at once and scanned their camp. Everyone appeared to be asleep.

"What are you doing?" Sloane whispered in return. She didn't want to risk waking anyone else who may have drifted off.

"Come on." Joah stood and beckoned her to follow him into the trees.

Sloane's heart pounded. She glanced toward Tolvar. His chest rose and fell deeply. Quietly, Sloane followed Joah into the grove, noting Hux, on guard duty, had his back to them.

When he stopped, she spotted two rucksacks leaning against a tree.

"What is this?" Sloane whispered.

"You may be able to fool the others, but you can't fool me. Something's wrong. You looked better when we found you in Kage Duna."

"Joah—"

"Stop pretending. Even if you *thought* you were the Unsung, I can tell. You don't want to be the Unsung anymore."

Joah's words were much too close to her heart. She dared not speak in case part of her said, aye.

"We don't have to stay here, Sloane. We can leave." Joah gestured toward the packs laying in the snow. "You have the Edan Stone. The Befallen can't hurt *us*. Why should you worry about everyone else? An entire country! Face it. You're not meant to do this, to be a hero."

He's right, thought the part of Sloane who could not tear her eyes from the packs.

What about Tolvar and Alvie? And the others?

You'll never be able to not hesitate in the end. You're not brave enough to be the Unsung.

"Besides, we're all we have left, Sloane," Joah said, his voice cracking. "I'll never be able to forgive myself for what happened with the Ravyns. Let me take care of you. Come with me. I can't take any more shadow cats or attacks by cursèd men or trekking around aimlessly in the snow. Mayhap we can go to Kestriel. Between the two of us, we can surely make a living there."

A living. She wanted that. A living. Part of Sloane's mind wandered into a future where she dared to think about a life with Tolvar. She could send word to him once in Kestriel. Mayhap she could even convince him to come with her and Joah. And Alvie, too. He'd come. She didn't want to die. Not for so many who'd treated her poorly or who were plain evil like the Brones. She and Tolvar could mayhap even sail to the Capella Realm. Leave all this...

Except Tolvar was more honorable than that. He'd never abandon his quest.

"Joah, I can't flee in the middle of the night." *Only a sook would do that.*

"We aren't fleeing. Sloane. You're not made for all this. 'Tis your life." His tone changed. "You don't have to do something simply because you think it's expected of you."

"You mean like you running away two years ago?" Sloane blurted out.

Joah snickered. "Not at all, Sloane, but since you brought it up, I'm not sorry that I made a choice. That's what I'm trying to tell you. You have a choice, and it doesn't have to be carrying around this weapon that's clearly killing you inside, searching for the Befallen, hoping we don't die in the process."

Go. Go with him. You know you can't do this. Sloane slung one of the packs on her back.

And a life with the Wolf was never going to happen anyway, the other part of Sloane resolved.

"I knew that I knew you." Joah picked up his own pack. "This is the right decision. Why don't you give me the weapon, and I'll leave it at the edge of the trees? They'll find it, and—"

"I can't go with you." Sloane bit her lip. *I am the weapon.*

"Sloane."

She shook her head. Joah had their mother's eyes. And even if only a sook would flee in the middle of the night, and oh, how she longed to go, she did see in those eyes that he only wanted to protect his sister. But that was why she couldn't go with him, wasn't it? She had to save the last of her family. Alvie, who'd been her best friend. Hux, who'd lost his brother. Lauge and Carrin, who'd felt like family when she'd needed it most. Henry, who'd been her first champion. And Tolvar, whom she could imagine a life with that no fate of death could touch.

"I'm sorry, Joah. I want to go. And you're right. Part of me doesn't want to be the Unsung. I don't know if that will change, but I cannot go with you."

Joah glared at her. It was a reminiscent moment. How many times would she say goodbye to her brother?

"Well, I can't stay. This is too much." Joah took a few steps before turning. "I hope you're not doing this for *him*. You have no chance of having a life with him."

A single tear slid down her cheek. "I know," she choked out. If only he knew how true that was.

Joah disappeared behind the trees.

It was the morning of the Solstice Moon, a night that should have been a celebration. Riding along to stars knew where, Sloane could almost smell Ma's roasted nuts, juice from a turnip candied and poured over them to give them a hint of sweetness.

As the shortest day of the year, the villagers of Mohn would begin their celebration well before dusk. There was no desire to work until sundown on this day, and far too many festivities to enjoy: songs, games, dancing. The Sloane of moons ago would no doubt spend her day wondering if this were the Solstice that Lonn would finally notice her, realize her leg didn't matter, and ask her to dance. She and Sherik would exchange trinkets, a tradition that would have been Sloane's last. Once turning eighteen, one did not participate in the ritual after the Prelude Moon passed. Her gift to Sherik would have been a small leather pouch for his treasures. Sherik had loved collecting rocks he found interesting.

When the Solstice Moon rose, her family would huddle together, basking in each other's love, and pray to the goddess to bless those who might not be as fortunate, who might need extra light and love, and to beseech the sun and stars to continue their protection of the heavens in the new year.

It was all she could do to keep Joah out of her thoughts. When she'd told the others he'd left, Tolvar appeared as though he would like the opportunity anew to kill him. Hux, too, actually. A flood of questions came from Alvie, and the other Ravyns exchanged looks.

Later, Alvie attempted to offer solace, but Sloane had only muttered that she didn't want to talk about Joah anymore.

A gust of wind snapped Sloane out of her trance, and through the morning sunbeams, she could still envision the cheerful firelight of the bonfire in the center of Mohn's village square.

There was no celebration, only tramping aimlessly through the snow. Thank the stars it hadn't snowed for a few days. When the Solstice Moon rose tonight, even though she knew she shouldn't ask for anything for herself, Sloane would simply pray for the gift of knowledge: where the Befallen would hit next.

In the afternoon, they came upon a cluster of cottages. Even though the ground was a snowy white, Sloane could tell these surrounding fields were farmland by the way it was lined with fencing.

"Maybe they'll add a few more to their Solstice party?" Alvie asked.

Tolvar stared at the cottages with a grievous expression. Ghlee bore it, also.

"There's no smoke rising from their chimneys."

Weapons drawn, they descended the hill to the cottages.

Everything was too still. The shutters or curtains on the windows were all open, but no movement could be detected inside.

Tolvar and Ghlee dismounted, moving toward the first cottage in a rhythm as if they had done this a thousand times before. The others dismounted, scanning the horizon. Hux took out a spyglass and surveyed the village. Sloane clutched the Edan Stone. It remained black and cold. Had the Brones come across these cottages?

"Together?" Tolvar asked Ghlee, who nodded in return.

The two opened the door and stepped inside the first cottage. It wasn't two breaths before Ghlee yelled, "Damnation!"

They were back through the doorway and stomping toward the

cottage next door. Everyone else stood wide-eyed and frozen. In a matter of moments, inside the cottage, Ghlee cursed again. When they came out of this cottage, their slumped shoulders said everything.

The Befallen.

"No," Sloane cried and moved toward the cottage.

"Sloane, don't go in there," Tolvar said, but she didn't listen.

Inside the cottage, the late sun streaming through the unshuttered windows, Sloane halted at the sight of the three children, mayhap close to Sherik's age, laying on the floor beside the hearth. Three dolls lay next to them, sprawled out in the same limp manner. Whether the lack of stench was due to the shortness of time or the coldness in the air, Sloane didn't know, but she longed to take them one by one in her arms and warm them. Their smooth faces wrapped in innocence, eyes closed, they might be sleeping, but for the stark paleness and blue lips.

Sloane sunk to the floor, barely aware Tolvar had come into the cottage behind her and placed his hand on her shoulder. Her low wince turned into a silent sob, for she didn't want to disturb them, didn't want to make any noise that may frighten them.

What are you thinking? They're dead! The part of Sloane, who wanted the other side to confess how much grief filled her, screamed in her mind.

"We have to stop this, Tolvar," she whimpered. "I must stop this."

The hand on her shoulder gave her a tender squeeze.

"Tolvar!" Ghlee yelled from outside. "You better get out here!"

"Who might you be?" An unfamiliar voice called from a distance.

Voices began talking, though she couldn't hear what they said. Then a woman's voice screamed. And Sloane felt it all the way to the bottom of her own pool of grief.

A frizzy-haired woman, red-faced from the cold, but mayhap more from the news she'd received, tears pouring down her cheeks, entered the cottage.

"No!" she cried, sinking next to Sloane, and enfolded the closest boy into her arms. "Pat! My Pat!" Still holding her son's body, she drew her little girl into her chest. "Nessie. Beautiful Nessie. My love." Her wails filled the cottage, the area, mayhap the whole island of Deogol in that moment. Sloane took in the scene, her own tears blurring the sight of the mother grasping for her third child while hugging the other two close to her. Without a word, Sloane crawled closer to the other son and brought his body closer to the mother so she could envelop him with the others. All three of her babies embraced in her arms, she rocked back and forth, wailing and muttering to herself. Part of Sloane told herself she should leave this woman to her raw grief, but the other part knew that to leave this woman alone would be an act of cowardice. So, she sat there and cried with her.

CHAPTER
58

Tolvar

"They left only me and Fren alive," the man who'd called himself Hugh said. "We raced back here to warn the others. Never thought more could befall us."

While Sloane had spent the afternoon with the frizzy-haired woman, Fren—and sounds from her cottage like the shrieks of a dying man on a battlefield—Tolvar and the others had spent the time building a pyre for the lost souls who had lain here for the last two days. It couldn't be clear if the Befallen had hit the day Hugh and four others had left on their hunting excursion in preparation for their Solstice celebration or the day after. The pyre wasn't as well-built as it should have been, but it was the best they could do. Tolvar had a pang in his throat when they'd taken some of the firewood from aside one of the cottages—carefully stacked and meant to last through the winter—to use for the pyre.

Hugh, an older man with a drooping mustache, had insisted on helping, even with a stab wound through his leg.

"I'll be the one to give my kin a proper send-off," he'd said earlier, carrying the first bundle of wood to the spot.

Now that the pyre was built, Hugh had been coaxed into sitting beside a cookfire Alvie had been working at for an hour to tell his story. The story wasn't good. While hunting, they'd stumbled upon a group of villains—the Brones, though Tolvar and the others gave away nothing.

"Their faces," Hugh kept repeating. "Their faces was sheer evil, I tell you."

Adrienne. The Curse was growing stronger within them.

"They was looking for a knight. Big man, they said..." Hugh trailed off, giving Tolvar a once over. "Thought we'd seen him in the woods. Tortured and killed everyone else. Told Fren and me to be grateful they'd left us alive." Hugh glanced back at his own cottage, where Tolvar knew his wife lay. "Wish they'd killed me."

If Hugh's hunting party had run into the Brones, they couldn't be far away. Tolvar's eyes were drawn to his sword—his father's sword—resting against the outside of one of the cottages. If they set this pyre aflame tonight, which surely Hugh would want, it'd attract attention. Should they pack up and carry on their way? It was a clear night, but it certainly would be good for Sloane to sleep in a bed this eve, to eat a good meal. It'd been a while. And what of the Solstice? That was ruined. Overrun by tragedy.

Tolvar knew Sloane had been looking forward to it, despite what had happened with her brother and her insistence it didn't matter. It did matter to her, for he'd heard enough about what her childhood Solstices were like that he'd wanted to recreate something of a festivity for her. At least give her a gift. He pulled the ruby earring that'd once been his mother's out of a pouch in his pocket. There was only one, the other lost long ago, and Sloane's ears weren't pierced, but it was the only precious thing he carried. He wanted Sloane to have it.

Ignoring the rest of what Hugh was saying, Ghlee and Hux carrying on the conversation for him, Tolvar turned toward Fren's cottage where Sloane still sat. The cries had ceased, but that didn't make the agony in the air any less poignant.

It was quieter, however, and over Hugh's repeated story, a raven cawed. But the bird wasn't in a nearby tree or in the sky. It cawed again. It was coming from one of the cottages.

"Have you a raven?" Tolvar interrupted.

"Aye," Hugh said, gesturing his arm to one of the cottages. "Guess it's good I brought Ol' Lars along."

Tolvar stood, set down his bowl of Solstice Stew, and went into the cottage. In a wooden cage, the black bird flapped its wings from the sudden intrusion. Ghlee appeared behind him.

"We can send word to Dara Keep," Ghlee said.

"Aye," Tolvar said. Pharrell would come. Henry would make sure of it. If they could stay here for a few days, keeping watch for the Brones, Pharrell could join them and bring the remaining Order knights with him. Tolvar had a feeling they were going to need them.

"What are you doing?" Sloane's voice from behind surprised both men.

"How is she?" Tolvar asked.

"She'll never be the same," Sloane responded without missing a heartbeat. Tolvar knew no truer words could be spoken. "But I have coaxed her into joining us for food. From the smell, I assume Alvie's cooked something?"

"Solstice Stew. Have you tried it before?" Ghlee asked.

"Aye, once this autumn. Feels like years ago." Sloane's face, blotchy and puckered from crying, attempted to slacken. "I suppose I can try it again."

"These last days have been awful, what with—you know." He did not want to bring up Joah. "And this day has been the worst."

Sloane could only nod. She turned to leave.

"Wait." Tolvar felt for the tiny earring in his pocket, giving Ghlee a sideways glance.

"I think I'll go join the others," Ghlee said, leaving them.

They stood in unbearable silence.

"Someone needs to do something, Tolvar." Sloane's voice was a near-whisper when she finally spoke. "I've been so uncertain that I could...do what's needed."

Tolvar wasn't entirely sure that she wasn't talking to herself.

"But, after Joah leaving and now...Fren's children." She stifled her sob. Mayhap she was out of tears. "They should have lived! And I think about Alvie, and Ghlee, and Henry, and Lauge and Carrin—you don't know them, they're good people—and, of course, you..." Sloane peered up at him with those enormous eyes, the glassiness therein making them appear like wet onyx. "No more." She shook her head emphatically. "No more. I cannot see any more people die from the Befallen. I must save you all."

Her emotions filled the cottage, and it took everything for Tolvar to not well up, also.

"You will," was all he could manage. He ignored the desire to throw her onto Valko and ride away.

Sloane bit her lip. "Anyway. What is it you wanted?"

"I wanted to give you something. I know it's not customary in Deogol for adults to exchange gifts at Solstice, but in the Capella Realm, gifts are given to anyone..." Could he get these words out? He felt like a fool. "Anyone you care for. Anyone whom you..."

Sloane was doing him no favors. Her eyes remained locked on his.

But Tolvar couldn't get the rest of his words out. Cursing himself silently, he grabbed Sloane's hand and placed the ruby earring in her palm. That broke her gaze.

"'Tis beautiful." Sloane turned the jewel over in her palm with her index finger. "Thank you."

"You are most welcome."

"I don't have anything for you."

The way your smile radiates brighter than any gem is a gift enough, he wanted to say. Their eyes linked once more. He needed to tell her. He needed to—

"Sloane, you comin'?" Alvie poked his head into the cottage. "The moon is rising."

"Aye," she said to Alvie, then turned back to him, the earring held fast between three fingers. "Thank you, Tolvar. I'll cherish this for the rest of my days."

He nodded, the moment broken. He lingered in the cottage, his eyes staring at the empty space she'd left behind. "Fool."

Ghlee returned, holding parchment, a quill, and ink.

"Hugh gave me this," he said, "Let's send this now."

"The sooner, the better," Tolvar agreed. Ghlee made no sign he was curious about Tolvar and Sloane's exchange. Well, that was gift enough.

"At least we'll be able to rest for a few days," Ghlee said, lighting a lamp so Tolvar could write. "We'll have to keep constant watch, but at least we'll have that."

BUT THEY WEREN'T GIVEN a few days. Two mornings after Solstice, a carcass of a wolf was clearly visible on the snowy field. The note this time read, *Give us the weapon.*

Tolvar and Ghlee began packing immediately, ignoring the complaints from Sy and the other Ravyns until Hux's threats stopped them altogether. Sloane helped, her shuffling steps evident that she wasn't as rested as Tolvar would have liked. They would make for the town of Clemen, less than a day's ride away.

"Do you think this plan is wise?" Hux asked.

"I'm not worried about someone in Clemen recognizing you as criminals, if that's what you mean." Tolvar folded another blanket and placed it in Valko's saddlebag.

"Ah, ever the barb waiting sharply on your tongue." Hux elbowed him. "Why not make for the mountains? We could set a trap of our own there."

"I won't risk Sloane." Tolvar continued his task.

"'Tis a long ride in the open fields to Clemen," Hux said, his mouth a firm line as he surveyed the wolf carcass in the distance. "But I suppose everything seems a risk now."

"You're free to leave." Tolvar cinched the flap of the saddlebag.

"And brighten your day? Never." Hux sauntered away. "Besides. The Edan Lore is about to come true. I wouldn't miss that. To Clemen or our graves it is."

Tolvar ignored Hux. Hugh and Fren exited one of the cottages, bearing four large stuffed saddlebags.

"We'll need all the food we can handle," Hugh said in passing to Tolvar as he made his way to the small shed that housed their horses.

"*We?*" Tolvar said.

"Aye, you don't think we're not going with you. Looks to me like you could use a couple more who know how to handle a weapon, even if it's only for hunting. Besides, there's nothin' left here for us now, 'specially if them men come back."

"But your leg—" Tolvar started.

"They's after you, after all." Hugh kept speaking like he hadn't heard Tolvar. "Fren and I are coming with you, even if it's to make our last stand."

Tolvar opened his mouth to speak, then shut it.

Hugh nodded in Sloane's direction. "She really the Unsung? That bit o' a girl?"

"Careful," Tolvar growled.

"Ease up, there." Hugh held up a palm. "I guess they don't call her the Unsung for nothin'. But she looks like she has some stamina in her."

"That she does," Tolvar said. "How'd you know?"

Hugh surveyed Sloane. "I been waitin' for this. Haven't we all been waitin' for the Edan Lore to come true...?"

Stars, can't I pack in peace?

"...that cursèd Befallen! She really have a weapon those bastards want?"

Tolvar rolled his shoulders and popped his neck. How much did he want to divulge to Hugh? "Aye."

"She'll do," Hugh said. "No doubt she's got heart. She has a friend for life in Fren, that's for sure. We better make haste." And Hugh continued his way to the shed.

Ghlee joined Tolvar. "You really told *him*." They snorted out a laugh together. What a band of misfits they were becoming. "I was hoping they'd tell Pharrell what direction we went. But, if it doesn't snow again, they'll see our tracks well enough. Course, so will the Brones."

Tolvar grunted in agreement.

"This is probably a trap," Ghlee said.

"Most definitely. But to stay here is a death sentence. Mayhap we can leave Sloane with the others in Clemen and then go out and track them ourselves. Lay a trap of our own."

Ghlee pondered the idea. "Sloane won't like it."

"True. But we don't need to tell her until we're there."

"And it's a risky plan, Wolf."

Siria's skirt. Not Ghlee, too. "You up for it?"

Ghlee's grin was his reply.

"'Tis time we ended this."

CHAPTER 59

Sloane

They'd stopped to rest the horses and have an afternoon meal. Sloane half-heartedly brushed Kenn, watching everyone go about their tasks. The sky was winter white, not cloudy, but pale, and blocked any bits of blue. The colorlessness of the sky melded into the mountains to the east, giving the impression that the peaks had simply faded into the horizon.

Clemen was only a couple of hours away, and she still argued with herself about whether she would be glad or not when it was in eyesight. She did *not* want to run away, and she didn't want to waste time.

Someone needs to do something.

That someone was Sloane. Fren's loss had been too much.

"As soon as Sy comes back, let's be off," Ghlee said, saddling his horse. Sy had ridden over the hill to scout out the next leg of their journey.

"When we get to Clemen, I'm gonna order the biggest ale I can get my hands on," Alvie said, standing. "Whatd'ya say, Tolvar? Ghlee? Hux?"

"Are we sure we should even be going to Clemen?" Sloane asked again.

"Aye," Tolvar said, saddling Valko.

"But I don't see how this is going to stop the Brones from tracking us. They'll know exactly where we are."

"Not if we find an inn to hide in first," Ghlee said. "We'll hide out for a few days and then leave after they've gone. And we can post scouts."

"Speaking of, why hasn't Sy come back?" Hux grimaced in the direction Sy had ridden.

"I'll go look," Alvie said, mounting onto his mare.

"Alvie, no," Sloane said.

"What? Nothin' to worry about. I'll just go look and see if I can see him. You'll still be able to see me."

Tolvar nodded, and Alvie cantered away. Sloane fidgeted with the saddle stirrup, unable to shake her anxiousness.

She struggled with Kenn's saddle momentarily before Tolvar effortlessly threw it onto the stallion's back, cinching it around his middle like it was a matter of snapping his fingers. They slung the last of their saddlebags onto the horses. Hux sent two of his Ravyns, finished with their preparations, off toward where Alvie was getting closer to the top of the hill. They had almost reached him when he spurred his horse back.

"Go back!" he yelled.

The drips of unease slid down the back of Sloane's neck.

Tolvar didn't wait to see who or what Alvie was fleeing. He threw Sloane onto Kenn, mounted Valko, and smacked Kenn's behind as he raced away. Kenn kept pace with Valko, and the two had made great lengths, the others close behind, before Sloane dared turn.

Alvie, still at a distance, was being chased by a group of crimson-cloaked riders. The Brones. They were gaining on him. She'd just turned her head back when Kenn slammed to a halt behind Valko.

In front of them was a line of more red-cloaked men, two dozen at least. At the center of the line, a clean-shaven older man sat atop a giant black horse. His sneer would have been the most nightmarish feature about him, save for the blotchy black...well, it could only be described as a rash that ran up his neck and halfway across his cheek. His comrades had similar rashes. Behind them, a storm was looming. The dimness shadowed their faces to appear more frightening.

"This is the end," the man shouted. "Give me the weapon you acquired in Ayla, and mayhap we'll make your deaths more pleasant."

Sloane regarded Tolvar, who seemed to be physically drawing power into himself. He exhaled steadily. She waited for him to speak, but he simply put his hand on the hilt of his sword. The coming storm breezed across her cheek.

"No more games. I know you have the weapon of the Edan Lore, Sir Tolvar," the Brones leader continued as his line of men began toward them.

"Told you it was a long ride," Hux said nearby.

"Douse out, Hux," Tolvar returned, though he remained staunch and still.

"What are we going to do?" Sloane said shakily, angry at the quake in her voice. The wind picked up and blew a strand of hair into her face. She could feel the others behind her waiting for Tolvar's command.

"We'll hold them off, and you will make toward the foot of the mountains. Then circle back and make for Clemen. You will carry out your quest and defeat the Befallen."

Tolvar hadn't so much as glanced at her. His voice was as steady as a stone.

"I can't leave you," Sloane whispered. *But you will anyway in the end,* she reminded herself.

"You won't," Tolvar said. "I'll have you here." And he put his hand to his chest and finally gazed at her. "Now go."

"But—"

"Go, Sloane," Tolvar said, before directing his attention back to the approaching Brones. "The only weapon I bear is this," yelled Tolvar, brandishing his sword.

The Brones paused, three men nocking bowstrings.

"Go, Sloane."

Then someone leaned to the leader and said something. The arrows were lowered and put back in their quivers.

"I beg you." Tolvar's eyes had never been so vulnerable.

Sloane tightened her grip on Kenn's reins, making an effort to draw courage into herself like Tolvar, when she gazed down.

The Edan Stone was beginning to turn color. From onyx black, the stone had transformed to a dark grey. Subtle. And mayhap if Sloane hadn't spent so much time studying the moonstone, she would have missed it, but she was certain.

The Befallen was coming.

"Tolvar," she whispered, still eyeing the stone. He glanced over and caught her meaning.

"This doesn't change anything. Go. Find it. Defeat it."

She wanted to scream. How could she leave him? How could she not tell him goodbye? But he'd never let her go if he knew. Never.

Sloane flicked Kenn's reins when the Brones charged. Sloane didn't need to tell Kenn to gallop. The horse bolted away from the battle, the sickening sounds of metal on metal mixed with cries of war and wounds stalking her. No one followed her, and for once, she didn't mind being a small woman, overlooked and underestimated.

She kept glancing at the Edan Stone to see if it grew lighter, but it remained the color of grey charcoal. Kenn galloped and galloped. She had no idea where she was going. The storm grew closer, the dark clouds filling the sky, the frigid wind making her teeth chatter.

Finally, she halted Kenn to scan behind her. The full melee of bodies was well underway. She could barely detect who Tolvar, Ghlee, and Hux were.

It was better this way. If she could find the Befallen and make her sacrifice while everyone else was busy, she could go through with this. But they weren't simply busy; they were going to be killed, she reminded herself.

On the other side of the hill in the far distance, it appeared as though a black cloud raced across the white fields to where the forest stood to the west. The Befallen? Nay, that was no cloud. Those were men on horseback. Sloane discerned the Order of Siria's black uniforms, looking like a gift from the stars. She kicked Kenn to move.

They were headed in the wrong direction. They were going to pass Tolvar and the others fighting for their lives.

"Wait!" Sloane screamed. "Wait!" She kicked at Kenn and sped toward them, screaming over and over.

At last, she got close enough. The Order knights heard and halted —though over the increasing wind, she couldn't believe it. In perfect synchronization, they backtracked to her.

"Sloane, is that you?" Henry called, when they were close enough to spot each other.

"Aye, come!" She pointed to where the others fought. "We must help."

Pharrell lost no time. He asked no questions, simply kicked his horse into a gallop, and made toward Tolvar and the others.

Sloane paused Kenn, then sucked in her breath as soon as she'd exhaled.

The Edan Stone had become a shade lighter.

CHAPTER 60

Tolvar

A ll other battles, Tolvar decided, had prepared him for this last one.

It'd been too long since he'd been able to scan the area to assess how his companions fared, but the knight in him knew surely half of them had been downed and were probably dead. At least he could still see Ghlee from the corner of his eye. Both had been forced to abandon their horses and were fighting two at once. Tolvar hadn't been injured yet, which meant he still probably had a dozen men he could take down before tiring and falling himself.

At least Sloane had escaped. That Brones lout thought Tolvar had the weapon. They'd completely ignored her when she'd ridden away. Fools.

The leader of the Brones, his thin facial features pursed, surveyed the scene from the bottom of the hill as if spectating a jousting match. Could Tolvar get to him before he commanded those cursèd arrows be brought out again? Kek and Clive's faces swam before him. Probably not. Siria's skirt. This was not how Tolvar thought he would go in the end.

The sky darkened with thick clouds and the winter wind whipped through him as he parried and blocked and swung and sliced his sword against his opponents. It was difficult to look upon these men. There was an emptiness to their eyes, and the visible mark of Adrienne that drew itself across their necks made Tolvar think that mayhap he should've been a praying man after all.

Three more down, and Tolvar's exhaustion intensified. Was it the Curse of Adrienne that was making him feel unwieldy? This leader was toying with him and Ghlee. In his last glance, he hadn't seen anyone else, not even Alvie or Hux.

Tolvar swung his sword into a man's arm, half-severing it and spraying the snowy ground with a fountain of red. The man's scream echoed through the wind.

The other man backed off, and Tolvar noticed that the men who fought Ghlee did the same. Tolvar gasped in lungfuls of air.

"Scared to fight the Wolf?" he shouted at the leader.

"That doesn't seem wise," the leader said through a thin-lipped smirk.

"Definitely not wise, but cowardly all the same," Tolvar said. "Much like your sovereign. Sending after us villains rather than facing us himself."

Damn. The Brones had surrounded him and Ghlee, drawing their circle in tighter.

"The sovereign is a fool. Desperate to help his people," the leader said, dismounting. "So desperate he's willing to put his faith in us. But he doesn't realize the *real* possibilities this weapon may have. A way to wield the Befallen to vanquish enemies. Wipe out armies. Crush empires."

The leader halted. Could Tolvar run him through before being run through himself?

"You're the fool," Ghlee said. "There is no wielding the Befallen. Just as there's no wielding the Curse of Adrienne."

"You know nothing," called a voice—familiar, but raspy—from behind the leader. A man strode into view and Tolvar's jaw slackened. His palms sweat as the rest of him went cold.

There, almost unrecognizable for his disheveled red hair covered much of his face that was half-blackened by Adrienne's Curse, stood his brother.

"Stars almighty," Ghlee spoke.

The chill burned through Tolvar, and every dark thought he'd ever savored about meeting his bastard-traitor-brother again coursed through his blood. Crevan. Standing here as his enemy once more.

Now the dying man's words, *I am not the leader,* made sense. The lowering of the arrows. The taunts with the wolf carcasses, for Crevan had always sneered at Tolvar's knight's title. Tolvar stanched the pricking in the pit of his stomach and gritted his teeth.

His brother.

"Siria's skirt, you look terrible," Tolvar shouted, stepping forward. Around him, the Brones tensed. "Worry not. You'll look better once you're dead."

The thin-lipped "leader," focused on the brothers' exchange, had left himself vulnerable when Tolvar had taken his last step. Tolvar owed this scrote for Kek and Clive's deaths. Without warning, Tolvar's sword drove so far through the man that he was almost able to touch him with his fist wrapped around the hilt. Tolvar stuck his foot up onto the man's chest and slid the sword out, black blood pouring from him. The man landed on his knees and then dropped to his face, crushing–Tolvar hoped–that stupid thin nose in the process.

Everyone stood frozen.

"Like him," Tolvar growled at Crevan, who replaced his astonishment with a hideous smirk.

Crevan sauntered forward. "I've missed your doltish humor. But, once again, I have the upper hand. You really must stop setting traps for yourself." He laughed. "My, King Rian is in for an awful surprise. All the Capella Realm is."

"You're a fool more times over than I can count." Tolvar took another step. "You cannot wield the power of Adrienne, Crevan." He snorted. "It has devoured you. And I see before me a shell of a man. Father would be disgusted with you."

"You'll not bait me, *brother.*" Crevan spit and it left an inky spot in the snow. "Now. Give me the weapon."

"I don't have it," Tolvar said so matter-of-factly there couldn't be a chance anyone would consider he was lying. Most of all Crevan, who furrowed his eyebrows, pursed his lips, and brought up a finger in question below his nose, ugly with blotchiness.

With the mark of Adrienne running across his neck like a tight scarf, he was difficult to look upon. Tolvar *almost* felt pity. Almost. Stars, every bit of Crevan was obviously trying to work out Tolvar's words. His face screwed up into a confused mess.

Tolvar almost laughed.

"You think to best me, *brother*," Tolvar said. Another step. Close now. "I am the Wolf. And you, you're naught but the worst of cowards. You hid behind me in battles. You've hidden behind the Brones. And you, a treacherous viper, shall finally pay."

Crevan kept the appearance he was still pondering the whereabouts of the weapon, but gave a sideways look and said, "I didn't hide when I killed our father."

Tolvar's fingers gripping the hilt itched. "I cannot wait until his sword ends you."

Crevan snapped his fingers. "Ah, I know. The girl who rode away has the weapon."

Tolvar wasn't prepared for those words and knew his expression gave it away for one brief second. But between the pause in fighting and the hatred pumping through his veins, a renewed energy burst through him, and he downed the man next to Crevan only a breath before Crevan had his sword out and had blocked Tolvar's thrust. An arrow missed Tolvar only because of his well-trained reflexes.

"No arrows yet!" Crevan yelled. "By my signal." He backed away, a ghastly grin slicing his face. "I've been training, *brother*." And swung his sword at Tolvar.

The battle broke anew, but six of Crevan's men mounted their horses and rode away from the fray. Sloane! But Tolvar couldn't follow. Crevan swung and swished his sword at him with a gusto Tolvar had never experienced from him. Nearby, Ghlee and Hux were combatting more than should have been possible.

Tolvar had sparred with Crevan many times and couldn't remember him ever beating him. At most, it'd been a draw. Crevan's technique came at Tolvar swift and calculating. Tolvar changed stance to adjust his own sword tactic. And all the while, Crevan attacked Tolvar with words meant to cut or distract. The description of King Rian's cousin when she bled out. The rumors he'd reveled in about Tolvar's disreputation. His plans for revenge on the Capella Realm.

Tolvar ignored each word and focused each movement on silencing Crevan for good.

The most difficult part was keeping one eye on the archers, but no one fired another arrow at them. On they fought. Soon, other Brones joined Crevan against Tolvar.

"You realize that you cannot defeat me without help?" Tolvar scoffed, ignoring how his arms screamed in exhaustion.

Crevan gave an exasperated squawk. Good, he was growing exhausted, too.

Dark clouds pressed upon them, the wind howled, blowing bits of falling snow into his face. The stench of black blood permeated the air. Tolvar had downed each man who'd joined Crevan, and Ghlee and Hux—still standing—had downed plenty themselves, but it wasn't long before they were tightly surrounded again. Where were all these men appearing from?

Crevan backed away from Tolvar. "That's enough," he said, stepping over a corpse. His men ceased fighting.

Tolvar didn't consider the gash near his hip he'd suffered, but taking a glance at Ghlee, he saw his shoulder was nothing more than a gaping wound. But his friend, his blonde hair soaked with sweat, simply switched his sword to his other hand. Hux panted for breath and had a gash on his head that drizzled blood.

"Face it." Crevan clicked his tongue. "You've lost again."

Tolvar's mind raced. Three against—however many this was.

Movement drew his attention from behind Crevan.

Tolvar relaxed his neck. "Guess I'm the one with tricks up my sleeve this time." And an arrow, shot from one of the Order of Siria knights, struck into the back of the man next to Crevan. The war cry of Pharrell was met by the rest of the Order, who, on horseback, plunged into the battle.

The Wolf willed himself to dig deep for more strength and took up his sword once more against attackers. Crevan slipped away in the commotion, Tolvar cursing that he'd lost him. Coward. He'd torn the arm from an opponent when he noticed the grey stallion. What was Sloane doing back here?

"Sloane, get out of here!" Tolvar bellowed, but through the uproar of the fray there was no way for her to hear. She wasn't in the mix of the fight but clutched something—the Edan Stone, no doubt—in her hand and focused east. Tolvar wished for Valko as he made his way toward her, knocking men over and slicing his way through the fray to get to her. Sloane seemed miles away from him.

"Sloane!" A few more feet and he'd be near enough to touch her knee, but she didn't notice. It was too blaring.

Movement shifted behind him. He turned. Crevan lunged for him. Tolvar was a split second too late. He braced himself; held up his sword in vain. It wouldn't be fast enough.

A *clang* hit Crevan's sword. Hux's sword held Crevan's in a braced parry. Their swords gritted against one another. Sweat mixed with blood dripped from Hux's forehead as he held off Crevan.

"Attacking from the back? *Tsk, tsk.*" Hux's voice was a contrast to his pained expression.

They broke off their swords from one another, Tolvar readying his at the same time. Crevan glanced toward Sloane. Damn. Tolvar had to get to her before the Brones did.

"Go, Lord Wolf. Your business lies elsewhere," Hux said, raising his sword and eyeing Sloane, who was riding away. "And the business of killing family members is not for you."

Crevan's face was losing its smugness; his shoulders sagged. Tolvar gripped his father's sword, torn.

"Trust me on that matter," the leader of the Ravyns said, giving Tolvar the impression that the words held many meanings for Hux.

Reluctantly, Tolvar pivoted toward Sloane, the ringing of Hux and Crevan's swords clashing behind him difficult to ignore. It should be him. But he recalled the ghost of his father and didn't look back. His place was with Sloane. He couldn't jog well, but a wound wouldn't stop him. He clomped through the battle, yelling to her with no success.

Sloane's back was to him. If she'd just hold still. A few more steps.

A horn sounded in the distance.

Stars, 'twas the sovereign's army. Even through the dark clouds and snow, Tolvar recognized the scores of men dressed in cobalt uniforms. And now, he couldn't find Sloane—or Crevan and Hux—in the throng. The horn sounded again, and the army rushed toward them.

"Order of Siria! You are commanded by His Majesty, the sovereign, to stand down and deliver us the weapon of the Edan Lore," a commanding voice rang out—from the Commander of the Guard, Tolvar assumed.

Pharrell, still on horseback, made his way to the front. "You've been deceived, Sir Gilbert. These men do not have the sovereign's interests in mind. They mean to take the weapon for themselves. They're under the influence of the Curse of Adrienne. Can you not see that for yourselves, or are you influenced as well?"

"You dare speak that word?" Sir Gilbert shouted back, ignoring the rest of what Pharrell said. "You have failed in your quest to find the Unsung. Now the sovereign himself will rid Deogol of the Befallen."

"Nay, he won't," Pharrell shouted back. "The Unsung has been found, and she alone will defeat the Befallen."

She? Pharrell! Tolvar wanted to strangle him. He wasn't the only one who'd picked up on Pharrell's words. Tolvar not so much watched but felt multiple pairs of eyes searching the horde.

"Then give us the Unsung," Gilbert commanded.

"Never!" Tolvar shouted and drove his sword through the nearest Brones member.

This motion spurred everyone on the battlefield into action. The sovereign's army joined in, set on crushing the Order of Siria and capturing Sloane. In a mess of men, horses, and swords, Tolvar still could not find her. The snow increased, obscuring the horizon and making everything a blurred scene of chaos.

But over the clamors of battle—sounds that no one should grow accustomed to, yet the Wolf certainly had—Tolvar thought Sloane yelled, "Cease! Run! The Befallen comes!"

CHAPTER 61

Sloane

It was chaos. It was devastation. It was desolation. And Sloane was right in the middle of it, her hand gripped around the Edan Stone, the shade of which was becoming lighter by the moment. She couldn't see the foul presence of it yet, but it was approaching. Stars, she didn't even need the Edan Stone to know it was coming. She felt its evil, its wrongness, in the air.

Sloane wiped snowflakes from her face, not wanting to focus on anything around her—for it was death, only death—and yelled, "The Befallen is coming! Run!"

The snow swept over everything. Even if Sloane had wanted to find anyone, there was no making out anyone's faces.

You need to find the Befallen before it gets here, part of Sloane thought. *Or everyone will die.*

But she couldn't move.

You must find the Befallen and walk into it without any hesitation. It will not be defeated until it's devoured bravery, the goddess of the Azure Moon had said. *Without any hesitation.*

She clasped her moon cuff. *Goddesses unseen, help me.*

Sloane snapped Kenn's reins, and they took off toward the east. He dodged other horsemen and those locked in combat. Sloane glanced at the Edan Stone. Aye, becoming whiter than charcoal ash now.

A horse slammed into Kenn, and Sloane dived onto the ground. Spooked, Kenn reared and trotted off.

Sloane lay on the ground, the wind knocked from her for a moment before she assessed what hurt more, her arms or her knees. All of it, she supposed. The horseman who'd knocked into her was combatting someone. She couldn't even tell who was on whose side, the snow covered everything. She groaned and planted her leg to stand. Something was wrong. Her right leg didn't want to support her. She put her weight on her left leg.

"No," Sloane whispered.

She looked around for a stick or something on which she could lean. Nothing. And all around her, the din of battle burned her ears. The Edan Stone grew a shade lighter.

Then something strange happened. The snow's color began to change. At first, Sloane thought it was her imagination. The flakes, white a second ago, looked like bits of ash cascading from the sky. Then they turned from grey to charcoal until, now, dark shards of snow tumbled down. Sloane studied her sleeve in disgusted amazement. The snow was black.

With another attempt, Sloane managed to stand, swiveling her head around her, ignoring the screaming pain of her knees, and stared wide-eyed at the snowstorm surrounding her, a thickness of black.

There'd be no seeing the Befallen advancing now.

And darkness drowned her, pouring an inky film over her shoulders, the blackness a weight upon them, dragging Sloane into the gloom that tortured her back to her knees.

Sloane's shoulders shook in terror. She was lost. She was weak. The vulgar sounds of the battle faded into shouts of confusion. Sloane could barely make out men's silhouettes here and there. She couldn't tell who was on her side or not. And it occurred to her that it didn't matter.

The scourge slipped into a passing silence and slowly sapped all who remained into figures stark and grotesque. Sloane seized her knife—the last remaining tool she'd ever clasp—choking for courage, breathing for stability, exhaling for what she knew was her demise.

The metallic stench of blood seeped into Sloane's nose and

trickled to the bottom of her being like an icy drip of frosted water drizzling down her neck, and it was here on this battlefield—where she didn't belong—that she realized for the first time what it meant to weather the storm called fear.

Sloane exhaled the coppery air, taking in goodness instead. Every moonbeam cascading from the heavens, every spirit skipping like stardust to the earth. She took in the pink petals of wild mountain flowers, their roots robust enough to hold them firm, the spring's droplets dancing down the peak, giving life along the way, the bursts of sunshine, concealed now, yet a promise all the same, and last, saw the girl inside, tilted on an emaciated field, but upright, nevertheless.

She bore her weight onto her right leg and heaved herself up and held her ground like every blade of grass was hers to defend.

Through the ebony air, Sloane sought out the silhouette of the man she loved. She had to say goodbye, even if he didn't know it was goodbye. When she caught sight of him—his imposing and razored outline like a wolf—at the other end of the infinite field, when she perceived how far away it was for her to hobble, when she resolved to try anyway, that is when she sensed the presence behind her.

Rhiner, his gruesome smirk a line across his filthy beard, gripping her Father's stabbing awl, she noted from the engraved handle, sauntered his way toward her through the black snow as if she were a friend he was meeting in a pub and not prey he was stalking.

No!

"You look like you seen a ghost." Two paces nearer and Sloane noticed he staggered. An effect of Tolvar's wound? He should be dead. "Found new friends, I did." He gave a brief nod, and she could only assume he meant the Brones.

She was no sook in an alley. And so, Sloane took in her last breath, regripped the knife in one hand and clenched the other around the Edan Stone hanging from her neck, solidified her stance, and with hardened brows, dared him to keep walking.

Movements scrimmaged in the background, shadows of those fighting, who were cloaked in the darkness that pressed heavier and heavier over the field. Cries and moans and shrieks of war from all directions, a barrage of both noise and an underlining soundlessness only she could sense in the approaching Befallen, and all the while, Rhiner crept closer.

"Been waitin' for this a long time, gimpy girl. You've ruined everything. And now, I'm gonna take that weapon from your warm, dead body."

Her knife trembled and convulsed. Then the blade caught an impossible singular streak of light that looked like a flicker of flame dancing: a reminder.

She, this girl with her cursèd leg, with a stature slight and small, who had been unlucky enough to thwart the Befallen three times, who had made a journey that felt like the size of the sky. This unlikely girl, battered from one place to the next, yet carrying faith like a candle, bearing nothing more than a blade and unbending shoulders, who was too far away from anyone's help—but who sensed the weight of the Edan Stone. She was no one's casualty.

"Don't you come near me." Sloane's steady voice was one she barely recognized.

Rhiner stalked closer.

"You heard her. Don't take another step." Joah came into view behind Rhiner.

"Joah!" Sloane shouted as Rhiner turned to face him.

"Kerr?"

"You're a dead man holding my father's tool," Joah said.

Rhiner lifted the stabbing awl above his head. But Joah was ready. And so was Alvie, who'd been standing behind Joah just out of eyesight. Blood sprayed from Rhiner's mouth as Alvie's club swung into his face. He fell. Joah swiped at his legs before stabbing into his torso. Sloane couldn't watch. Alvie's club made another horrible noise as it found its mark against his skull. Rhiner's last moans were that of a coward. Joah spit on Rhiner's body. Sloane felt no joy at his death. As evil as he'd been, she'd resolved to stop death. No matter who.

Through a daze, she heard Joah say her name.

Alvie's voice brought her back, "Holy goddesses of the moon! Look!" Alvie's club had cracked and underneath it was—shining. The metal underneath was shining. "It *is* starstone! Now I'm really keepin' this."

Sloane and Joah gawked at the crack in the club, before Alvie pointed and exclaimed, "Sloane, the Edan Stone!"

"Aye. I—" It sunk in that her brother stood before her. "Joah, how did you get here?"

"I ran into Alvie. I was riding here from Clemen with a group of men. The town received a raven from the Order of Siria saying the Unsung needed help. I've been trying to find you again since I left. I never should have left you, Sloane. I am a coward thrice over."

"You can say that again," Alvie said, giving a low whistle.

"I hope this is the last time in our lives I need beg for your forgiveness."

Sloane couldn't linger on those words. It'd be her downfall.

"Of course, I forgive you, Joah." The two embraced; it was a good farewell, Sloan decided.

The weight of the darkness made Sloane's knees buckle.

"Sloane, you alright?" Joah said.

"The Befallen is here." She nodded toward the moonstone. "Get everyone out of here."

"Don't worry, Sloane. This will all be over soon. You're our lucky charm," Alvie said. Sloane couldn't bear to reply. Instead, she hugged Alvie, too.

"Lucky to have you as my friend, even though you're a heretic."

Alvie grinned against her shoulder before he released her. "I can stay with you."

"Nay, I have to do this alone, Alvie." He nodded in understanding, even though he didn't.

"Find that Befallen, Unsung," Joah said over his shoulder before they ran back into the battle, yelling to take cover, disappearing for the last time from Sloane's eyesight. She said a prayer of thanks that, at least, she'd been afforded those goodbyes.

She hobbled in the direction that felt heaviest, the Edan Stone like a boulder held in both hands clasped like a prayer.

One foot in front of the other. Right. Shuffle. Right. Shuffle.

By and by, the sounds of the battle were behind her. If only she'd been able to say goodbye to Tolvar.

Right. Shuffle. Right. Shuffle.

The snowfall had begun to slack, though it remained black. The voice of darkness inched toward her: "*Adrienne, I come.*"

She paused. Would the war within herself never be over?

Be brave. You cannot hesitate. You cannot—

"Sloane!"

"Oh no," Sloane whispered.

Tolvar rode toward her. He led Kenn beside him.

She'd never been so gladdened and yet so sorrowful to see anyone. Tolvar. Aye, she wanted him to be the last person she saw. And yet, seeing him, broad and intense on his steed, made it all the more difficult to not hesitate.

"Sloane!" he said, sliding from Valko and wrapping her in his arms. "I thought I'd never find you."

She clung to him in return, smelling the musky leathery scent of him.

"The Befallen comes," she said, holding up the Edan Stone, a smoky white rock. "I have to go."

"Let me take the weapon. Let me do this for you," Tolvar said. "Please, Sloane. I do not have the forbearance that was Seen in my fortune. And it isn't because I doubt you. 'Tis because I love you, Sloane. I want naught to happen to you. Let me take the weapon into the Befallen for you."

"You cannot," Sloane said, holding back her tears. "I—"

Kenn neighed, and for a moment, Sloane pictured again the two of them mounting their horses and riding away. Away from this dark, faithless place.

The tears found their way down Sloane's cheeks. "Tolvar, I lo—"

Four men bolted past them on horseback, Ghlee, one Order knight, one sovereign, and one Brones. So engrossed in their own fighting, they barely noticed Tolvar and Sloane. But their closeness spooked the horses. Valko reared and ran.

"Valko!" Tolvar called.

In the distance, Ghlee was struck and knocked from his horse. He didn't stir and there was no one to defend him. "Ghlee!" Tolvar took off toward Valko, a wound impeding his speed.

"*Aaaaadriennnnne.*" The Befallen was here.

The hairs on the back of her neck rose. Darkness, thick and evil, was visible on the horizon. "*Adrienne.*"

Kenn jerked. Sloane held tight to his reins. Tolvar still jogged after Valko shouting Ghlee's name. There was no time left. Brushing away tears and black snow from her face, Sloane swung herself into Kenn's saddle.

Tolvar noticed she'd mounted and immediately changed direction back toward her. "Nay, stop! Sloane, let me take the weapon!"

She rode to him, peered into his eyes, and said, "You can't. I *am* the weapon."

Without waiting for his reaction, Sloane leaned down and planted her lips on his. They were warm and rough and exactly as she'd imagined. When she broke away from him, she placed something in his hand. "I love you, Tolvar. Keep this safe."

And with that, she kicked Kenn into motion away from him.

She looked back; she couldn't help it. His eyes moved from the smoky white Edan Stone in his hand to gaze at her. It broke her heart. His expression went from confusion to understanding to a mix between dread and distress.

"No!" he shouted.

He knew then.

"No! Sloane, come back. No!" He raced to catch up with her and Kenn, and, for a moment, Sloane wondered if, despite his wound, he might. But she knew how to ride a horse now—because he'd taught her—and she kicked Kenn into a gallop, straight for the Befallen, wishing the whole time she couldn't hear Tolvar's anguished cries.

Kenn was lightning. The wind and snow against her cheeks made her feel so alive. The distant battle sounds and Tolvar's voice faded away. The only sound was Kenn's hooves thundering across the snow.

When the Befallen was mere yards away, Sloane halted Kenn. It wasn't snowing here. A distinct border between the darkness, waiting to engulf all life, and the snow—still white here—was drawn.

The mass of darkness grew motionless, but Sloane heard the voice calling, its hideous timbre like a chisel on metal. "*Adrienne.*"

Sloane dismounted and stared into darkness.

"That curse and you shall never be one. I am the Unsung. Weapon to defeat. You shall corrupt no more."

"*Adrienne.*" The voice sounded far away, an echo.

She took a deep breath. There could be no hesitation.

"*And what can you possibly think to do against me?*" Now the voice was butted up against her ear. A monstrous thing sounding as if it were inside her. She gasped and faltered. The sound of heinous laughter twisted in her other ear. "*Weak. Like all who are devoured by me.*"

Weak. That is what part of Sloane had taunted at her all these moons, hadn't it? It was as if the Befallen's voice had always been with her.

Don't listen. You're the Unsung. You're the weapon.

"My faith is a flame," she whimpered the old saying.

"*The weak believe in such foolishness as faith,*" the voice buzzed, making Sloane feel as though its voice had turned into tiny bugs, which crept and crawled all over her. "*The servant of Adrienne scorns the weak, which is all humankind, for they need not the Curse to be filled with weakness, to be filled with darkness.*"

Sloane covered her ears. This voice was coming from inside her. It was true. Too few carried faith. Too few were brave. Too few saw the good and truth in others; they only ridiculed. Hadn't that happened to Sloane her entire life?

"Stop," she whispered, tears streaming. "Stop talking. Stop thinking."

The laughter erupted again. It made her teeth grind. Sloane's leg wavered, her tears kept coming. She was going to fall again.

And she almost did.

A candle's flame burned in her heart, glittering and glowing, warming the very depths of her soul. It was then she understood the candle's flame grew, flickering and flaring, bracing the very core of her being.

She steeled her stance, stood still, and knew a flame blazed through her core, coursing and connecting her to herself. It was all she needed. *She* was all she needed.

She recognized that a candle's flame, though small, built bravery. Expanded into endurance. Climbed into one's courage until it rushed through the recesses of the self, creating an inferno of strength.

She peered into her heart—that bold, valiant heart—and saw the candle's flame was a wildfire, upholding her spirit, racing through the epitome of what she knew was true.

She was strong.

And the candle inside her, which could never be doused, would remind her.

It was then she decided she was the weapon.

Sloane heard no more of the taunts grappling to drench her in fear, to drown her in weakness. She focused on love's murmur. The resonance of Alvie's and Sherik's laughs. So different, yet infectious all the same. Ma's sweet singing. Father's gentle encouragements. Joah's last tone of sincerity. And Tolvar's beautiful gravelly voice.

Step after step, Sloane walked head-on into the Befallen, never even noticing when she'd crossed the border into the darkness.

A light burned inside her, and there was no hesitation. Because she was born for this.

CHAPTER
62

Tolvar

First, it was as if the enclosing darkness had always been there. It was cold and cascaded over him like he'd know misery for the rest of his days. Then suddenly, a flash of blue light, blinding him, swallowed the darkness. And in a blink, it was gone.

Tolvar doubled over, dry heaving, noticing first how strange the snow appeared now that it was white again. Around him, and stranger still, was the scatter of ashen bodies—Brones or sovereign soldiers—who'd dropped lifeless next to Order knights or Clemen townsfolk fighting them. Had being infected with the Curse of Adrienne caused that? He paled at the thought. What'd become of Crevan? Some sovereign soldiers stood dumbly, looking around as though not sure how they were there.

In his hand, the Edan Stone was onyx black once more, but a strange azure crack now sliced through it. Like it could be snapped in half.

But the strangest sight was in front of him. Nothing. The darkness of the Befallen had been before him, edging closer and closer. Then, he'd felt it rush over and tear into him, severing air from his lungs. Then nothing. There was nothing but a pure white horizon ahead, save for a grey stallion standing next to what seemed to be a person lying in the snow.

"Sloane."

Tolvar picked himself up, and ran, ignoring the wound at his hip. She'd thwarted the Befallen before. She'd survived before. She would survive again. She was the weapon. He'd misunderstood the expression on her face, he told himself.

She hadn't sacrificed herself.

She was the weapon. Promised in the Edan Lore as the Unsung.

He paused to catch any motion. There was none.

"Sloane!" he called, dashing forward.

His thoughts raced: *She survived. She must survive. She had to survive. She must survive.*

Tolvar halted, kicking up snow as he did. She was so still, curled up with her legs tucked under her, with her eyes closed. Just like last time.

Except it wasn't like last time.

Tolvar held up the Edan Stone. *He* had survived the Befallen, not Sloane. Because she was the Unsung hero who'd sacrificed everything—her life—for everyone else.

The Wolf was known for his animal-like battle cry. It was a fearsome sound. But the bellow from Tolvar was unlike any sound he'd ever made. He fell to his knees, tossed the Edan Stone away, and cradled Sloane, looking so peaceful in death. A small ruby earring fell from her hand.

He roared in torment.

"WOLF, 'TIS TIME," Ghlee said from the doorway, making Tolvar come out of his trance.

Tolvar sat in the sovereign's private solar, the Edan Stone tucked in his pocket. The sovereign wasn't there, of course. He'd been sent to the dungeons a fortnight ago. In his place, Princess Benetha had been crowned the new sovereign. It was strange thinking of that tart, little woman as the new ruler of Deogol, but of course, Tolvar wouldn't be here much longer to see how she'd do. He was going home.

King Rian had officially lifted Tolvar's banishment, restored his title, and was anxiously awaiting the return of the hero, his letter had said. Again, Tolvar pushed down his inner turmoil. Hero. He was no hero. Sloane the Unsung was the only true hero in this story.

But, as Ghlee had pointed out one night when Tolvar had refused to take to drink in his grief, she'd made him a better man. And that was something. No more the wallowing sot. No more the self-loathing, grieving son. At least there was that. Tolvar, the Wolf, would go home to Thorin Court, and with luck and practiced forbearance, would do Sloane's memory proud.

"Aye, I'm ready," Tolvar said to Ghlee, standing gingerly against his hip injury. "But I still don't know why I must be there."

"Come now, what's a celebration without the famous Wolf?" Ghlee said, clapping him on the back.

"Careful," Tolvar said as they both winced.

They were both quite a sight, even these weeks later. Ghlee's other arm was in a sling. He hadn't been able to lift his arm since the Battle for Sloane—as it was being called—and time would tell if it would heal to where he could. But Ghlee had only laughed. "If Alvie can be knighted with only one leg, I think I may remain a knight with only one arm just fine."

Ghlee and Alvie were headed back to Dara Keep in the morning, where Ghlee was to be the new commander there—Pharrell had died in battle. Too many had. Ravyns. Order knights. He needed to cease thinking. Aye, too many had. One body that hadn't been found was Crevan's, he'd checked thrice. Tolvar drove these thoughts of death away.

Benetha had declared Deogol would maintain its Order of Siria headquarters, with the permission of the Capella Realm, of course. It was one of many first declarations that made Tolvar wonder what was in store between the two lands. A renewed partnership, mayhap? That the island of the moon and the empire of the stars could bring their two faiths together again in harmony was quite a thought, even for a man who didn't pray.

Tolvar followed Ghlee through the castle's corridors to the outer bailey. As they walked, Ghlee handed Tolvar a note. "This won't cheer you, but I said I'd deliver it nonetheless."

Tolvar unfolded the parchment. The first words were condoling Tolvar's loss. He skipped to the end.

...What a tale we have now. Wish I could share in the festivities, but I like my head much too much to venture to the castle. I hear you return to the Capella Realm soon. As I have no comrades of my own left and I understand you're losing yours to Dara Keep, I thought I might offer you my services. I'll be at the docks. –Hux

"Stars' shadow. Absolutely not. When did he give this to you?"

"He did save you in battle, you know."

"Bah. The only reason he was there to do so was because I spared his life."

"True." Ghlee opened the door to the outer bailey. "But mayhap you can help him form a new life."

Tolvar's only response was a snort.

He surveyed the crowds. Stars, he wasn't ready to be around people. The gates of the castle stood open to allow all of Kestriel to join in the festivities. Though it was mid-winter, the Prelude Moon Celebration never took place indoors.

Tolvar spotted Alvie, Sir Henry, and some man named Lauge, who Alvie had introduced Tolvar to last week, laughing heartily together. Would that man ever run out of jokes? Alvie caught Tolvar's eye and made his way to him. It was an unspoken understanding, but they'd avoided each other. Sloane had been the person who'd tied them together, and Tolvar knew it was as painful for Alvie to speak to him without her there.

"Didn't think you'd make it," Alvie said, taking a swig of the moon mead he held.

"Ghlee made me." Tolvar kept his arms folded across his chest.

The lively music, the many people dancing in the evening light—everyone wearing a moon cuff—and the scent of the many pies and meats being served, did naught to lighten his mood. Almost an entire moon had gone by since Sloane the Unsung had defeated the

Befallen, but the ache in Tolvar's heart burned as if it had been yesterday.

"Sure is strange without Sloane here." Alvie kept his voice light, but the expression he carried was a weighty thing indeed.

"Aye. You ready to join the Order of Siria?" Tolvar said, wanting to change the subject.

"Sure am. Sloane would be right proud of me, I think." Alvie snickered. "She always called me a heretic. Well, guess you'd have to be pretty dense to not have faith now." He held up a new, well-oiled moon cuff.

"Certain you're not doing it because everyone else is?" Tolvar asked.

Alvie shrugged. "We'll see. Fact o'matter, I've learned a thing or two about faith. 'Specially after hearing the legend behind starstone." Alvie winked.

"Stars." Tolvar shook his head good-naturedly.

Alvie downed his last sip. "After I return Kenn to the Cibil and show him my club, maybe he'll help me find a quest of my own." He eyeballed what Tolvar had been fidgeting with. "You know you can put that on. She wouldn't mind," he said, gesturing to Sloane's moon cuff.

"It doesn't fit." And to Tolvar, that statement meant more than the size of his wrist compared to her delicate one. Aye, there was a reason why Sloane had been the Unsung.

"Join me for a drink." Alvie turned over his empty mug.

"Mayhap in a bit," Tolvar said and Alvie nodded in understanding.

Tolvar made his way through the crowd, feeling like an outsider in many ways. Though he received numerous gawks from people, recognizing the Wolf in their midst, he appreciated he was left alone. Finally, he found a solitary wall to lean against.

"I thought I might find you someplace like this," said Princess Benetha—or the sovereign now, Tolvar reminded himself—coming toward him. She was followed by four ladies-in-waiting. "Leave us," she commanded, being instantly obeyed.

"Your grief is palpable, sir knight. Or I suppose 'tis truly Lord Tolvar now." Her pale blue eyes twinkled.

"What a memory you have, Your Highness," Tolvar said, referring to that late summer day in the courtyard.

"Quite a long one, I'm afraid," the sovereign said. "But 'twill be good for my people. For Deogol. I want you to know that though I and most of Deogol never knew your Sloane, she will not go unsung. Tales and songs will be written and spread throughout all of Tasia."

Tolvar half-smiled, half-frowned. He ached so fiercely. "Her brother will be honored by that, I'm certain."

He eyed Joah in the crowd. The only Ravyn—besides irksome Hux—to survive. Tolvar couldn't sort out his mixed feelings about Sloane's brother. Alvie had told him about the end with Rhiner. Ghlee had offered to take Joah to train. And although he'd said he was unworthy to be a knight, he'd asked if mayhap the Order of Siria could use a good leatherworker.

"I am certain her brother will be, but I wanted you to be the first to know." She held out a piece of parchment and, though Tolvar could not read what it said in the dim light, he knew it was a verse penned in Sloane's honor. "The Chief Scholar, herself, wrote it."

Tolvar rolled it up and placed it in his pocket. He would read it later when he was alone and could better let out his emotions.

"Do you think the Curse of Adrienne is gone from this land once more?" the sovereign asked, her face grave.

Tolvar had been pondering the same matter over the last moon. What he'd seen on the battlefield that day would certainly suggest it.

"I hope so, Your Highness. In my experience with the Curse, I find the more faith and goodness that can be spread, the better chance we have that no one will be tempted into its darkness."

Her expression appeared wise despite her youth. "I agree, m'lord." She stepped away, then turned back. "She will always be with you. You know, in Deogol, we believe the Prelude Moon symbolizes new beginnings. It does not mean we do not miss those who have been taken from us forever, but I hope new tales of the Wolf will reach my ears in due time."

She nodded in farewell.

Tolvar, alone again, studied the engravings of Sloane's moon cuff. He'd noticed each moon had a different symbol but hadn't paid too much attention to them before now. He'd been too filled with grief in looking at it.

But now, Tolvar noted the symbol of the Prelude Moon. A candle.

The full moon came out. Nothing had ever appeared so white, so pure, before. And for a moment, just a moment, while gazing at the brilliant moon of new beginnings, Tolvar felt the warmth of something placed over his hand, and a delicate, small squeeze.

ACKNOWLEDGMENTS

The Befallen began as a spark of a tale on a midnight road trip with my husband. But when Sloane and Tolvar decided to make their entrances on the page, it was all I could do to keep up with their journey of hope, redemption, forgiveness, and perseverance. There have been many people who've helped me make this journey into a reality.

To you, my readers, thank you for taking on this quest with Sloane and me. It is because of *you* that the world shines brighter. No one who is loved goes unsung, including you, dear reader.

To booksellers, librarians, reviewers, bloggers, and my fellow authors, the writing community is remarkable, and I feel so fortunate to be part of it.

To my editor, Lindsay Flanagan, who started as a voice of encouragement and challenge and who became a friend and champion. Every writer needs an editor like you.

To Holli Anderson, thank you for seeing Sloane and for believing in and taking a chance on a hopeful writer.

To the rest of the Immortal Works team: Jason King, Staci Olsen, Ashley Literski, John M. Olsen, and so many others: *Mwah* and my thanks. I'm proud of the work we've done together. Special thanks to my editor, Krista Olsen, who helped me take *The Befallen* to the next level. Thank you for asking tough questions until I discovered the answers.

To Mayank Sharma, my fantastic mapmaker who made the island kingdom of Deogol come to life. You were extremely patient and professional. Thank you.

To my dear beta readers: Kathy Dale, Julie Quintero, Annica Slaugh, Brooke Hanink, and Emilie Kingsford. Your advice, critiques, and cheerleading was invaluable as *The Befallen* came together. To Kathy, you always know what to say. You're truly my mentor in all things. To Julie, you read the way you live life: with your heart. I knew I was on the right track by your reactions. To Annica, you and your critiques were perfect. To Brooke, one character owes you his life. He's tremendously grateful. As am I. And to Emilie, my beautiful sister and *very* best friend, the hours-long phone calls, brainstorming, laughing, reassuring me, and your rallying to make the world of Tasia a richer place saved me more times than you know. I owe you.

To my incredible MFA professors: Tony D'Souza, Nicole McInnes, Kali VanBaale, and Zachary Tyler Vickers. Truly, *The Befallen* could not have been written without you. You taught me to never shy away from challenging myself, never settle, and never let doubt be the loudest voice in my head. Thank you.

I am blessed with an exceptional support group of fabulous friends, family, and framily. To all of you (you know who you are), you have all carried me at some point and kept me going. To the Fab Five, especially, "I love you more than my luggage." Writing is a lonely business, but with cheerleaders like all of you, I know I'm never alone.

To Franklin and Carol Williams, the most wonderful in-laws. You embraced me into your family without hesitation, and have encouraged and inspired me. I love you.

To my parents, Wayne and Debra Demke, I love you. You read to me, patiently listened to me tell stories, and emboldened me. A girl can do anything when she knows she has her two biggest fans cheering her on.

To my amazing children, Sawyer Williams and Annabel Williams. You inspire me every day. Without a doubt, raising you has been the best part of my existence. Never stop dreaming. And never stop working for your dreams. I love you all the way.

My final and most wholehearted acknowledgement is for my husband, Stuart Williams. Without your support, strength, and love none of this would be possible. You are my everything. "I am the luckiest." In the story of my life, *you* are my hero.

ABOUT THE AUTHOR

 Cambria Williams believes that storytelling is a collective experience that is both limitless and timeless in its transformative nature. Cambria writes fantasy fiction that emphasizes the magic of hope. *The Befallen* is her debut novel. When not writing, Cambria is reading. She's built a sizable library despite the fact she's long since run out of shelf space. She loves traveling, dining al fresco, and taking walks all over the world with her husband, two children, and dog. Cambria has a Master of Fine Arts in Writing and lives in Utah. Visit her online at cambriawilliams.com.

This has been an
Immortal Production

Printed in the USA
CPSIA information can be obtained
at www.ICGtesting.com
CBHW031343041023
1229CB00004B/11